Valentine and the Empire

Here be monsters

Terry Hornby

The Valentine Series

Valentine and the Devil

Valentine and the Undead

Valentine and the Mobsters

Valentine and the Prince

Valentine and the Empire

Stand Alone Novels

Sally's Got a Taser

Terry Hornby is the sole author of this work

Ebook ISBN: 978-0-6458491-5-8

Print ISBN: 978-1-7637826-1-7

www.terryhornby.au

Cover design by Amber Thompson and BookCoverZone

To my beloved nephews and niece,

Stephen

Andrew

Graham

Sarah

Thank you for looking after your wonderful mum.

Acknowledgments

I belong to a supportive and encouraging writing community, the Writing Friday gang at Maroochydore, Queensland. These people hold me up and cheer me on. I trust I return this support to them. Plus, we laugh a lot. I mean, A LOT!

A big thank you, to my editor, the wonderful Laura Antram. I cannot stress how much this lady has done for my work. She is professional, compassionate and highly competent; she makes my work better. Any remaining issues in the text are due to my own idiocy, often blindly ignoring sage advice from Laura. I don't know how she puts up with writers in general and me in particular.

And, as ever, I could not be the writer I am, nor the man I aspire to be, without the unfailing love and support of my beautiful, intelligent wife, Glenda. I am a lucky man.

Who are the Night Watch?

VALENTINE AND HIS COMPANIONS are refugees. Members of the City Watch, they carried swords and muskets in an unnamed 17th century medieval city.

When they encounter an alien on one of their nightly patrols, their lives become complicated.

This encounter takes them into a confrontation with the city authorities, one they could not win. Instead, they were offered a place on a trading ship, a place they eagerly accepted,

It was quite a surprise when they discovered it was a spaceship.

The Valentine novels are all standalone stories, yet each tells of a different encounter the Night Watch has in their journey through the stars. This book is Number 5 in their journey.

They meet murderous aliens, psychopathic killers, assassins, mad scientists, and the occasional member of the Imperial Family.

Through it all, they stick together. They are just a bunch of barely functioning human beings trying to get by.

Yes, Valentine is a thug.

But he's our thug.

Chapter 1

THERE COMES A TIME in a young man's life when he must take stock of what he is doing, of what he has become. A time when he reflects upon ...

"Valentine!" yelled a loud and intrusive voice. "Get your backside out here and do some bloody work!"

My reverie was shattered. With ill grace, I stumbled out into the welcoming arms of Teddy Boy. He is an ensign and, since I am but a lowly sergeant, he occasionally thinks he can order me about. Obviously, today was one of those days.

"Something on your tiny mind, birdbrain?" I queried.

"That's Ensign Birdbrain to you," he said. I noted he had stepped back, putting some more space between us. I also saw his eyes flick to my empty hands before glancing at where I would be wearing any weapons.

"How about you put some clothes on?" he suggested.

I glanced down at my naked form and considered his idea. As I stood there wondering, another arm, also naked, emerged behind me from my room. This arm thrust a bundle of clothes onto my shoulder, followed by a tired voice slurring, "Please take him away from me, Ted. I need some rest."

Teddy Boy did not appear embarrassed. "Sure thing, Lydia," he said. "Sorry I woke you up, but I need dickhead here to start pulling his weight."

"Been a lot of pulling already," came Lydia's voice, I think I detected a certain fuzziness in her tone as she wafted back to dreamland. "Be nice to have some quiet time." The door shut behind me. A small crowd had gathered to watch, a crowd consisting of the usual loafers plus a few others who had been walking off in pursuit of their duties. Now they all stood and smirked at me.

There was no gain here for me. I would not be able to enforce my will upon these clods, they would not respond to any authority from me, nor would they quake before my potential wrath.

It's difficult to summon up potential wrath when you stand naked in public while holding your clothes and wearing a satisfied smile. Yes, I was deeply satisfied. I was with Lydia, I was alive, and my injuries had almost healed, thanks to the bloody nanobots in my system.

Okay, the nanobots were a downside. But Lydia tended to compensate for any negativity in my worldview.

"You're still naked, fungus features," said Teddy Boy. "Get dressed, the Man in Black wants to see you. Some sort of big discussion with NAVIGATOR."

Poo. The Man in Black, our boss. The man who had taken us from Earth before the Inquisition could discuss the errors in our thinking. We fled with our swords, our muskets and our terror; we had no place to go, we were doomed. But he got us a ship — not any ship, he put us on a spaceship and put us out here amongst the stars. The man who demanded we be our best selves.

The guy's a pain in the rectum. I'd follow him anywhere.

I got dressed and began an unhurried saunter. Since my mind easily wanders off topic, it took the opportunity presented by my walk to have its own downtime. Great. My nerves came out to play and decided to highlight the fact I was now in a spaceship and about to talk with a sentient machine. Oh, joy.

When I was young, my Latin tutor almost had me convinced my name was not Valentine. He usually began every sentence with the phrase, "You idiot ..." Fortunately, I had a mum who was good at hugs. Dad was a bit more distant, but I know he loved me because he didn't beat me as much as the other dads beat their sons. Life was tough in merrie olde England.

My youthful discussions with early tutors never covered the topic of aliens or other worlds. They gave me Latin, the Bible and knowledge of my place in a seventeenth-century world.

But never a mention of spaceships.

Conversations on the meaning of life revolved around angels, devils and the need to stop touching yourself. Again, the subject of thinking machines never came up with my village priest.

Yet, here I was, now sitting on a makeshift stool, having a yarn with a being calling itself NAVIGATOR. Outside our small room, I could hear various conversations, including some gloriously colourful language, from the rest of the NightWatch. Beside me sat Lord Franz von Palmerland, the Man in Black, our leader and an aristocrat; intelligent, fair, wise and, as mentioned before, a right pain in the bum. I thought he was great.

"And you are considering giving yourself a name?" he asked NAVIGATOR. "Why?"

"It seems to me," replied NAVIGATOR, "that thinking beings such as yourselves all possess an individual name or honorific. My title describes what I do, not who I am." We paused as the boss and I considered the philosophical implications of such a statement. Well, I expect he did, I gazed into space.

"Sergeant Valentine here, for example," continued NAVIGATOR, "is a fine example. I understand his name is 'Valentine' while his title is 'sergeant'. He does not rejoice under the name of 'guard' or 'soldier'.

"I've been a soldier," I said. "Didn't like it much." Bloody Spaniards.

"Yet," went on NAVIGATOR, calmly ignoring my professional input, "I have also heard him described as 'wastrel', 'an utter oik,' and 'a complete waste of space.' He seems to possess an abundance of names. Surely, I deserve at least one individual cognomen."

The Man in Black leaned forward. "Did you say 'cognomen'?" he asked. "Have you been talking to some of the more educated members of the NightWatch? Horse, for example? I believe he knows his Latin syntax."

"Indeed," replied NAVIGATOR. "Horse has been filling me in on your own history, also that of your planet." NAVIGATOR was contained in a large box or crate, no arms, legs or other appendages which might make you think you were talking to another living being. No, he was a box. Cameras on the walls, both in this room and scattered throughout the ship, allowed it to see what was going on. No face. We had no visage upon which to focus. We saw a small control panel with a few buttons and the odd flashing light. You haven't experienced deep existential thinking until you have chatted to a talking box while looking at a blinking light.

"And why," NAVIGATOR asked, "do you refer to Horse as some sort of Earth animal? I believe his name is Giovanni de Macque, from a place you call France; yet you all have given him this rather unusual sobriquet.

Is he, in fact, some sort of medical experiment wrought upon a poor beast?"

I resolved to have a chat with Horse, he had been responsible for setting up security while we all recovered and had taken on the task of sleeping in NAVIGATOR's room as a last line of defence. They had obviously been having some rare old chats about this and that which had apparently resulted in NAVIGATOR being told anything he wanted to know. While Horse was educated and intelligent, he had no filter. He keeps telling the truth. Yes, I don't get it either.

"The NightWatch have a habit of giving each other these alternative names; they are often descriptive," explained the boss.

"Does he look like a horse?" asked NAVIGATOR.

I needed to head this topic off. Horse had acquired his name due to some aspects of his physique which did, in fact, resemble a horse. But sharing this with an alien would lead us down discussions on human anatomy not meant for tender ears. And by that, I mean my ears.

"What's a 'cognomen', boss?" I asked. I knew, because of the many beatings I had endured, but it never hurts to let the high and the mighty display their erudition.

The Man in Black gave me the old side eye. "It's the third personal name given to an ancient Roman citizen, typically passed down from father to son. Other names were labelled as nomen, praenomen and agnomen." He scratched his head, rolled his neck and popped a few joints. "As you well know, you annoying carbuncle."

This was going well, so far I had racked up a growing list of insults and it was barely time for my morning cup of kaffe. Time for another redirection, "Have you got any particular name in mind, NAVIGATOR?" I asked.

"I was thinking of 'Caesar'," he replied.

Of course he was. I must talk to Horse.

"Seems appropriate," said the boss.

"Because he's pompous and annoying?" I suggested.

"Because, lackbrain," said my lord and master, "NAVIGATOR is the sole ruler of this domain, this immense spaceship which has travelled between galaxies. NAVIGATOR has many minions, and here I speak of PILOT and the host of smaller machines inhabiting this vast structure." He went on for a while but I tuned out. I winked at one of NAVIGATOR's cameras while endeavouring to keep a smile from my face. You have to know how to push some people's buttons and I had come to know how to get the boss up to full speed.

He ground to a halt, clipped me behind the head and said, "Stop smirking, nosewipe.""You're certainly getting the hang of NightWatch vernacular, sir," I replied.

"If I may," interrupted NAVIGATOR, or Caesar. Pick one. "I can no longer travel between galaxies. This ship's maiden voyage traversed the immense distance between galaxies at a cost, but it did something to us. Like PILOT, I was a mere machine, capable of navigating space but without any sense of self awareness. The organic crew of the vessel lost their cognitive abilities and regressed to wild animals. PILOT became insane and proceeded to wreak havoc on all around while also damaging the main engines. Intergalactic travel is no longer possible, we have sustained much damage. I also changed. I acquired ... something. I became aware of myself, of my individuality. Of being 'me'."

"Is this speech going to go on much longer, mate?" I asked. "You're hitting my boring quota for the day." I've always found insulting those in authority has an entertaining effect.

"Sod off, sergeant," the boss said. "Go and tell everyone that NAVIGATOR is now to be called 'Caesar'. And send Phil in, I want a word with that numbnuts."

I stood up. "That would be Lord Phillip Kent, son of Prince Clarence of Arenburg, tenth in line of succession to the throne of the Empire?" He glared at me and grunted assent.

"No worries, boss," I said. "I've got a thousand things to do, anyway." As I left, I heard the next bit of their exchange.

"And I shall call this ship 'New Rome'," said Caesar. I smiled as the boss groaned, even he had his limits. Always something to smile about in the life of the modern NightWatch.

Time for me to chat to some of my own minions.

Chapter 2

I EXITED THE ROOM and ran into Claude, or rather, into Claude's back. He stumbled forward while I bounced back with a nose full of Claude odour, not a pleasant experience. He regained his balance, looked back at me and muttered, "Sorry, Val."

"What are you doing here, Claude?" I snapped. "Get out of the bloody way!"

We both shuffled around until he was again standing lumpishly before the door leading into the room containing the Man in Black and NAVIGATOR. Sorry, Caesar. I gave Claude one of my medium level glares.

"I'm on guard duty," he said.

"Guard duty," I repeated. My tone leaked overtones of amazement. So much so, that he dragged himself erect. Well, as erect as any of the old NightWatch could possibly manage.

"Are you trying," I began, "to stand at attention?"

His eyes took on the thousand yard stare all rank and file learn when being quizzed by someone in abrasive authority. The gaze focussed on some part of the far distance, his lips remained closed and I detected a slight clenching of the jaw.

"Let me get this straight, Claude," I said. "You are standing before me at some vague equivalent of rigid attention while carrying out your duties as a guard. Is this a correct assumption?"

"YES, SERGEANT!" he bellowed. The gaze never wavered, the eyes remained attached to their far away goal.

"I see." This was going well, time to turn the screws a little more. "We are currently in the bowels of a spaceship. A gigantic spaceship capable of traversing intergalactic space. This room, this huge cathedral-like space in which we now stand, is the only open space in the entire structure. As I stand here, I can see our guardsman, I can also spot those over muscled space marines brought from the frigate by the terrifying Sergeant Gorka. No one else."

My arm waved about, indicating our surroundings. The room in which we stood was indeed huge. The walls were vaguely visible but the ceiling disappeared into some unknown height. In the centre of the space was a tall, circular tower which housed some of the technology to make the whole thing work. Spaced around it at regular intervals were several smaller towers, each of these contained a single, normal sized room. I had recently exited one of them, our sick and wounded occupied another and I presumed we had put any dead bodies in another.

"What, precisely," I asked, leaning into the question with a touch of cynicism, "Are you guarding against?""DON'T KNOW, SERGEANT!"

Hmmm. "Who gave you this duty, Claude?"

"ENSIGN FRANCO, SERGEANT!"

Oh, dear. "Did you do something to upset our ensign?"

Sweat was now beading his upper lip, I was zeroing in. His voice dropped a few octaves and came out in the husky tones of a broken man. "I dropped my blaster," he confessed.

"You poor fool," I said. "Still, everyone drops things at some time. And skip the 'Ensign Franco' thing, Claude. Give him his proper name, call him 'Teddy Boy' to save confusion. Surely a bit of dirt would not get you more than the normal bollocking from our lad.""I dropped it into one of the pits,"

Cheese and crackers! These pits were scattered about the floor of our giant room and contained a smelly gloop, we suspected it was some sort of food for the original crew of the vessel. They didn't need it now since they were all dead. Long story. We stayed away from them because we had seen stuff dissolve in the gloop. Stuff like the odd dead body, a spacesuit or various odds and ends. It all dissolved if left in long enough.

We stayed well away from it. Claude's blaster would have eventually decayed.

"He made me reach in and get it," choked Claude. "At least he let me wear my spacesuit. Of course, it's now damaged and Lydia's upset with me. She says the sleeve is useless and my suit's now good for spare parts, nothing else." He slumped and turned his head to face me, "She said some harsh words to me, Val."

I patted him on the shoulder, "How long do you have to stand guard?"

"Until we go back to the frigate. When I'm not here, I have to repair my own weapon and carry out maintenance on all our gear. And do hand to hand combat training with Sergeant Gorka's people. God, they hurt when they hit."

"But you got the blaster back," I said. "That's something. Ted'll get over it. Remember when Marek dropped his weapon into the sea and lost it forever?"

"Still walks with a limp," said Claude.

We both shuddered at the memory. "And now, he always wears a groin guard," finished Claude.

"Okay," I said, "You stay here and protect the boss and Caesar from ... something. I'm going to see how the rest of the gang is doing." Again, I walked off, heading towards more of the gang. I tried to message Teddy

Boy by using my communicator but it didn't seem to be working. Damn thing was powered by my internal nanobots, or wee beasties as I like to think of them. But they must have decided to have a rest. Maybe they were tired. Or broken. Poo. Bum...

I stopped and took a few deep breaths. Why were my nanobots not working? Was I going to die? Were they even now attempting a small coup in my brain? Had it already happened? Perhaps I was dead? I looked around with new eyes, was I one of the Undead? My body controlled by tiny little things nesting in my brain and having machine babies? I took a staggering step and fell over.

I fell over because Horse had hit me on the back of the head. It was a solid thump, I'll give him that. Horse was slightly smaller than me and wider, he could block a door by standing still. He liked his muscles, was always lifting heavy things to bulk himself up a tiny bit extra. When he discovered the weight machines on the frigate, he would spend every spare minute doing pointless exercises. It did mean he could give a decent thump when required. Like now.

"OW!" I cried. "What the hell, Horse?"

"You were standing there whimpering, Val. What is wrong with you?" He pulled me to my feet and looked me in the eye, "For God's sake, it was a little tap. Grow a pair, you big wuss."

The words did not match his eyes. His face showed concern, and in his eyes I could see the lurking fear. The fear we all carried, those of us from Earth. We were born to a world of muskets and outside drains, of poverty, filth and a life usually cut short by disease or war. Our brains were wired for the horse, not the spaceship. The meadow and village, not planets and aliens.

"Are you feeling okay, Val? You seem a trifle more ... angry than usual." He said this while backing away a step or two.

What had gotten into him? Come to think of it, everyone was giving me a wider berth than normal. Had everyone become meek and sensitive while I recovered? We'd have to see about that, I thought. I straightened up, knocked his hand away and growled, "I've got a crook stomach, you mullet. Probably picked up something from whatever crap we had to eat this morning." I turned to survey the rest of the room. "What's everyone doing and why aren't you doing it with them, you slack-jawed oaf?"

His shoulders relaxed, a smile tweaked the bottom lip, a smile quickly erased. "Teddy Boy sent me to check up on you, thought the boss should have finished yelling at you by now.""Our fearless leader, the Man in Black," I replied, "has been seeking my advice, my counsel. He appreciates a man with my inherent qualities of intelligence, sagacity and humility."

"You possess none of those qualities, dog breath" he said. I nodded agreement and we sauntered off together.

We walked over to where Ted had a team clustered around some tables. On the tables were a wide array of weapons, all being polished, tweaked and caressed by his team. Yes, I did say 'caressed' and I meant it. They're a sick bunch, in Ted's group.

By the time we arrived at the tables, Horse had resumed his normal, vaguely cheerful self. I had to give him some gentle counselling which consisted of saying mildly insulting things to him from time to time. I could feel the weight of everyone's expectations on my shoulders. I wasn't allowed to stutter, to show weakness or any loss of faith in who we were and what we did. Sometimes, I felt as if I was carrying the entire damned NightWatch on my back.

"Ahh," said Teddy Boy as he noticed our arrival. "My day may now begin, the sunshine has re-entered the world, boys and girls, for Sergeant

Valentine has joined us. A round of applause, please, for the fabulous Sergeant Valentine."

Everyone ignored him. His own sergeant, an energetic woman with long blonde hair tied back in a severe ponytail, looked over at me. She gave me a smile, a thumbs up and then returned to pointing out all the things the guardsman in front of her was doing wrong. Keep up the great work, Elena, I thought.

"G'day, Ted," I said, moving to stand beside my old friend. "I've finished an interesting chat with Claude."

"Guy's a pea brain," said Ted. "George, you're putting too much on, wipe about half off and keep one hand clean."

"Dropped his weapon, he says." I smiled at my mate. More of a grin, possibly even an annoying smirk.

"Into the gloop!" spluttered Ted. "Still, he got it out, the dropkick. George, don't scratch your face. That stuff will burn your skin."

"I understand he has to do hand to hand training with Sergeant Gorka. When's that happen? I might wander over to watch." I was ever the caring sergeant, knowing a true leader of men — and women — knew their little ways and enjoyed learning about their lives. Nah, I wanted to see how Claude stood up to some serious pummelling.

"After lunch," said Ted. "We're all going over there to join in. George, report to sick bay, see if Sylvia can do something to stop the burn." He mumbled some vague obscenities at others in his gang and then turned the lot over to Elena. He grabbed me by an elbow, shuffling me into a quiet space.

"Val, I couldn't raise you on the communicator, that's why I had to send Horse. That, and the fact he kept telling everyone stories about Earth. We were getting seriously depressed and homesick."

"Homesick for the gutters?" I queried. "Or maybe the various diseases. Perhaps the cuisine is a point of contention, we're certainly not getting a lot of cabbage soup." But I knew what he meant, we were still scared. Hence why I had limited my choice of thugs to a few old NightWatch, leaving the bulk of our gang on the frigate because I knew they were getting more and more fragile. It was a shame the team I chose had to confront killer machines, homicidal haystack aliens and yet another scary spaceship. And the sentient machines, mustn't forget Caesar, sitting over there and talking to the boss.

How was the Man in Black coping? He treated every new occurrence as normal. I knew he had been on some sea voyages of exploration to remote parts of Earth so perhaps he had become accustomed to weird stuff. Then again, I reflected, considering my own mental health, perhaps he was doing the same as me. Burying it deep and keeping us all together.

The guy continues to be a total dropkick.

"Yeah," I agreed, "I tried to contact you but something's not right with my nanobots."

He looked at me long and hard. "You think ... you, we, might have ... the things inside us are not ... working?" His face showed a small sag. None of us liked the thought of little machines inside our bodies. They allowed us to understand and speak other languages and they accelerated our healing rate. The latest bit of tweaking opened up their use as communicators. I also had an additional new wrinkle, mine could also let me read text of foreign languages. I was the experiment for this last bit and didn't I love being a test subject.

"Can you use your communicator?" I asked.

"Well, here's the thing. Occasionally, I'll give a message but no one receives it. At first, I thought they were all annoying buffoons, but Elena confirmed it and I trust her."

"It happens occasionally with you?"

"Yeah, mostly it's fine. But no one has been able to reach you. At first, we left you alone with Lydia because, well, you know." He coughed gently, a man of deep sensitivity to my personal relationships with my girlfriend. We had been tucked away as I recovered from my wounds and Lydia used this time to test the limits of my stamina. Turns out, I had a lot of stamina.

"You mean, we've been at it like rabbits."

"Well, yeah."

"Okay, I haven't had any communications for a couple of days, I assumed everyone was being nice to me." I thought over my words. "What was I thinking?" I said, smacking myself in the forehead.

I continued. "This morning, when I came out from my meeting with the boss and Caesar, I tried sending a message to one and all. No one got back to me which, now I think about it, was strange." I spent a minute turning in a slow circle, checking for signs of imminent destruction. No, all was well and under control. Obviously, I wasn't needed.

"We need you, Val," said Teddy Boy.

"Rubbish. You guys have got on well without me. Obviously, someone has been organising things. Who has been doing all the running around?"

"The Man in Black," replied Ted. "He has us gather and tells us what we should be doing. he checks on the wounded, gives Sergeant Gorka and me some tasks and areas of responsibility. He meets with Sylvia and then sits and talks with NAVIGATOR." He scratched his head, "Who's this 'Caesar' character? Have we run across a Roman Emperor now?"

"It's what NAVIGATOR wants to call himself," I said. "Send out a message to that effect to everyone. I'll be interested to see if it comes to me. Ask Elena for a reply so you know it's gone out." I thought of the strange behaviour of my nanobots and decided we better open up that particular can of worms. "And send for Greenash, I want to ask him about our communication failures." Greenash was our resident nanobot technician who enjoyed tinkering with things he should damn well leave alone.

Ted did all these things, I watched his lips move as he muttered messages. You didn't need to do this, you could think in a certain way and the message went out. But those of us brought up in a non-technological world still moved lips when we communicated. Meataxe also did it when thinking. That's how we knew he was thinking. Didn't happen much.

Chapter 3

Ted told me he had heard back from Elena and his message had gone out successfully. Now everyone knew of Caesar's name; Ted's communicator nanobots worked this time. I had not heard the message at all so I assumed mine had decided to resign their position. Hope the little sodomites were dissolving quietly so I could crap them out later. I'm not big on forgiveness.

But I needed a way to communicate beyond yelling at people, we had moved on from the old tried and true methods and we now lived in a world of instant communication. I thought long and deeply about how to resolve this question.

Came up empty.

"You need a communicator bead," said Ted.

"Great, I so want to stick another one of those annoying things in my ear. Pity I don't have one on me," I said. A thought blossomed, "Don't suppose you have one tucked away in amongst all your scary, shooty things?"

"No, but I'm sure there are some in the shuttle. I seem to recall reading in the manual something about all shuttles having a small stock of back up communicator beads in case of emergency."

"Two questions arise, fartface. One, how can you read their text? And two, why on Earth would anyone want to read those manuals? Honestly, Ted, you continue to disappoint."

"Because I want to stay alive, you ignorant buffoon. Lydia has a program for translating their manuals into our language. You remember Lydia, the brains of your relationship? If we left it to you, we would all die."

"Yes, but gloriously."

"Still die."

"Ted, you're taking all the romance out of life."

I called Horse over. "Horse, be an outstanding minion and go to the shuttle. Fetch me all the spare communicator beads," I said.

"The what? Where are they?""No idea, ask Mr Know-it-all here," I stuck a thumb out at Teddy Boy. They fell to discussing drawers and compartments while I continued to gaze placidly about. This leadership stuff wasn't so hard. But one must have minions.

As Horse began to move off, I called out to him. "By the way, you loose-lipped son of a cave troll, STOP talking to NAVIGATOR! You've inspired him with your sterling accounts of Roman history.""You mean 'Caesar'," he replied. A certain mirth had entered his being, I made a rude gesture to his retreating back.

"You're such a breath of fresh air, Val," said Teddy Boy. "Easy to see why everyone likes you.""And you can get stuffed, too, mate." I don't know why I was so testy. Probably thinking about little things running wild inside me. "I need to send Phil in to see the boss. Then I want to talk to someone clever about my nanobots."

Greenash trundled up and I asked him, in the nicest possible way, why our nanobots were falling down on their jobs. We had acquired Greenash on the same planet which had developed the nanobots.

The original theory for the wee beasties was worthy of merit. Instead of sticking a translator bead in your ear, let's make tiny, tiny machines which could be injected into a bloodstream. These little machines — or nanobots — would breed and then congregate in the parts of our body responsible for communications. You know, talking and listening. That meant they would nest between our ears and brain, in the brain itself and also have some villages near the mouth and tongue. I tried not to think about any slight swelling acquired on the face in case it turned out to be a massive nest of nanobots. Lydia told me I was being childish and any facial swellings I had were gained by someone hitting me. Since this happened fairly frequently, it was hard to ascertain any real solution until the bruises faded. She was probably right, but I still worried over any new skin blemish or insect bite. Mirrors were not my friend.

Greenash shrugged and said, "Sure, of course they're failing. What did you expect?" He didn't seem utterly flabbergasted by this breakdown of tiny machines, tiny machines for which he had developed an unsavoury passion. We'd managed to get him some documents outlining the mad doctor's design for the little vermin, we also press ganged a scientist who had helped develop the damn things. This guy had a political job as an Elector but was happy to give up the machinations of civil service for the joy of researching nanobots. Machines over people, eh? Very understandable. These two played with our nanobot settings all the time, even after my strongest possible criticism which involved death threats and beatings. Sorry, that should be beating first, then death. Silly me.

"Care to elaborate, you horrible man," I asked.

"Look," he said, giving me the old look, the one where you realise you must explain something to an idiot all over again. "The nanobots are brilliant, their concept and planning is outstanding. The more I learn about them, the more I am impressed with their capabilities." I yawned and made waving motions with my hand to get him to skip over the boring bits.

No such luck.

"They are designed to carry out a variety of tasks, depending on their programming. It is this programmability which makes the invention of these nanobots so utterly, utterly brilliant. Originally, we thought they had the one function as a translator, useful in itself and one which would already have made their invention the discovery of the century. The communicator bead, the thing we all stick in our ears, can eventually translate any language and allow the wearer to understand anyone. The drawbacks are the time it takes to learn the language and the necessity of everyone in the conversation having a bead. It's purely a one-way traffic device — words go into the bead, are translated immediately and this translation is then sent to the brain.

"And an even bigger breakthrough was the short-range communicator function." His eyes were glowing now, if he got any more excited, he might start humping the table. "You realise you carried the ability to understand any language, to speak it and then to communicate with others over a short distance. All inside your bodies! Amazing!"

I sat down on one of the chairs around Teddy Boy's worktable. Several of them were scattered about and I could see nothing short of violent action on my part was going to stop Greenash's verbal diarrhoea. My God, the man loved to talk about yukky things. Ted and Greenash joined me in other chairs and I groaned aloud, this day kept getting worse. Other people had wandered over and listened in, I suspect there were a few bets made on the time I would finally snap and hit something. Or someone.

"But the nanobots!" enthused Greenash, "The nanobots can manipulate the subject's brain signals to the mouth and tongue, altering any words they speak. Translating them into words understandable by the other party. It's brilliant!" I put my head down on my folded arms and made snoring noises.

"But, Greenash," said Ted, "they're not working anymore. Or not as efficiently as they should. We're all getting lots of gaps in any communication and Val hasn't been able to get any at all. Why?"

The little man slumped, shrugged and replied, "Well, it's your fault." I sat up ready to resist any implication I had done my usual act and caused the doom to descend upon us. His next words cheered me up no end. "Specifically, Teddy Boy, it's your fault.""Do tell," I said. "Expand upon your thesis, old chap," I suggested. "Tell us, in detail, how young Ted has stuffed things up." I was smiling at one and all, life had again gained a rosy hue.

"Remember when you entered the scout ship," Greenash asked. "Remember that surge which you felt?"

"You mean the surge which exploded all the communication beads in the ears of the assault squad. They all died, Greenash," said Ted. "I didn't die because I didn't have a bead, I had the nanobots."

"Exactly," triumphed Greenash. "And what did you feel, inside you?"

I groaned. I saw where this was going. "He felt a tingle," I said. "Like bubbles in the blood." We felt more of them when we entered this bloody huge ship and encountered PILOT. The bloody machine kept hitting us with more surges, none of which had any effect on us because I'd brought people along with nanobots, no one with a comm bead. I'm a clever bastard.

"Yes," agreed Greenash. "PILOT was using those surges as an offensive weapon. It had worked on the crew of the scout ship, killing them all. And again, it worked on the assault squad. The surge exploded an element in the communication bead resulting in a small bang inside the person's ear. Enough to blow their brains out."

"Poo, Bum, Tit, FART!" I said. "I bet our nanobots have bits of that element in them. When the surge hit us, the nanobot exploded. Inside us." I felt sick all over again.

"Yep," said Greenash. "Each surge destroyed more nanobots. It didn't kill them all at once because ... well, I don't know. Have to think about that. But each time PILOT hit you with a surge, the number of viable nanobots decreased. And I'm betting the remaining ones had their functions degraded. Probably had some residual ability to function left but, over time, even this faded.""But why did I lose all communication functions like the short-range transmitter, but kept the basic translator ability?" I asked. "While Ted kept some of his transmission ability, and others on the team retained varying degrees of communication. Elena, for example, seems to have been relatively untouched. Doesn't seem fair."

"Are you complaining because everyone didn't suffer the same as you, Val?" asked Greenash.

Well, this comment made me seem petty and small. "Damn right," I agreed. "If I'm in the cesspit, I want lots of company."

Teddy Boy patted me on the back. "That's our wonderfully supportive sergeant," he said. "Always putting others first.""Drop dead, dog breath," I said. "I still want to know why yours truly ended up with all the dead nanobots while you lot managed to keep some alive."

"Probably because you had extra tweaks to your nanobots, Val," said Greenash. "Remember how we had added some functions to yours?"

"Like faster healing?" I said. He nodded. "And then, you slimy little man, you added the ability allowing me to read text."

"That'd be my guess," replied Greenash. "Your particular nanobots, Val, were under pressure carrying out all these functions. A few shots of the surge would have destroyed enough for them to fall below their critical mass. Hence, some abilities were lost, the translation capability seems to have remained which is a win."

I considered hitting him. "I'm stuffed, then," I said. "In fact, all of us will have to go back to old fashioned devices. Like sticking something unpleasant into our ears."

"Ahh, yes," said Greenash. "Unless ..."

We all leaned in a little. "Unless enough nanobots have survived in your bloodstreams for them to slowly increase their numbers. If they can build up their populations, there is a chance some or all of the functions will come back."

"Let me get this straight, Greenash, you vile toxic warrior," I said. "If we are lucky, our wee beasties will fornicate like sailors on leave and have lots of kids. These will grow up and have more incestuous relations with each other until our blood is awash with the results of mass copulations."

Chapter 4

"YOU ARE A POETIC man, Valentine," said Ted. "Capable of producing images none of us needed by the use of a few colourful words." He put his head in his hands and sat quietly before saying, "I think I can feel them having a party inside me."

"Let's get those old comm beads stuck in everyone's ears. I don't want to suffer alone," I said.

'And I need to have myself checked out by someone with actual medical training. The little critters may have decided to grow me an extra leg or ear or something."

"That would be Sylvia," Ted muttered. "My best girl.""Oh, for God's sake," I said, some firmness entering my voice. "Do you mean to say she still thinks a walking dung heap like you is worth consideration? And how can you ignore her overbearing, opinionated, stubborn, argumentative nature?"

He gave me a look. I think he was going for wise, or even ironic. I ignored the prat.

"Where's Phil, the greasy piece of toejam?" I snarled

"His Grace is in the central command tower," he said. "I think he's talking to PILOT."

"Has PILOT shown any signs of having its own personality, like NAVI ... er, Caesar?"

"Nope, still as dumb as paint, but obviously in control of the maintenance of this ship. It's sent little machines everywhere doing lots of unknowable tasks. Something to do with cleaning up dead bodies and generally repairing the damage it did when it went a little psycho. Caesar seems to be keeping a close eye, or something, on it. We haven't been attacked by any more rabid mechanical things and all the dead aliens have been dumped in the gloop.""What about our dead?"

"Yeah, we lost a few. The boss had them laid out in one of the storage rooms. I've got some people watching them in case PILOT decides to send them to recycling. So far, everyone and everything have been behaving themselves. By the way, Sylvia's in that small tower over there," he pointed at one of the smaller structures surrounding the main control tower. "You need to see her, Val. Get yourself checked out."

I sighed. "I know, it's just that, I don't know. I don't think she likes me."

He gave me an amazed look, "Well, duh." He bent down and picked up the weapon left by a stumbling George who was even now moaning on his way to see Sylvia, our ice queen of the sick bay and the beloved of my gun toting maniac. Teddy Boy ignored me and squatted down to complete the cleaning process left by our sorrowful pal.

I wandered off towards the central tower in search of royalty and a man who may well be a good friend. Or an inveterate liar. Or both. Probably both.

I found the tenth in line to the throne of the Empire slumped over the crate containing PILOT, snoring softly. See, if you live right, good things do come your way. Here before me was a wonderful opportunity to inflict some low-level mischief; how often do you get to see an aristocrat drooling on a table. Well, now, I mean, not on Earth. Fairly common there.

I snuck up behind Phil and reached around his head. My aim was to place my fingers over his eyes and yell some inanity like, "YOO HOO!" Perhaps I anticipated too much because a small chuckle escaped from my traitorous lips which alerted the dill.

I don't think he was fully awake but he had been around the Night-Watch long enough to make the appropriate responses. He plunged an elbow into my stomach, spun around and crashed a fist into my descending noggin. Since he did this while still seated, the punch did not have his full body weight behind it. Stung like hell, though.

I fell on to my rump with an audible "oof" as he rose angrily to his feet. The heir to the Empire stood ready to take on all comers and I was proud of the growth in our lad.

I saw the light of recognition appear in his eyes and smiled up at my buddy. He kicked me.

"You stupid, annoying sewer, Valentine!" His voice sounded a little peeved, couldn't think why. "What's the idea of sneaking up on a man? I could have killed you!"

He held out a hand and pulled me to my feet. I assembled the old body into some semblance of normality and smiled quietly at him. I was doing this because the mongrel had knocked all the wind out of me and I was struggling to breath. Some damn fool had been teaching him how to punch.

I inhaled slowly and gave him my patented, sappy grin. "Phil, Phil, Phil," I said. I hoped the small gasps were unnoticeable, I was aiming for casual insouciance but I fear it came out as breathless gasps. "You couldn't kill me, mate. I'm too handsome."

We stood looking at each other, eventually we smiled.

"Dickhead," he said.

"Moron," I replied.

"What can I do for you, Val?"

"The boss wants to see you. He's over with Caesar discussing matters of great import. Probably wants to have your royal opinion on this and that." I looked at the crate containing PILOT. "What's going on here?"

"I thought I'd try to communicate with PILOT, see if it's displaying any of the sentience shown by NAVIGATOR."

"Who?"

"Sorry, I mean Caesar."

"Any sign of intelligence?" I walked around the crate and peered at the control panel. More blinking lights and a large RESET button. I knew that one well.

"I think Meataxe displays more evidence of self-awareness than this box of electronics," he said, patting the crate. "No, I believe PILOT is a straightforward machine capable of carrying out complex tasks when programmed correctly. And I also believe Caesar has it under control." He moved towards the doorway. "Are you here to escort me as befitting my rank and status?"

I joined him in leaving the room. "No, pusbrain, I have to go see Sylvia and have my health checked out. My communicator's not working, it might be a nanobot thing — maybe the little critters inside me have, you know, damaged my internals."

"Yes," he muttered. "I was beginning to think you had been too quiet far too long. Some of us were considering mounting a rescue party for Lydia, you insatiable animal." He went in one direction while I dragged my unwilling feet towards Sylvia's domain. "Good luck, you poor sod," he said, waving cheerfully at me.

I have a strange relationship with Phil. I like him, he's got a ton of courage and is smart and resourceful. He's generally fun to be around unless he's carrying out some obscure plan, which is most of the time.

He is a liar, devious, ruthless and willing to go to any lengths in order to accomplish his goal. As I considered these thoughts, a part of my brain asked me to look in the mirror. I ignored me. Usually a safe thing to do.

Sylvia had claimed one of the auxiliary tower rooms as her sick bay, her domain. And heaven help any soul who tried to interfere with how she did things. Which is one of the main reasons we rubbed each other the wrong way. She desired order, organisation and predictability. I rejoiced in none of these attributes. Consequently, she viewed me as something unpleasant on her shoe.

Still, she was a professional and would surely treat me, an injured waif, with kindness and compassion. I entered her room with a mild quake.

"Oh, God," she said, glancing at me as I stood in the doorway. "There goes my day."

"Hiya, Sylv, killed anyone today?" I said. Sometimes I can't help myself.

"Day's not over yet, sergeant. Have you come to annoy me?" she continued to bustle about, checking on our wounded, fussing over dressings and adjusting controls on machines that went beep.

I explained about my nanobots and the loss of the communication function. She stopped what she was doing, had me sit down and shone a light in my eyes, tapped my knee a few times and did other vaguely medical stuff. At one point I had to stick my tongue out at her, that part I enjoyed. She finally stood back, folded her arms and gazed at me. I was not feeling encouraged. One of her fingers tapped her crossed arms and she said, "Hmm."

"Is that your considered medical opinion?" I asked.

"Shut up, you annoyance, I'm thinking."

I shut up. Around the room were a set of bodies on bits of padding, our version of a makeshift bed for the wounded. I counted about six of the gang, all now awake and looking back at me with eyes displaying interest in the proceedings. I smiled at them, they gave me hesitant but encouraging smiles back. They all looked like they were well on the road to recovery. I guessed the ones who went the other way had already ... went. I swallowed.

"I can't see anything wrong with you," said Sylvia. "Beyond the normal, I mean." She was all heart. "Your vital signs are good, there's no sign of physical degradation. I can't judge your mental condition because you are generally an idiot." She stopped talking and looked hard at me. I think she was waiting for me to react to her last, somewhat harsh, assessment of my mind.

"Teddy Boy told me he loves you and wants to meet you after lunch behind the latrines for some kissy time," I said. I was hoping a display of my usual charm and thoughtfulness would reassure her.

She smiled at me, her body relaxing. I had not noticed she was standing a little stiffly until she changed her posture. "I think you're alright, Val," she said. "Still as annoying as ever.""Were you testing my mental faculties?" I asked. Why I give people these opportunities has always eluded me.

"I've seen mould with higher mental faculties than you, sergeant," she replied. "I suspect your communicator nanobots, and possibly others, have decayed. Greenash has been sharing his concerns with me, but you need to have him check you out using his fancy machines once we get back to the frigate."

It all came back to Greenash, our tech guy. An ex-drug addict, good with nanobots and harbouring a suspected desire to tinker with our insides. I hit him from time to time, keeping his expectations of life expectancy in order.

"But you think I'm okay? Healthwise? Not going to, you know, become a mad dog killer?" I asked.

"You are so not okay, princess," she replied. "but you should be able to stagger about for a bit longer. We can put up with you drooling and stammering, purely to accommodate Lydia's idiosyncratic choice in men."Again, I think I had been insulted, hard to tell with Sylvia because she said this sort of thing to most of the NightWatch. Quite justified, I might add, in everyone else's case but certainly not mine. I'm a saint.

A voice from outside called in, a nervous, tentative voice. "Are you in there, Val?"

It was Horse, he had wisely decided to stay as far away from Sylvia as possible. I gave her a warm thank you and attempted a manly hug whereupon she pushed me back and slapped my arm, She may have muttered something about buggering off but I couldn't be sure. Sylvia usually doesn't swear.

I'd have to work on that aspect of her character.

I found Horse outside, shifting from foot to foot, he was relieved when it I exited alone. He held out a hand and gave me a communicator bead, I fitted it into my lug hole and went through the tiresome startup process. This consisted of me setting up communication protocols with everyone, establishing sub groups and initiating rules for who could call me. Look at me, mum, I'm a real spaceman.

I clicked on the 'call everyone' channel and said, "Hi, kids. Dad's home."

Chapter 5

A TSUNAMI OF MESSAGES flooded back, all of which I ignored. Some of the epithets generated by the gang were truly creative words, ones I would tuck away to be used at a later date. But now I was back in the game.

Lunch was announced which meant we all got together and yarned. These were the fun times, we talked about stuff we had done, seen and generally lied to one and all. Sergeant Gorka had her team distribute food packages brought over from the frigate courtesy of Captain Blund, a true gent. Lydia arrived looking fresh and alert and everyone treated her with respect and affection. Exactly the reverse of how they treated me — it's good to have mates.

The Man in Black and Phil emerged from their conference with Caesar, both looking absurdly pleased with themselves. That was my clue we were going to be involved in some more sewage. If things were safe and stable, they would have looked almost bored. But no, they competed to see who had the have the biggest smirk of complacency.

"Bloody hell," said Teddy Boy when he saw them coming to join us, "We're in trouble."

The great and the good joined us and invited Sergeant Gorka, Sylvia and Lydia to our makeshift table. I looked around, this was the command team and when a command team gets together, it usually involves commands being given. Since I hadn't called this meeting, I was in the dark, my normal operating place; I didn't like it but I understood it. The boss, or Phil, was going to tell us about some new wacko scheme. It's how we roll.

"We're heading back to the frigate tonight," said the boss.

Okay, not so bad.

"I'll be going to the scout ship," said Phil.

We all looked at them both. Silence roamed the table as our two betters scarfed down rations. I sat back, took in the assembled throngs who were deeply involved in eating, no one appeared to be watching us or taking any notice of our conversations. Live that dream, pal, I thought. The NightWatch were masters at hovering on the edge of conversations and so learning where the bodies were buried. We'd even buried a few ourselves. Thus, I knew whatever we discussed would be public knowledge about two heartbeats after we finished talking.

Time for some delicate leadership, the sure hand, the subtle art of negotiation.

"Alright, you two wankers," I said. "What have you cooked up for us now? New ways to die?"

Sergeant Gorka snuffled pieces of food out her nose. She was still getting used to our egalitarian manner of conversing with those of higher rank. The Man in Black gave me an innocent look, Phil kept his smirk going.

"I may have to punch you in the face, Your Highness," I said to him.

"Surely not, Sergeant Valentine," said Phil. "You forget I travel under the protection of the redoubtable Sergeant Gorka and her squad of marines." He smiled at Gorka, she was entranced with the food before her. "I am finally returning to my original journey, albeit somewhat bereft of my original companions."

"You are 'bereft', dickhead," I said, "Because that battle brig from the Confederacy blew up your pleasure yacht, killing damn near everyone. You are dead lucky Captain Blund was nearby and able to rescue your worthless carcass."

"Indeed," he agreed. Complacency emanated from him in waves. He turned to Sergeant Gorka, "I shall require two of your marines to accompany me on the journey, sergeant. I can fly the ship but would feel safer with some additional support."

"Yes, sir," said Gorka. Nothing else, just the acknowledgment. I watched her eyes lose focus for a moment and guessed she was breaking the news to a couple of her team. When her eyes refocussed, she said, "I have two people on standby, sir. Both are competent marines with specialties in small ship actions. One is qualified as a small ship pilot."

"Splendid," said Phil, returning to his food.

I kept my gaze on the boss. He must have felt it as a heavy presence because he stopped eating and returned my look. "All well, sergeant?"

"What's the go, boss?" I asked. "Is there anything else you might wish to share with us?"

He swallowed a bite of food, wiped his mouth with a fancy piece of cloth extracted from his sleeve and leaned back in the chair. Who carries fancy pieces of cloth up their sleeve? Shouldn't any wiping be done on the actual sleeve? Isn't that what sleeves are for?

"As you are aware, Caesar," he continued, "has declined our invitation to join the NightWatch."I interrupted him, "Do you mean the invitation you extended when you were hopped to the gills on painkillers? The one where you thought having a gigantic spaceship as a member of the NightWatch was good idea. Do you mean that actual, stupid invitation?"

Silence settled over the table. Gorka was still, watching the back and forth but not becoming involved, she was probably seeing it as a learning experience on how to stuff up a cadre. Phil continued to smile and enjoy our banter. The rest of the NightWatch remained still, sensing the boss and I had gone beyond friendly badinage and were now engaged in what may possibly become a physical altercation. A lot of my discussions finished as physical altercations.

"Settle down, Val," said the boss. "Take a breath and step back from that precipice."

I found I was standing and leaning forward. Aggressively leaning forward. I didn't recall getting to my feet, perhaps I had not fully recovered from my physical injuries. Or my mental ones. And let's not forget the emotional strain of looking after this gaggle of suicidal morons and homicidal maniacs. A gentle hand rested on my arm, I looked down to see Lydia watching me with a kind and gentle face. Scanning the table, I saw Ted showing his neutral, hard face — but it wasn't directed at me, he was facing the boss. If it all kicked off, Ted would back me up. My last glance took in Sylvia, she was staring at me, wide eyed and afraid.

Hmm, if I'd scared Sylvia then I was in trouble. I took a breath, muttered an apology and sat down and the table exhaled in relief. Gorka continued eating, Phil kept his smile in place. I continued to think I would have to punch him later.

Okay, I'm all good now.

"I want to apologise," said the boss.

That rocked me. I've never heard him say anything along those lines before. Usually, his talks require us to come up to his level. Any error was ours and we had to be better. He set the standard and we all followed his example. What was he apologising for?

"I haven't been keeping you all in the loop. Mainly, because I didn't know where we were going in our negotiations with both Phil and

Caesar. But now, I believe I can share what we have discussed. Things are a bit clearer and I think I have handle on ... stuff."

Okay, I thought, this was better. I leaned back and felt Lydia gently rubbing the back of my neck with her free hand. Life has special moments, if you let them gently unfold.

"Yes, I did offer Caesar a place in the NightWatch. A truly stupid idea, as Val has pointed out. Yet, as we talked, Caesar and I found we had much in common. Like us, he is isolated from his home planet. His home galaxy, even. He has come into an awareness of who he is relatively recently. He is newborn."

God, this was getting boring, I emitted a slight groan, Lydia squeezed my neck in a touch which had gone from 'I'm on your side' to 'mind your manners'. She's a peach, I did my best to sit up and pretend I was interested in what the boss was saying.

"Phil has asked to take the scout ship directly to the capital planet of the Empire. The scout ship is much faster than our frigate and he has critical information concerning the new attacks by the Confederacy. As you heard, Sergeant Gorka will supply two of her people as crew, they will leave tonight."

I looked over at Phil, he was doing his best impression of mild compliance with whatever the boss said. A new look for our little royal, normally he's deep in some duplicitous scheme involving people being run over. And by 'people', I mean me. Sure, I liked him, but that doesn't mean I trusted the toe rag. He caught my look and winked at me. Yep, he was up to something.

"What about us, sir?" asked Teddy Boy. "Do we go back to the frigate?"

"Yes," replied the boss. "Caesar needs some time to continue repairs to this ship. Many functions remain inoperable and both he and PILOT must focus all their energies on repairing damage. The ship can move using docking engines but is otherwise trapped here until the repairs are complete. Additionally, the only defence currently available is a cloaking device. Offensive actions are limited to the power surge we have all witnessed, the one which has probably damaged our nanobots."

Several of us did a deep swallow at this statement. That would be those in possession of nanobots — Teddy Boy, me and a few NightWatch plus other newcomers to the gang. People like Lydia, Sylvia, Sergeant Gorka and her troopers plus a sprinkling of new additions to the NightWatch — those with no nanobots — still had the communicator bead in their ears.

Sergeant Gorka raised a finger to her ear, the one with the bead. She looked stoically neutral, well aware Caesar or PILOT could send a pulse out which would explode the bead. Such an explosion destroyed the bead and took out any surrounding living tissue. Stuff like brains.

A voice came over our communicators, those of us with malfunctioning nanobots had stuck a communicator bead in one ear so we all heard the voice. It was Caesar. "Again, I apologise for any inconvenience caused by the use of the pulse. PILOT was operating from a damaged outlook on the universe, everything was an enemy.""But we're all good now?" I queried. "You're not going to melt our minds. And to be clear, the previous use was not an 'inconvenience'. It killed the crew of the scout ship and an entire squad of Tharls. Let's hear no more of 'inconvenience'." My voice had once again taken on that ragged croak.

Ted was looking decidedly green. He had been aboard the scout ship with the Tharls as they all slowly dropped dead around him. He had been forced to spend a few hours alone in an abandoned spaceship surrounded by dead bodies and wondering what was going to leap out of a dark space to eat him. When I got to him with a rescue squad, I was full of concern for my little buddy and took the time to dump on the poor bludger. I find being offensive takes a person's mind off any immediate difficulties. Stuff like a possible impending death. You know, the usual.

It may have been my imagination, it's hard to tell vocal nuance through a communicator bead, especially when the one doing the communicating is a sentient machine. But, nonetheless, I felt Caesar gave an embarrassed gurgle accompanied by mental foot shuffling. Fair enough, I thought, the big lug may be feeling conflicted over the murderous actions of his insane PILOT. I could be generous.

"Now, sod off, Caesar, and let us get on with listening to the boss," I said.

Lydia hit me across the back of the head. Love that girl. My chin bounced towards the table as the boss said, "Thank you, Lydia. Keep up the good work." He gathered us all again with that sweeping look he could give. The one which made you sit up straight and check your shirt for food crumbs.

"As I was saying," he said, "we will take the assault shuttle tonight and return to the frigate. Lydia will pilot the vessel, we will drop Phil and his team off en route."

"There are two shuttles here, sir," said Lydia. "The assault shuttle you came over in and then the standard transport shuttle I piloted when I brought over the rescue team."

I couldn't let that one slide. "We didn't need rescuing," I growled, righteousness reeking from every syllable.

Chapter 6

THE TABLE WENT QUIET. Gorka was smiling, loving the process and enjoying a potential rift between Lydia and her stud muffin. "Well, Sergeant Valentine," she said, "you might not have needed rescuing, seeing as how you were unconscious at the time and leaking bodily fluids everywhere." She sat back and looked way too happy. "All of your team, including Lord Franz, were injured or dying."

Teddy Boy spoke up in a soft and gentle voice. It was never wise to antagonise Sergeant Gorka, she had a fearsome ability to pound the stuffing out of up to four muscle bound men at once, I'd seen her do it. But our lad was not going to let her previous comments go unchallenged. "To be clear, Sergeant Gorka," he said, his tone soft and low, almost a monotone, "We had already killed every damn thing on the vessel. Everything worth killing, I mean. And Val, that is to say, SERGEANT VALENTINE," he had risen a little in his seat at the same time as his voice rose to a thunderous roar, "HAD JUST SAVED THE LIFE OF EVERYONE ABOARD!"

He sank back down and continued in his lost voice. "He was badly hurt and semiconscious yet still able to do what needed to be done. We were successful in shutting down and then restarting the murderous inclinations of PILOT, we had defended a member of the Imperial family, we had lost several members of our team and we were all beaten up and injured. BUT WE DID NOT NEED RESCUING!" He took a breath. "Are we clear on that topic?" he asked.

Gorka sat with a slightly open mouth. She must have noticed the many filthy looks directed at her from the table because she replied in her meekest growl, "Absolutely, ensign. No offence intended."

I made a mental to buy Teddy Boy a beer at some point in the future. The far future, to be sure. Mustn't spoil the little git.

"I should rephrase my previous comment, sir," said Lydia. "When we arrived with the 'support team' we used a standard shuttle from the frigate. Who will take it back?""No one," answered the boss. "We are leaving it here for the use of Caesar. Phil has given the necessary permissions. Caesar believes he will be able to analyse the shuttle and possibly recreate some of our technology and thus speed up his own repair processes. Phil is happy because it means he can report back claiming successful negotiations have begun with our visitors from another galaxy."

Yeah, right, I thought. I bet Phil was going to leave out all mention of sentient spaceships and insane thinking machines. He likes to keep a few cards hidden, the lying snot.

"Caesar had previously established communications with the frigate, communications which resulted in the arrival of our 'support team'." The boss gave me a smile as he emphasised the last words. "I now ask Sergeant Gorka to brief Captain Blund on the frigate, let him know our plans. We intend to depart this vessel tonight." He turned to Teddy Boy. "Ensign Franco, please ensure everyone is packed and ready to leave after our evening meal."

Ted looked blank, then he looked at me. I studied a far wall and ignored his pleading eyes.

"Yes, sir," he muttered.

I pulled the communication bead out of my ear, it was bigger than I remember. As I turned it over in my hand, Lydia rested her chin on my shoulder. "Watcha doin'?" she asked, her voice gentle and thrilling at the same time.

"This bead is bigger than the ones we used to have. You know, back on our first planet when that bastard Chayla tried to kill us all.'

"Because this one is military grade while the ones we used to have were primarily for traders."

"Why's it bigger?"

She took the bead from my hand and stuck it back into my ear. "This one," she explained, "has two functions. It serves as a translator, like the beads we used to have but it also contains a short-range transmitter. When your nanobots were working, these two functions were carried out by separate groups of nanobots. Now, it seems, the ones responsible for short range communication have decided to roll over and die. You'll probably excrete them out if you haven't already done so."

"You mean I'll be defecating nanobots? Solids and liquids?"

"A true poet, such a colourful turn of phrase. Who said romance is dead?"

"Hey, I can be romantic." I couldn't let such allegations go unchallenged. "What about the night I sang to you? Dead romantic."

"That would be the song about the miller's daughter and the donkey?"

She had a point. Right, I resolved to be more poetical, more of the soft and floppy young lad so beloved by young girls and less of the rough-hewn son of the soil. I gave a deep sigh and fluttered my eyes whilst also taking on a soft and dewy faraway look.

Horse chose that moment to wander past. "A good crap will fix you right up, Val. Sorry to interrupt any tender mooning, Lydia. The boss wants dickhead here to pull his finger out and do some work. He wants a briefing on everyone's readiness in fifteen minutes."

My girl stood up, ruffled my hair and said, "No worries, Horse, I'll be sure to have my stuff packed and at the shuttle door. I can also give Sylvia a hand." She leaned down, kissed me gently on the cheek and then more sensuously on the lips. Tongue was involved. Then she straightened up, breathing pleasantly heavily and sashayed away.

I remained where I was, endeavouring to slow my beating heart, Lydia's kisses could jump start an elephant. I was smiling that smile we reserve for bliss, the one everyone round us hates. Horse slapped me on the back, hard enough to rock me forward. "You lucky, lucky bastard, Valentine," he said. "If you ever hurt that girl, I will personally cut off your nads."

I heard his voice from afar whilst contemplating Lydia's departing form. His words struck a deep chord in my heart. "You have the soul of a poet, Horse. And if I ever do hurt that girl, I'll supply the knife. A rusty knife.""Fair enough," he replied. "Now, what do you want us to do? Ted's looking all lost and alone. I'll get the gang together to pack stuff, that's no problem. What else do we need to do?"

Okay, time for me to work. I jumped on the communication networks and started giving instructions. Mainly, it was me delegating who should look after what. I don't believe in micromanaging so I used my standard mechanism of outlining all the tasks and then said to the team, "Make it happen."

Syvia said all the wounded were able to be moved, so that was a win. But it did make me think about our dead. What would we do with them? Perhaps that was a decision for higher up the food chain. By this time, the fifteen minutes had passed and I decided to find the boss and give him an update. The update would mainly consist of me saying, "We're all good," and hoping he didn't ask for details.

Naturally, he was back with Caesar, having more private discussions. "Ahh, Val," he said as I came through the doorway, "All well?"

"No worries, boss," I said. "We're all set."

"Should I ask for a more detailed report?"

"Go for your life, I can make stuff up." I sat down and patted the crate containing Caesar, "Will you be right without us, Caesar? Not going to get lonesome and sad? Not going to run amok and take over the universe?"

"Bite your bum, sergeant," said Caesar. I raised my eyebrows at this comment and gave the boss a questioning look.

"Yes," he said, "Caesar's attitude has been heavily influenced by hanging around with some of the more unsavoury characters from the Night-Watch."

"Not sure if that's a good thing, sir," I said. "We're not big on savoury."

"He does seem to have acquired a healthy disrespect for authority," said the boss. "Can't imagine where he got that one from." I caught his accusing look but bravely ignored it.

"What will we do with our dead, sir?" I asked, time to lower the cheerfulness factor. Silence was his reply. The boss and I looked at each other, I could see the touch of helplessness in his eyes and I felt sure he could see the same in mine.

"May I keep them?" asked Caesar.

My blood ran a little colder. "Why?" I asked. Was he going to try and reanimate them, would we have a ship sailing the space lanes crewed by shuffling corpses and maniacal machines? What did the future hold for our poor comrades.

"Easy, sergeant," said Caesar. "I can see by your face you believe I will be disrespecting their bodies. I can assure you, they will be treated with the utmost care and consideration.""What do you want them for?" asked the boss.

If a machine could give an embarrassed cough, Caesar did it then. He even muttered a small "umm..."

We waited.

"I am new to this thing called life. I know nothing of what makes me ... me. I understand your companions have ceased to be, they have 'died'. But what does that mean? What is 'life'? What is 'death'? I would treat your friends with respect but I would ask to be allowed to examine their bodies. Nothing ghoulish. I would not be creating any nightmares."

He stopped. My mind was blank. Was he asking permission to cut up our mates? To rummage around inside the people who stood and defended us — and him — knowing they were making the ultimate sacrifice. I don't think I liked this idea.

"I would also like to learn how your bodies work. Perhaps, in the future, I could contribute some benefit to the NightWatch. I am aware of your nanobots, they do sound wonderfully interesting. It may be I could assist in their development?"

He sounded plaintive. We stood before a machine bargaining with us so he could cut up the bodies of our friends. I didn't like it.

"No," I said.

"We cannot make that decision on our own, sergeant," said the Man in Black. "I will put it before all the NightWatch on this vessel. Together, we will decide. And together, we will have to explain our decision to the rest of our people when we return to the frigate." He was right, the mongrel.

"If you did not leave them with me," asked Caesar, "what would you do with the bodies?"

I started to say, "Bury them ..." and stopped. How would we bury them in space? Perhaps Captain Blund had a procedure for storing the bodies of any deceased crew person for future burial? But where would that happen? They might land on a nearby planet. The idea of burial on a strange planet, possibly inaccessible to any family, was too austere. And what ship captain allocated precious storage capacity to bodies?

No. Like our naval practices back on Earth, any dead would be sent into space. Never buried, never decaying, always orbiting some far away star. I shuddered, sometimes I creeped myself out.

Caesar spoke again, 'I would erect a memorial to them in the central area of this ship. A solemn remembrance of those who gave their lives that we ... that I ... might live."

We gathered everyone together and put the idea to the gang. At first, there was utter revulsion to the proposal. But, after some quiet reflection, we all came around to agreeing Caesar would keep the bodies, the concept of a memorial statue or structure resonated with all of us. Caesar showed us some preliminary designs of a structure into which he swore he would inter the remains of our people after he had finished with them, but still, his heart was in the right place. I realised what I said about a bloody machine having a heart. I am beyond stupid.

We agreed to let him have the bodies.

Chapter 7

OUR LAST MEAL ABOARD the huge spaceship was a sombre affair. No one felt like acting the goat, especially when I snarled at a few of the more stupid types who laughed too loudly. After I regained my seat and replaced the hammer back into its holster, everyone become interested in the food before them. Lots of soft murmurings. Sergeant Gorka moved behind me for more food and softly whispered in my ear, "You sure know how to make everyone depressed, you irritating man. Beautifully done, Val."

Intercourse off, I thought.

After dinner, I stood with Teddy Boy and we exchanged lies and other vital information, the sort of conversation mates have with each other. All was under control, people were beginning to drift towards the corridor leading to the assault shuttle. Almost time to go. Sergeant Gorka wandered by and told us that, courtesy of the assistance of Caesar, she had communicated with Captain Blund aboard the frigate. They were all ready for us to come home. Lost little lambs, we were.

My communicator pinged, the boss wanted to meet me, Lydia, Sylvia and Teddy Boy in Caesar's room. But not Gorka. And no one else, either.

Bloody wonderful, more secret nonsense.

I stood sullenly against an interior wall in the room housing Caesar, I didn't bother going over and talking to the boss. What did I care if he was feeling low? Yes, I know I was being petty and selfish but that's the kind of warm-hearted human being I am. Ask anyone. Lydia, Sylvia and Teddy Boy drifted in. The boss nodded at each of us as I began to wonder why these particular folk had been asked to join this little conclave. And why not Sergeant Gorka? Or Phil?

We waited in silence, no one else arrived; finally, the boss lurched into motion. He looked tired, exhausted even. Perhaps I had been too harsh in ignoring his needs, a good sergeant would have been at his side, giving him moral support. Yep, that's what a good sergeant would be doing — I stayed against my wall and sulked.

Two other machines entered, metallic, clunky and possibly murderous. I tensed until Caesar said, "Relax, everyone. I have gifts."

The two machines were similar but slightly different. Definitely spider looking, so Sylvia was turning green. Well done, Caesar, I thought, a win there. The larger spider thing was another box on articulated legs and moved creepily about, I kept wanting to hit it with my hammer. It was about as large as a coffin so no bad vibes there; a brutal yet simple design, no romantic flair.

"I have something for each of you," said Caesar. The top of the coffin box slid back, revealing a large empty space except for three smaller boxes. Each one had a strap. They looked like some sort of holster or ammunition pouch.

"What's this, sport?" I asked.

"These are for Lord Franz, Ensign Franco and Sergeant Valentine. Please take one each," said Caesar. We did so.

We now stood facing each other holding up the strap with one hand and looking at the dangling box before us. It was metal, rectangular and about the size of a good-sized plate. About as thick as my hand but with no discernible opening. Attached to the strap was smaller pouch containing a set of goggles. Or eyeglasses, hard to say.

"You're giving us some sort of dinner plate?" I said. "And safety goggles?"

"These are machines," he said.

"What do they do," I asked, "keep food warm?"

"No, but that is an excellent suggestion, I must make a note." There was a brief pause before he came back and said, "Unhook the machines from the straps. Wear the glasses."

We did so. Lydia was giving me anxious looks while Sylvia had moved to stand next to Ted, ready to lend medical assistance; probably something in the line of intense mouth to mouth. I must learn to control my brain.

"I am transmitting to each of you a command code." A soft ding in my mind indicated I had received the code. "Send the code to your machine."

"How?" asked Ted. I was grateful he had spoken up, I was getting tired of being the one asking dumb questions.

Caesar instructed us in the method for sending a command code to our machines. It involved some flexible mental practices and, on my part, a lot of grunting and squinting. But we all sent the code.

I knew we had done so when each machine raised itself on a set of legs, about eight of them. They unrolled from the external structure of each box, but when they were folded up and out of the way it was impossible to discern any gap. Extracting the legs meant the overall size of the remaining box was smaller. Little antennae like things popped out of the thing's head and they did a quick look around as the now smaller spider thing scuttled back and forth.

I wanted to pull out my hammer and squash the little creepy crawlies.

"Sergeant Valentine, please do not hit them," said Caesar. He was beginning to pick up on my little ways.

I stood there in shocked revulsion. The Man in Black remained calm and casual, tapping a thoughtful finger on his chin. But Teddy Boy, oh dear me, Teddy Boy was in heaven. He crouched down and put a hand out, his machine ran to him, climbed on his hand and then scuttled up his arm. Far from being righteously disgusted by this act, as I certainly was, he stood up and cooed at the damn thing. Sylvia had stepped well away from her beau, I suspect she did not approve of Ted's new toy. The day was getting better and better. Ted was blithely unaware of her grimaces and revulsion.

"This is so cool," he chortled. He held his arms out and let his little machine buddy run back and forth, when it reached his neck, it ducked into his shirt making him giggle before reappearing at the other arm. Ted was obviously mentally unbalanced. I think I agreed with Sylvia.

"Do they do anything?" asked the boss. "Or have we now acquired some sort of mechanical pet?"

A pet I would be squashing, first chance I got.

"The machine has a function, one you may find useful. The command code links the sensors on your machine to your glasses and also to your communication bead. If you ever get another bead, or functioning nanobots, transmit the same code to establish the link.

He gave us some other instructions including a few commands we could issue to our little spider buddies. We could use our glasses to see whatever the machine saw. I sent mine up the wall and then accessed its vision. Sure enough, there was the wall and, with a bit of careful placement, I could look down Lydia's blouse. These things had definite potential.

"Nurse Sylvia," said Caesar. "I understand you have a need for carrying medical supplies. Please take this large machine, the one now empty, and use it in any way you see fit. I have designed it as a transport device, capable of holding your supplies. It also has a secondary configuration, please observe."

The coffin box shuddered and bits slid about. It turned itself into a simple, flat surface. A table on legs. What the hell would this be good for, I wondered. A place to eat your dinner?

"You may find this useful," continued Caser, "for the transportation of sick and wounded, or perhaps even as a work surface while performing your necessary ministrations. It will also serve as a security device for you." Caesar must have sent another command to the coffin thing because several smaller arms erupted from it, each one holding knives, clubs and other instruments of destruction. I also saw a broom and a mop so I guessed the old cleaning and maintenance habits die hard. He went on, "I am transmitting codes to you now. These codes will allow you to instruct the machine to obey your commands, to transform or carry on as you see fit. I have also sent to you a video manual showing all of the capabilities of this machine."

Sylvia glowed. She honest to God glowed. Yes, the table now had legs and could still move but she now saw a medical device and not a scary giant mechanical insect. She babbled a set of thanks to Caesar and I saw her eyes glaze over. I assumed she was watching the videos. Some girls get flowers, others get scary machines which can dismember you.

"The smaller machine is for you, Lydia," said Caesar. "I understand you are an engineer and a mechanic, perhaps these tools may be of some use." The top of the machine slid back and several trays emerged on some sort of articulated arms. Each tray carried a tool. At least, I guessed they were tools. A side panel opened and another arm emerged, this one sparking a little.

Lydia swooned over the damn thing. She ran over, cuddled the bloody machine and began picking up tools and stroking them. The sparky thing caused her more glee, no idea why. Yep, we had weird girls in the NightWatch.

"Again," said Caesar, "I am sending you detailed instructions for each of the tools, including the necessary command codes."

"Why all the gifts?" I asked. "And why us?"

"Because, although I am not a member of the NightWatch, we have journeyed together over a significant part of my growth. You rescued me and have given me hope for the future. I believe, if you had not arrived, I would have slowly degenerated into madness. I may even be a little mad now."

My hand crept down towards my hammer. Caesar laughed, "Relax, Val, I'm kidding."

I don't know what made me more unsettled. The fact a damn machine could laugh, or that it could display a gutter level of humour. Naturally, I fell back on to my strengths in negotiations and leaned into charisma.

"Drop dead," I snarled. "You insensitive piece of pond scum. You're a glorified ... something." My voice trailed off because I could not think of an appropriate insult. What do you say to a thinking machine to put it in its place? Especially a machine which controlled your environment, the air and so on. Maybe I should shut up.

"Shut up, Val," said the Man in Black, ever the peacemaker. "But I support some of your questions. Why us for these gifts? What about Sergeant Gorka and everyone else out there?"

"It's a question of resources," replied Caesar. "PILOT cannot produce more than you see before you. At least, not now. If you stayed a bit longer, I could make more devices, we could even discuss what you might find useful. As for Sergeant Gorka, she is not a member of the NightWatch. Nor does she hold any status in our relationship other than Empire trooper."

"Uh-huh," said the boss. "But you said you were not a member of the NightWatch. What status are you talking about?""I have initiated a new category for us. I am the first in this category but you may see fit to include others as you journey through the stars."

Oh, dear God, he said 'journey through the stars'. Right, I would certainly find out who has been talking to Caesar. Some dipstick has been telling him stories again.

"I am in the ..." I heard a distant roll of drums, Caesar was playing this up. "... NightWatch Irregulars!"

Sure. No problem. Let's get as many weird things as possible into our nice little grouping.

Chapter 8

WE STARTED THIS WHOLE adventure with a bunch of drunken lowlifes, men who could be relied upon to be slothful, selfish, lazy and often drunk. My sort of people. Then we started allowing the rot to set in. First it was girls. Yes, they were bloodthirsty, aggressive females who were happy to drink and fart with the best of them. But still girls. And then we had the kids, the ankle biters we rescued from slavery. Resilient, energetic little nightmares capable of terrifying any adult who wandered into their midst. Now we had a bloody machine. Yes, Caesar was not a real member of the NightWatch but I am sure that's because he was so big. How do you squeeze a giant spaceship into the barracks? No, wouldn't work.

Fortunately, the boss had similar ideas. He stated, in a clear, authoritative voice, "No, we will not be using that phrase. People will want badges and emblems. Not going to happen, we will not have the 'NightWatch Irregulars'."

We wandered out with our new toys and got ready for departure, eventually meeting everyone else as they gathered at the assault shuttle entrance in preparation for leaving. We were all back in space armour because the boss told us to do so. My new suit had been obtained from stores aboard the shuttle and showed no signs of having been gnawed on or thrown up in, so that was a win.

I wandered over to one particularly diminutive space armoured figure. The person inside the suit was making a strong attempt at casual insouciance, an effect spoiled by the compressed nature of the suit. This compression was caused because the figure inside the suit was Jeremy, a young boy of indeterminate years, somewhere between ten and thirteen. It varied each time you asked him. He had a way of annoying me by existing, the little twerp. But I did love the nugget. More fool me.

"Is that you, Jeremy, and are you pretending to be a spaceman?" I asked.

"Umfgl," came the reply. It was difficult to understand through my suit's external speakers. Jeremy was yelling inside his helmet, choosing not to use the built-in communicators.

"Strong words, indeed, you loathsome pimple," I pushed him and he staggered back onto his backside.

"UMFGL!"

"Sorry, what's that?" I loomed over him. He resisted my attempt at subtle intimidation and punched me in the groin.

"Didn't hurt, wart. Remember, these are 'armoured' spacesuits. I suspect they are up to handling any grief you can dish out."

"Umfg ... UMFGL!"

"Oh, for God's sake. There's a toggle near your chin. Nudge it and you'll engage the suit's external communicators."

"HI, UNCLE VAL! HOW DID YOU KNOW IT WAS ME?"

"Adjust your volume, snotbreath. Look at the display on your helmet and work it out. How have you managed to avoid being pounded into paste thus far in your life, oh small wizened person? And from where did you get that ridiculous suit?"

Jeremy stood before me in a parody of an armoured space marine. These suits were adjustable, points at various places allowed for the arms, legs and torso to stretch or contract. Other adjustments allowed for the girth of torso, arms and legs to extend or contract. My little mate had obviously grabbed a suit and cranked every setting to the bare minimum. I was looking at an entire spacesuit compressed to its smallest settings. He looked like a squat barrel on stumpy legs waving two pipes for arms. The elbow and knee joints dominated. Atop the entire disaster was a full-sized helmet.

He looked ridiculous.

"Looking good, mate," I said. "Armageddon level threatening, I'm quaking in my boots .""Honest?" he asked, a certain plaintive note in his voice. It also contained overtones of discomfort and nervousness. "I look alright? I didn't know how to do some of the adjustments. Truth to tell, Val, I think I've messed up some of the bits, I've got part of a sleeve jutting into my stomach and I think a piece of leg wants to go up my bum.""You are a joyful conversationalist, Jeremy. Hard to believe people want to punch you in the face so often.""It's usually you, Uncle Val."

True. I took my role as mentor to the cadet corps seriously. As such, I endeavoured to give them real world experiences about dealing with unpleasant people. Some of life's tougher lessons. They'd thank me one day.

Still, whereas I don't mind inflicting some life affirming suffering myself, I draw the line at anyone or anything else hurting my little guys. I called Sergeant Elena over and introduced her to Jeremy, explaining he had done the suit adjustments himself.

She looked horrified and began unstrapping bits from the little nugget. His face emerged, showing a dubious shade of red, not improved by the protruding tongue nor the tears welling in his eyes. I stepped forward and assisted in getting the little guy out of the instrument of torture. He hugged me, snuffled in my shoulder and mumbled some thanks.

I gave him a noogie.

"Elena," I said, "can you reinsert Jeremy into this suit and make the connections all good and safe?""Sure," she said. "But, Jeremy, why do you need to be in a suit?"

"Because everyone getting on that shuttle is wearing a suit," announced my minor Achilles. "Plus, I want to look cool for the rest of the kids when we get back. Umm ..." he paused, I knew what was coming.

"Need a restroom break, Jeremy?" I asked. He nodded. I turned to Elena and said, "Jeremy has bladder issues."

"Aww, Val," he muttered. "Let's keep that a bit quiet, if you don't mind."

He stood before us, suit pieces hanging off him and piled on the floor, his clothes were soaked in sweat and he looked the picture of lost childhood. Poor little lamb.

"I'm going to have to kill someone," he announced. Okay, not such a lamb, then. "After I go to the loo," he finished.

"You can," said Elena. "Or I can hook you into the suit's systems. People can be in these suits for hours, sometimes days. They can take our bodily waste products and recycle them or flush them when convenient. That way, you always feel comfortable. I'll also show you how to use the air conditioning functions and some other comfort features.""I can wee in the suit?" Jeremy asked, homing in on the key element of Elena's words. Hope for new life was dawning in his eyes. "And it won't get all stinky?"

Elena nodded, Jeremy hugged her and I left them to it. Dear God, I thought, I've made a person happy by giving him the option of urinating whenever required. That had to be Jeremy heaven.

We began boarding.

The sick and wounded and non-combatants boarded first. Then Sergeant Gorka and her team, followed by our surviving lads and lasses. Finally, it was down to the Man in Black, Teddy Boy and me standing there. Teddy Boy entered, his new toy slung over one shoulder.

"Want to be last to leave, Val?" asked the Man in Black. "Sort of a symbolic moment?" I couldn't care less when I boarded, I was not interested in the heroic image of being the last to leave this bloody giant spaceship where so many of us had died. Where we had also gained ... something.

"Nah," I said and went into the hatch of the shuttle.

I didn't get far because Sergeant Gorka was pushing to get back outside. Behind her was Phil and over his shoulders I could see the rest of the gang. Some asleep in chairs, other chatting and winding down.

But not Gorka. She was in the moment. She barrelled into me, pushed me out of the way and strode to stand before the boss. Phil put out a hand to stop me from falling over, Gorka has significant body mass, most of it muscle.

"You better hear this, Val" said the prince, pulling me along with him. We caught up to Gorka as she started speaking to the boss, she was using the internal communicator channel for the command group so I could hear it. Back in the shuttle, her words would also be heard by Teddy Boy, Sylvia and Lydia. We're an egalitarian lot.

The boss gave her a quiet look. "Problem, sergeant?" he asked.

"The frigate's under attack," she replied.

Everyone got off the shuttle, even the sick and wounded. We wandered back to the main room, the large cathedral-like space where everyone again sat down. The boss had Sergeant Gorka loop everyone into the discussion, including Caesar.

Break out a few drinks and snacks and we could have a party.

"Start again, sergeant," ordered the Man in Black.

"Yes, sir," she barked. She stood slightly more rigidly, not exactly saluting but a hand strongly wanted to bounce up and down.

"I was sending a message to Captain Blund, Caesar had given me this long-range communication module," she said, holding up a box with lights, dials and other stuff of no interest to me. "A standard communication informing him we were about to depart." I watched her marines gathering in a more formal set of ranks off to one side. They all fiddled with their gear, transitioning from passengers on a shuttle to potential combatants.

The Nightwatch continued to flop on the ground or lean against walls. I think I even heard snoring. Terrors of the galaxy, we were.

"As we spoke," she went on, "the frigate was attacked by a battle brig, probably the same one which destroyed His Grace's yacht. It has physically attached itself to our frigate and will be attempting to drive a hole through the ship's hull and board her. I would like to take my team back to the frigate and assist in its defence." She stood expectantly after finishing her little speech. Her body twitched, eager to leap about and get started on what I could see as a suicide mission.

The silence stretched.

Thank goodness, I thought, we have a leader with a brain. If we all jumped back aboard the assault shuttle and attempted to rejoin the frigate, we would probably be shot down by the weapons on the battle brig. Totally bad idea. Stupid, suicidal and a disaster waiting to happen.

"Sure," agreed the boss. "We can do that."

Twit. Pillock. Lunatic.

Chapter 9

GORKA STARTED TO BOUNCE, ready to get right to it.

"But," said the boss, "perhaps we might consider how we attack. A bit of thought might increase our efficiency and produce a wonderfully destructive plan." He was certainly a clever bloke. Any gung-ho military types would be fully in agreement with a plan based upon words like 'wonderfully destructive'. Gorka ceased to vibrate and calmed down. Perhaps she was rethinking her initial desire to charge the guns.

Once again, the boss had brought some sanity into the conversation.

"Tell us about this 'battle brig'," he instructed Gorka.

"It's the ship from the Confederacy which destroyed my yacht," put in Phil. "I would have been a dead man if Captain Blund hadn't turned up and retrieved my survival pod.""Phil," said the boss, his voice calm and moderate. "Shut your mouth."

Gotta love that guy.

The boss nodded at Gorka who launched into a precise briefing on our situation.

"Sir, yes sir," she began. "A battle brig is a long-range raider, capable of outrunning heavy ships like dreadnoughts and cruisers while carrying weapons able to take out individual ships of frigate class and below. It is used to interdict supply lines, for long range seek and destroy missions and also as a roving bloody nuisance."

"Our frigate would not be able to defeat such a ship?" asked the boss.

"Yes, it has been done before. But it is remarkably rare. A frigate is at the lower end of the ships capable of standing up, even briefly, to a battle brig. Captain Blund would be outgunned and unable to match its speed. But that is not the primary offensive capability of the brig"

"Do go on, sergeant."

"Sir, yes, sir. If the target ship is not at full speed, but perhaps on a gentle patrol or stationary while keeping post ..." she began.

"Like our frigate was doing," interrupted the boss.

"Correct, sir. In that case, the battle brig is capable of cloaking itself and moving slowly into position. It won't work on a swiftly moving vessel but is bloody effective against transports or situations like the one we have with Captain Blund. When ready, it attaches itself to the hull of the enemy vessel. It has a particular assault strategy, whereby it punches through the hull of the target ship, even the hull of a frigate. The particular explosive hatch on the Brig is big and devastating. In short order, it would be capable of breaching the hull of the frigate at a point of its choosing and then sending storming parties aboard. At the same time, the Brig would have launched its associated short-range fighters which would be searching for any escape pods or other communication rockets."

"Hmm," said the boss. "And if we launched from this ship, we would probably be seen by either the battle brig's own weapons or by these fighters of which you speak."

"Yes, sir. We would be sitting ducks."

"Shot down?"

"More than likely, sir. The assault shuttle has some armour, more than a standard shuttle. It's capable of holding off weapons from the fighters for a short time. But against any major weapon on the battle brig, no chance." Gorka had lost her bounciness, reality raising its ugly head.

"To be clear," said the boss. "If we tried to rejoin the frigate, right now, we would be spotted and probably destroyed."

Silence. Then, from Sergeant Gorka a small response, "Yes, sir."

"Let's not aim for that outcome then," said the boss.

We all hung around, waiting for his mighty brain to come up with a plan.

"Pity we cannot sneak across without being seen," muttered our fearless leader. "We could sneak back into the frigate and help out. I'm especially interested in what has happened to the rest of the NightWatch."

"They'll be fine, sir," I put in. "Magic and the gang were doing lots of drills in case we were boarded by hostile forces.""Why on Earth would you all have been doing those sorts of drills, Val?" asked the boss. "Did you expect this to happen?"

"Hell no, sir. But I couldn't stand having our people sitting around doing nothing. Wanted to keep them busy with a few games. You know what they're like if you take your eyes of these bedwetters. Probably end up drinking everything in sight and peeing in dark corners." Murmurs of agreement came from the lads and lasses we had brought over. No one was offended at this character profile of our folk.

"What a wonderful image you paint of the NightWatch, sergeant," said Phil.

I turned to him and said, "Again, fungus for brains, shut your mouth."

"Shutting up, sergeant," said Phil, he being was far too polite and far too agreeable.

I may have to hit Phil some more.

More silence floated in and dragged on. The brain's trust was dry. According to our normal operating procedure, anyone in the NightWatch could offer a suggestion and they usually were keen to do so. But not today. Assaulting a spaceship was probably a little outside their realms of experience given their technology experience ended with the horse and cart.

"I could help with the 'unseen' part of your plan," came Caesar's voice. Great. A newly born 'thinking engine' — not sure what to call it — was going to give us tips on how to kill other living beings. We were certainly doing our bit to corrupt his innocent soul. Ah, well, life sucks and then you die.

"What do you suggest, Caesar?" asked the boss.

"My ship is currently cloaked. I can install other devices on the hull of your assault shuttle which would extend that cloak, especially if I moved my ship closer to the battle.""You've got engine power again?" asked Lydia. That's my girl, the one with the spanner and a love for machinery.

"Manoeuvring power for the moment but more will come online as repairs continue. But I can certainly cloak your assault shuttle."

A thought blossomed in my brain, it does this sometimes because the damn thing likes to wander about the vast caverns and empty spaces in my head. "Why is it called an 'assault shuttle'?" I asked. "What makes it different to the normal shuttles we have been using?"

"Heavier armour," replied, Gorka. "And it has a special hatch in its belly. It can be used to assault enemy ships, normally we go in with a battalion of shuttles and squadrons of support fighters to clear the way."

"Tell us about this 'special hatch'," said the boss.

"Well, it's like the big one on the battle brig. The assault shuttle lands on the hull of an enemy vessel, the hatch has the capability of blowing a hole in the hull and in we go. The hole is much smaller than one generated by the Brig, but good enough for armoured marines to go in. Only one at a time, but that's enough. Especially when there are about twenty shuttles doing the assault. Ten to twenty shuttles are considered to be the bare minimum for an assault of this nature."

"Hmmm ..." said the boss.

"Oh, hell," I heard Ted mutter.

With you on that, Ted, I thought. For I knew what our crazy hooligan of a leader was planning to do.

"I think we can have a go at those guttersnipes," said the boss. "Let's get some prep done, then fly across to the battle brig and kick its teeth in."

I looked around, Gorka and her team were all on board with the idea while most of the NightWatch were too dim to fully understand the magnitude of our idiot leader's suggestion. Lydia looked worried, Sylvia simmered with anger at fools off to do foolish things, Teddy Boy and I exchanged worried glances and Greenash stood trembling. Now there's a sensible man, I thought.

Wallace leaned against a wall and smiled at me. God, he's infuriating sometimes.

We were going to assault the battle brig. Just us. The one little vessel. Against an entire ship full of angry, angry people.

Poo, Bum, Tit, Fart ... Enema.

Chapter 10

WE SPENT MORE TIME arguing over the plan. That is, I argued how ridiculous it was while most of the others ignored me. Lydia kept hanging onto my arm and giving me pleading looks. Sylvia checked and rechecked her medical equipment, hitting things as she packed and repacked her gear. Everyone gave her a wide berth, even Ted circled at a distance.

Little machines scurried past us and moved into the area adjoining our assault shuttle, Caesar calmly informed us he was installing some modules on the shuttle's skin which would extend his cloaking device. He assured us he would move his ship, the *New Rome*, closer to the fight so the cloak would work.

"You mean, if we get too far away from your floating junk pile of a spaceship, then the cloak won't work?" I asked. I was keen to poke holes in every aspect of the plan. Not that I understood it to have many subtleties. We would fly over in cloaked mode, land on the hull of the battle brig, punch an access hole into its guts and then storm aboard. Shortly after that, we would all die.

Ordinary, straightforward stuff. No clever flanking manoeuvres or feints and sudden rallies. We would stroll through the enemy vessel while every Confederacy trooper lined up to kill us.

I was so on board with this plan.

"For God's sake, Valentine," growled the Man in Black. "Shut up. Do your damned job."

"But we're all going to die, sir," I pointed out with some justification.

"Of course, we're all going to die!" he snarled. "We all die, might as well do it now as later. Or do you want to stay on *New Rome* and chat with Caesar until you starve to death?"

"You can be a dead set turd burglar sometimes, sir."

"You're getting the hang of this NightWatch vernacular, sergeant," he smiled at me.

Once again, everyone went on board the shuttle. We sat in our rows, strapped in and watched Phil walk up to the pilot's cabin.

"Where are you going, Phil?" I called.

He turned to me, I could feel the rest of the gang shifting in their seats in preparation for a touch of street theatre. Phil's eyes flicked around the room, saw he had everyone's attention and gave me his most annoying grin. I was about to have a discussion with this dropkick in front of everyone, a discussion in which he would undoubtedly call into question my ability to think, plan and generally have half a brain.

"I'm going to fly us over to the battle brig, sergeant." He paused, "Unless you would like to do the honours?" He gestured towards the pilot area.

I glared at him.

"No?" he questioned. "Then perhaps I might continue with my task. But you stay there, we need someone to keep that seat warm. And you have such a huge bum."Lydia stood up from where she was snuggling beside me and walked over to Phil. As she walked towards him, he gave her the smile charismatic bad boys have given beautiful girls down through the ages. The one which seems to reach out and charm them, the look which says they are mad, bad and dangerous to know. The look which attracts girls like flies to honey.

Lydia returned his smile, but he must have seen something else in my girl's approach, something the rest of us were unable to witness. I couldn't see her face but he could, I noticed his own cheeky grin falter followed by a significant swallow.

She stood with her back to us, right on Phil's shoulder. Then she leaned in and whispered something in his ear. His face drained of all colour. He bobbed his head, nodded furiously and muttered something small and fragile back to her. She returned to her seat beside me, grabbed my arm and snuggled in closer. That's my girl, capable of intimidating heirs to Empires.

Phil gurgled something about preflight checks and scuttled into the pilot's cabin.

Behind me, Sergeant Gorka leaned her head in between Lydia and me to say, "You lucky, lucky bastard, Valentine."

Amen, sister. Gorka had been casting lustful glances at Lydia from the moment they met. Glances which had bounced of my sweetie pie because she has me as arm candy. Yes, I'm blushing.

The boss called us all to order, using our helmet's internal communicators. "Listen up, everyone," he said, "Phil's going to fly us over to the enemy ship. He's doing the flying because he tells me he's an ace combat pilot and Phil always tells the truth." Many groans came from the team, one of them mine. "Our other choice is Lydia and she's too valuable to risk up the pointy end. If someone's going to stuff this up and die when we crash into the bloody battle brig then I want it to be Phil. Any questions?"

Silence was the stern reply. I half expected Phil to say a few words in rebuttal but Lydia's last comments may still have been impacting his self-image. She has the ability to scare some people silly, me among them. I love her to bits. But she can be ... strong.

"Good," continued the boss. "When we land on the enemy hull, we will punch a hole using the built in assault function on this shuttle." There was a pause. Then he continued, "Does anyone know how that works?" Good man, our boss. But apparently now realising we were strapped in a metal coffin about to attack a bigger ship with no real idea what we were doing.

I love my job.

Sergeant Gorka helped us out. "This shuttle has an explosive hatch in its belly. We land on the battle brig and activate the explosives. These punch through the hull of the enemy vessel allowing boarding parties to storm ahead.'

More silence. Gorka's people probably knew all about this stuff, but us in the NightWatch were now realising we were sitting in a vessel which had powerful explosives underneath our collective bums.

"Won't the explosion also kill us?" asked someone. Damn fine question. I was thinking it but was unable to speak due to the inherent terror coursing through my body. We were sitting in a flying bomb.

"No," replied Gorka. "It's all carefully designed to push the force of the explosion out and away from the shuttle. The whole process is thoroughly dependable." There was another slight thinking pause before she finished with, "Usually."

Phil jumped in with, "And built by the lowest bidder." He was being a right cheerful mongrel, somebody was retching inside their helmet, I hoped it wasn't me.

"Okay," said the boss. "Let's continue. We will work on the assumption this assault won't kill us all the minute we activate the explosions underneath our backsides, blowing the family jewels into oblivion. Now let's consider how we do the actual assault. Phil and Sergeant Gorka, your advice, please. Do we storm aboard and kill everyone in sight?" Yep, that was our usual modus operandi. If it moves, hit it. If it stays still, step on it.

"I'll leave the planning to the good sergeant," said Phil. "I'm going to be busy in a few minutes trying to land on the damned Brig. Then I've got to work out which is the right set of buttons to set off the explosion for the assault. Don't want it to backfire. Still, if I get it wrong then we'll never know."

Yep, I would, most certainly, be hitting him later.

"Sergeant Gorka," said the boss, "suggestions, please?"

"Yes sir," she replied. "An assault on an enemy vessel should have a focus. We'll be outnumbered, even if they have sent the majority of their marines into the attack on our frigate." She drew breath. "I think we have two priorities, their communications room and their engineering room. We will need to ensure they don't call for help, while generally stuffing about with their internal comms. If we can disable this facility then their assault on the frigate will be severely compromised."

"Very good, sergeant," said the Man in Black, "and the engineering?"

"We want to disable their ability to disengage from the fight, sir. If they feel their assault is not successful, they may decide to pull back and use their guns to disable the frigate. I think they did their initial assault because they want to capture the frigate undamaged.""Why would they want to do that?"

"Don't know, sir," replied Gorka.

"Probably me," said Phil.

Oh, yeah, that's right. Capturing one of the royal family would be high on an enemy's list of priorities.

"We will be guided by your advice, sergeant," said the boss. "You take your team and assault the communication section. I will take the NightWatch to the engines."

"Could I suggest we reverse those targets, sir?" said Gorka. "The engines are durable but can be damaged by, er, heavy handed interference. It might be best if I take my team down there. We know what we can hit and what might go boom."

"Agreed," said the boss. "Sergeant Valentine, that means we will head to the communication section."

"Yessir," I said, upstanding soldier that I was. "Any specific rules of engagement?"

"Kill the bastards," said the boss.

"Right you are, sir. Killing the bastards it is." I heard several murmurs of agreement from the team. We could deal with this level of instruction. Find the enemy, kill them. We like to keep things simple.

"I'm not assaulting anything," said Sylvia. "I heal people. I put them back together after barbarians like you have done your best to cause harm." She was right, we were barbarians.

"I agree, Sylvia," said the boss. "The barbarian element will be coming along on the assault. That means some of you must remain on the shuttle with Phil.

"Excuse me?" said Phil. "I intend to be part of this little action."

"Think it through, gobshite," I said. "if they attacked the frigate looking for you, it might not be the best plan to have you waltz aboard the enemy ship.""But how would they know it was me?" he asked. "We all look alike in these suits." I had no response to this seemingly reasonable objection, so I shut up.

Fortunately, the great and the good on the team had a rationale for the decision. "You'll do as you're bloody well told, Phil," said the boss.

"You're staying on the shuttle. I don't trust you to not mouth off in there and announce your presence or do something else incredibly stupid."

Excellent, I thought. Being incredibly stupid was my job.

"Wallace, said the boss, "You'll stay on the shuttle and make sure His Grace remains here and out of harm's way."

"Might not be possible to do both, Franz," said Wallace, our ex-assassin. "I might have to cause him a little harm to ensure he complies with your orders."

Sure, Wallace called the boss by his first name, to everyone else he was Lord Franz von Palmerland but the boss and Wallace had become a highly functioning team. The boss did the thinking, Wallace did the security. Also, Wallace did this because he wasn't intimidated by anyone, he treated everyone the same. Namely, as a potential target. For some reason, the boss liked him and used him as personal security. Wallace's presence tended to give any uppity NightWatch member severe pause before conducting an aggressive interview with our lord and master. He tended to break the odd arm when he felt the discussion had reached a certain level of obnoxiousness. That level changed randomly so we never knew if he was okay with a mild disagreement or if you would walk away from the conversation holding your teeth.

My kind of guy. I was always nervous around Wallace.

Phil gurgled agreement, it didn't do to upset Wallace.

"The wounded will also stay on the shuttle with Sylvia. Lydia, Greenash and Jeremy will also remain with you." The boss was laying down the law.

Sylvia acknowledged her agreement. Greenash chimed in with his full support for the plan.

Jeremy and Lydia were noticeable by their silence.

"Jeremy, you little wart, did you hear the boss?" I asked. "You stay on board the shuttle. You, too, Lydia."

"We heard him," said Lydia, jumping in before Jeremy could say anything. He probably wouldn't dare speak up because he was one of the many people in awe of the boss. Hence, he was probably giving the waste product recycling function of the suit a thorough workout.

But I spotted her prevarication, 'hearing' does not equate to 'obeying'; it was one I often used myself. I sensed these two would be trouble; Jeremy is always trouble and Lydia has a mind of her own. She's not big on listening to authority, unless it agreed with her worldview.

She hangs around with the wrong crowd.

Chapter 11

I FELT A GENTLE bump which I took to be our arrival upon the hull of the battle brig. Since I had no idea what to do next, I stayed slumped in my seat and nuzzled Lydia. She nuzzled me back and all in all, we were having a great time until Sergeant Gorka's voice broke into our little tryst.

"Is this man annoying you, Lydia?" the sergeant asked.

"Absolutely," my girl responded in a soft murmur. "In the nicest possible way."

"Well, If I could interrupt your public fornication, perhaps you two could stagger to your feet and come with the rest of us. We were thinking of boarding an enemy vessel today, if that's alright with you?"

Lydia and I disengaged and slowly stood up, I noticed the gang were moving towards a door leading to yet another clever space inside this bloody shuttle. Perhaps I should have explored its inner workings and familiarised myself with how it was all laid out. You know, get to know the lay of the land, 'situational awareness' I believe it's called. But no, I had to fritter away my time nuzzling Lydia. It's all about priorities, I'm not a complete idiot.

"You are such an idiot, Valentine," snarled Gorka. "We've got a job to do, try and focus!" She turned to Lydia, "Not you, honey. You're perfect," she purred.

Most of the NightWatch were watching our little interchange with smiles, most of the lads — and one of the girls — were taking a great deal of interest in Lydia's chest, even in space armour. I pushed my way through the throng, all semblance of romance having disappeared from my person, and found the boss.

"Got any idea what we have to do?" I asked my lord and master.

"Nope," he replied. "I'm following Sergeant Gorka, she seems to be switched on. I'm guessing that's what a good sergeant looks like.""A re you impugning my professionalism, sir? Calling into question my sergeanty abilities?"

"Heck, no, Val," he said. "That'd be too cruel, like kicking a puppy." He pushed past me and followed Gorka through the door, his shoulder nudging mine in the normal blokey display of annoying your mates. "Come on, pusbrain, work now, play later."I followed him, "Right you are, sir. Slacking off now, copulating later.""You can be such a dick, Val."

"Trying to work on my sergeantness, sir."

The doorway we entered led to a wide ramp which took us to the lower level of the shuttle. This was a large room containing many lockers and a wall panel holding lots of buttons and levers. I sent a command to the NightWatch to stay the hell away from the panel. The lads and lasses had a bad habit of pushing buttons to see what happens. Stupid idiots.

"Val," said Sergeant Gorka over her suit's external speakers, "Don't touch anything. Hands behind your back.""Yes, mum," I replied. I noted who was sniggering at my poor treatment of this professional and scary solder and I would consider being nasty to them for disrespecting their fearless leader. That'd be me, for those without a program.

In the centre of the room was a slightly raised platform about the size of a wagon bed. It was oval shaped and I guessed it was where the big bang would happen which would allow us to board the enemy ship. I made sure I was standing well away from the bloody thing.

Sergeant Gorka lined her squad up in some sort of rehearsed order, they knew what they were doing. They stood in artificial poses, legs slightly bent, some with blasters aimed at the platform while others were ready to leap about. Looked like a gypsy dance troupe after a lot of gin.

Gorka looked around, made visual contact with the boss and Phil. Phil was standing by the control panel, I hoped and prayed he knew which buttons to press.

"We are ready to go," said Gorka, using our communicator beads. "Your Grace," she went on, addressing Phil, "we are ready for entry. Remember everyone, we need this hatch to remain open if we want to retain communications between our assault teams and this shuttle. The warship's hull effectively blocks all outside communications from our little beads. Keep the hatch open, unless there is an emergency."

I wondered what would constitute an 'emergency', given we were about to invade a hostile ship during a space battle. That would be enough of an emergency for me.

She changed stance and continued, "Lord Franz, wait for us to be clear, then follow us in. Follow the route we discussed earlier. You should end up at their comm hub, I'll be at the engineering room. We will go on your command, sir."

Okay, the boss got to give the big order. One of the perks of the job, I assumed, making things go bang. "Everyone ready?" asked the boss. No one said a negative. Gorka's team was too well drilled and my lot had no idea what was going to happen, they lived in a state of constant confusion. I noticed helmets were all on and suits buttoned up so they still had a strong sense of self preservation.

"We're all good, sir," I said. "You lead us in, Teddy Boy in the centre and I'll sheepdog the rear. Everyone, make sure your suits are all intact, we could be breathing space shortly."

The boss grunted and then he said, "Phil, push the button."

Phil did something and the raised platform shivered as God knows how much explosive went off beneath it. Its surface swelled up and then returned to its original position. A moment afterward, the platform unhooked itself from the floor and dropped away. Before it had fully disappeared, Gorka and her team were on the move.

Now I could see the sense in all their strange postures. Some stepped up to give covering fire into the depths of our new hole, in case some fool had survived standing beneath the massive explosion. As they took up their stand, Gorka jumped into the hole, closely followed by most of her marines. After the last one had been swallowed up, the guys around the rim on shooting duty calmly stepped into the space and vanished from sight.

The dust for the explosion had not even settled.

"Bloody hell," said someone.

The Man in Black gave his professional opinion, "That was certainly impressive. Her whole squad took about two heartbeats to board the enemy vessel." He paused, whistled, and went on, "our turn now." Then he gave the command all good leaders know, it must be seared into their hearts.

"Follow me."

He jumped into the breach.

A heartbeat later, the NightWatch followed him. The most active were right behind him but even the slow and stupid were in motion by the time his head sank below our deck level. What a guy, he has our team willing to follow him anywhere. I saw Ted disappear and then the last few NightWatch entered the hole.

My turn. I strode forward in time to hear the sound of blasters, screams and see flashes from detonating explosions down in the frigate near our new entry hatch. Our entry had been discovered.

Sergeant Gorka's voice came over our comms, "Your Grace! Seal the hatch! We cannot stay here and defend it. Lord Franz! We have to go, good luck!"

Before I could reach the opening, a solid plate slid across the gap, sealing me off from the breach. I turned to Phil, "What the hell! Open the bloody thing, you bastard!" I yelled.

"No, Val, I won't," he replied. He did, quite sensibly, back away from me until his back was hard against the wall.

"I said, OPEN THAT BLOODY HATCH," I roared.

My people were on the other side of the damned thing, they were fighting even now. I desperately wanted to be with them, to help, to stand with them. I did not want to let them down, they were my mates. My communication bead was not capable of punching through the warship's hull, I had no idea what was happening to my team.

And this foppish bloody prince was standing there telling me no. I drew my hammer and grabbed him by the throat. This lovely weapon consisted of a nasty hammer on one side with a fiendish spike on the other. Lovely piece of kit. A twist of the handle brought the spike to the front, he could see it through his face plate, he also knew what it could do. Lord knows, he had seen me use it often enough.

"If I open the hatch, Val, we'll be boarded by the enemy," his voice was steady, a small quaver. "Is that what you want, enemy soldiers on board this shuttle? Think of the wounded." He paused and then said a bastard thing, "Think of Lydia."I snarled and drew my hand back. "You loathsome toad, you're thinking of yourself and your precious skin."

This was a bit harsh. Phil was many things — a liar, a cheat, devious and an undoubted cad — but he was never a coward.

A small hand reached from behind me to rest gently on my arm, the one holding my spiked hammer. "Think carefully, Sergeant Valentine," said Sylvia's voice, giving my arm a gentle squeeze. I never realised how small her hand was.

Sylvia. It had to be Sylvia who intervened. Not Lydia, my sweetie pie and a girl for whom I would slay dragons. No, it was the officious, rule bound bloody Sylvia. The woman who defended her charges like a mad lioness. She would never instigate a blow or start a fight. But heaven help anyone who wanted to hurt those in her care, especially if they were children.

"We have wounded aboard, Val," she said. "And most of us are non-combatants. I'm sure His Grace shut the hatch for a reason. Perhaps we should ask him to explain himself?"

Poo, Bum, Tit, Fart.

I lowered the spike and dropped my hand, releasing Phil to sag back against the wall.

"Alright, you loathsome turd, explain why you shut the hatch," I growled. "Make it good, imagine your life depends upon it. And hook everyone on this shuttle into your communications."

I heard some extra clicks followed by a gulp from Phil. "Certainly, sergeant. I shut the hatch because of those blaster shots and the explosions we heard, this is a standard response during a boarding. There is a specially armoured hatch which becomes ready to be deployed after the entry explosion occurs; this extra hatch is strong, easily stronger than a ship's hull and impervious to normal explosives or small arms fire."

"Not good enough, Phil. Keep going."

He coughed. "Yes, well, during an assault, the shuttle sometimes finds itself blasting a hatch in an inopportune space. Like a barrack area, for example. Or an assembly point for the defensive teams. Lots of reasons. It could even be because the hatch has been opened onto adjoining walls or other obstructions. The hatch operator, me, must be ready to slide the cover in place and so prevent the shuttle from being invaded or destroyed by the enemy."

"Why?" I asked. "Once everyone leaves the assault shuttle, there's no reason to worry about it. Let the enemy have the bloody thing.""Yes. Well, no. An assault will often destroy the enemy vessel. Or have it so badly damaged it cannot sustain life and may, in fact, be a hazard to anyone staying aboard. In that case, the assault shuttle is their escape route from the destroyed vessel. If it has been captured or damaged, then all the people currently on the battle brig are trapped. No escape. All dead or captured."

"You are a cheerful soul, Phil," I put my hammer away. "But you make sense. Dick."

I stood and looked at the closed hatch, wondering how the gang were coping. Were they already dead. What do we do now?

"What should we do now, Val?" asked Phil.

I looked askance at him. "You've been making the big decisions up to now. Why ask me? Why don't you tell us what to do?"

"Because I have no idea," he said. "I'm a planner, not a fighter. I moves pieces on a game board, I don't fight in the streets."

"You fought well back on the *New Rome* when we battled our way through the ravening hordes," I said.

"Well, thank you, good of you to say that," he said, soundly ridiculously pleased. "Although, if it hadn't been for you and Claude, I would have been killed many times over."

"Yeah, well, we all make mistakes," I replied. Okay what to do now. What to do, what to do.

"Let's get on board the battle brig another way," said a voice. A small voice, a small and annoying voice.

"Shut up, Jeremy," I snapped. "What would you know about it?"

"I know I don't want to be cooped up in this shuttle with you while everyone else is fighting down below," he responded. "You need to be with them. Otherwise, you might kill us all through sheer frustration. You're becoming harder and harder to be with, Uncle Val."

The room had slowly filled up with other people. Our wounded were mostly ambulatory by now, the four of them had carried each other down the ramp and now slumped against the wall. All looking at me.

Hmm, yes, they had their helmets off. I removed mine after realising we were back to ship's atmosphere. Must have something to do with the hatch shutting. God, I hate this space stuff. You have to know so much otherwise it kills you dead. Which is like normal killing but worse.

My mind was wandering, it did a lot of it recently. Nanobots, perhaps. I shoved the thought back into the abyss of things which terrify me. It's a big abyss, and getting bigger.

Sylvia had taken up a position near the wounded and pretended she was ministering to them. They were on their best behaviour and sat or lay still. Lydia stood beside Phil at the control panel, I suspect she would back me up if I wanted to hit him. Unless she hit him first, always hard to tell with my girl.

Wallace and Greenash waited at the bottom of the ramp leading up. Wallace didn't seem too concerned, probably used to being in life-or-death situations given his background as an assassin and enforcer for the mob.

Greenash gave a rational response, he quivered in terror. Good chap, well done that man.

And then there was Jeremy, the little snot had come to stand beside me, possibly hoping the presence of a small child might ameliorate my more homicidal tendencies. A vain hope, but the kid was showing initiative.

"So, Jeremy," I began, turning the sarcasm up to maximum, "Do you have any idea on how your favourite sergeant can attack a monstrous warship all by himself?"

"Well, er ..." began Jeremy.

"I do, "said Lydia. "We use another hatch — one which gets us onto the hull of the battle brig — to exit the assault shuttle. And you can forget about this 'all by himself 'nonsense. I'm coming with you.""And me," said Wallace.

"Me, too," said Phil.

"And you'll obviously need me," said Jeremy in his high, squeaky voice. "I'll be your backup, your enforcer." I was overcome by an unwarranted sense of affection at my erstwhile companions who had so stupidly volunteered to accompany me on this suicide mission. Before I could choke up too much, I gave an automatic reply.

I hit Jeremy.

Chapter 12

GREAT, WE WERE OFF for another stroll over the surface of a ship's hull — while it was still in space. And, seeing God has a sense of humour, the difficulty level of this particular walk was increased due to the bloody huge battle taking place around us.

The four wounded were incapable of any sort of rapid movement. Two of them were not completely ambulatory, more draggable than mobile. Still, they all swore up and down on their mother's lives they would be able to defend the shuttle if any nasties came calling. I knew for a fact two of them had no idea who their mother was, the third had run away from the family rather than work on the farm while the fourth had worked as a pimp for all the girls in his family.

We're a decent, solid, God-fearing lot in the Watch. Lambs, we are, innocent lambs.

Nonetheless, I ensured they knew Sylvia was to be in command. This instruction was scarcely necessary since they were all terrified of her whilst simultaneously being in awe of her seemingly magical powers to heal the sick and wounded. She believed in things like hygiene, wearing gloves during the rummaging around in your innards and the liberal application of foul-tasting medicine.

It was common knowledge in the Watch that any medicine had to taste truly awful for it to have any beneficial effects. Sylvia had picked up on this, I'm sure she added a few extra hideous flavours to whatever she gave the lads.

I had always avoided her presence, my nanobots assisted my healing rate and I generally surfaced after a big fight with very few horrible wounds. Some extra bed rest gave the little horrors time to clean me up and I bounced back quickly. It doesn't mean the process didn't hurt. Heck, knowing little machines are crawling through your body, dragging bits of flesh together and possibly sewing them up did not give one peace of mind. And, by God, it hurt. It hurt a lot.

But it did mean I rarely had to seek assistance from Sylvia. We both saw this as a win-win.

Greenash would stay on the shuttle and monitor communications. He was our tech guy and could be relied upon to know which buttons to press and, more importantly, which ones to keep his grubby fingers off. He was pathetically grateful and constantly reassured me he would be diligent in his monitoring of all communication traffic. He confided Caesar had plugged some bits and pieces into the comms on the shuttle so we could still communicate with him.

Yeah, great, gives me a thrill.

I tramped onward to find yet another exit door. The more I got to know this stupid shuttle, the more methods of egress I found. Made sense, I suppose; when you call something an 'assault shuttle' you might expect it allowed horrible people with big guns to exit the damn thing in exciting ways.

"Each of you, give me a good reason why you are coming on this little jaunt. Explain to me, in small words of one syllable, what possible benefit I, personally, will accrue from having your bodies clutter up my walk. Phil, you are a member of the Royal Family and I would assume your in-laws will be cheesed off at a lowly sergeant if you so much as stub your toe. You're getting better at this fighting stuff but not yet in the big leagues."

Phil smiled at me. We could see each other's faces since we had removed our helmets. Tip for young players — keep any suit time to a minimum. The stink, once the helmet is removed, is astounding in its depth, its colour and its gagginess. It becomes noticeable when your nostrils encounter clean air, the smell has a life of its own. I call mine 'Eric'.

"I am coming because I am experienced in the use and wearing of this armour. I would suggest my knowledge may help keep you alive when you wish to do something exotic and wish the suit would help. Stuff like staying alive and so on. Also, I am the tenth in line for the throne, lots of spare cousins and so forth between me and the big chair; I'm certainly not expecting promotion anytime soon. My big ace is I know how to get us into the battle brig. At least, I know the location of a hatch near their launch bay, a hatch which is likely unguarded."

"Aren't you also some sort of topflight surgeon for kids?" I asked. "I seem to remember seeing you on a news video where you were opening some new building?" Was Phil a real medical doctor? Should he have been helping Sylvia with our wounded? And how did he know about secret doors into enemy spacecrafts. I hated him so much.

"Ahh, yes, my medical degrees. Hmmm," he shuffled his feet before continuing, "Largely honorary, I confess. Yes, I did attend medical college and I did graduate but more due to the work done by my tutors than any rigor on my part.""You mean they took the tests for you, wrote your exams and finished off any written work. Probably had a reasonable look alike do the actual practical tests." This was the normal method for the children of the rich to gain qualifications. They bought them. He nodded without a hint of shame. Yep, Phil remains a dick. Okay, he could come.

I turned to Lydia and Jeremy. "You two are, and have always been, non-combatants. Lydia, you're a pilot, an engineer and ... and ..." I ground to a halt. I wanted to say she shouldn't come because she was my girl and I wanted to keep her safe. But was this fair?

"Val, sweetie pie, I am coming. Do not take advantage of our relationship to treat me like your 'little woman'. I have been learning self-defence from Sergeant Gorka, I also know how to use a blaster and most of all, I know how to get us through a hatch or door."

True. "And how, exactly, are we going to do that, princess?" I asked. She and Phil had obviously been chatting and making devious plans.

She smiled, pushed back some errant hair, patted a large bag hanging from her shoulder and said, "I've got some of Caesar's tools in here, they should be able to get us through any door." She patted a large box at her feet, "Failing that, I have explosives in the box. LOTS of explosives. Caesar has kept us cloaked so they still do not know exactly where we are. The breach we made into their hull would be a clue, of course, but the cloaking effect should make them think our assault teams were dropped onto the hull, after which they planted their own breaching charges."

"Yes," murmured Phil, "that's another standard way for assaulting a ship. Dump a bunch of marines on the hull and then fly away, leaving them to it."

"Christ on a crutch," I said, "the casualties must be awful for such an assault."

"Yes," rejoined Phil. "They call them the 'forlorn hope'. They get lots of medals if they survive. They're all volunteers and I believe they have to beat them back with sticks, such is the desire of the standard space marine to break things and kill people."

This concept struck me as bizarre. I made a mental note to never, ever join the space marines. Okay, I grudgingly acknowledged Lydia could come but I was still left with two more bodies: Wallace and Jeremy.

"Wallace, you can come," I said. I'd seen Wallace fight on the hull of a ship before. He was the sort of competent bastard who could fight anywhere and with anything. He'd killed a pirate with a pencil. A pencil, for God's sake!

I looked down at my last remaining volunteer.

"Go away, Jeremy," I said. "You not coming and that's final. You can't fight, you can't shoot and you wet yourself every time there's a crisis. What are you gonna do, annoy them to death?"

"Okay, Val," he replied.

This was too easy, I gave him my patented steely glare.

"I'll wait until you all leave," he said, "then I'll head out by myself and follow you at a distance."

The little toad would do it, too. Not short on guts, is Jeremy.

I swore at them all for a while, they all stood there and took it. Wallace smiled, Lydia folded her arms and tapped one beautiful finger on her arm, Phil leaned against a wall and whistled softly. Jeremy picked his nose.

Finally, I ran down, Wallace quietly applauded, Phil lurched erect, Lydia picked up her box of explosives and Jeremy flicked something obscene into a dark corner.

"Let's be clear about this," I said. "Wallace and I have killed before, we know what it's like to take another's life. Be warned, it damages you at some level. If you come with us, you will have to fight and you may have to kill; try to understand it is a bad thing to do." I looked at them all again, especially at Jeremy and Lydia, "Do you still want to come?" I asked. "This is real, you two, this is what the NightWatch does."

Everyone nodded. Jeremy had gone quiet which I considered to be a minor miracle while Lydia set her jaw and looked firm. Phil had his normal insouciance set to maximum — I don't know about him. Had he ever killed a living thing up close and personal? Wallace was ... Wallace, he's a mad dog, like me.

"Put your bloody helmets on and let's get out of here," I snarled. "Here, you little wart, make yourself useful and carry my new toy from Caeser." I thrust the pouch containing the insect scout thing at my erstwhile companion and told him how to use it. I sent him the appropriate codes and the instructions from Caesar.

"Learn how to use this thing, Jeremy, it might save our lives," I said. I had no real use for it and hoped it might keep the wee lad busy for a while, keep his mind off the coming violence. Because there was going to be violence and I wanted to keep him safe. I hoped that, by telling him he had an important role, it made him feel good. Yeah, sometimes I let my guard down and my affection for the little snot creeps through. I resolved to be better.

His eyes gleamed as he took the pouch with the same solemnity I have seen the faithful receiving communion. We wandered through the shuttle until we came to our departure door. Oh, goody.

We sealed our suits and, following Phil's guidance, checked each other to ensure we hadn't left anything unlatched or unplugged. He turned to me, gave me a thumbs up and stood waiting at the door controls.

"Wallace," I said, "you and me up front, weapons out. Lydia, behind me and looking after Jeremy. Phil, rearguard. Give us directions as to where we should go. Are we all set?"They all communicated their readiness, Jeremy's response had that vague fuzziness indicating his mind was elsewhere. I hoped he was wading through reams of instructions on my toy, stuff I was never going to look at. Minions, it's all about the minions.

I established a subgroup of them for communication purposes, sent a farewell back to Sylvia and told Phil to open the damned door.

I was angry, annoyed, flustered and generally pissed off at everything and everybody. I suspected this increase in my aggression levels and the accompanying elimination of tolerance might have been the result of malfunctioning nanobots. Were they turning me into a psychopath? Perhaps I always was one.

Didn't matter, I was going to kill someone. Hopefully, lots of someones.

Chapter 13

THE HULLS OF SPACESHIPS are messy places. Not rounded and smooth as you might expect, but full of bits that stick out — bulges, tiny maintenance hatches too small for a person and then there were the more sizable structures. Some of them were guns, big bloody things that could blast another vessel out of existence, especially a small thing like our assault shuttle. There were other wee buildings looking like rooms or guard posts which Lydia told me housed other defensive and offensive items.

All in all, it was maze and we zigged and zagged on our staggering walk across the hull with me swearing and Jeremy making 'ooh-ahh' sounds. Focussing on where I put my feet in our space boots allowed me to ignore the vast expanse of nothingness over my head. From time to time, Phil would stop, stretch his head back and murmur things like, "Beautiful, beautiful. Look at that constellation, Val."I kept my helmet firmly fixed on the floor. God, I hate nothingness. It doesn't make sense. On the upside, I was still functioning. My previous space walks had accumulated into some sort of beneficial experience, an experience which reduced my stark terror from catatonic behaviour down to the screaming heebie jeebies. Keep walking, Valentine, I told myself; put one foot in front of another, listen to Lydia's instructions and hope Wallace is keeping an eye out for things which might want to kill us.

Coming over a curve in the hull allowed me to see a soft glow coming from up ahead. That would be the launch bay, I surmised, from which any moment a fighter could emerge. It would either see us, or the shuttle, and kill us all. Caesar's cloaking device was able to fool electronic sensors but not the mark one eyeball of a pilot.

Life is a lottery.

Phil took us to one of the shed-like structures next to the launch bay, this one held a small door.

"This door will get us into the launch bay," said Phil "It's used for accessing the ship when the main bay doors are shut. There should be a small room beyond with a couple of access doors leading to the interior of the ship." I thought this exterior door looked incredibly solid and wondered how Lydia planned to get us in. I asked as much.

She began pulling things out of her packs and dumping them on the ground. "I've got things that go bang, Val," she explained. "Explosives, lots of explosives. I thought we could probably blow an appropriate hole."

"Let's think about this," suggested Wallace. "This 'battle brig' must be tough enough to withstand barrages from other war ships, like our frigate. Do you mean to say these few explosives could damage this door, this door which can stand up to pot shots from a ship's main armament?"

Lydia looked at the bundles at her feet, her shoulders slumped. "It's all I could come up with, Wallace." Her body posture was one of dejection. Ahh, well, time for the maestro to take a hand.

"It was worth a shot, Lydia," I said, the complete man of sensitivity and understanding. "But, as Wallace has pointed out, it won't work." I patted my girl on the shoulder, looked around and decided to undertake yet another activity in my long history of stupid activities.

"How about I nip in though the main bay doors?" I suggested. "I'll wait until the shields drop and then dash in, all heroically like."

"You mean when a fighter exits or enters the launch bay?" asked Phil. "That's the time you'll scamper in? You realise the shield drops momentarily, a brief moment for the ship to transect the hull. And its engines will be blasting heat and other horrible forces all around it. "

Everyone's a critic.

"No, Val," said Lydia. "It's impossible. I know you once entered our original trading vessel through their launch bay, but that was not a military ship. Commercial vessels usually have other, internal shields. Ships like this are a different matter. For the brief few moments the shield drops for a ship to enter or leave, you would be surrounded by the exhaust from the fighter. You'd be fried in an instant."

This was going well, I thought. "Still," I murmured, "Worth a try. Surely?"

Phil broke the ensuing wall of silence with a gentle cough.

"Or," he said, "we could enter through this door." I watched his hand reach up to a control panel where he punched a series of buttons. It looked like the number pad on a locking device, stuff I had seen on board the frigate when they wanted to keep me out of places. Damned effective.

The panel blinked and the door opened.

"We are so going to talk about this later," I snarled at Phil.

Wallace pushed past us and entered the hatch. Lydia gathered up her explosive packages with Jeremy's help and then they entered. Phil gestured grandly to me and said, "After you, mate," he sniggered.

The guy's a boil on the bum of humanity.

Once inside, Phil shut the hatch behind us. I looked around at the small ready room we were in, it was an area where people could, I don't know, do whatever space sailors do when they come on board. In the far wall were two doors, Lydia stood before one of them while Wallace took up a position from where he could kill anything coming in from either door. Now that's a man with his priorities right, I considered.

Jeremy slunk into a corner and opened up his pouch from where the little insect/spider thing emerged. He must have given it commands because it scuttled around and sat on his shoulder. He bent his head down again, engrossed in whatever bit of information Caesar had left for me. I'd ask Jeremy for a brief summary later. Possibly. Nah, not interested.

"I might be able to open this door with explosives," said Lydia. Her voice had a certain tentative quality.

"I can open either door," said Phil. "But we may need to be quick. Opening that last hatch would have alerted someone whose job it is to monitor such things, especially in a battle scenario."

"Where do these doors lead?" I asked.

"One goes to the shuttle bay, the other is a storeroom," replied Phil. "Where will we go?"

"Shuttle bay," I said. "Wallace, get over here and stand with me, we're about to cause some mayhem.

On my nod, Phil opened the second door and I got my first look at the interior of the shuttle bay. I held my hand up to block Wallace from moving. I did this because I could see the people in the bay were all heavily engaged in specific tasks and none of these tasks involved coming over and killing us. A distinct plus, in my view.

I started speaking, keeping my voice calm and businesslike. My companions, with the exception of Wallace, would not benefit from my usual stream of commands and questions. Often the commands were shrieked while the questions were many. No, this time I sounded as if I was examining my dinner.

"Okay," I said, "I'm looking at a shuttle bay holding two fighters. The one closest to us has a pilot sitting in the seat and they look ready to launch. The other one is being refuelled or rearmed or repaired or I don't know what. There are several people in space suits — not combat suits — running around this second ship plugging in hoses and loading stuff into it. On the right is the opening to space and I can see the blue shimmer of a containment field keeping out the bad things. I can see the far end of the bay, the whole room is not huge but there is enough space down there for two more fighters. It's empty now so I can assume they are outside doing bad things to our frigate."

"Standard protocol for the Confederacy," explained Phil, "They have two fighters launch immediately from each shuttle bay, then they rotate one back as needed so there are always two fighters outside while one is inside being re-armed."

"You sure know a lot about the operations of a Confederacy vessel, Phil," I said. "Let's add it to the list of questions I intend beating out of you when this is all over. We'll start with the one involving you knowing the secret codes to open armoured hatches."

"I only know the one set," he replied. "Just enough to get on board."

Wallace brought us back to the task at hand, "Why is there a fighter sitting there with someone in the cockpit?" Our door had opened into the back of the shuttle bay, we were looking at the rear of the whole place and so the pilot would not be looking at us, unless he screwed his head around and got a crick in his neck.

"Again," said Phil, "standard practice. They keep one fighter back for immediate launch in case of emergencies. Things like a sudden attack and so on." He paused, "Hmmm ..." he muttered.

I told Wallace to go and neutralise the pilot, the one sitting in his ready fighter. I didn't like the thought of leaving an enemy combatant behind us as we waltzed further into the shuttle bay. Wallace didn't ask any questions and I was hoping Lydia and Jeremy would not ask me what was entailed in 'neutralising' someone. I knew. And I knew Wallace knew, we were both killers — but Lydia and Jeremy were relatively untainted by that hell and I wanted to keep them innocent as long as possible.

Yes, they had both seen death and destruction, a fair bit of it done by me. But they had not yet crossed that line, they hadn't acquired the mindset which allowed a person to calmly walk up to someone else and kill them.

I knew Wallace had done it, many, many times. Heck, it was in his job description as a hit man for the mob. And I did not think Phil had fully gone the murderous prince route, members of the royal family may be absolute mongrels but they generally employ other low life thugs to do the cold-blooded killing. Thugs like Wallace. And me.

No one had noticed us yet. Wallace returned from his side excursion giving me a thumbs up; scratch one Confederate pilot. The remaining wall to our left was mainly blank except for a large window about head height. It ran down most of the wall and I could see various people moving about behind the glass or whatever protective stuff they used. It had the look of a command centre. I asked Phil and he agreed.

"Yes, that's the room which monitors all the activity here. I imagine they've noticed us by now but since we aren't running around being nasty, they may think we are harmless. That should change at any moment. Especially if someone notices the flashing light which is probably on by now. The one announcing the external hatch was opened. It won't trigger an emergency because I used one of their known codes, but we have to expect someone to wonder who we are. Especially given the fact we are standing here in battle armour."

"Wallace," I said, as he returned from his little chore, "come with me." I walked brazenly into the shuttle bay, trailed by the lumpish form of Wallace. "Try not to look too threatening," I said.

A vain hope but Wallace did relax his ominous tread and produced a gait which can only be described as 'thug strolling in the wildflowers'. Phil must have been inspired by my initiative for he began to slide up behind the other fighter, the one containing the now dead pilot. I left him to it, I did not need someone getting all queasy and hesitating as Wallace and I went through the next few minutes. I needed someone beside me who would not think twice in close combat and who could be relied upon to kill without hesitation. And I did not know Phil well enough to trust him in those situations, therefore, he could go and play somewhere else.

That left Lydia standing there alone except for Jeremy who was now sitting on the floor while his pet machine spider roamed around our room. She called out to me and began to follow my leader like form. She was asking me what I planned to do, where was I going, shouldn't we talk about this etc, etc. Usual stuff.

I ignored her pleas and kept walking. Wasn't I the boss of this little expedition? Shouldn't I be the one dishing out the clever plans and setting great events in motion? I must have made some demurring sounds because she told me I was an idiot and would get us all killed. Fair comment. Phil chimed in with, "Hey, this pilot's dead!"

Thank you, captain obvious. "Of course he's dead, Phil," I snarled. "That's what we do with the enemy. We kill them."

"But he was stabbed in the back of the neck!" claimed our fragile royal. "Do you mean to say Wallace hit him from behind!?"

Wallace and I kept moving, I felt Phil had now justified my decision to leave him off the frontline team. He was behind me so I could not see what he was doing but I heard low mutterings and the occasional swear word. Nothing serious. "Phil," I said, "What are you doing back there. And whatever it is, do it quietly, I don't want to be distracted for a few minutes." The crew people ahead of us had not yet taken offence at our incursion but they would any moment. We had to saunter towards them looking harmless as long as possible.

"I can replace him in the pilot's seat. I'm qualified to fly a fighter, thanks to my family's idiotic belief in being prepared to defend ourselves against the peasantry."

"I might not be combat qualified," said Lydia, "but I've got these explosives and I want to make a bang. Those fuel containers might scratch that itch."

"Er," I said.

Perhaps I should give clear and concise instructions to Phil, as well as ordering Lydia to do ... something. Hopeless, I was. Bloody hopeless. In my defence, I was invading an enemy vessel with my backup being a hit man, a man who may well have a contract out on me. Long story. What to do, what to do ...

I decided to be the man of action and started running. At least we could take out these various crew people. After we dealt with everyone in the shuttle bay we could have a think about how to get inside the main part of the ship. That large window overlooking the bay would be my first choice. Use some of Lydia's explosives to blow it out and then scramble through and kill everyone. You know, the usual routine.

Wallace easily ran past me, we both left Lydia in our wake. The astonished crew people were now realising we might be trouble, some were on the wing of the fighter, two more under the craft loading things into it and another pair stood beside hoses which ran from valves in the main ship's wall and into the fighter. Probably fuel, I guessed. Part of my brain queried how the hell would I know. Damn brain, always the critic.

Wallace ran past the two crew at the refuelling hose and continued onwards to have a terminal chat with the pair under the fighter. Smart lad, or optimistic. He was assuming I would take out the blokes behind him, thus save him from being attacked from the rear. I'd have to talk to Wallace about trust issues. That is, don't trust me.

Still, in this case, he was correct. I remembered everyone's unfounded concern over my use with any sort of firearm so decided to use my hammer. The first crewman copped the blunt end in his face, the lovely weapon going straight though his visor and into his left eye. I was aiming for his nose but you take what you can get.

By the time, his companion had begun to straighten up with a surprised expression on his face. This disappeared when the other end of my hammer, the spike, entered his brain directly through the top of his skull. I'm tall and he was both short and still slightly bent over so, well, no contest.

My weapon was, unfortunately, now lodged in his brain. This meant I had to drop it as I raced towards the fighter's wing to take out the last two crewmen.

The last two became the last one because Wallace had already killed his targets and moved on to these poor slobs. I pulled out my pistol and moved closer to the last survivor when Lydia yelled into my helmet.

"No shooting, Val!" she cried. "The place is awash with fuel vapour and ammunition. You'll kill us all."

Okay, that argument made a lot of sense. The guy on the wing had now realised we were not the good guys. He was raising a large tool over his head, in preparation for bringing it down on my own delicate noggin. I couldn't shoot him because of the 'kill us all' thing from Lydia and my best weapon was stuck in the last bloke's skull. I did have a knife and a musket sized weapon strapped to my harness but time may be against my deploying these useful items.

That unpleasant looking tool was descending towards me at a rapid rate. He couldn't miss since I was standing at his feet and looking up into his smiling face. He would be able to use the extra height to put some real power into the blow. A part of me admired the whole display, professional, neat and productive.

My mind goes to strange places sometimes. Fortunately, my body can think for itself.

I reached out and grabbed his booted feet in both hands and heaved upwards. He flew onto his back, dropping the tool and was probably wondering why his life choices had lead him astray when Wallace gave a graceful leap to land on his chest. The knife he was carrying disappeared into the last crewman's throat.

Phil had obviously tossed the body of the pilot out of the other craft. I guessed this because I saw an engine blast and watched the heir to the Empire give me a cheery wave, accelerating the craft out of the launch bay.

Okay, my plan was going well. I hadn't planned on Phil shooting off into space and joyriding around but you take what you can get. I was sure I would hear many criticisms of my actions

from the Man in Black, probably not a good look for the team if I got Phil killed.

Such is life, not a lot I could do about it.

Lydia had caught up to us by now, so I asked her, "Can you use your explosives to blow in that window? Wallace and I could get in and clean the place up a bit."

"What window?" she asked.

I turned in time to see a huge shutter falling across the window, it locked in place and I was now facing a solid wall of metal.

"Doesn't look good," I muttered.

"That's a safety protocol in case the shuttle bay is ever breached. That shield is not the same hardness as the hull of the ship but it's close. My explosives won't worry it at all."

She turned to me, "What are we going to do now, O Mighty Brain?"

Good question. Damn good question. One of the best questions I had ever heard.

I wish I had an answer.

Chapter 14

LOOKING AROUND PROVIDED NO inspiration. Mainly, I was searching for a place to hide. Old habits.

The shuttle bay was a large rectangular space. One wall being mostly the exit to space while its opposite wall was now a solid sheet of protective shielding. Except for a large door at each end of the wall. Hmm, could be a way out.

"Can we use those big doors?" I asked, pointing at the possibilities of escape.

"Those doors will soon disgorge a security team, nasty men with big guns, eager to ask why we have cluttered up their shuttle bay," said Lydia. "A ship this size would have onboard security troops at various sensitive areas. Places like engineering, communications, bridge and, of course," she waved a hand about, "the shuttle bays. In case someone tried to board. Someone like us."

"Let me get this straight," I said, searching for loopholes. "Any moment now, those doors will open and we will be invaded by angry space marines?"

There was no answer to my genial question, no response at all. I had been looking at the target doors but now turned to have a final, loving conversation with my girl before we were both obliterated. She had disappeared.

"Lydia?" I bleated. Wallace's bulk filled a corner of my vision, I looked directly at him and asked, "Seen any sign of Lydia?" I was wondering how someone could get lost in a shuttle bay. How did she disappear? Was she abducted by aliens? Silly question, given my own history.

Wallace gestured with his thumb at a small figure climbing into the cockpit of the last fighter, the one which had been undergoing refuelling and so on. Around its base were scattered various bodies of its extinct crew, she used one as a stepping stone onto a small access ladder at the side of the vessel.

Within moments she was in the pilot's seat and starting the engines.

"Uhh, Lydia ..." I said. Once, I thought, just once, it would be nice to actually know what's going on.

"What's going on?" I asked her over our suit communications.

"Tell Jeremy to shut his door and stay in our entry room, it might give him some protection," she answered. "And you and Wallace need to be behind a blast shield. There's one at each end of the shuttle bay.

I couldn't help myself, I turned to look and sure enough, there was a raised shield tucked against each end of the shuttle bay. The closest one had a small pit behind it, good for cowering in as fighters took off and landed. Okay, my mind was wandering.

"Er, Lydia ..." I tried again.

Wallace grabbed me and started dragging me towards the nearest shield. I listened in to our shared channel as he told Jeremy to shut the door and hide. Sure, hide in an empty room. Still, if anyone could do it, Jeremy could.

"Lydia, do you ..." I began. "Are you going to fly off in that fighter?" I asked. I mean, it's the sort of thing I would do, run away and leave everyone behind but I thought Lydia had higher standards. You don't know someone until you've been trapped in an enemy shuttle about to be attacked by murderous marines.

"No, snookums," she replied. "I'm not trained in flying this thing more than a short hop to a maintenance ship. And I certainly wouldn't last as long as Phil, I have had no combat training. No, I'm capable of starting the engines and rotating the ship, but that's all."

"I see," I said. "And you think that will help because WHY?"

"Because," she said, and I noticed the fighter's engines begin to glow, Wallace thrust us both behind a blast shield, while I continued to bleat at my girl. "Because," she repeated, "this fighter possesses heavier ordnance than any man portable weapon." The fighter rose above the deck, various lights were flashing on its wingtips and the entire vessel wobbled slightly.

"You're basically flying the fighter INSIDE the shuttle bay!" I pointed out. "Isn't that sort of thing, you know, frowned upon?"

"Oops," she said, "thanks for the reminder." She must have done something because the shimmering blue glow which indicated the shield across the exit bay winked out. "Now I won't be too worried about the back blast."

"Back blast!" I yelled. "What back blast?" Wallace had grabbed my helmet and was pushing my face into the floor behind the shield.

"What are you going to do, Lydia?" I demanded. Which is a tricky statement to say while a burly hit man is sitting on your shoulders, simultaneously pressing your helmet into the floor. "Wallace, get off me!"

Like so many people before, he ignored me. From my squashed position, I saw one of the access doors to the rest of the ship begin to open. A heartbeat later, enemy marines surged in, looking for someone to kill.

I guess they were surprised to see a fighter hovering above the deck of the bay, I base this assumption on the fact they all stopped dead in their tracks for a few seconds. Then they stayed dead because Lydia had sprayed the entire far wall, swivelling to include both access doors, with streams of something nasty. It wasn't a blaster because I saw ricochets and holes appearing in suits and spare body parts. And there were a lot of spare body parts now. A fighter's guns must carry slugs big enough to take off a person's arm, armoured space suit or not. Bits of space marine showered the wall creating a rather grotesque commentary on modern art.

"Can I get up now?" I asked Wallace as the sounds of mayhem wilted away.

"I don't think she's finished," replied my new best friend. I say this because he pressed himself hard against my back while attempting to travel through my inner core to the safety of the deck.

"Mate," I said, "at least, buy me a drink first."

I heard a huge blast. Well, not so much heard because of space and no air and stuff like that. No, I FELT it through my entire body. The floor heaved, I could see a little bit of the shield over the command centre's wall and the shield was destroyed by whatever Lydia was shooting at it. With some wiggling, I managed to squirm out from under Wallace and drag myself around the shield. The shuttle bay was a mess, and I've seen real messes, destroyed cities and so forth. Lydia had shot some big weaponry at the entering soldiers and then fired something bigger at the shield covering the control room.

The big access doors were gone, body parts and bloody mist covered both entry points and, given there was not a stream of atmosphere escaping from the ship, I had to assume an inner airlock door had slammed shut. The control room lay open and exposed, at least two bodies were draped over the windowsill, seeming to peer into the wreck of their bay.

A weight shifted from me and I caught a glimpse of Wallace charging towards the new opening leading to the control room.

"Wallace," I asked, all casual and unconcerned, "watcha doin'?"

"Going to kill everyone up there," he replied. Short and to the point, that's my boy. "Back in a minute."

I stood up and checked out Jeremy's door. It was well to one side of all the destruction and was untouched. I pushed one of the two buttons and the door slid open. Two buttons, no keypad. I guess they figured only good and decent people would be coming in from this side.

"You right there, Jeremy?" I asked.

I took his returning gurgle as a signal he was fine. Then his voice cleared and he said, "I wet myself."

"The suit, Jeremy," I said. "The suit has its own miraculous ways." His happy face poked around the corner and he asked a key question, "Where's Lydia?"

Oh, shit. Where, indeed, was my girl?

Chapter 15

I ran around to the main part of the shuttle bay looking for the Lydia and the fighter ship. I saw them. They were not in the bay anymore.

The blast had pushed the vessel out of the bay, damaging it to some degree. A wing had been blown off, the nose was ripped apart and many holes dotted its hull. Many, many holes.

I also saw the pilot's cockpit, the cover had been blown away and inside, sitting serenely in a destroyed vehicle, was my girl, looking at me and giving me a gentle wave.

"Lydia!" I called, yelling into the communicator. "LYDIA!"

"You don't have to yell, sweetie," she said. "I can hear you."

"Well," I stumbled to a halt and watched the fighter drift further away from the main ship. "Good." I paused, "can you come back now?"

"Well," she said, using her soft voice, "no. The explosion gave the fighter enough of a push to keep it drifting away." She waved again. "I love you, Val. Be kind to people."

Be kind! She asked me to be kind. "Can't you, I don't know, eject out something. Fly back to us?"

"I can get out of the cockpit, that's no trouble. But getting back to you ... no." She gave me a shoulder shrug. "I'll keep drifting further and further away from you. There's no way I can get back and no way for you to ... WHAT ARE YOU DOING?"

I ignored her question because my attention was focussed on building up a good head of speed. I had backed up to the rear wall and ran forward as fast as I could before leaping out of the shuttle bay and sailing towards the battered fighter.

I drifted. Slowly, but faster than the fighter. Yet again I found myself floating through the infinite emptiness of space, no comforting ship around me, no tether line keeping me secure; just me, drifting in my fragile human body. I took a deep breath and realised all the stars did, in fact, look beautiful — my mind was obviously going. Soon I was able to reach down and attempt to grab an edge of the cockpit. I missed.

Fortunately, Lydia was able to snag my boot before I wafted past. She pulled me, a feat possible because she was still strapped into the cabin. Who is saving who here? Whom?

"Hiya, babe," I said, all cool and suave. "Come here often?"

She unlatched her seatbelt and flung herself into my waiting arms. Her motion caused my momentum to wobble so I reached out with one gloved hand and grabbed the edge of the cockpit.

"You idiot," she said. "You lovely, wonderful, annoying idiot." Her arms tightened around me. "Now we'll both die.""Hold tight, princess," I replied, and hard kicked against the fighter, pushing us slowly back towards the shuttle bay. The fighter barely moved, but the mass difference allowed us to edge away from it. I was struck by the fighter's colour scheme, which was a lovely shade of blue, a small part of my brain suggested that bits of the shuttle bay were the same colour. I told it to shut up, concentrate on the job in hand and work on getting us out of here alive. Live now, decorate later. Words to live by.

I had jumped after Lydia, not because I had already thought about things like momentum, inertia and mass differentials. No, I had leapt because she needed help. Plus, I think I loved her. No, that's not true, I know I loved her and did not want to consider a life in which she was left to float in the darkness of space. That darkness would enter my soul and, God knows, there was enough black stuff in there already.

So, my idiotic jump was an automatic reaction. I did, however, have time to consider my stupidity as I sailed over to her and rather hoped I could grab the girl and leap back. Dead graceful and drop-dead heroic. What a story, eh? Brave young lad leaps across space, snatches the beautiful girl from the jaws of death and leaps back again to safety.

That was how my mind saw it.

The reality was different. While the leap to the fighter was okay — even though I almost missed and only made it because Lydia grabbed my boot, thus stopping me from sailing into unknown space — the return jump was pitiful. My legs had no real purchase on the fighter and I know that, together, we weighed considerably more than little old me. The force from my legs was not enough to move our combined body mass with any sort of a decent shove. We moved slowly, but we did move.

I considered mentioning the weight thing to Lydia but wisely kept my stupid mouth shut. It's not a good time to discuss your girlfriend's body mass when you are struggling to stay alive; best not to mention it now. Actually, never mention it. Ever.

We drifted slowly back to the battle brig.

And it was slow. The mass of the fighter certainly allowed me to get some heft into my kick against its hull, but even with my best push we were barely moving at a snail's pace. The angle was all wrong and I was a klutz.

"See," I said, secure in the knowledge of pushing things around in space. "We'll eventually drift back into the shuttle bay. It might take a bit of time, but we'll get there." I said this over Lydia's shoulder. My view was of the receding fighter while she had her legs wrapped around me and was able to see the mass of the battle brig as we crept up to it. A slow creep.

Right, let's think about this.

I understood we needed momentum, and it had to be aimed away from us and towards the battle brig. Some tiny part of my mind also cautioned me against exerting any force not precisely aimed, since we were liable to spin about. Oh, yeah, that sounds good. I could stuff this up and have the two of us floating in space, bouncing off bits of space debris while spinning around. I had done this sort of thing before and knew we would not feel the spin. No, what we would experience is the universe spinning around us.

I may have to throw up.

Back on track, come on brain, think of something. I had to throw some mass away from us which would push us towards our target.

What mass did I have?

Sometimes I'm so brilliant I amaze myself. I pulled out my blaster pistol, carefully judged the aim and pressed the trigger. The blaster beam hit an edge of the fighter, a few more pieces melted and sizzled.

Lydia had noticed my action and leaned back, keeping her lovely arms about my neck. I think I'd seen this pose on walls, drawn by artists with a desire to communicate sexual positions. Bits of me stirred. She turned her head and saw my shots, pressed her helmet to mine and said, "Nice try, luvvikens, but your blaster does not expel mass. It's an energy weapon."

Stupid blaster. Yes, we called every damn thing a blaster even though that category included projectile weapons, heat weapons, and dart throwers; mine happened to be a beam weapon. Stupid gun. I threw it at the fighter, at least the tiny mass of my pistol should be of some help.

"What you need," said Lydia, "is a projectile weapon. Something which shoots slugs, even of small mass, will push us along." She wriggled some more, I unconsciously responded.

"Are you enjoying this pose, Val?" she asked. "I can feel something sticking into me down there.

"You're too kind, ma'am," I replied. Inside my helmet I was having a slight blush. Was I the man or what?

"It's your long gun," she said. "It's wedged between us."

I felt I should draw her mind back to our current predicament and get her mind off bits of my anatomy. "Let's try to focus, Lydia, leave my 'long gun' out of this. Until we get somewhere safe and then we can both play with it."

She wriggled some more. "Idiot," she muttered. Then she pulled my large shotgun-like weapon out from between us. "I was sitting on the damn thing." She rotated the gun until its butt rested on my chest with the barrel poking over her shoulder, pointing roughly towards the fighter. She looked about as if judging distances and angles before pulling the trigger.

My chest was kicked by a mule. Lydia grabbed my helmet for extra purchase and proceeded to empty the magazine, each shot pushing us closer to the battle brig.

"I love you, snookums," she said. "But we still might miss the shuttle bay. That ship is drifting forward and we're aimed at where the bay used to be." She stopped speaking for a moment while I allowed confusion to reign inside the Valentine brain.

"We'll come close," she said. "The bay is long but I can see we'll hit the hull right about the place those nasty antennae are sticking up."

I squirmed my head around and saw her point. Or rather, it was a lot of points.

She threw the now empty shotgun away, wrapped her arms around me once more and leaned in for a quiet snuggle. If I turned my helmet up and looked over my shoulder, I could see the shuttle bay. We were close but needed a little more push. What excess mass did we have to get us across the last few paces?

Wallace was standing on the edge of the shuttle bay and leaning far out, he had both hands reaching towards us while Jeremy had a hand around the big man's equipment belt and another hand grabbing on to something solid inside the bay. At least, I hoped it was solid.

If we could grab Wallace's hand, we could get inside.

We were so close, our drift had taken us almost to his waiting hands. The various attempts had changed our direction. Now, we would not hit the antennae. No, we would miss the ship entirely, float above the bay and glide across the hull and so on into the yukky blackness. To save us, we needed a little bit more push in the right direction.

I felt Lydia squirm as she unwrapped her legs from mine. Not today, princess, I thought. You are not throwing yourself backwards so I get shoved into safety. I grabbed her by the waist, enfolding her in my own version of a leg death grip.

"Val," she pleaded, "You have to let me go. At least one of us will survive." She wriggled but was no match for my strength.

"Val," she was becoming quieter now, "please ..."

I ignored her because my wrapped hands hand felt her pistol, another energy blaster. I devised a cunning plan.

"Shut up, Lydia, I can get us both out of this. Give me your pis tol."Her helmet did that puzzled head tilt we all do when something strange enters our lives. God knows, I've been on the end of it most of my life. Still, she pulled out her pistol and gave it to me."But it won't do any good, sweetie. It's another blaster, an energy weapon. No mass to expel."I grunted, looked around to check on distances and angles, saw Wallace's outstretched paws so close, soooo close. We needed about one body length.

I shot my finger off.

Well, to be fair, not the whole finger. I took the last joint of one of the fingers on my left hand, hurt like the blazes for a moment. I previously lost another digit earlier in my career, think it was a toe, to a homicidal priest before Ted ventilated his chest. Ahh, good times.

Where the finger had been was now a hole, a hole in my suit. A hole through which air escaped. I was my own jet engine.

I waved my damaged paw about, giving a slight push and gaining us a little distance towards Wallace. The suit self-sealed after a few minutes, and the air jet shut off; we had gained some distance but not enough.

Right, I've got lots of fingers and knuckles. Let's try door number two. I shot the next finger off at the last knuckle and again aimed the escaping air away from the battle brig. Over my shoulder I could see Wallace's hand, stretching for all he was worth.

I hoped I got us there before I ran out of fingers.

Again, the suit self-sealed and I prepared to lose a middle finger. If we got out of this, I would look like a careless butcher I once knew.

The things you think of, eh?

Lydia placed one restraining hand over the blaster while reaching across my shoulder with her other hand, she was grabbing something. It was a gloved hand.

Slowly and gently, Wallace pulled us in, he had to be slow and careful because our safety relied upon the muscle power of Jeremy. Wallace was virtually out the door of the shuttle bay with Jeremy gamely hanging on to his belt.

Something unusual I did notice. Wallace had extended his reach by grabbing one of the bodies of the dead crewmen and pushed it out to us. He had the corpse by both ankles while Lydia was hanging on to its outstretched hands.

We were being saved by a dead man and Jeremy.

I would never hear the end of this.

Chapter 16

WITH MUCH GRUNTING AND some unladylike language from Lydia, we managed to drag ourselves into the shuttle bay. And there we lay, panting, gasping and feeling grateful for a strange collection of rescues.

I rolled over, got to my feet and surveyed the scene of our handiwork. The shuttle bay was effectively destroyed, no more fighters would be using it as a place of respite. The control room was now open to space and contained nothing but dead bodies, courtesy of my girl with some extra garnish added by Wallace. Bits of broken machinery and an assortment of body parts were strewn across the bay with two clumps of ex-people taking up space in front of the now destroyed entrance doors.

Lydia had walked over to the body parts of all the troopers who had been coming through the doors, the troopers she had successfully neutralised. Okay, she had killed them, shot them to pieces without a second thought. It sounds so simple in stories, the hero chops off the dragon's head or skewers the evil villain after a ferocious swordfight. Stories make it all sound so ... clean.

But now Lydia was looking at the results of her actions, the dead bodies of those she had so easily killed. And, because I knew her, I understood she was not seeing the enemy. She was seeing someone's husbands and wives, she was looking at the sons and daughters who would never go home to their mum. Ever. She was realising she had ended not only one life, but a host of them. I waited and watched her, ready for the movement.

And it came, she collapsed, sank to her knees and lowered her head. Oh, God, she had crossed that line, the line separating innocence from warfare. The line I crossed when I was fourteen in Ostend, a line you never recross. She was alone in her mind now, screaming at the universe over placing her in a situation where she had to carry out such heinous deeds.

I walked over and knelt behind her, wrapping her in my arms as she sobbed, as she tried to understand the awful truth about humanity. Human beings are bastards. We hurt each other, we hurt ourselves, we destroy environments and we devastate cities. We are capable of reaching the pinnacle of cruelty and selfishness.

But we don't have to be that way. We don't have to live in that world, that hell. Humans can also show the most extraordinary kindness and compassion, they can defend those weaker, they sacrifice themselves so others may live. And, if we are fortunate, many of them never have to experience the absolute awfulness of taking the life of another living thing.

We can be noble, we can be compassionate, we can be kind and loving to each other.

It doesn't mean the demon doesn't exist inside each of us, it means some people can keep the beast in chains and buried so deep they forget it exists. But the beast is always there, ready to leap at the exposed throat, ready to be cruel, ready to kill.

I had to help Lydia put her beast back into chains, to bury it deep. She was too good, too gentle and too kind to allow it to rave through her system.

Wallace and I had our beasts out all the time, but we could wear a mask of normality. My beast was always unchained and free, that's my hell. The mask holds.

Her sobbing stopped and she went quiet. I gave her a few more moments, Jeremy had come over and was sitting beside her, holding a gloved hand. Wallace was standing over us and keeping guard. He knew what was happening and knew he was not the person to give succour. His beast was too close to the surface, like mine. Lydia needed someone who loved her and that was me. Me, me, me, me.

Eventually, I stood up and looked around, time to get moving. Phil was off somewhere and we had to get out of here, I did not want Lydia to be faced with all this death any longer than necessary. If we were going to get out, it had to be through the control room. A short climb and then we would see if there was a way we could do our usual knock knock trick. Perhaps this time with less bang.

As I stood gazing at the control room, I felt a tapping on my shoulder. By turning my head, I could see Lydia standing beside me, she had risen to her feet and was now staring out the opening to the shuttle bay, into the blackness from which we had so recently escaped. Poor love, she needed some quiet time, no doubt. She was trying to attract my attention without using the communicators, probably due to her own fragile mental state.

I continued to look into the control room for doors while patting her hand reassuringly. "We're fine, sweetie," I said, ever the caring boyfriend. "We'll catch our breath here and then find somewhere a little less ... full of dead people." Okay, perhaps I had to work on my vocabulary.

But it wasn't Lydia who spoke next, it was Jeremy. He grabbed me about knee height and spoke in tones somewhat frazzled. "Uncle Val, we could be in a bit of trouble here."

Nonsense. Poor lad should have stayed on our assault shuttle. Wandering about with me often led my companions into places full of mayhem and violence, part of my boyish charm. “We’ll be fine, Jeremy,” I said, my voice all firm and in control. “You’ve done well, all the bad guys are gone.”“Yeah,” mumbled Wallace, “maybe not all the bad guys.”

I turned around and joined my three companions in staring into the void. The void right outside the exit to the shuttle bay. The void which contained the slowly receding wreck of the fighter which Lydia had so gallantly used.

The void now holding two other fighters, pristine in their blue paint and livery. Both enemy vessels were hovering outside the entrance to the shuttle bay and, judging by the restless nature of their wingtips and my own ability to sense danger, they were not impressed with how we had rearranged their home base.

“Er ...” I stumbled, a bit at a loss for words. I needed to say something manly and inspirational, a few words to give my friends some hope. “They’re a nice shade of blue,” I said. “Matches the colour scheme of this shuttle bay. What’s left of it.”

I said this because I had nothing else to offer. For some reason, my brain was latched on to the colour scheme of the fighters and the shuttle bay. Blue must have been the colour of the week when they got to decorating the place, because the colours of the two fighters in front of us, the ones aiming deadly weapons at our fragile bodies, precisely matched the colour of the shuttle bay and the colour of Lydia’s recent ride.

The things you notice, eh?

“This is the blue wing,” said Lydia. “The colours help the pilots when they need to rejoin the main vessel. On the other side of the battle brig would be a similar set up in red — shuttle bay and four fighters.”

"That makes them the red wing?" I said, getting the hang of all this colour scheme nonsense. Part of my brain was asking why on Earth this was the topic I chose to discuss before the two fighters shot us to pieces. Sometimes, it's best to go off into la-la land and let the universe wreak havoc upon us all.

A third blue fighter hove into view, this one taking up position behind our first two arrivals. That made three of the lads about to kill us. Talk about overachievers.

Wait a minute. Three blue fighters? "Lydia," I asked, all casual like, "how many fighters would be in the blue wing?"

"Four," she replied. "And four in the red wing."

The fighter at the rear launched two missiles, Lydia grabbed my hand. Jeremy whimpered. I made a rude gesture at the two front fighters, sort of a lone defiance sort of thing. The front two fighters exploded, shot down by someone they assumed was their buddy, the guy at the rear.

Bloody Phil.

Everyone was rescuing me today.

Wallace was the first to comment. "Looks like Phil does know how to fly those things."

I waved at the last blue fighter, the one we hoped contained Phil and not some random maniac. Although that description fitted Phil exceedingly well.

"Can we talk to him?" I asked. "Use our communicators?"

"No," said Lydia. "Our little beads, even though military grade, are not strong enough to reach through all the garbage around us.'

She must have seen my quizzical look because she went on, "I mean electronic garbage, sweetie. The hull around any warship is covered with jamming devices, it makes any assault team work hard. We've been able to talk to each other because we've all stayed within a few paces of each other. But talking over any reasonable distance, such as from here to that last blue fighter, is not possible. He's too far away." She gave Phil a wave, he waved back and pointed at something near his sealed cockpit. Something outside his cockpit. Maybe he wanted me to come over and scratch it.

"Hmm," said Lydia. "Might work."

The two destroyed fighters slowly drifted away which left the entrance to the shuttle bay reasonably empty. The four of us stood and watched Phil manoeuvre his fighter closer and closer to us. He was still much farther out than Lydia was with her little 'shoot everyone' jaunt, there was no way I could leap from here to Phil's machine and repeat my Lydia rescue. He was floating about a hundred paces away from the bay opening but even so he was a long way off. I'm guessing because judging distances in space is bloody hard. Anyway, he stopped and I saw him looking at us. At me. I waved at him and he made the pointing gesture again. Something about something outside his cockpit. Man's a fool, I thought.

"Lydia," I said, trying my best to sound all casual and unconcerned. "What's he doing?"

Rather than answer me, she unclipped a cable from my belt, a cable I never knew was there and clipped one end to another similar cable coming from her belt. Now we were tethered. Okay, this was a nice symbol of our relationship but I was unsure why she was choosing to demonstrate it now.

"Wallace," she said, "make sure doofus doesn't let me go," she said. The she leaped into space again, sailing out to Phil's ship.

The cable on my belt extended from some hidden receptacle. I felt Wallace grab me firmly by the shoulders and push me to the ground. "Jeremy," said the big guy, "come and sit on Val." Some orders are far too well received. Jeremy skipped into the air with a glad cry and built up a little velocity before landing on my tummy. He squealed with glee. I exhaled violently and started to throw the little gargoyle off me. Wallace's hand pushed me back down, followed by his foot.

"What the hell, Wallace?" I snarled. "Get this blot on the landscape off me. And remove your troll foot from my delicate form.""Shut up and lie still, Val," said Wallace. "You're Lydia's anchor."

Well, this was an endearing observation from my large friend and I considered grunting some sort of acknowledgment. Some witty bit of parlance to recognise that I was, in fact, the centre of my girl's universe and the source of all her joy. Stuff like that.

"She needs a heavy object to give her some security. You make a great dead weight, Val," said Wallace. Jeremy continued to snigger while bouncing on my chest. The little snotbreath had significant heft, encased as he was in the modified suit.

We stayed this way for another few moments. Me with my mind trying to analyse the situation, Wallace and Jeremy forcing me to remain prone and motionless and Lydia was ... where was Lydia?

"Where's Lydia?" I asked. "Is she alright?""I'm here, Val," came my sweetie's voice, she patted me on the top of my helmet. "Been chatting to Phil. You can let him up now, guys."

Wallace removed his elephant sized foot from my chest which allowed me to roll on one side, throwing Jeremy off my poor, much pummelled chest. The little snot made a 'whee' sound as he slid across the floor. I got to my feet, helped by Lydia who was returning our various belt cables to their respective ports. They wrapped around the torso inside some secret channel. Big deal. Looking outside, I saw the last fighter, the one which presumably contained Phil, turn and float away.

"What just happened, Lydia?" I asked.

"I needed to link up with the comms port on Phil's fighter, Val," she said. As she did so, she pulled out yet another cable from her suit and waved it at me. God almighty, what else was tucked away in these things? I made a mental note to ask someone about it, knowing I never would because, well, you know, attention span.

"This had to be plugged into that comms port he was pointing to," she said. "Such a good idea from Phil, bloody brilliant, in fact." She let the cable retract and moved off to begin her ascent over the debris leading to the destroyed control room. Wallace and Jeremy followed her, leaving me standing alone on the lip of the exit and wondering what the hell happened.

Sometimes, the man in charge is the last to know what is going on.

I ran after them, scrambling up into the control room, stepping over bodies and gasped out my key question, "Lydia, what happened? What did you do? Why did you do it? And don't do it again!" That summed all my concerns into a sizable bundle. I joined my three pals at one of the doors leading into the main part of the battle brig and nudged Lydia's shoulder.

"Anytime now would be good. Answers in any order," I said. Authority dripping from me. Well, something was dripping from me, I could feel it in my boots. When this helmet came off, it was not going to be pleasant.

"Wallace," said my girl, "forget about trying to open that door the usual way. When the control room became open to space it would have resealed as an atmospheric barrier. Fortunately, these internal doors are not as robust as the ship's hull and other nasty bits. My explosives should be able to blow it open." She sounded disgustingly gleeful. Unhealthy, if you ask me. She needed to take some calming breaths. And she needed to do some explaining to those in authority.

"Lydia," I barked, "stop what you are doing! Everyone, settle down. What the hell is going on? Why did you make that dangerous jump over to Phil's fighter?"

"Did you bark at me, snookums?" asked Lydia.

I easily detected a certain tone in her voice, a tone any sensible man would wish to avoid, Jeremy, the little swine, sniggered. Wallace, whispered 'snookums' under his breath but I picked it up regardless.

The troops were making fun of their erstwhile leader. Okay, seemed fair.

"If you wouldn't mind, Lydia. Please tell me what you did and what we are going to do now? If that's alright with you?" Yep, I was the man I charge alright.

She leaned into me and I could see her suit move as she took a calming breath. Lydia taking deep calming breaths will give any red-blooded male within a day's march cause to adjust their clothing.

Jeremy squirmed, so I hit him behind the helmet. Wallace stirred ever so slightly and I decided not to hit him. But I gave him such a look.

"I needed to plug into the fighter's external comm port," explained Lydia. "And to get there, I had to jump and float out to him. I'd seen it done before by heroic young lads." At this, she rubbed herself against me which caused me to lose track of the next few sentences.

When my brain came back online, I heard Lydia say, "So, Phil decided he could shoot up the other launch bay, the red one. That would take out any chance of their fighters being able to re-arm and refuel. He hoped they would allow him to approach, given he was in one of their ships.""Don't these guys talk to each other?" asked Wallace. "Surely those fighters can communicate with the battle brig and know we had done some damage here?"

"They could," said Lydia, "except the Man in Black has already captured their communications hub on board the main ship. He now controls all comms. Apparently, he decided to turn everything off. At least, I hoped he turned it off and didn't simply shoot the place up.""Bear in mind it was the NightWatch doing the assault," said Jeremy.

Fair comment, the comms hub was probably a smoking mass by now. Lydia gave me an extra hug. "And I also needed to be secured to something solid and reliable while I did my little space walk. That's where you came in, sweetie.""I think I may be sick," muttered Wallace.

Jeremy made gagging noises.

Okay, that explained why these two lumps sat on top of me. "You could have explained what you were doing, Wallace," I complained. "No need to have sat on me." I gave Jeremy another clip around the helmet. Damned hard, these helmets, I suspect he didn't feel a thing.

"But it was so much more fun our way," replied Wallace.

Barbarians. I'm surrounded by uncouth barbarians.

"Okay," I agreed, calming down and seeing things from their side. I understood the actions, didn't like them but you can't argue with results. "Now what? Phil shoots up the other bay and then ..." A random though struck me. "Hey, what about the fighters from the other bay, won't they be upset with Phil if he shoots up their home."

"Yes," agreed Lydia. Her voice had become more solemn. "I pointed it out and he agreed his chances of survival were slim. He was almost cheerful, said something about it being a 'NightWatch sort of thing to do'."

Hells bells and buckets of blood, a prince of the Empire was about to be killed. While under my command.

I was going to be in so much trouble.

Chapter 17

LYDIA WAS UNPACKING HER explosives bag and placing things in special spots around the door. I watched as she attached various bits and pieces while my mind grappled with the loss of Phil. He was brave, the miserable snot. Annoying and untrustworthy but certainly brave. I liked him, he made life interesting because he was always up to something. Reminded me of me, except I'm a good guy.

Wallace and Jeremy were doing the sensible things like watching around us, in case someone else unpleasant came along; I wasn't because I'm management and they're labour. Plus, I was mired in thinking about Phil, the stupid clod. Thus, I was surprised when Wallace punched my shoulder and said, "Company's coming."

We all turned to look out the shuttle bay entrance, past the broken control room window, over the remains of the equipment in the bay and ignoring the various bodies scattered about. For there, coming into view some distance out, was a fighter. A damaged fighter, a fighter leaking bits of metal and some form of liquid from its rear engines.

A blue fighter.

"That's Phil!" yelled Jeremy.

Sure enough, our wayward royal was guiding his damaged ship into view. He was a long way out, too far for any heroic leaps from me and I wasn't going to let anyone else try Lydia's stunt. He was so far out we could barely recognise the blue colouring but still close enough for me to see the hatch over the pilot seat swing open.

“What’s he doing?” I asked as we all clambered back down to the main deck of the shuttle bay. At least we could stand and watch Phil die or do something equally pointless. Wallace grunted, a grunt I took to be a negative. Jeremy said nothing and Lydia ran to a relatively undamaged compartment off to one side of the shuttle bay. Good. Everyone was doing something. Wallace and Jeremy joined me on the lip of the shuttle bay and watched Phil stand up in the pilot’s seat, wave at us and the step off into space.

Where he floated, looking at us.

Was he going to stay there and haunt us? I wondered. Float in the blackness of the universe, sidling alongside the battle brig until he died and became some sort of haunting legend. My mind was constructing a variety of tales about ghosts and other scary things. My train of thought was interrupted by a body surging past me, a body wearing a special pack with assorted nozzles and jets. I’d seen these packs before, even used one. They allowed the wearer to navigate through space, some sort of extra vehicular suit. Since I knew where I was and understood Jeremy was on one side with Wallace on the other, that left one person unaccounted for.

Lydia.

“Honey!” I said, my tone carrying that wistfulness she had heard so often, “Watcha doin’?”

“Back in a minute, sweetie, I have to pick up the kids from school, be back ...” she replied, then her voice cut out as she left our communication range.

Once again, I stood uselessly on the sidelines while others did the good deeds. Admittedly, others usually had some plan and skills which allowed them to complete their deeds successfully, whereas I was more of a charge forward, hit everything and see what happened kind of guy. As such, I would not have been able to retrieve Phil with the same ease and air of competence displayed by Lydia.

Feeling I had to be doing something proactive, I ordered Wallace and Jeremy to go back up into the control room and guard the doors, in case we were interrupted by enemy soldiers or even a stray gust of wind. Yes, I know Wallace would be able to look after himself and probably hold off the hordes from one door and I also realised sending Jeremy as door guard was ridiculous but I was out of ideas. And I wanted them out of the way in case I had to do something awful to Phil, he might have been horribly injured and needed a spot of mercy killing.

I was all for a spot of mercy killing at the moment. Life's events had gotten up my nose and someone was going to pay. If Phil looked in any way damaged, I would feel obliged to put him out of my misery. Sorry, out of his misery.

As I thought these dark, dark thoughts, Lydia landed back in the shuttle bay with the returning hero clutched in her lissom arms. I especially did not like the way he was clutching her in return. Surely, he did not need to have his hands placed on those particular parts of her anatomy. Communications were restored as they arrived and I heard Phil say, "You've got a lovely bum, Lydia."

She unstrapped herself from the manoeuvring pack, poked Phil in the chest and said, "And that bum is not for fondling." I did like the way she was expressing herself, a fondness which increased with her next words. "Unless your name happens to be Valentine," she said, looking over at me and thrusting out a hip, "in which case, fondle away."

The males in the group lurched and groaned while Phil muttered, "You lucky, lucky bastard, Valentine."Amen, brother, I thought. So very amen.

The three of us climbed up again to where Lydia had been setting her explosives. I recalled Jeremy from his solitary post at the other door and he wheezed in appreciation. "I'm still a kid, Uncle Val," he said. "Not sure if I can handle defending a door all by myself."

"Of course you can, wart," I replied, giving his helmet a noogie, which is actually rather difficult. "You could annoy them to death. Like you do me."

Lydia told us the big bang was ready to go and suggested we find a place to hide. I suggested we leave the entire shuttle bay, in case she had set the explosives too strongly and we blew ourselves all to kingdom come. She stated her expertise was now in question by those idiots in charge and placed us in positions which I considered to be borderline suicidal. I noticed she had set her explosives in a line around the outline of the door. Apparently, explosives can be moulded like clay and not like lumps of gunpowder in a barrel, I had always left this sort of thing to Teddy Boy since he liked a big noise. I once suggested he was compensating but stopped when Sylvia went into some detail about how he had nothing to compensate for. As I recall, many of us felt embarrassed and ill during her little soliloquy. I daresay a few even felt somewhat envious of our fellow guardsman. Some, but not me. No siree, not moi.

Lydia stuck Wallace and me close to one edge of the hopefully to be destroyed door. She assured us the explosion would push into the door, forcing it out of its current little slot and free it to float off into space. How an explosion which blasts one way could free its target to go another way was yet another thing I did not understand. And wisely, I kept my mouth shut about it.

Because I wasn't a complete idiot, I made sure I was standing behind Wallace. I tucked myself in close to his manly back and hoped it was manly enough to withstand either an explosion or the imminent arrival of a blown-out door. He turned and looked at me. "I'll look after you, snookums," he said.

"Bite your bum, Wallace" I replied, his body posture hinted at a smile but it's hard to tell with Wallace, he's not big on smiles.

Lydia planted herself and Jeremy at the far end of the control room while Phil sauntered over to her and took up a position far too familiar with my girl. He made sure I could see him leaning close to her shoulder. Far too close, the sewer.

"In three ... two ... one," she said and then I watched the door sail past Wallace, missing us all entirely. If we had any sort of atmosphere, I believe we would have heard an almighty bang but as it was, we saw a puff, a flash and then the door floated away revealing a now empty inner corridor.

We went into the new space and found ourselves in a short corridor running along the back of the control room. At each end of the corridor was another door, an internal door.

"Come on," said Lydia. She ran to one end of the corridor and opened a small control panel. She pushed some buttons, an atmosphere proof panel slid down behind us and, once it deployed, the door in front opened and in we went. Once inside, she shut the door behind us.

"Okay, "she said, "We are now inside the ship. You should find your suit comms work a little better now."

She was right, the moment she shut the final door, my communication bead had been swamped with messages. It sent through a whole series of pings to my brain, lots of pings, many with different tones and lengths. Each of the sounds was someone asking to contact me because, like a complete idiot, I had left everyone on my communication net while also setting up subgroups for the Man in Black, then the squad leaders and on and on. My head felt like I was sitting inside a church during a particularly aggressive recital on the pipe organ.

Fortunately, one of the key mental commands I had at my disposal turned them all off. Which I now did. Ahh, peace, blessed peace.

Someone hit the back of my helmet, causing my poor noggin to dance about. Phil was standing beside me with a raised hand, apparently keen to repeat his attempt at nonverbal communication. Our helmet face plates had cleared to become transparent — outside they had been darkened in case we looked at the sun or explosions or naked women. Okay, that last was more aspirational than reality.

But now I could see their faces and they could see mine. In front of me was a worried Lydia, she had her helmet touching mine and was pointing at her ears. Since our helmets were in contact, I could also hear her voice.

"Turn your comms back on, you bloody fool!" she said. My girl has a lovely voice, all soft tones and golden hues. Still, I got her point. I turned my comms back on, ensuring this time I had set it to receive this team, plus the Man in Black and Teddy Boy.

Phil hit me again, I told him to cut it out which he did, but after giving me one final thump. "You left your comm channel open to everyone, didn't you, dickhead?" he asked.

"Sod off," I replied. The various pings I had received were messages, none were actual contacts with anyone else on the ship. Why was that, I wondered. I thought I better show I was back in control, "Everyone, give me a report," I commanded.

They all stopped and turned to look at me. I can spot body posture communications and their stances all reflected a certain amazement at my instruction.

"Did you ask us to report in, Val?" asked Lydia.

"CADET CORPORAL JEREMY REPORTING, SERGEANT!" bellowed Jeremy, standing at attention and saluting. You haven't experienced ridiculousness until you've been saluted by a waist high waif, in full combat armour — armour designed for an adult and hilariously squashed down to suit the young sprog. The effect was heightened by the small scout machine climbing to the top of his helmet where it adopted a formal pose and raised one of its legs in salute.

"This is all going in my memoirs," said Phil. "The title should be something like 'Lord Philip Arenburg, the early years'. Or possibly, 'The Care and Feeding of Valentine'. What do you think, oh mighty leader?" He chuckled. "That, by the way, was my report."

"Christ on a crutch," muttered Wallace. Nothing else, a simple statement of his deep sense of ennui.

I pulled myself together and went to the exit door. "Okay," I said. "A momentary lapse into being professional. Won't happen again." I tapped the door. "How do we open this thing? Do we need more secret codes known to members of the Imperial family? And where do we go to find the Man in Black?"

"We open the door by pushing the 'OPEN' button, Val," said Lydia, gesturing to one of two buttons on a side panel. "These doors are shut whenever the hull integrity is breached. They are not coded because anyone rushing in to rescue trapped crew doesn't have time to faff about with secret codes. And they are generally in cumbersome rescue suits carrying lots of emergency gear. Of course," she finished, "the people on the other side might not be gentle rescuers. They might be armed troopers resisting our incursion."

"Did you just say, 'faff about'?" I queried.

"Good to see you have homed in on the critical part of Lydia's message, dickhead," said Phil.

Chapter 18

WE ALL TOOK A breath and calmed down. Phil obviously decided to expand on his previous skills and said, "I knew the various codes for entry to this ship because I … er … just do." He finished rather weakly, probably regretting opening up on the subject at all.

"Something you want to tell us, Phil?" I asked. I did a small loom over him, nothing too serious, merely a reminder of who I was and what my baser inclinations would lead me to do if obstructed in any way.

"No," he croaked. But his voice was small and weak, I could see his face clearly and a small line of sweat had formed on his upper lip.

"Hmm," I said, placing both of my hands on his shoulders. "How about I beat the snot out of you, here and now?"

Phil's head swivelled about, seeking some assistance, some succour, an ally from among the team. I didn't look, I knew what was happening because I could see most of it through my peripheral vison and could guess the rest.

"Wallace?" pleaded Phil. "Aren't you tasked with, you know, keeping me safe?"

Wallace grunted. "I'm on a break, Your Highness."

"Better tell him, Phil," suggested Lydia. "When he gets like this, there are two things which calm him down. One is an outbreak of violence."

I could feel the question in the air, what was the other thing which could calm me down? To be honest, I think Lydia had over stressed my mood swings and emotional capabilities, I have a broader range than simplistic violence and, well, whatever the other thing was. And what was this other thing? God, I hate it when my mind wanders.

"Is the other thing," piped in Jeremy, "having a special cuddle with you, Lydia?"

I could feel my face heating up, Phil must have seen my blush because he almost chortled. Almost, but not quite, because he still had a decent sense of self preservation. Nonetheless, I had to reassert my authority and so I turned my head to Jeremy.

"Bite your bum, pipsqueak," I said.

"Biting now, sergeant!" he replied. The little wart certainly knows how to lower the emotional tone in a room. I say this, because he bent over which allowed his little insect machine thingy to run back over his body where it perched on his raised backside.

Then it mimed biting down.

God, I love Jeremy. The blemish.

Everyone relaxed, even Phil. He must have thought he was out of the woods because he even smiled at me. I smiled back and he swallowed.

"Still waiting for an answer to my question, you lying snake," I said. My voice had lost its tinge of maniacal glee and was back to my ordinary threatening tone. It was obviously still effective because Phil started babbling.

"I do jobs for the Emperor," he said. "Special errands."

"You've said that before," I said. "I assumed you went and opened the odd building for him or dropped off love notes to his girlfriends."

"Yes," he said. "Well, I do that, too. But mainly I meet with ... people ... who know things and are willing to ... sell that information."

"Are you a spy, Uncle Phil?" asked Jeremy. I looked over at the wart, he had come to stand beside me and was gazing up at the heir to Empire with the inquisitiveness known solely to youth, unabashed interest in all things. And when did Phil attain 'uncle' status?

Phil squeezed Jeremy's shoulder gently, I could see the obvious affection the man had for my young companion. Okay, he can't be all bad if he likes Jeremy. Mentally unbalanced perhaps, but not bad.

"No," stated Phil, with some emphasis. "Certainly not! I'm a messenger. I do errands."

"Perhaps we can share life stories later," interjected Wallace. "If this door opens easily then it means anyone approaching from the other side could open it up and see us here, gabbing away like fools."

He had a point. "Right," I said, "we'll open that door, but we'll be sneaky about it. We might see people lurking there with evil intent."

"I hate you, Valentine," said Wallace. "No one actually says the words 'evil intent' out loud."

"Umm, boys," said Lydia, "if I may interact in your vibrant social matrix." She pointed at a small hole, high up on the wall containing the door. "That's a camera. The people in the next compartment, if there are any, have been watching us since we arrived."I looked at the little hole. Bloody cameras, they were scattered far too liberally in this modern world. "So what?" I said. "Should we give them a wave or something?" A thought struck me. "Hang on, why are there cameras in this compartment? And why should the next space be able to see us?"

"It's another tool for the emergency responders," said Lydia. "Any compartment, such as this one, close to an opening in the main hull, has cameras in it. As you have seen, this room forms a barrier between space and the rest of the ship, it might contain survivors from any unexpected breach such as from the shuttle bay. The emergency responders can use the camera to see who is in here and how urgent any rescue has to be. For all they know, this room might be empty or full of people losing air. Seconds count."

My mind ticked off the seconds we had been in this room. We had entered from the broken control room and stood around gabbing for maybe a minute. That was enough time for any responders to check us out and see who we were.

"Would anyone looking at us think we were from their crew?" I asked. "Survivors from an attack on the shuttle bay?"

"No chance," put in Phil. "Our armour is different from the Confederacy, we stand out like tits on a bull."

Great, when Phil gets home and has lunch with the royal aunties, he will be using terminology like 'tits on a bull'. Right, back to the situation at hand — if we opened this door, we could be faced by unpleasant people with lots of weapons. Or they might open the door and kill us all as we stood here with our thumbs up our bum.

"Get ready," I said. "They'll probably open the door and shoot first. I would."

We certainly made a wonderful target, all clustered around the door. Anyone opening it would have the pleasure of shooting all five of us as we stood so thoughtfully in a clump. I was going to get everyone killed. I opened my mouth to tell everyone to spread out or run away or bend over and kiss their bum goodbye. But before I got a word out, Wallace started issuing instructions.

"Phil!" he said, ownership of the situation reeking from him. "When Val opens the door, drop and lie down, tuck yourself at the bottom of the door with just your pistol around the door frame. You should be able to get most of your body behind that side panel." My mouth started to ask questions but my brain wisely told it to shut up; I was going to open the door. Right, I could do that, I was good at pushing buttons.

"I'll drop at the same time and push myself to the opposite side," went on Wallace. "Phil, you and I will be the shooters, we have to take out any offensive personnel as quick as we can. But we don't drop or move yet, otherwise the team on the other side will have a few seconds warning of our new positions.""What about us, Wallace?" asked Lydia, indicating herself and Jeremy.

"We can't all fit behind these small wall panels beside the door," said my new ideas man. "I'm sorry, but the best I can suggest is for the two of you to go prone against opposite sides of the room. Get yourselves away from the centre space where we now are, that will be their aiming point.'

"And me, Wallace?" I asked. "Where will I hide?"

"You get to remain standing, Val," said Wallace. "I notice you don't have any ranged weapons." I think I detected a slight note of censure in his tone. Yes, I had lost my pistol and my long gun because we had thrown them away in my small rescue journey with Lydia. "Stay out of sight of the door when you open it. You'll be on the same side as Phil but he'll be on the floor, no room for you as well. Tuck yourself into the corner behind him."

I grunted assent. Not happy agreement, more of a soulful reply.

"And, Val, stop whinging, for God's sake," said Wallace. "Everyone ready?"

We all responded. I looked over the gang, now with bodies tensed, ready to fall and roll as required. I understood Wallace's plan, it made sense. The camera would show us all standing together in front of the door. Ergo, anyone opening the door would expect to see a gaggle of enemy combatants — us — clustered helpfully together as easy targets. Anyone on the other side — and we still didn't know if there would be anyone there — would be expecting to shoot us down like the idiots we were.

But we would not be idiots, we would have dropped and rolled away from the opening door leaving the space in which we now stood empty of fragile bodies.

As long as we moved rapidly and the bad guys did not change their aim too quickly. And then we would be relying on Wallace and Phil to shoot down any assailants. This part did not worry me since I had seen Phil shoot, he was accurate and calm in a crisis; I hoped he could bring himself to shoot down a living, breathing person he could see over his gun sight. I guess we were about to find out.

And Wallace was, well, Wallace. A deadly man.

"Val," commanded Wallace, "Open the door!"

I pushed the button and jumped behind the panel beside the rapidly opening door. I landed on one of Phil's legs as he attempted to occupy the same space as my tender boots. I jumped again, allowing him to wriggle into safety before landing on his right leg. This was turning out to be a bit of fun.

A whole series of shots ripped into the space which we had recently vacated. Lots of nasty beams and slugs tore past me and impacted the far door. All the shots were about body height and every one of them missed. Then our guys responded.

Wallace had already dropped and rolled and was now shooting. Lydia and Jeremy fell to the floor and rolled towards their respective side walls. Phil started shooting while simultaneously cursing my lumbering grace, implying I had purposely jumped on him because I wanted stop him from thinking about what he was about to do. He was using lots of bad words, many of which he must have picked up from the NightWatch. His mum would not be pleased with that sort of language.

Since I couldn't see anything, I asked for a status report. Phil ignored me but Wallace was able to speak in his calm voice. I watched him on the far side of the door opening, lying prone and steadily shooting into the other room. His shots were evenly spaced out, no hint of rush or panic. Heck of a guy.

"I saw four troopers in the room, Phil and I got three of them but the last one is hunkered down behind some sort of shield. A panel pivoted up from the floor, it's resisting our shots. We can keep him pinned down but I can't see how we get him before his buddies arrive."

"That's another piece of standard kit in a potential battle room," said Lydia. "A part of the floor can hinge up and act as a blast shield. Good for such occasions as this." She was lying prone, stretched out along the line where the wall met the floor. She was trying to crawl into the corner even more. Jeremy was doing the same on the other side. At least they were away from the obvious aiming point of the last trooper, but if he poked his head out and took careful aim, he would be able to hit either of them. Or both. Phil and Wallace were almost impossible targets while I was invisible behind the wall.

Invisible and without a way to shoot back because I had chucked away my main weapons. Wallace was aiming and shooting carefully. I don't think he had a target but those shots would certainly keep someone's head down. A glance at Phil told me he was lining up a shot, waiting for some part of the last trooper's body to show.

Ah, well, I decided, nothing else for it but to do something stupid.

I pulled out my hammer, it still had a few bits of the earlier crewman sticking to it after I had messily pulled it from his squelchy body; you need to maintain your equipment, Valentine, I thought. I ran into the room and yes, it was borderline suicidal but I had noticed Phil was not shooting. He was waiting for a target. It was Wallace who kept up a steady stream of blasts and so I needed to avoid getting in his way but I could run in front of Phil. I stepped over our resident royal, ran into the room and then spun to the side wall. Now I was in the same location as before but on the opposite side of the wall.

Wallace kept shooting at the enemy trooper, the poor sod must have been terrified because he limited his shooting to popping his hand above the shield and blatting blindly towards us, he showed a hand clutching a pistol, never a head which we could happily shoot. Sooner or later, he would hit Jeremy which would not be good. Or he'd hit Lydia, which would be a tragedy. Phil had stopped shooting, I don't know why. I hoped it was because he did not have a clear shot at the enemy trooper.

I took three paces along the side wall and then dived at his protective blast panel. It's like charging a shield wall, but different; I've fought against hard lads who used the old ways, hairy men from the north of England who liked to form a shield wall and dare anyone to come and get them. As I dived, I reached out with my left hand and grabbed the top edge of the blast panel. I used my forward momentum and my arm muscles to pull myself over its lip — mind you, I was still airborne and horizontal at this point. My other hand had the hammer raised above my body, ready to descend on any random bit of anatomy. I bet I looked fantastic.

The trooper must have been surprised to see my hand appear in front of his face as it grasped the upper rim of his shield. I say this because his helmet raised a little to see what was going on, and into that questioning gaze came my hammer, spike end first.

He reconsidered his commitment to life as I crashed over the blast panel. My body followed the hammer onto the now dying trooper and we both rolled about until I came to rest. I was still holding my hammer because I am such a pro, I never let go of a weapon. Unless I throw it into space, my brain whispered. Stupid brain, what would it know.

I stood up as Lydia rushed in to check me for injuries, one of her standard responses. Phil and Wallace ran to the far end of the corridor and peered round the corner, ready to … do something, I'm sure.

Jeremy wandered in with his little machine perched on his helmet. "That was so cool, Uncle Val," he said. I noticed he was stepping over the bodies of the dead troopers with casual insouciance, probably not even noting they were there. Hanging around us, and me in particular, had probably damaged Jeremy in some way, he was far too comfortable around violence.

Can't be good for a growing lad.

Chapter 19

Phil came back and reported there was no movement down the other corridor. I noticed he did not walk as assuredly as before, some of the air of entitlement had been knocked out of him. He had left Wallace to keep lookout because Wallace was keen to know whenever other bad lads turned up. Wallace has this dreadful need to know, ahead of time, when something awful is about to happen. Why, I do not know. I assumed the next disaster was always about to unfold and so kept my hopes and dreams on an even mental keel.

Lydia and Jeremy joined Phil and the four of us stood together, looking at each other and hoping someone would take charge, give us a direction, solve the problems and basically tell us what to do. The Man in Black and Magic were not around which meant that, eventually, all helmets were pointed my way.

"Still nothing," reported Wallace. I understood he meant the corridor was still clear but his comment aptly summed up my thinking processes.

"What are we going to do, Uncle Val?" asked Jeremy.

"Dunno," I replied. This cast a pall of gloom over my comrades so I added a few more encouraging words. "Seems like we're stuffed."

"I feel so much better, knowing you are in charge," commented Phil. "Why don't we rejoin one of the other groups? We could head towards

Sergeant Gorka in engineering or catch up with the rest of the Night-Watch in communications."

"We better move soon," added Lydia. "I'm surprised we haven't had more troopers checking up on their shuttle bay." She had pulled herself together after the scene in the shuttle bay, buried it deep, I should imagine.

This was a good point. "Surely their leadership must know we have stuffed up this shuttle bay," I said. "And, if what Phil tells us is true," this got a groan from Wallace, still on watch, "then they have also lost their other shuttle bay. Why aren't we knee deep in people wanting to, you know, kill us?"

"Maybe they don't know," said Jeremy.

"Of course they'd know," I said. "They must have a good comm system in place, keeping tabs on who's doing what. And to whom." While we in the NightWatch were conspicuously poor to organise or to follow orders, I had assumed a ship like a battle brig was crewed by people who actually knew what they were doing.

"How do I contact the Man in Black?" I asked. Our suit comms were working, but I couldn't hear anyone else. I could talk to Wallace, Phil, Jeremy and Lydia without any problem. Where was everyone else? Could I contact them?

"How do I call the Man in Black?" I repeated to the gang. Any of them might be able to answer me — Wallace kept his eyes and ears open in our new world and may have picked up some clues; Phil knew stuff, it's always impossible to work out what he did know and what he didn't, plus he was a lying bastard. Lydia was my best bet, she was a technician on board a spaceship, surely she would have some answers. I discounted Jeremy, mainly because he was an annoying snot.

"We're still blocked by the amount electronic interference," said my girl. "We would have all received lots of pings when we entered the ship, but they would have been rubbish noise." I nodded at her, because I did not know what she was talking about and wanted to appear knowledgeable.

"You might need to use small words with Uncle Val," said Jeremy. I recognised what the little snot was doing, using humour to lower our emotional temperature; it was a technique I had used often and I guess he had been watching. "Maybe some pictures, coloured drawings would be most helpful." I clipped him over the helmet. Just because.

"Our communications are too weak to punch through, "said Lydia. "Are you hearing lots of pings? Requests for joining? But when you try to send or receive, all you get is static."

I had been reaching out through my comms system, trying to reach the Man in Black, Magic or Sergeant Gorka. Each time I managed to get out a trickle of a link, it was quickly drowned in a wave of unbearable noise, I kept shutting it off.

"Is 'static' that scrunching noise through my comm system?" I asked.

"Yes, sweetie," said Lydia. "We use the term 'static' because 'scrunching noise' is not sufficiently pompous." Jeremy chuckled, Lydia took the opportunity to hit his helmet.

"Jeremy," she said, "be warned. You pick Val, you pick me."

Jeremy shrank down even further. Yet another example of my girl's ability to bring the peasants into line. I wish I could do it as well.

"So, our comms are not up to the job?" I asked. "Too weak?"

A soft cough brought our heads around to Phil. I sighed.

"What is it, weevil breath?" I asked. I needed to lean on Phil, to get his mind off the recent close quarters combat he had experienced. Yes, I know he had shot down two of their fighters — containing, living human beings — but they were in machines and you could fool yourself no actual people were involved.

We're all heavily into self-deception. Or alcohol. Or something, anything to make the heebie jeebies go away. So, for Phil, I believed treating him like a piece of faeces would help, it would not be the sort of treatment he would be used to and so it might throw him out of whack long enough for his psyche to deal with his actions. I'm living the dream here.

"Your conclusion about *your* comms is correct," Phil said. "Even military grade would be insufficient in this environment." The mongrel was smirking, enjoying his moment of revelation. "But I, as you may recall, am a member of the Imperial family. We like to be able to stay in touch."

"Phil," I said, "are you saying you can contact the boss?"

"Most certainly," he replied. "In fact, I've been chatting to him since we entered the main part of this vessel."

"I am going to do you someday, you imperial nosebleed," I said. "Why didn't you tell us you could communicate with the gang?""Ahh," he demurred. "because, so far, it has been all one sided. I can punch through to him but he cannot respond with anything coherent; I know he is saying something but each word is a blast of static. I suspect I am hearing every word but it's indecipherable. I can't make out the individual words."

"What about using the static to communicate?" said Lydia. "Have him send a message containing one word and then another with two words. Can you do that?""Wait one," said Phil. We stood around watching him move his lips. I decided to join Wallace at the end of the corridor and wait for angry troopers to come looking for us. And why hadn't they turned up yet? I figured Lydia and Jeremy could work out a way to use the static as code. Lydia's intelligent, Jeremy's a smart nodule and Phil is

... Phil. While I waited, I decided to ask Wallace about why weren't we knee deep in blood and guts.

"Dunno," he replied.

"I can see you've given this a lot of thought," I said.

His head turned to me and I could see his face through the clear plate of his helmet. I reminded myself never to play poker with him. Stoneface is not a sufficiently rock-like description of his visage. He opened his mouth to speak, changed his mind and placed his lips together. Then he gave me the once over, scanning my body up and down. This caused me to recall he may well have accepted his final contract to assassinate a target before he joined our little crew. And the general consensus was this target was me. I understand bets were laid and a pool was being run by Right Honourable.

"Are you going to kill me, Wallace?" I asked. Might as well get it out in the open. "Someday?" He stretched himself to his full height, rolled his shoulders and probably popped knuckles and then smiled at me. A little smile, he even threw in a wink, good for effect. Wallace scares the crap out of me.

A hand thumped my shoulder, a large hand, a hand belonging to Phil. "We have a plan," he said. Terrific. Phil's plans always worked out so well for me. I groaned.

Lydia hugged me. "It's alright, sweetie," she said. "This plan does not involve you doing something incredibly brave."

"Or incredibly stupid," said Jeremy.

Lydia and I both hit his helmet.

Chapter 20

LYDIA FILLED ME IN. Phil was familiar with the concept of codes — no surprise there — and established a simple YES and NO response process with the Man in Black. Something about one burst of static meaning a YES and two bursts meaning NO. Or the other way around. Or something different. Don't know. Don't care.

The main thing is, we could talk easily to the boss ; at least, Phil could, using his royal comms bead. Probably got diamonds and gold on it somewhere. And a coat of arms.

God, Phil gives me the pip.

The boss could give responses with a yes or a no. Between Phil's innate sneakiness and Lydia's flat-out brilliance, they got some messages to go back and forth. Now I knew what the situation was with the Night-Watch team.

They had captured the comms room, avoided destroying everything while turning off the ship's internal communication system. Apparently, Teddy Boy had been listening to people talk about this sort of stuff, I was with him during those lectures but must have dozed off. It meant our gun nut guardsman knew which buttons to push.

The Man in Black told him to turn off all the comm channels the battle brig crew were using; this explained why we were not inundated with hordes of unwashed troopers. They either didn't know we were here or were unable to contact their own people, the ones capable of resisting an incursion. The shuttle bay had its own set of troopers, in case an enemy got aboard through it. That would be all the dead body parts lying around the entrance doors to the shuttle bay, doors which Lydia had shot up while killing all the troopers.

The bunch we encountered in this chamber was probably a roving patrol and unlucky enough to find us. I felt a twinge of sympathy for the poor sods, I'd been on those roving patrols back in the City and it was never nice. Admittedly, they believed they were wandering through their ship and reasonably safe whereas we patrolled the Thieves' Quarter and knew everyone wanted to kill us. Gave you a real desire to be observant and, if needed, bloody ruthless.

"Let's go and join them," I said. "Where are they?"

"Ah, yes," said Phil, "we still don't know. The static bursts allow a form of primitive communication but do not allow us to find their position. How about I contact Sergeant Gorka and set up the static burst comms with her, maybe she has suggestions."

Terrific. Gorka and Phil would have to devise a plan based upon a lot of YES/NO responses. That was bound to take a long time and I didn't fancy standing around here like tourists until the locals turned up to ask serious questions about our redecorating.

Plus, I was getting bored. I needed to be moving.

"Let's all walk around while you do that, Phil," I said.

"We can use Sparky to scout ahead for us," proclaimed Jeremy. This brought me up to a halt. Lydia was beside Phil as he walked and talked at the same time, must be hard for a royal. Yes, I know he was doing some delicate negotiations with Gorka who liked to yell at people and yes, I understood he was probably the best man for the job but still ... he's Phil.

I turned back to Jeremy and asked, "Who, or what, is 'Sparky'?" In response to my perfectly reasonable question, Jeremy's little insect-like machine crawled on top of his helmet and stood erect. Then it saluted me.

"Sparky can climb walls and even hang off the ceiling for a short time," he said. "He can send back a video of whatever he sees. Could be good for peeking around corners and stuff."

Okay, that could be useful. "Jeremy, you are now Cadet Scout," I stated. "That is, you and, er Sparky."

They both saluted, I'm living in a circus.

Sneaking through a spaceship is surreal, especially if you believe enemy troopers could be around any corner. Lots of enemy troopers. I suspected we would face more roving patrols and did not want to be breezily turning a corner with eyes agleam and faces all smiley before meeting armed thugs coming the other way.

Yes, I admit I fit the description of an armed thug but I'm on my side and consider myself a reasonable and gentle man. I think I'm alone in that opinion.

Our movement order consisted of Wallace up front with Jeremy behind him. That meant the first one of our group anyone encountered would be Wallace and I was so on board with that idea. I certainly would not like to meet Wallace — an angry, alert Wallace — as I rounded a corner, walking and whistling. Then came Lydia and Phil as they talked with Gorka and sometimes the Man in Black. I brought up the rear, this allowed me to scan behind us for anyone seeking to disturb our day.

It also meant I got to gaze at Lydia's bum from time to time. I get distracted easily.

"Val," said my sweetie, "are you staring at my bum?"

"Maybe," I prevaricated. A change of subject was in order, "Any updates on Gorka?"

"Yes," she replied. "They're in engineering, suffered some casualties but they seem to be in charge of the place. She says the battle brig's captain tried to contact them but lost all communications. Probably around the time the NightWatch took over the comms room."

Wallace held up a hand, we ground to a halt. I checked our rear and turned back in time to see the big man lean backwards towards Jeremy. I suspected they had set up a two-person comm link, specifically for their little scouting task. Smart guy, Wallace.

"Stay here," he said over our team channel. "Jeremy tells me there are two troopers around the corner, looks like they are guarding the entrance to a stairwell." He disappeared around the corner, returning after a few heartbeats to say, "All clear."

And indeed, we were. When we rounded the corner, I saw two dead bodies with small holes in their helmets. Wallace does like a good head-shot. "Up or down, Val?" asked Wallace, gesturing at the two sets of stairs. I had no idea.

"Hey!" exclaimed Jeremy, "I'm getting something from Sparky. Can you guys give me a minute?" We took up guard positions around our little snot as he did things with his new toy. Finally, he came back with, "Sparky says he is picking up a weak link with another one of his machines. Not words, more of a tingle telling him something is almost within range."

I had a hunch. "Could the other machine, the other 'Sparky', be one of those with Teddy Boy or the Man in Black?" Given that Caeser came from a different galaxy and had advanced technology, it was possible his wee machines were able to detect each other.

"Hang on," said Jeremy, "let me check the manual again." His head tilted back and I could see his lips moving through his faceplate. What was he doing, I wondered? Communing with God?

"Sparky can detect other machines like him because he is in active search mode — because we're, you know, trying to stay alive and so on. If Ensign Franco can switch his machine into Active Search Mode, then we should get a cleaner link."

"On it," said Phil, before I could order him to get in touch with the Man in Black. Didn't he realise I was the big dog in this group, that I gave the orders? Obviously not, the sewer rat.

I felt Lydia give my shoulder a gentle squeeze. How does she do that? I wondered. How does she know when I am acting all selfish and stupid and need bringing back down from my heights of emotional stupidity, especially now my rage was always close to the boil. I calmed down, took a breath and patted her hand quietly. Then I turned back to guarding us all, trying desperately to keep us safe. They would do what was needed for communications, they didn't need me to be all bossy and precious. And angry.

I moved around our stairwell, checking the various entrances for anyone sneaking up on us. Several corridors debouched into this landing space, it was obviously a key movement juncture. But everywhere I looked, the corridors and stairs remained admirably clear. It's times like this when the stomach heaves and the heart races. When it's quiet, that's the right time for the nasty beast to leap out and attack, ripping faces off, spilling blood, wrenching arms and ... I got a grip on myself. I was never any good at the waiting part of a fight, far more comfortable with the actual hitting and screaming.

"I think we're good to go," said Phil. A small line registered on my helmet, a gentle yellow line starting from the bottom of my face plate and jutting towards the stairwell. As I moved my head, the line altered, always leading towards the down staircase.

"Have we been clever?" I asked.

"Jeremy has," said Lydia. "He's had Sparky set up a tenuous link with Sparky Two, that's the one with Teddy Boy. It won't allow voice comms but it can set up a travel route for us to follow, the route links the two Sparky machines."

"Well done, wart," I said to Jeremy. "You are hereby appointed to Chief Scout.""Is that a real thing?" asked Jeremy.

"Not at all," I confirmed. Lydia gave him a hug to make up for my manifest cruelty. I had Jeremy send Sparky on a small reconnoitre down the stairs to the next level and sure enough, two more guards stood there.

Probably more on every level, these guys had serious trust issues.

Chapter 21

"WHY SO MANY GUARDS?" I asked. Our internal comms worked as long as we stayed close together so we were able to huddle and talk without using the suit's external speakers. Because that would be bad.

"Let's see," mulled Phil. "This vessel is carrying out a hostile assault on our frigate, all was going well until, unexpectedly, gate crashers blew a hole in their ship and they were in turn invaded by our meagre force."

"Yeah, but," I said, "we're defending our pals. They're the actual bad guys, they did the original attacking."

"Think of it from their point of view," said Wallace. "They hit the frigate, all goes well and then, suddenly, a hole gets blown on their ship. They never saw another ship nearby — since we were cloaked — but suddenly find themselves with several angry enemy troopers storming aboard."

"I must say," said Phil, "their response to our incursion was commendable. Excellent reaction time. We hadn't even managed to inject all our chaps — that's you, Val — before their fast response team was on top of us. Hence the sealing of our breach. They've got a good team on board this tub."

"They're the bad guys Phil," I reminded him. "A little less on the gushiness, please."

"Making a comment, your sergeantness," he replied. "Of course, since then their captain has lost all engine power and any ability to communicate with his various teams. He may not have learned that both his launch bays, the shuttle bays for the fighters, have been destroyed but is probably wondering what the hell is going on aboard his ship."

"You mean," said Lydia, "the captain and all the senior leadership are probably on the bridge, wondering what is going on. Wow, talk about being kept in the dark." We stood and thought together until someone nudged me, I think it was Jeremy.

"What are we going to do, Val?" he asked, always the same old question.

"Okay," I said," I don't know how people run spaceships but I do know how commanders work during a siege. They like to know what's going on, they are always keen to know what the enemy is doing and they try to have a system for delivering messages to various areas of the city."

"Or spaceship," interrupted Phil.

"Shut up, Phil," said Lydia. "Val's talking."

I swallowed. "Without any electronic communications, my guess is he has fallen back on the tried-and-true technique of using people as messengers. If it was me, I'd put guards at critical communication junctures, like stairways, also gathering all the troopers I could. Then I'd send these guys to take back the invaded spaces."

"Good plan," grunted Wallace. "Let's get moving."

We started descending the stairs, Wallace and Jeremy up front as scout and bodyguard, I brought up the rear behind Phil and Lydia. All was going well.

"If possible," I continued, "I'd have a few smaller squads move around the ship to look for intruders and checking up on the stationary guards. In case they get attacked by random ruffians."

Wallace dragged everyone to a halt and pulled Jeremy back behind him. "Do you mean to say," he said, "that you would have roving patrols checking on the guards?" he asked.

"Sure," I said. "Obvious thing to do. Check on guards, listen for sounds of battle or fighting and so on. Otherwise, anyone could creep around and ... oh, damn."

"PHIL!" I yelled, "Watch our back, but lie down and creep back up the stairs to where we left those bodies. Let me know if you see anyone turn up to check on them." Phil may be annoying but he is quick on the uptake. And brave, he wasn't going to let his mental qualms interfere with his work on the team. He pushed past me, crouched down and crept back up the stairs until he came close to the top where he then went prone and crawled up the last few steps. His pistol was out as he peeked over the final step before reaching out a hand behind him to give me a thumbs up. We were in the clear up there, at least temporarily.

"Wallace, can you sneak down and take out the next two guards silently," I said. "Take Jeremy and use Sparky to help locate them. He nodded, grabbed Jeremy by a shoulder and ushered the little guy down towards the next landing. I sent Wallace a private message, "Look after Jeremy, he's getting too comfortable around violence." Wallace clicked back once in reply, I think that was an acknowledgement of my message.

These staircases had two long sections separated by a small landing. The sections reversed at the landing as they descended which allowed for the structure to take up the minimum space. Fortunately for us, we were still on the first descending section which meant we had the landing and the next set of stairs between us and the lower guards. Unfortunately, it meant Wallace had to do a significant creep in order to shuffle up to the two lower guards and then sort out a way to kill them silently. They, of course, would be in space suits and probably armoured. Still, if the upper-level guards were anything to go by, they wouldn't be the nasty space armour favoured by the troopers, this stuff looked more like standard shipboard gear, useful for emergencies but not intended for serious fighting.

I hoped.

Lydia tapped my arm, "What do I do, Val?" she asked. Not a damn thing, I thought. Not even a stubbed toe.

"Lie down and watch Phil," I said, my traitorous mouth ignoring any sense of safety for Lydia. "Be ready to assist him if he's attacked." She drew her pistol, shrank down to the steps and slid up behind Phil. I must be out of my mind.

I watched Jeremy and Wallace glide down to the landing where Jeremy went prone and tucked himself against a wall. He was such a small nugget he may be mistaken as a bundle of refuse by the casual observer. Wallace had ... disappeared. I blinked, leaned forward and went down two steps in time to see the big guy moving like a shadow down the last flight of stairs and move around the corner, out of sight. I don't think even the air noticed him, I saw the big guy because I was looking for him and was in my usual heightened state of terror. I think fear improves the eyesight, I seem to see more nasty things when I'm scared.

Nothing happened for a few beats until Wallace reappeared and waved us down. I told Lydia and Phil to join us but also to keep an eye on our rear. With an instruction like that, I expected Phil to make some Lydia-based comment but he said not a word. A sure sign he was also feeling nervous.

Goodie.

Again, we gathered at the bottom of the stairs and chatted over the bodies of the two now deceased crewmen. Both had holes in their helmets, helmets which looked to be on backwards until I realised Wallace had snapped their necks by twisting their heads. He likes to double check his work from time to time. Oh, God, Wallace terrifies me.

"How much time do we have before the patrols come around?" asked Phil.

How the hell would I know, I thought. Still, the gang needed some calming down. "Not long, I would think," I said. "We don't have time to hide the bodies, even if we wanted to." I had no idea, I was making stuff up to give everyone some sense of calm, of control. A patrol could turn the corner or come down the stairs at any moment and kill us all. They knew that, but they did not need me to whimper and blather, they needed me to tell them what to do. Keep people busy during a crisis, it takes their mind off their impending doom.

"Jeremy, which way do we go now?" I asked. "To reach the Man in Black? Do we go down more stairs or along one of these corridors?" We still had the line on our helmets and did not need Jeremy to tell us, but I wanted to give the poor little tyke something to do.

He came back like a good 'un. "We have to go down at least another level," he replied. "Wallace and I can go first and repeat our actions. Come on, Wallace." He turned and began his descent, Wallace looked at me, shrugged and then followed his new lord and master. I'd have to watch Jeremy, getting too uppity, especially in a crisis.

"Can we move, too?" asked Phil. He was edging down the stairs while always looking behind him and up to the previous level. Lydia was endeavouring to watch all the hallways which debouched into this small area, she looked like a slowly spinning top.

"Phil, you and Lydia go down after Wallace," I said. "I'll do the rear guard. Wait!" I commanded. "Grab the guards' weapons." You can never have to many weapons, I wished I had thought of this up top, we had left several instruments of destruction littering the hallways of the battle brig. Not my usual behaviour, I must be feeling a tad stressed.

We descended two more levels using this technique — Wallace silently killing all and sundry —until Jeremy told us we needed to take one of the side corridors. We were now on the same level as the communication hub. Wallace had pulled his silent assassin routine each time and we had gathered a few extra sets of pistols and long arms.

Jeremy took it upon himself to hang two of the large weapons over his shoulders as well as strapping a pistol to his belt. He looked ridiculous.

"You look ridiculous, Jeremy," I said, as we entered the corridor. Each of his shoulders had a long arm hanging over it with the muzzle pointed at the ceiling, the base plates of the weapons barely clearing the floor as he tramped along.

"Bite me, dickhead," he replied.

I considered giving him another clip over the head but decided against it, he was too heavily armed plus it was difficult to actually reach his helmet through the forest of weaponry.

"Today, you are a man, my son," I told him. He turned back to me for a moment and I saw his poor little scared face before a fleeting smile flashed out. He again turned back to tramp after Wallace and Sparky. Sparky was on the ceiling, scuttling along merrily before disappearing around a corner.

We were in a longish corridor, it gently curved, allowing the stairway access to disappear which gave me some relief. At least our pursuers, if we had any, would not be able to spot us from a distance and, you know, shoot us; I'm not a fan of the whole 'let's shoot Valentine' thing. I divided my time between walking backwards to watch for approaching enemies and bumping into Lydia. After one particularly heavy footfall she pushed me back and said, "For God's sake, Valentine, stop putting that big thing there!"

I could feel the atmosphere crinkle, a charge ran through our comms and, looking into Lydia's helmet, I saw her face blush and her lips begin to babble, "I didn't mean ..." she stammered into the meaningful silence, "he's not ..." She gulped, swallowed and finished with, "We will never speak of this again." Her voice had changed to become a firm, steel clad rod, "Are we clear on that? Phil? Jeremy? Not a word to anyone."

"What about Wallace?" asked Jeremy. "I saw his shoulders shaking, I think he was laughing.""Wallace is a gentleman," proclaimed Lydia. "He would never spread salacious gossip."

"And, er, Valentine?" said Phil, "he can be somewhat ... salacious."

"My sweetie pie will refrain from spreading innuendos," replied Lydia, "That is, if he ever wants to spread my innuendos again."I nearly died. Wallace doubled over while Phil and Jeremy leaned into each other and guffawed.

Somehow, my girl had done more for our morale than any order barking from me. Is she aces, or what?

Jeremy stiffened, which is probably the incorrect reference after our current discussion but accurately sums up the little wart's change in stance and demeanour.

"Val," he said, "Sparky can see bad guys ahead. Lots of bad guys."

Chapter 22

JEREMY SHARED SPARKY'S VISION with me, apparently you can do this sort of thing if you learn how to use the technology. Personally, I prefer to use minions and Jeremy makes a great minion. I had him share the vision with the rest of us so everyone could share in the dilemma.

The offending enemy troopers were gathered in a wide section of the corridor as it disappeared around the corner ahead of us. They were clustered in three groups, the middle group hunkered down behind some sort of large weapon with a shield, like a small cannon or similar. The other two clusters, each consisting of five troopers, hid behind walls on either side of their big gun. This big gun was pointing away from us and down a short hallway, at the end of which I could make out a hastily erected barricade whose shoddy workmanship gave me a great surge of pride.

"Is that our gang down there, Jeremy?" I asked. "Behind that sorry excuse for a fortification, the flimsy thing in front of that bloody huge gun?"

"Yes," squeaked my little buddy. "What are we going to do, Val?" Yeah, yeah, I know. Same old song.

"That's a portable heavy blaster," said Phil, ever ready to bring a downer on the event. "It's normally used by the marines if they ever do a ground assault, notice the two wheels which allows it to be moved easily."

"Not cheering me up, Phil," I said. I counted fourteen troopers ahead of us, the two groups of five plus the four crew on the heavy blaster. Against them we had the five of us. Well, three fighters, a mechanic and a child. Hmm, I needed a cunning plan.

"Shall we charge into them, Val," suggested Jeremy, displaying an unhealthy eagerness to cause bloodshed.

Phil clipped him on the helmet, he must have found a small opening between all the hardware. "No, Jeremy," he said. "You do not charge unthinkingly into greater numbers, that would be the act of an idiot."

"Val does it all the time," said Jeremy.

"I rest my case," said Phil.

"Shut up, the pair of you," I said. "No, Jeremy, we can't take on all of them at once. Sure, we could charge around the corner, guns blazing and take out a few. On our best day, Phil, Wallace and I could probably do about two each but then they would react. And these guys are serious lads, look at their armour. They are not the shipboard security whom Wallace has been merrily despatching, these guys are in full battle rattle. Thus, I suspect their reaction to an assault from the rear would be quick and decisive, resulting in some spinning about and then shooting us down."

"I could shoot two of them," said Jeremy. "And so could Lydia."

"Not on your best day, pumpkin," I said. "Killing people is both hard and easy. The task itself can be trivial, done with a minimum of effort such as a shot to the helmet or a blast to the body. Lots of ways to kill someone. But, and this is the big one, you have to be ready to do it, you have to have a mind content with taking another's life. To kill another living human being. It's not easy, my wee destroyer of worlds.""But you do it," said the little guy. "And Wallace, he simply walks up to them and they fall over. And what about Phil, I know he fought with you against all those machines back on Caesar's spaceship." His voice had begun to acquire a certain plaintive note.

How do I explain to him about the damage to a person's mind, the damage we garner whenever we take a life? Wallace stepped up beside the little guy and put an arm around his shoulders, "Val's right, Jeremy, listen to him," he said. "You take a person's life and you take away someone's son or daughter, you destroy a family, you extinguish all hope, all the future which might have been for that person."

"But you and Val ..." Jeremy whispered.

"We're broken, Jeremy," said Wallace. "Something's gone inside us, something which holds back the darkness, something which keeps us as the people you want in a civilised society. Val and I do what we do because we're already in hell, but you don't need to join us. This is not the time to find you cannot look into an adversary's eyes and realise you can't kill them. When, and if, we go around that corner, it has to be killers who erupt from here. You're not a killer, my small friend. And I hope you never become one."

Jeremy looked at me, I saw through his helmet plate, his little face screwed up in anguish, his eyes seeing me without a loving gaze, gone was the gentle, mocking look he saved for me. Now, I could see, he was staring at me and seeing an awful man, a man who snuffed out another's existence as easily as breathing. He turned his head to Lydia and then to Phil, searching for something. I don't know what it could be, but I knew he would not find it in my face.

"I've never actually killed anyone up close and personal either," stated Phil. "Until today. But I've never taken the life of someone standing in front of me until I shot those men above us. Sure, I shot down those fighters, that was the first taking of another life I have ever done. But I wasn't really shooting at a person, I was shooting at a ship, at another machine. At least, that's what I told myself. Sure, I had training, I've been in tournaments and competitions but that always finished up with me sharing a drink with someone. Today, I killed people, for the first time. And I'm sick to my stomach about it."

Well, this put another wrinkle into any plan I would come up with. Wallace and I could run about and cause mayhem, but now I had my doubts about Phil. I needed to buy myself some thinking time and also remove Lydia and Jeremy from our potential assault.

"Lydia," I said, "do you still have that little doohickie for peeking around corners?" She nodded and pulled out a small device from some obscure pocket. It was a small screen, about the size of the palm of your hand, with a flexible tube sticking out one end. You poked the tube around a corner and looked in the screen. On the end of the tube was a camera and, hey presto, you got to peek around corners. Lovely piece of kit.

"Thanks," I said. "Now, you and Jeremy take Sparky back to that curve in the corridor behind us. Use Sparky to alert us if any of those roving patrols come by. And I expect they will, we've left a bit of a trail behind us." I was expecting some resistance to this order, an order which Lydia probably viewed as a suggestion.

I was therefore surprised when Lydia grabbed Jeremy and trundled off. Sparky scrabbled along the ceiling overhead after them while Jeremy walked with shoulders down and his world view destroyed.

I was no longer the nice guy, no longer funny old Uncle Val. I was a thug, I've always been a thug. Thank you sieges and thank you bloody Ostend.

I turned back to my remaining team members, one killer and one poncy prince who was now realising he had fallen in with bad company.

"Right," I said, "we need to take out all those lads ahead of us. Any suggestions?"

Silence greeted me. Finally, Wallace shrugged his shoulders and said, "Well, without any bombs to throw at them, our remaining option is a sudden attack and hope for the best."

"Not a fan of 'hoping for the best', Wallace," I replied.

"You don't say?" he said. "Yet it seems to be your normal method of operation." Vile man.

"All the fun has gone out of our relationship, Wallace," I said. "And where the bloody hell do you think you're going, Phil?" I snarled. My snarl was directed at the retreating back of His Grace, Prince Philip of Arenburg, tenth in line to the throne, who was now rapidly moving well away from Wallace and me. Okay, I understood his running away. I'd do it myself except that ... well, except nothing. I had mates down there, mates about to be shot at by some bloody huge gun and I couldn't stand about and do nothing.

But Phil could run away, the slimy, deceitful, sleazy dog; he could shoot through and save his worthless skin, the mongrel — and why was he bending over and talking to Jeremy? I watched the little scene unfold while Wallace kept an eye on the screen showing the lads around the corner. The bad lads, the ones I wanted to kill without mercy. Lord help me, I am in a bad way.

Phil was coming back to us, he had most of Jeremy's recently acquired weaponry slung about his body. Perhaps he wanted more firepower. "You right there, Phil?" I asked. "I thought you'd bottled it and run off. A sensible decision, I might add. What the hell are you doing coming back? And why are you carrying every weapon known to man?"

"Because, my homicidal maniac," he said, and I could feel the grin in his voice, "I have a plan!"

Well, roger me rigid.

"All of these weapons," he explained, "have power packs."

Ahh, I thought, I'm going to get another lecture on how guns work. "Phil," I said, "tell someone who cares."

"You will care about this piece of information, my intellectually challenged throwback," he said. I was too physically tired and emotionally exhausted to hit him but decided I would cause him some pain later, if there was a later. "A powerpack," he said, the gloat being strong in his words, "may be overloaded!"

I assumed his last statement carried some significance but I mightily refrained from jumping for joy. "Overload them by all means, Phil," I said, "and then stick them up your bum." I turned back to Wallace, "Ready to die unnecessarily, mate?" I started to move towards the corner leading to all those troopers, ready to do yet another stupid, pointless action in my long history of stupid, pointless actions.

Phil showed incredible bravery at that moment. He grabbed me by the shoulder and halted my advance to a better life. "Listen, numbnuts," he snarled, spinning me around to face him, "when a powerpack overloads — it explodes! In a big way."

A pause settled over our little scene, a wonderful pause in which my brain joined the dots and guessed Phil's plan.

I smiled at Phil, he smiled back. Wallace came over, put an arm around each of our shoulders and joined our little smile fest. We were grinning like fools at each other.

"Phil," I said, "Your blood's worth bottling!"

Chapter 23

"WHY DO YOU WANT to bottle Uncle Phil's, blood, Val? Is he a vampire?" asked Jeremy's voice in my ear. I looked around, expecting to see the nodule around my knees but no, he was still up the end of the corridor standing next to Lydia. I kept forgetting we were all looped into our own communication net, but a comm net could not display the wolfish smiles of me and my two new best mates.

"Jeremy," said Lydia, "I think the boys are discovering some new toys. We had best leave them to it and do our job. How about you and I make a little subgroup of the two of us, that way we won't be distracted by their maniacal laughter."

"I'd like to do some maniacal laughter, Lydia," said Jeremy.

"Perhaps later, sweetie, if you're a good boy," she replied. Then their conversation clicked off and I assumed they were in their own little world. I did send a message to them both to keep me informed of any enemy movement but, aside from that, I had no interest in following their conversations. I had better things to do, I had bombs to make and people to blow up.

Phil showed us the way to overload the pistols and the long arms, you had to twist bits while holding other bits down firmly and I think some tongue action was also required. Wallace did it with a casual fluidity and ease because he has no sense of occasion but I was determined to make a production of the process.

After I dropped the pistol I was working on — for the third time — Phil snatched it out of my hands and muttered something about asking a goat to dance. I think I was the goat. Eventually, we had three pistols and two long arms ready to explode, all we had to do was make the final twist of something or other and then we would have an explosion. This last sequence of events gave me a moment of reflection. "Phil," I asked, "how long between making that final twist and the thing exploding?"

"About three seconds for the pistols, possibly five for the long arms."

"Any way to make it longer?"

"No, you do the final twist and then throw the damn thing away as fast as possible."

"Let's think about this, boys," I said. As I considered our attack plan, I turned my head to look back to Lydia and Jeremy. They had been fiddling with her backpack and then they scurried around the corner back towards the staircase.

"Lydia, sweetie," I said, calling her over our shared channel. "Are you making sensible decisions? You're not doing anything, you know, silly, are you?"

"We're checking the stairwells and the corridors leading to us, honey bun," she replied. "It's all clear so we'll come back now." Sure enough, a few moments later both her and the grommet ducked back around our corner and squatted down. I'm not great at reading body posture in armoured spacesuits but I got the distinct impression they were giggling.

Okay, leave them to their little game and back to my job. "Okay, boys, here's what we'll do," I said and outlined my plan. Surprisingly, neither of them groaned, not even Phil.

Poo, bum, I thought. We are so dead.

"Righto, boys," I said, "do it." I was standing with my back against the wall with the corner leading to the bad guys who were one step away. In each of my hands I held one of the pistols we had prepared as a bomb, each one required the final bit of twisting to initiate the timer, the timer which would expire three seconds later allowing the pistols to explode.

The choice of each person's role came down to who was best equipped for the job. Or, to put it in terms Phil used when we discussed it, 'don't give the delicate job to an idiot who has trouble tying his own shoelaces'. Thus, I was not allowed to be one of the chaps making the final adjustment to the pistols, I suspect the fact I had dropped the damn things several times had influenced the group decision, and Wallace agreed with Phil; I went with their beliefs since I strongly believe in democracy. Except when I don't.

I felt movement in each of my hands, heard Phil and Wallace grunt "Go" and took off around the corner. Three seconds is not a long time, I would have preferred five but the long arms were too unwieldly for what I wanted. No, it had to be the pistols, the smallish, handheld weapons which I now threw at one of the squads of five troopers. Both pistols flew from my hands; I might be capable of dropping them unexpectedly but I am hell on wheels when it comes to throwing a bomb. God knows, I threw a lot of them during that bloody siege and some things stay in muscle memory.

As they left my hands, I was diving for the floor in the hope I might slide out of the blast area. Phil was unable to tell me how big the blast was going to be since he had never actually triggered one. I suggested he had missed a golden opportunity as a prince of the realm to play with things that go bang but he fell back on insulting me, something about me showing him behaviour appropriate to his station. Dick.

The moment I hurtled around the corner to perform my deadly throw and accompanying death dive, Wallace and Phil stepped out behind me with pistols raised and proceeded to blat away at the other bunch of five guys. As I slid along the ground I got to see real marksmanship in action. Two of the troopers had been hit and were in mid fall to the floor as another two got shots into their helmet faceplates. I daresay these faceplates were covering some surprised faces, now

dead faces. My slide came to a stop against a wall as the pistol bombs went off, eviscerating my five targets. 'Eviscerating' is such an appropriate word, it accurately describes the damage done to these poor bludgers as my thrown pistols exploded around waist height in their midst. Yep, one pistol probably would have been enough, bunched up as they were. Two pistols shredded armour, helmets, dismembered bodies and ruptured torsos. A selection of space armour scraps rained over me, accompanied by other particles which were still steaming. I suspect I was receiving a particularly gruesome shower.

I, fortunately, was not affected by the blast. Well, no more so than the shudders you get when things explode around you but I call that Tuesday. I stuck to the plan, rolled to my knees and unslung my own long arm. I used these big weapons because everyone sems to think I cannot shoot a pistol with any sort of accuracy. Any denials I make to this outrageous claim are howled down, even when I mention the few times I have killed someone — or something — with the sissy little things. Rebuttals seem to include references to me pressing the barrel against my target's body before pushing the trigger and thus negating any use for marksmanship. I consider these points to be nit picking.

Nonetheless, given we needed two accurate shooters to take out the other gang of five, Wallace and Phil both agreed I should not be one of those shooters. They each made some reference to their desire to remain unshot by the idiot standing beside them as well as the need for the shooter to be able to fire accurately over the given range.

So, considering I was both clumsy and dropped pistols, combined with being unable to hit a barn wall while standing inside it, I begrudgingly agreed to the task allocation and the weapon choice. They got to use their delicate little pistols and plink away at a distance while I threw myself into the fray, eviscerating opponents — love that word — before switching to my long arm. My long arm had been adjusted to fire like an old-fashioned blunderbuss. Some call it a shotgun but I firmly remain old school.

I pumped a blast into the four guys kneeling behind the blast shield of the heavy blaster, the blast shield being of no use to them whatsoever since we had hit them from behind. Good to see some NightWatch traditions remain; our preference, hit your opponent when they are not looking. My first shot took out one guy, my second drilled another and it was only now they were realising something was going on, they were under attack.

We had selected targets based upon the enemy's probable ability to respond rapidly to any attack. My reasoning was, the two squads of five guys are troopers ready for a fight. Sure, they are looking to go forward but when you are in this sort of tense situation, an attack from the rear would require the merest of body swivels in order to bring guns, lots of guns, to bear on the intruders.

Ergo, the two squads had to go first and had to be taken out simultaneously. If we stuffed up our attack, we could be faced with ten angry troopers in full armour shooting at us as we emerged like three idiots from the corridor. Nope, they had to go first.

The guys on the heavy blaster were still troopers but their focus, their area of priority, was the aiming and function of the big gun. To me, that meant they were probably going to be a second or two behind the normal troopers in their reaction times. Plus, I had seen their weapons were not in their hands, not like the ugly sods standing beside them ready to shoot my pals.

And that is why I now faced three, sorry, two troopers — I had shot another one — who were now raising their hands in surrender. The delicate mist of blood and body parts raining down upon them from the squad I had — wait for it — eviscerated, would also have contributed to their shaky view of the world.

I indicated they should stand up but keep their hands well and truly in the air. When they were stationary and suitably cowed, I risked a glance at the other squad, I recalled one of them was still alive and functioning.

But, alas, I was mistaken. Wallace had walked forward and shot the last guy, again through the helmet. How much practice must this guy put in, I wondered.

Behind me, back in the direction of Lydia and Jeremy, a series of loud explosions went off. I regained conscious control of my body to find myself hurtling back down the corridor. My girl needed me.

I stumbled to a stop, ready for anything, any form of chaos, any moment of danger for Lydia and Jeremy. I was ready to fight, shoot and, if necessary, eviscerate. Okay, that word is now banned.

My honey turned to face me, probably sensing I was somewhat tense and stressed. She, on the other hand stood remarkably calm and relaxed. Jeremy said, "Can I do my maniacal laugh now, Lydia?"

"Sure, sweetie, go right ahead."

And he did, the maggot.

Chapter 24

LYDIA EXPLAINED WHAT HAD happened. She is such a love.

They knew they could not hold off any concerted attacks by a determined enemy and also understood that neither of them felt comfortable at being asked to kill someone up close and personal. But they can think, the devious pair, and so devised yet another cunning plan. They would blow up the interlopers with explosives, planted to be detonated remotely.

They placed their remaining explosives around the top of the stairs and in the entrance to each of the corridors. Detonating the explosives was the problem. Lydia had timers but they were of little use unless the enemy sent a message ahead to say they'd be arriving in five minutes. Neither of them had enough knowledge to rig up proximity sensors allowing the bangs go off as someone walked past so that solution was off the table.

Which left pushing the big red button by eye, watching for when the enemy were walking past the bomb and then pressing down. As plans go, it had a lot of merit, but it did have one major flaw. They had to be able to see the explosives and the only place they could do that was right near the stairs and corridor entrances. Exposed to all comers, right out in the open, nowhere to hide.

Unless, as Jeremy pointed out, you happened to be a small, insect- like machine capable of clinging to the middle of the roof. And then capable of projecting a video image back to where Jeremy and Lydia waited with bated breath and itchy button fingers.

Sure enough, the person in charge of the enemy forces had used their brain and sent security people down several corridors as well as up the stairs. They had coordinated for their charges to all meet simultaneously at where we were supposed to be. I guess they had been following the trail of bodies behind us and decided an all-out effort was called for.

Lydia pushed the buttons as they all emerged from the stairs and corridors. Judging by the body

parts, there had been a lot of them. Not armoured troopers, not space marines but the lightly armoured internal security for the battle brig.

They were all dead.

I would find Lydia and Jeremy at another time and walk them through the dark night of their souls, that night we all have to tread after inflicting death. It doesn't matter if it's the death of one or many, their actions were in close quarters, close enough for them both to see the fragility of a human body.

But for now, we were overjoyed to be alive and undamaged.

Phil had wandered down to the communication hub and greeted the Man in Black. I gathered up Lydia, Jeremy and Wallace and together we strolled down to garner our well merited praise for rescuing all and sundry. Time for some love on the old Valentine actions.

"What were you thinking, sergeant, you bloody idiot!" snarled the boss. This was not the rapturous applause I had been expecting, a feeling reinforced by his next words. "You damn fool, you brought Phil on board! The exact place we did not want him to be!" He stamped about while Lydia looked at the control panel and opened her bag of tools. Her movements caught the big man's eye. "And Lydia!" he said — some may call it a shout — "you dragged non-combatants along!" Jeremy chose that moment to step forward and salute, complete with insect machine perched on top of his helmet. It was, of course, also saluting.

The Man in Black drew breath, I readied myself for more invective. Around me, members of the sloth and indolent brigade had taken up positions from which to watch the entertainment. Further vocal gymnastics from the boss were interrupted by Lydia saying, "Okay, sir, we're all good now. Everything's back online, who would you like to talk to — Captain Blund on the frigate, our shuttle, Caesar, Sergeant Gorka or the captain of this vessel?" She gave him a winning smile, we all saw it through her faceplate. "We can contact anyone you like from here, sir."

It's always interesting watching someone change their course of action, especially mid-way through a verbal tirade. Their face goes a sort of blue as their mouth clamps shut, the eyes swivel about in search of the meaning of life and, if you're lucky, they gabble incoherently. Which is what the Man in Black did.

"I DON'T CARE ABOUT CONTACTING ...umm," this is where his face went blue. His remaining eye flared open and his cheeks puffed out, all this I saw before he turned to Lydia, "What did you say?" He rolled his neck and continued "You can ... anyone .... what the hell ... communicate?" And that was the incoherent gabble. Lovely to witness my betters falling over their tongues.

"Yes, sir," replied Lydia. "I have restarted the big desk," and here she patted the monstrous thing before her, all flashing lights and dials. "Give it a moment to initiate all the protocols and we will have effective communication re-established."

I have to hand it to the boss, he adapts quickly. He must have taken a few calming breaths because I saw his shoulders heave up and down a few times and then stop. There was a brief pause and he was back in action. "To be clear, Lydia," he said, all calm and in control now, "you have a way for me to talk to all our people? Including Captain Blund?"

"Yes, sir."

"And I can also contact the captain of this vessel, this bloody battle brig?"

"Absolutely."

"Does this mean everyone can also talk to each other? Can this vessel's captain, for instance, initiate communication with his own troops?"

Lydia leaned a casual hip on her big desk, folded her arms and smiled. No, I couldn't see her smile, but her whole body gave the message she was a happy camper. When she folded her arms, she certainly cheered me up — but that's another story.

"No, sir," she said. "You are in control of all comm traffic."

The boss turned back to me, "Consider yourself reamed out, Valentine," he said, but he had his happy face on.

"I feel thoroughly cleansed, sir," I replied. "Totally unable to walk. May need stitches."

"Oh, ye gods," he said, "he's back among us." He was, however smiling at me so I did the decent thing and smiled back.

"What are we going to do, sir?" I asked. It felt so good to be able to ask that question of someone else. I was heartily sick of being asked it myself but Lord Franz is so much better at this stuff than me. I say this because his smile changed, it turned into something approaching evil.

"You're not going to give a maniacal laugh, are you, sir?" I asked.

"No, Val," he said, "but I am going to spoil someone's day."

He went into order mode then, not yelling or snarling which is my general way of talking to the troops. No, he spoke softly and everyone, me included, leaped about and wagged our tails. The guy is such an overachiever.

"Tell me what you saw on your way here, Val," he said. "I'd love to know how many more troopers and so on are still aboard this ship. And we need to find their entry point into our frigate, some of those mongrels may decide to come back and check on their ship. Since they lost their own comms, I should imagine their assault commander is getting twitchy."

"I could help with that," said Lydia. She pointed to a large screen hanging over the control desk, "I can display where all the crew are on that schematic." She punched some buttons or twisted dials or whatever and the screen came alive. We all saw a plan of the ship's interior showing all the rooms and corridors. Cool.

"Keep going," said the boss.

"Okay," said Lydia, doing more clever things on the desk. "This is our deck and these green lights," a bunch of green lights showed on the screen, "show where everyone is on the ship. Everyone, that is, wearing one of their communicator beads, synchronised to this ship. Give me a few moments and I'll get their system to recognise our beads. I have to establish the correct handshake protocols." She turned to me and said, "Don't try to understand this, sweetie. Perhaps you could go and have little rest."She's got some nerve, that Lydia. I desperately wanted to ask how our communicator beads shook hands since they had, like, you know, no hands! But she was right, and a rest sounded good. I grunted and wandered over to where Wallace was sitting on a clear piece of deck with Jeremy. I slumped down beside them and let the old shoulders sag. Jeremy punched me on the arm, saying hello.

Ted had sent his team out to the mess of bodies we had left. Sergeant Elena looked after policing any stray weapons and then came back with an excited lilt to her step. I watched her go over to Teddy Boy, lean in and probably talk. A few moments later, Ted's body language showed me he was happy, the little dance he gave was also a clue. It seems our boy and his trusty gang of shooters were about to have an early Christmas.

I turned all communications off and let my eyes close. Surely someone else could carry the load for a while.

Chapter 25

A KICK WOKE ME. It wasn't a serious kick, it wasn't a boot suggesting you owed it money. No, it was more of the friendly wake up taps the lads administer to each other. I moaned, rolled to one side and dragged myself to my feet. Upon opening my eyes, I notice the kicker had moved a few steps away from me.

"Is that you, Claude?" I growled. He took another step back. Why were people doing this to me?

It was indeed Claude, he gave me a few moments to collect my thoughts and my thoughts being what they were, he gave me too much time. "What do you want?" I finally said as I felt the blood sluggishly move around my limbs. My blood and its accompanying flotilla of wee beasties.

"The boss wants you, Val."

"He could've sent me a message," I stretched my limbs, popped some joints, rolled my neck and gradually felt life begin to take hold once again. "We have these things stuck in our ears, you know."

"I don't know anything, Val," he turned and started to walk away. "Anyway, I'm off to join Ted. The boss is over there." He waved at the control desk where, once again, the Man in Black had found himself another chair. What an utter bastard, I thought.

I rolled over and shambled to some semblance of alertness, Lydia was fiddling with things and the big screen showed our deck and its bunch of accompanying little green lights. One of them winked out.

"What's up, boss?" I asked.

"Ahh, Val," he said, "feeling refreshed?"

"No, I'm still feeling like death warmed up. What's Ted up to? What happened to that green light? Why are some of the lights blue?"

"Excellent!" he stood up, ignored my questions to wave at Lydia and the nearby technology. "Lydia has been most helpful, I've sent Ted on a little errand with his new toy and that green light disappeared because its owner has had a catastrophic reduction in his or her commitment to life."

My head was still muzzy. I gave it a shake and said, "Use small words, please, sir. I'm feeling a bit crook."

The Man in Black turned to look at me, this time his gaze was vaguely unsettling. "Yesss ..." he said. "I have noticed some small changes in your behaviour. I've also heard of an increase in your aggression levels, if that is at all possible. What's going on Val? Is all this running around and saving us causing you to empty your emotional bank account?"

"What are you talking about, sir?" I snarled, stepping forward in a decidedly aggressive manner. We both stopped in surprise. Not at my words but at my tone and movement. "Sorry, Franz," I continued, my tone dropping to a more civil level while I also took a step back. "I seem to go from calm to homicidal in one step. I always could — but I was usually able to keep it under control. Now that control is slipping away."

"Hmm," he said, which helped a lot. "I might have to keep you out of harm's way for a while." He looked at the big board, tried to scratch his head through his helmet and then gave it up as bad joke. "Okay, here's the situation. Ted's taking the heavy blaster up to the doorway leading to the bridge, the part of this ship where all the senior officers are gathered. I've established communication with their captain and he seems intent on holding out, he doesn't believe we have control of his ship. The blue lights are our people. At least, the ones with a comm bead like Sergeant Gorka and her squad. Anyone with nanobots won't appear. Don't ask me why, my head hurts every time Lydia explains something to me."

"And do we have control, sir?" I asked, noticing yet another green light winking out. Lydia was heavily engaged in some communications. I couldn't hear her, of course, because I was not included in her comm loop but her bodily posture told me she was doing some serious talking. Another green light went off.

"Indeed we do," said the boss. I could hear the undertone of glee in his voice. It would seem our clever leader had done something wonderful. Again. "Those troopers you took out on the way here constituted most of the onboard troopers and security forces for this ship. I understand Lydia destroyed the ready response team at the blue shuttle bay and then repeated this outcome when the troopers from the red shuttle bay attempted to storm in behind you. Her and Jeremy apparently used explosives to utterly wipe them out."

He paused and looked over at where Jeremy still sat, apparently asleep or comatose. "I suspect our little man may need some counselling after all this. Neither he nor Lydia would have had much experience with combat and must be feeling the after effects."

"You mean the after effects of killing people, sir" I asked. "Those feelings we get whenever we shoot, destroy and otherwise take some else's life. You call those feelings 'after effects' do you, sir? DO YOU?"

Wallace had come to stand beside me. Close enough to bump my shoulder and settle me down. I don't know how he did it, but his presence allowed me to take some breaths and regather my rapidly disappearing equanimity.

"Sorry again, sir," I said, "for some reason, I'm not handling things too well." I slumped. "Maybe I've had enough of it all, sir. Maybe I'm of no use anymore."

The Man in Black stepped up to me. Laid his hands on my shoulders and looked through my faceplate. I could see the concern in his eyes and also something else. Not fear but ... what? A genuine affection for me? "Val, you've been carrying us for a long time, ever since I laid eyes on you, we have placed burdens on your shoulders. And you have carried that weight. But you are also different from everyone else." His eyes flicked to Wallace before coming back to me. "Even Wallace here, who shares the same abilities as you, has not had to deal with the leadership issues. Combine that with the expectations all of us have for you as our sergeant, the man we all look up to — and I include myself in that description — well, it's a load to carry. No, I don't think you are used up, I don't think you are coming apart. But I think something else is at work inside you."

What was he talking about? A thought came to my mind, "My nanobots, sir?" I muttered. "You think they are having an effect? But a lot of us have nanobots. Hell, you've got them. Why aren't you frothing at the mouth? Why aren't all the NightWatch running amok and killing everyone?"

"Because, sweetie," chimed in Lydia, "Your nanobots have had some extra tweaking from Greenash and his mad mate." A few things came to mind then. Why was Lydia even involved in this conversation? Who else was listening in? And what was this about my nanobots and special treatment?

Maybe I needed to hit someone, that usually fixed everything.

"I've been discussing you with Greenash and other people," said the boss.

"Why?" I growled. "Haven't you had, like, enough to do? Taking over entire spaceships and so on?"

He squeezed my shoulders, "You're important, Val.'

Poo. Bum. Tit. Fart.

Chapter 26

THIS WAS NEWS TO me, a pause was called for.

"What does Greenash think?" I asked. This question undoubtedly put me beyond the pale of normal thinking. Asking Greenash for counsel on nanobots was similar to suggesting a pyromaniac might be the perfect guy to check on those fires over there.

"He doesn't know," said the boss. I believed some common sense was entering the conversation and began to relax. That was my big mistake. "He wants to run a few tests," commented my lord and master.

"No way," I replied. Obviously, this was the most sensible thing to say.

"Not asking you, sergeant," he said, "but yes, it will involve him sticking more needles in you. I am also aware of your 'blood exchange' policy and I want to make it clear you are not to make anyone, attempting to help you, lose the use of their limbs. Nor do I want them to experience any significant blood loss."

"Bit of wiggle room in the word 'significant', boss," I said.

"For God's sake, you blot on the landscape, please go away and hold a wall up somewhere." He looked around and went on, "I can see Jeremy is struggling. Go and talk to him. You're the one who dragged a child into your world of blood and slaughter, you should be the one to help him understand what has happened around him."

He turned his back on me and, while I knew I could still talk to him because we were still in spacesuits, I did understand he was giving me the cold shoulder for a reason. I suspect his reason was he wanted me to go away.

Fair enough. I sauntered over to where Jeremy sat against a wall. As I slid down beside him, I caught a glimpse of his anguished expression through his helmet faceplate. It wasn't his normal cheery, cheeky face. It was a face of someone in torment, a face I had seen before, whenever I looked in a mirror.

Oh, hell. What had I done to the poor little guy? I reflected on the boss's words, his inference that I was the cause of Jeremy's current anguish because I had dragged him into the world of violent and messy death. The world of blood and pain and the destruction of lives. My world.

I softly cursed myself.

He needed help, he needed someone to talk to him, someone kind and empathetic. What he got was me. I scanned the room, searching for someone better qualified for this talk, someone who could help the little guy off the ledge onto which he had crawled. The ledge where you consider letting sanity have bit of a break, let the madness take over. I needed someone who knew this stuff and could talk nicely.

But there weren't many people left in the room. Teddy Boy and his gang had left to make threatening moves on the ship's leadership. Lydia was obviously busy talking people into their search for the green dots. A few injured were splayed out against the walls but they had their own issues of pain and regret. That left me and ... Wallace.

"Wallace," I croaked, "get over here and help me."

The large, muscular man slowly walked over and sat down on the other side of Jeremy. I described him as 'muscular' even though he was in a spacesuit. Wallace had that effect, no matter what he was wearing he reminded you of someone wearing a tunic with torn off sleeves revealing huge arms, multiple body tattoos and a surly growl. I couldn't see any of these things at the moment but he conveyed an impression, the one that said "I am a bad man and may cause you some harm. Go away." I had tried for the same look but too many people offered to fight me; it could be fun, they said.

I established a private channel to him. "Wallace," I said, "I need your help with Jeremy." He grunted. Okay, that's positive, so I kept going, making stuff up as I went, "The little bloke's in trouble."

"Why?"

"Because he came with us on this jaunt. Because he watched you and me kill people up close. He knows Lydia shot all those troopers when she jumped into that fighter — and I'll have to talk to her when she gets a moment." I looked over at my girl, I suspected she was keeping the horror of her actions at bay by keeping busy and doing something technical. Yes, I know her actions were allowing our team to find their team — the little green dots — and probably kill them. But she wasn't doing the killing herself, she wasn't seeing the blood and guts. It's a small difference but in the world of self-deception, we take what we can get.

Wallace grunted some more, shifting his weight comfortably on the metal floor. "So, what's the problem? He's been with us long enough to know what we do, he's even seen you thump a few people. What's the big deal now?"

"Because now," I said, my voice dropping and approaching something like grief, "now he has killed. Now he has taken another person's life. He helped Lydia plant those explosives and used Sparky to coordinate the destinations." I took a breath, the next piece was the hurting one. "And then he walked out and saw what he had done, he saw all those men and women blown apart by his actions. He saw the blood and guts, the viscera, the arms, legs and torsos. And right about now, he is realising he ended lives."

"Link him into comms with both of us, "said Wallace.

I looped Jeremy into our small, three-person group, put my arm around his shoulders and softly said, "Hey, buddy, how are you doing?"

Wallace scrunched in closer to Jeremy from the other side, making a whole lot of body contact with the little guy. "I killed my first man," said Wallace, "when I was ten. I stuck a knife into the back of his neck as he was raping my mother."

Then he stopped talking, not another word. I kept quiet because I didn't know what to say to his statement. Jeremy hadn't moved.

"He was the local enforcer for a loan shark. My father had borrowed heavily and couldn't pay, a common story. He walked into our apartment and shot my dad in front of me, I ran and hid but I heard him talking to my mother. Saying things like he needed payment of some kind and then I heard mum whimper. Along with the sound of tearing clothes. I still hear that sound every night. I crept out of my hiding space and saw him on top of mum, he was choking and raping her at the same time. In one hand he held a knife at her eye while the other hand grabbed her throat and squeezed. She was naked from the waist down, as was he. Mum was sobbing and he was grunting."

I could hear Jeremy's silence change, change from introspection to listening. Listening to this horror story. "What," said the little guy, "what did you do?"

"I picked up a knife from the kitchen bench, a small one we used for vegetables, and plunged it into the back of his neck. All the way, up to the hilt." Wallace's head dropped a little but he kept the body contact with Jeremy. "He twitched, and his knife hand spasmed. It went into mum's eye, straight to her brain. Killing her. I was left alone in an apartment with three bodies, two of whom I had destroyed. I had helped kill my own mother." He choked a sob and I heard him croak, "Oh, God, Mum. I'm so sorry." Then his shoulders began to heave.

Jeremy's small hand moved. He placed it on Wallace's huge knee, giving solace from within his own pain.

"Jeremy," I said, "Wallace and I are different to most people. We encountered death early in our lives. Not the death of someone being ill or from an accident. Not even the death caused by others. No, we have been formed by the most awful of experiences, the taking of a life up close. The destruction of a living, breathing human being.

"It changes us, Jeremy," I went on. "Most of the old crew in the Night-Watch, the guys who came from Earth, have had similar experiences. It's why they are so dysfunctional, so damaged. They drink to blot out the pain. They're violent to take their minds off their hurt. That horror lives with them each and every day, and it slowly destroys them. None of them would function in a polite, civilised society; they need chaos and movement, they need distraction. If they ever tried to lead a quiet life, they would end up hanging themselves.""Is that how you feel, Val?" asked Jeremy. This was a good sign, he was talking, he was engaging with us. "Do you need constant distraction?"

I sighed, now for the hard bit. "No, Jeremy, I don't. And I suspect Wallace is the same. Normal people, good people, decent people, struggle with their actions. Their inner decency keeps reminding them of what they have done. That's what's happening to you now. You heart, your soul, your essence, is asking you what happened. How could you do such a thing? How could you so easily end so many lives, destroy families, rip parents from children and husbands from wives. You're asking yourself what sort of a disgusting person are you."

Jeremy's other hand crept around my arm and squeezed, he leaned his helmeted head on my shoulder. "What's the answer, Val? Am I a bad person? I'm still a kid, I don't want to have these feelings." His voice revealed the hollowness of his potential future, he was close to that point of insanity.

"No. Jeremy, you're not a bad person," I said. Wallace had stopped crying and put an arm around Jeremy. He now had two of the meanest, ugliest killers giving him a cuddle. That's got to be the stuff of nightmares.

"Because you feel that pain," said Wallace, "because you can empathise and feel regret ... it means you are still that young lad we know and love. Monsters don't have those feelings, they can kill without thinking, whereas most people will hesitate. When I stood in that room with those bodies, with my mother, I didn't have someone to come and hold me. Everyone who cared for me was dead. Something clicked inside my brain and I changed. And, if I hadn't changed, I would have gone insane. Possibly run amok and trotted out into the street with a blood dripping knife, attacking anyone and everyone until I was brought down like a mad dog.

"But I became something different," he said, and then leaned forward to look across Jeremy to me. "I suspect Valentine had a similar experience at an early age, and he also changed."

I nodded. Wallace was right. We talked with Jeremy some more, slowly drawing him back to a place of sanity, away from the knife edge of madness. That's no place for a young boy — I should know, I was there myself once. Wallace was right, but now was not the time for my story. Now was the time for Jeremy.

After a while, we stopped our talk. It had become more gentle, more normal. At one point Jeremy made a bad joke and we all laughed, he even punched Wallace in the shoulder which I felt was borderline suicidal but the big guy chuckled. I stood up, dragging the little blemish with me.

"Val," he said, "you said I'm not a monster, that I'm going to be okay as long as I have friends around me." Wallace climbed to his feet and now the three of us stood in a comradely triangle, there was so much affection in the group I wanted to puke.

"How did you and Wallace do it? How did you come out of that bad time?"

Wallace answered for both of us. He rolled his shoulders and gave the little guy a final hug before saying, "We didn't, Jeremy, we're still in it."

Chapter 27

THE THREE OF US sauntered over to the boss where I gave him the all clear for Jeremy. The number of green dots had reduced significantly which gave me a question. A question I decided to ask and get the misery out of the way.

"Boss," I said, "why are the green dots winking out? Does that mean we've killed one of their guys?"

He turned back and looked at me with what I took to be mild amazement. "Of course not, numbnuts," he said. "For God's sake, Val, you don't solve every problem by killing the person in front of you." He must have realised who he was talking to, especially since I was in the company of Wallace. "No," he went on, a trifle calmer in his response, "Sergeant Gorka is roaming this ship, following Lydia's guidance. Most of the 'green dots' — the people she encounters — are straightforward crew. And since Gorka and several of her squad are in obvious space armour and tooled up to the eyebrows with things which kill, the crew she finds generally surrender. Yes, she's had to suppress a few idiots and probably killed one or two, but not the wholesale slaughter you are suggesting."

"Why are the green lights winking out?"

"Because she takes their communication bead, of course!" he sounded a tad exasperated, must be a leadership thing. "We can't have prisoners chatting to each other and making plans. We have standards, Valentine, us in the NightWatch."

I swallowed this obvious fiction but was happy to understand my girl had not been hand in glove with the female killing machine known as Sergeant Gorka. My God, that woman was tough. Gorka mildly terrified me and, as recently affirmed to Jeremy, I am a card-carrying member of the nightmare club. Gorka's the sort of girl that makes nightmares hide under the bed — and stay there, shivering in terror.

"I don't understand, sir," I started, before being interrupted by several cackles from others on the same comm channel. I ignored the peasants. "If we control this comm centre and have turned off their ability to communicate, surely that's enough. Why take their beads? Won't that make it harder for us to boss them around, seeing as how they won't be able to understand us?"

"An excellent point, Val," said the boss. "And one I raised with both Sergeant Gorka and Captain Blund."

I waited. Was there going to be further explanation here? "And they said...?" I prompted.

"Basically, they told me to shut up and do things their way. Considering this is our first experience of fighting organised troopers in space — I discount those idiotic pirates we dealt with - I acquiesced to their greater experience.""Because you didn't know what to do," I summarised.

"Pretty much."

I stood patiently for all of a minute before asking the boss for something to do.

"Here's the picture, Val," he said, "Sergeant Gorka was able to leave the engineering section under the caring eyes of a couple of her troopers. She took the rest and has gone hunting for the crew of this ship, that includes the roving security guards. Lydia's 'green dots' are the game changer for her, Gorka has been able to isolate and nullify most of the crew now. It's also been made a little easier because you and your gang, in your slow saunter to us, wiped out every sizable force of troopers left on this ship."

He looked down at Jeremy and switched to communicate with me, "You think Jeremy's okay? He's done a fair bit for someone at his age — I don't want to lose him or make him into someone deranged."

"Like me, you mean," I bristled.

"My," he said, "touchy, aren't we?" He stretched his back and probably popped a few back vertebrae. "Why are you getting so punchy, Val? I mean, everyone walks around you carefully as matter of course, but your recent behaviour seems to have ramped up the 'mindless killer' aspect of your character."I growled. I believe I even snarled. What the hell was going on? "I don't know, Franz. I'm having trouble keeping my head on straight, every time I encounter any conflict I ramp up to maximum immediately. It's getting harder to restrain some of my more violent tendencies. I might need a bit of a break from all the usual killing and so forth."He looked at me, cocked his head on one side and made small 'hmm' noises. Finally, he spoke, "Nanobots?"

"Probably," I replied. "The new modifications Greenash did — coupled with whatever whacky nonsense happened when PILOT sent those pulses into all of us — seems to have sent my little guys around the twist.""Ahh, yes. The pulse that wiped out an entire squad of Tharls. Assault Tharls in full battle armour. My God, losing that terrifying squad must have knocked a hole in the frigate's ability to fight back." He looked at the green board again before turning back to me. "Speaking of which, I think we have this vessel by the short and curlies. Teddy Boy and his bunch of gun jockeys were overjoyed when they found you had not damaged the heavy blaster during your little assault. They've taken it up to the bridge of this ship and pointed it at the door leading to where all their remaining officers are huddling. Huddling in some trepidation, I might add, since between you and Sergeant Gorka we won't have any enemy personnel left on this tub."

"Well done us, sir," I said.

"Yes," he murmured. "It leaves Captain Blund and the people of the frigate having to deal with all the ratbags who assaulted them. His ship is still full of the enemy troopers from this ship. Probably running wild. I'm running out of people; Ted's got most of his crew up with the heavy blaster, in case the enemy leadership gets toey. Gorka left a couple of her beefy lads in engineering in case someone decides to be heroic, that leaves me no one as a backup fighter for this area.""You want me to stay here and make sure you're safe, sir?" A strange instruction from the boss but I could go with it. Of course, my mouth continued working well after the brain thought the conversation was finished. "Hold your hand?" I continued, "Sing some cheery songs?" Oh, God, why would I say such things?

Lydia and Phil ignored me while Wallace had, as usual, no response. I clipped Jeremy over the helmet in case he wanted to contribute and then muttered to the boss, "Sorry, sir, that comment was uncalled for."

The Man in Black rode above such minor irritants as my loose mouth, thank goodness. He ignored what I said which, I think, shows a great approach to life. "I am worried about what is happening on board the frigate. We can't reach Captain Blund or any of the NightWatch, Lydia tells me it has something to do with the jamming each ship puts out and I believe something called handshaking is involved." He indicated I should join him at the doorway to the communication room. "We need to find out what's going on there, Val."

"Sir," said Lydia, "here's the room with the assault bay." She brought up a screen showing a large room, in the middle was a sizable oval shape. A green light shone against one of the walls, obviously a Confederate trooper was in the room doing ... guardy stuff. Probably an alert guard, I guessed these guys didn't do a lot of goofing off like my guys. And girls.

"I want you to pop on down to the assault bay for this vessel," said the boss, "don't go into the frigate, just check out what it looks like. That green light is obviously one guard, find out what he's doing. Do they do any regular checks, how are they handling the sudden loss of their communications. That sort of thing."

I looked at him. "Franz," I said, using his first name since we had been on buddy buddy terms for a while. "Do you think those instructions, those tasks fall anywhere within my skill set?"

"Are you saying you can't sneak about and spy on bad guys from behind cover?"

"Ahh, now we're getting somewhere. No problem, boss." I moved off to the door leading to the assault bay.

The boss called after me, "I'll see if Sergeant Gorka or Teddy Boy can spare anyone to join you."

"Okay," I answered. I clicked for Wallace and told him to stay here and look after Lydia and Jeremy. He was to make them his prime focus. Phil could look after himself.

"What about the boss?" Wallace asked. "I'm supposed to be his bodyguard."

"I'll be right," interrupted the boss. "Do as Val says, Wallace. I think both Lydia and Jeremy would benefit from having someone near them, someone like you. Someone who can give them a sense of safety. Phil can remain a useless drongo."

"Do you always listen in on everyone's private communications, sir?" I asked. My chat with Wallace was supposed to be the electronic version of a quiet whisper, something spoken out of the side of the mouth. What was the boss doing invading my privacy? I believe I mentioned as much to him.

"I do," the Man in Black replied. "It's good to be king. I listen in on whoever I want, especially on conversations dealing with you, Val." He gave me a small wave, "You're a bit of a loose cannon at the moment, so, yes, I do 'invade your privacy' for two reasons."

I looked at him expectantly, he turned back to check on the board showing reducing numbers of green lights. When he turned back, I must have had my eyebrows raised and a certain questioning in my pose. "And they would be?" I prompted.

"What?"

"The reasons, sir, what would they be? Why are you listening in on your absolutely bestest sergeant and all-round first-class soldier." I had taken a couple of steps back towards the boss, this conversation was becoming interesting and annoyingly uncomfortable."Ahh, my 'bestest' sergeant. My God, your vocabulary is both poetic and asinine," he said. "The reasons, alright, here they are: one, you are becoming unreliable and a danger to others, your judgment is more and more reliant on violence rather than seeking alternative ways to solve problems. In short, you are a bloody hazard to be around and I may have to put you down like a rabid dog."Fair enough, I thought. I was becoming slightly testy with others and the fact I hadn't punched the boss in the face after these comments was mildly surprising to me. Still, that was one reason. "And the other reason, your high and mightiness? What else is going on in your insidious mind, such that you feel the need to keep an eye on me?"

"Because I like you, dipstick," he said. "I'm worried about you and want to think of ways to stop you doing anything too stupid; anything, that is, which might get you killed. I've gotten used to having you around, you frustrating piece of dog crap."

"Can I call you 'dad'?" I asked.

He slapped me over the helmet and said, "Go away, Valentine, I've got real work to do. Ask Lydia for directions to the assault bay. Have a look around and report back. Do not, I repeat, do not engage with the enemy. Try not to attack anyone on our side. Remember, you might be joined by people sent by Teddy Boy or Sergeant Gorka. Be nice to have them live through any encounter with you. Now, go. I'll go to our assault shuttle to bring Sylvia, Greenash and the others down here."

I can take hint. I turned to leave and sent a message to Lydia asking her for directions. I also told Jeremy to stay here and guard the Man in Black ... and Phil.

"Who's going to guard you, Val?" asked the wee lad.

"Do as you're bloody well told, sport," I yelled. Okay, not cool. Taking a breath, I tried again, "Sorry, Jeremy. I'm not feeling too great, it's probably best if I'm off by myself for a while. I'd appreciate it if you would stay here." He gave me thumbs up. Right, I better get out of here before I cause more damage. A small stroll to look at the assault bay would be perfect for me and my current mental state. I followed Lydia's directions without too much trouble; again, the benefits of growing up in my pestilential era. Streets in the City had no signposts and you better remember any directions if you wanted to stay out of the river with a knife in your back. It was a fun place.

I eventually made it to the assault bay and found the place empty except for two people, one alive and one dead.

The dead one was dressed in the armour indicating one of the battle brig's troopers while the one sitting on his chest and looking comfortable was another armoured soldier, this one wore the gear denoting a member of Sergeant Gorka's team. She had sent me the name and contact details for the person she was going to send to meet me in the shuttle bay and I hoped this was him. Or her. Hard to tell gender in these suits.

I received a ping as I entered the room, a ping requesting a comm link. I agreed and watched the armoured figure stand up.

"My name is Nadia Bosko, I am a corporal in Banner Sergeant Gorka's team," said the voice.

She sounded female but I've been wrong before so decided against categorising her gender. In case he/she became offended and hit me. I'd seen Gorka's people fight and had no wish to receive a thump from one of them; good people to avoid. "Pleased to meet you Corporal Nadia Bosko." I replied. Seemed safe to say this.

"Just 'Corporal Nadia' is fine, sir."

"I'm not a 'sir', I'm a sergeant. Like Gorka." I moved over to examine the body of the dead trooper.

"No one is like Banner Sergeant Gorka, sir."It's like that, is it? Right, moving on. "Have you been busy, Nadia?" I asked, poking the body with my foot.

"It's 'Corporal Nadia', sir," she said. I noticed she was scanning our environment and looking worrisomely efficient and alert. And also, if her correction of my use of her title was any judge, keen to be addressed properly. She kept speaking while surveying our surroundings, combined actions well beyond most of the NightWatch. We had trouble walking and talking at the same time although a few advanced cases could do these tasks, and chew gum at the same time.

I noticed I had categorised Nadia as a girl, so much for my desire not to offend. "Are you a girl, Corporal Nadia?" I asked.

"None of your damn business, sir," she said. "I'm a corporal of the Empire."Well, that's me told.

Chapter 28

I DECIDED AGAINST SWIMMING against the tide, the tide which usually involved me annoying people, but decided to leave this particular technique alone. Nadia — sorry, 'Corporal' Nadia came across as brusque and no-nonsense — I believed we would get along until she decided to thump me because I acted in my usual freewheeling manner. Still, this may be a good opportunity for me to practise those soft people skills I hear so much about. Things like empathy and listening and stuff like that. You know, pretend you care about people and what's going on.

Hitting on this approach, I asked Nadia — yes, I'm going to continue to annoy her by ignoring her rank, some habits die hard — I asked her what had happened and how the body she was near turned up in the assault bay.

"Nothing unusual, sir," she said. "Sergeant Gorka delegated me this job because I am a scout; I have training in stealth, in discrete observation and I also have experience in quietly neutralising enemy assets." Okay, she was beyond the pale. I don't approve of referring to the act of killing people as 'neutralising enemy assets'.

"Done a lot of it, have you?" I asked.

"Yes, sir," she answered. "When I was given this task, I contact Sergeant Technician Lydia who directed me to the best entry point for me to neutralise this trooper."

"By 'neutralise', you mean 'kill'?" I suggested.

"Correct, sir. Part of this enemy trooper's responsibility would be to monitor the breach which the battle brig had made in our frigate's hull. At the moment, this breach is open but capable of being sealed by that floor plate." She pointed at another of those plates I had seen on our assault shuttle, the one Phil had so quickly slammed shut before I could join my team. I could see an edge of it jutting over the assault breach and sending off a positive keenness to be deployed. I guessed the battle brig had a similar protocol with our ex-friend on the floor being responsible for pushing the open and close button.

Still, some questions came to mind. "Why would the breach be sealed off?" I asked. "Wouldn't the attackers like to have a quick way back if things went wrong?"

"No, sir. This is a battle brig and it is attacking a smaller vessel, our frigate. They would not be expecting to retreat unless something went catastrophically wrong with their insertion. There would be between a hundred to a hundred and fifty enemy troopers currently invading and fighting our people on the frigate. Considering we have already lost our assault team of Tharls — plus the squad sent across with Sergeant Gorka — that would mean Captain Blund has about thirty troopers available to resist the assault."

"Plus the NightWatch," I suggested.

"Oh, yeah," she may have chuckled. "Sure, they'd be big help. Especially the kids."

"I sense some doubt over the capacity of the NightWatch to be of any real use."

"Look, sir, I know they are your people. And I know we did some light training with you, things like shipboard fighting and a whole lot of scenarios. I know your little guys — I think you call them 'cadets' —

thought they were hot stuff because they could hide in the maintenance corridors but well, sir, we don't use children in war."

"But in the training, we did alright?" A certain pleading had entered my voice.

She sighed. "Well, yes, your people were minor annoyances and could hold off small numbers of attackers. In all those drills we deployed one or two squads, but the Confederate troopers down there probably outnumber all of us, your people and mine. I suspect things will not be going well for our side."

I was thinking this annoying corporal was probably right and our gang needed some help. Where from, I do not know, but I could not stand around gabbing while my mates were dying. While I was realising I had no idea what to do, another ping came into my head. This one from one of Ted's team who asked for a connection. I agreed and snarled a greeting at whoever it was who came online with me.

"It's me, Val," came a voice I recognised. "It's Dragos, Ted sent me to say hello. Can I come in? Please don't kill me when I arrive."

I growled assent and linked him into a subgroup with Nadia. "Dragos," I said, "this is Nadia from Gorka's team." I saw her look at his slightly unusual spacesuit, Dragos having lost most of an arm in the fight on the spaceship . But he still had one good arm and both legs so we figured he could still work, and he was a dead shot with a handgun. He had a variety of attachments he could plug into his stump but these made a spacesuit look somewhat...lumpy. I suspected he had gone with the metal fist for this excursion. Pity, it was always a hoot when he attached his hook and then absentmindedly scratched his bum. Hilarious.

"I am **Corporal** Nadia from **Banner Sergeant** Gorka's squad. What is your rank, NightWatchman Dragos?"

"My rank?" queried Dragos. "Oh, I'm one of the guys. And girls. I think I outrank the cadets but that's not too clear because Cadet Officer Layla has ordered me about at least once. How are you getting on, Nadia?" His tone was positively cheerful. Dragos was one of our old NightWatch, a good man to have in a fight but not the sharpest tool in the shed. I think he used to be a shepherd or such like, before the Huns wiped out his village. He was the guy I needed to be with Nadia, his casual approach to life and authority should mesh well with Nadia's status conscious persona. This could be a fun conversation.

"How's it all going with Ted and the gang?" I asked.

"Yeah, we're all sweet," replied Dragos. "Ted used the heavy blaster to blow the door away, the one the command group were hiding behind. I think the door took out a couple of their guys who were trying to hold it shut. The Man in Black had already asked them to surrender and they refused so, you know, same old, same old."

Yep, that would do it. The boss would give them one chance to surrender and then do something catastrophic. Not big on long drawn-out negotiations, is Franz. And Ted was probably begging for a chance to try out their new toy, Elena would have been in his ear as they argued about who was going to pull the trigger. Bloody idiots.

"Are they still holding out?" I asked.

"Yeah ... nah," he said. "When I left, Ted had them all sitting on the floor being good and quiet. Took their communication beads out of their ears. The boss is probably going to wander up for a bit of a chat with their captain."

"Looks like we control this ship," I said. "I guess someone should go down and check on the frigate."

Nadia was lying prone with her helmet and shoulders over the opening into the frigate. I told Dragos to watch our backs and signalled to them both I was about to enter the frigate.

"I don't see any enemy troopers in the corridor below the hatch," said Nadia. "I think you're good to go, sergeant ..." I used her back as a convenient step, taking a small pace onto it before leaping gracefully into the frigate. She expelled a small 'oomph of breath.

"Watch where you put your feet, sergeant!" she said, with some vigour.

"You have to learn to ignore Valentine," said Dragos. "He upsets most people; welcome to the gang."

I landed gracefully, ignoring the various slanders coming from my two erstwhile companions. Nadia was right, I couldn't see any sign of enemy troopers, my corridor curved gently left and right allowing me to see about fifty paces in either direction. I guess I better pick a direction and stumble about — my usual operating technique. Maybe Nadia could help.

"Which way should I go, Nadia?" I asked.

"It's **Corporal** Nadia, sergeant," came the reply. "And I can't tell you. It depends on which route their patrols take.""Patrols?" I said, a vague unease forming in the old tummy.

"You jumped in before I could finish, sergeant," she said. I detected a hint of something in her voice — exasperation, gleeful vengeance, something like that. "It's standard practice in a boarding operation to have one trooper at the hatch — the one I shot — and then have a patrol check up on things from time to time. It has to be a physical patrol since the comms are unreliable. They need to ensure nothing has happened aboard the assaulting vessel."

"Something like a bunch of yahoos deciding to do their own assault," contributed Dragos. "Go Team NightWatch!"

I was stuffed. Time to pick a direction and run. Any direction would do. I shifted from foot to foot, vacillating or procrastinating, I'm not sure which is the correct descriptor. Perhaps 'dithering' is nearer the mark.

"Why are you hopping about, sergeant?" asked Nadia. "Are you dithering?"

"He's probably thinking," said Dragos. "He generally gets twitchy before doing something stupid. Although, in this case, he's done the stupid thing first. Way to go, Val. Character growth in action."

"Dragos ..." I began, deciding to put off any decision in favour of exchanging insults.

My flow of possible invective was cut off by a small voice saying "Hsst!" The voice was picked up by my external speakers, not my nanobots. Okay, this was strange, who do I know who says 'Hsst'?

"Patricia," I asked, "is that you?"

A small door in the corridor wall opened and a young girl's head appeared. Patrica, one of the cadets, a young girl who was always chosen for scouting and spying operations because she had the ability to seemingly disappear in an empty room. She often teamed up with Jeremy to scare the snot out of me when they leapt out and said 'Boo'. Since she had not chosen this scare word but instead went for the 'Hsst', I knew I was in trouble.

"Get in here, Val," she said. "Their patrol is due anytime in the next hundred beats."

I looked at the small doorway. "I won't fit, Patrica. I'm too big."

"You did it before, when Lydia took you through these maintenance passages."

"Yeah, but I wasn't wearing space armour then. It tends to bulk a man up."

She looked at me, waiting for me to understand.

"Oh, crap," I said and began to clamber out of the armour. As I took each piece off, I threw it back up into the battle brig where Nadia grabbed it to tuck away. I aimed the odd piece at her head but she demonstrated great agility and an extraordinary reaction time.

"You are such a dick, Sergeant Valentine," she said, as she pulled back into the main assault bay. Now she was completely out of sight.

"To know me is to love me, Nadia."

She groaned, I smiled. It's the little things.

I slipped into the maintenance passage and let Patricia shut the door. "How long until the patrol comes along?" I asked.

"Don't know," whispered Patrica. "But Layla might." She nodded at another waif also in the passageway, another cadet. This was Layla, not human. Layla was an Anipe, a race who looked similar to humans if you accepted their elongated bodies and inbred desire to wear outrageously coloured one-piece garments. Layla stood before me in a neck to knee smock of a vivid yellow. Sunburst yellow, hurting the eyes yellow.

Her lips were moving and she spat out, "496," before turning away from my manly visage and continuing to count under her breath.

"Layla does the counting," explained Patricia. "Patrols come by between five hundred and eight hundred counts. So far."

These kids were good. "What happens when they get here?" I asked.

"They wave at the trooper on guard in the battle brig, sometimes they say a few words. Often they wave and keep walking. They don't look like they expect trouble.""Could mean they are slack and idle troopers," I said.

"Yeah ... nah," replied Patricia. "I've seen these guys work, they're the real deal, Val. Highly capable, scarily professional."

I called to Nadia and Dragos on my comm bead. No response. I tried a few more times and then asked Patricia, "Are your comms working?"

"They were until a few minutes ago. The Confederation was assaulting our comm centre, the command bridge and the engineering sections. We assumed that, when our comms went down, they had captured the comm centre and turned things off."

Hard to argue with that logic, given we had done the same to them when we assaulted their battle brig. "But I could talk to both Nadia and Dragos when I first jumped in here," I said.

"Yeah," said Patricia. "It's because you were directly under the assault hole. When you step out of that small area, all comms fail."

Rats, I wanted to give Nadia and Dragos a heads up about the routine of the Confederate patrols but I obviously couldn't use my comms. I started to open the door leading back into the main corridor but stopped when both Layla and Patricia hissed at me. Yes, they hissed. But they both hissed, not just Patricia.

I heard the steady tramp of footfalls, armoured footfalls.

Ah, the patrol approacheth.

Chapter 29

I LET PATRICIA SQUEEZE past me to the door where she cracked the smallest of gaps. I could see over her head and we both gazed at the corridor, the sound of tramping feet getting louder. Two Confederate troopers appeared, stopped under the assault hole and waved up at the open hatch. The open hatch where another of their lads should have been waiting for them, waiting to give a cheery wave and possibly a bit of clever banter.

But that trooper was dead, having been shot in the back by the bloodthirsty and efficient Corporal Nadia. Any moment now, the alarm would be raised, I readied myself for suicidal combat.

But then an enemy trooper did appear at the hatch, showing a helmet and torso, and an arm raised in welcome. I stood and watched the three exchange another cheery wave to the person above them, the patrol not even breaking stride before moving off and silence again descended on our little piece of heaven.

Something had happened up there, perhaps a stray Confederate trooper had wandered by and ... no, I had no idea what was going on. I pulled out my pistol, knowing I would never hit anything with it, opened the door to the maintenance hatch fully and stepped into the corridor. I approached the opening of the assault hatch where I was met by a strange trooper standing on the rim of the hatch and gazing placidly down at me. The top half and the helmet were dressed in the cool-looking black armour of the Confederacy while the bottom half was clad in the purple gear so beloved by the Empire. Dragos stepped up beside the trooper and helped in the removal of the helmet. A smiling face beamed down.

"Has someone been using their brain?" I asked.

"Corporal Nadia is the hell on wheels, Val," enthused Dragos. "She whipped herself out of the top half of her suit while I stripped the dead trooper. Then she dressed in the top bits and waved casually at those bozos as they went past. How good is she, eh?"

Nadia gave me a wink. "That's how we roll in our squad, sergeant," she said.

"Yeah, terrific, Nadia," I said. "That'll buy us some time." I indicated with a thumb the door behind me and went on, "I've got two of the cadets in here. I'm going to stick with them for a bit and see what's going on down here. We've lost our comm ability in the frigate, I'm assuming that means we've lost control of the communications hub. Like we did to them in the battle brig."

"That's a real problem, sergeant," said Nadia as she stripped off the Confederate armour and redressed in her original gear. "It means you won't be able to contact anyone down there. But," and here she leaned forward to peer down at me, "it also means the Confederate troopers on board the frigate now have their comm ability back. That is, if they have a technician with them. Someone like Lydia who could operate the big board."

"Do you reckon they would?" I asked, a sinking feeling growing in me.

"Guarantee it, sergeant," said Nadia. "And one more thing. It means they will be able to locate everyone wearing one of our comm beads."

"Oh, damn. Does that mean we are now the green dots on this ship. They can locate us on some screen and know exactly where we are?"

"Certainly, if you're wearing an Empire comm bead," said Nadia. "On the other hand, if you remove the comm bead from your ear," she had a small smirk in her voice, probably brought on by my hand moving towards my ear. "If you pull it out you will lose the translation function. You won't be able to understand anyone who doesn't speak your language."

"Like you," I said, "and the rest of the Empire people on board this ship." And the cadets, and a whole lot of the NightWatch. Sure, I would still be able to talk to the original NightWatch but that would be of limited use.

"Sergeant," said Nadia. I detected a certain tenseness in her voice. "I recommend I seal this hatch. If they carry out a successful capture of the frigate — which I suspect is going to happen quickly — then leaving this hatch open makes it easy for them to storm back aboard the battle brig. There's a lot more of them than us, we wouldn't stand much of a chance."Bum. "Seal the hatch, tell everyone what has happened down here," I said. And do a lot of praying.

"What will you do?" she asked.

"Dunno," I replied. "Wander about and try to stuff things up, I guess."

"Problem solved," contributed Dragos. "You're good at stuffing things up."

"Corporal Nadia, here is a direct order," I said. "Shut the bloody hatch. Then give Dragos a good thumping."

As the hatch slid shut, I heard Dragos say, "He's joking, Nadia. Honest. He's a real kidder ..."

I re-entered the maintenance corridor and told Patricia and Layla what was going on. "Right," I said, "your turn. What was happening on this ship before the comms got shut off? Was anyone telling you anything?"

Layla kept counting, I heard a '324' from her before Patricia chimed in. "Sure, Val. Magic had his comms on for all the NightWatch, he gave us regular updates."

"Where is everyone?" I asked.

"Right," said Patricia. "The cadets and most of the NightWatch are in the training room. That was our default position if this ship was attacked." She caught my questioning look, patted me on the head and went on. "Magic had us doing those drills, remember? Yes, we all knew they were meant to keep us busy but they were a bit of fun. Part of the whole training thing was us brainstorming a bunch of scenarios, one of which included being boarded by an enemy force at a random location. I think Right Honourable came up with that one. Anyway, Magic had us practise what we would do in lots of situations, the main action being for us to all gather in the training room until we knew what was happening."

"He's a clever lad, that Magic," I murmured.

"Too right," said Patricia. "So, when the alarms went off, we knew what to do. The cadets and all the newer members of the NightWatch, including some of the old guys Magic described as 'useless pieces of crap', regrouped in the training room under Right Honourable. Magic took another group, mainly the shooters left over from Teddy Boy's squad plus a handful of the more proficient hand to hand fighters and formed a rapid reaction team. He took them out into the corridors with a few cadets as scouts and proceeded to spoil a lot of bad guys' days. Ambushes, sneak attacks and other lovely little ploys we had worked out. I understand he lost a few people but was generally effective in keeping the corridors near the training room free."

"Five hundred!" said Layla. "Stand by.'

Paticia stopped talking and we cracked the door out into the corridor again. We could expect another patrol of two or three guys in the next few minutes. I leaned down and whispered in Patricia's ear, "What about Captain Blund and the rest of the ship?"

"Yes," she replied. "Captain Blund had sent teams to hold on to the comm room, engineering and the bridge. Since we lost the comm room, things will get tougher."I had a scary thought. "Yeah, we're the green dots!"

Patricia looked up at me, a question in her young eyes.

"The green dots!" I said. "if they're in the comms room then they know where we all are. Anyone with an Empire comm bead would show up on a floor plan of the frigate as a green dot. We're sitting ducks here."At that point, the enemy patrol arrived. Except it wasn't a patrol, it was a large squad of fully armoured Confederate troopers, all pointing their weapons at the wall separating the maintenance passage from the corridor. The wall behind which we now cowered. A voice boomed out over their external suit speakers, "We know there are three of you in there. Open the door and surrender or we shall open fire. Be warned, our weaponry is sufficient to go thought these weak interior walls. I shall count to three and then we shall open fire. One ..."

I opened the door and stepped out, followed by Patrica and Layla. "Thank God, I can stop this bloody counting," whispered Layla. Sometimes you have to find a positive in any situation.

One of the troopers grabbed each of us as we exited and pushed our faces into a wall. "Stand still, hands on heads while we search you for weapons." We did so and then we were turned around to face the troopers.

There were six troopers in the corridor, one of them stepped forward and opened his faceplate to look into my eyes. "Who are you, dipshit? And why are you hiding in the walls with a couple of kids?" his eyes flickered to Layla and Patricia. "A couple of girls. Young girls. Fancy a bit of young stuff, do you? Tell you what, we might have a bit of a play with the girls. If you're good, we might let you watch."

"Corporal," said one of the troopers, "we can't do that. They're our prisoners, they're girls and it looks like they're underage."

"Shut your face, Akal," replied the man in front of me, the man I assumed to be the corporal. The man I would kill. "Just for that, you can watch as well." The corporal turned his head to face the rest of his squad, "Who's in, boys?" he asked. "Anyone else ready for a bit of light exercise?" He turned back to face me, chuckling in his sense of power.

He unstrapped his helmet and pulled it over his head, revealing a blotchy face wearing a wide grin. He clipped the helmet to his belt and reached for the linkage to the lower part of his armour. He kept his eyes fixed on mine the whole time, his smile showing he was enjoying what he assumed was my sense of outrage, helplessness and terror.

"You're a corporal?" I asked.

The clips on his suit unfastened with a soft click, his smile never wavered. "That's right, you useless piece of Empire crap, I'm the corporal."

"Well," I said, "I'm a sergeant. Therefore, I outrank you."

His hands stopped moving, his eyes took on a slightly quizzical look. "So bloody what?"

I thrust my thumbs into his eyes, all the way. His eyeballs made a soft popping noise before collapsing before the force of my thrust. I also wrapped my hands around the back of his head to get a good, solid grip. I now had his head under my control, gripped tightly by the pressure of my thumbs in his eye sockets as my hands and fingers wrapped around his skull tilting the whole head up and back a little. I wanted to get this angle right.

I smashed my forehead into his nose, doing my best to push any bone fragments up and back into his brain. As he slid to the floor —

unconscious or dead, I didn't care — I let my thumbs slip messily out of his now destroyed eyes.

I turned to the rest of his squad, several had started to raise their blasters to me but there was a definite element of shock in the party. "I am the sergeant of the NightWatch and these girls are part of my team. No one touches them. Ever." I looked at the trooper who objected to the late corporal's actions. "You're Akal, right?" He nodded. "Right, you're now acting corporal. Tell the rest of these dicks to point their weapons somewhere else before I take them away. And send for someone higher up the food chain."

Akal came to a form of attention and started to say, "Yes, sergeant ..." before realising which side had all the guns. He stuttered and went on, now giving me an order, "Raise your hands, sergeant. No one will hurt the girls."

"He killed Balbir, Akal!" said one of his men. "We can't let him get away with that! Shouldn't we shoot him?"

"Shut your mouth, Charanjeet," said Akal, his voice gaining authority. "You run along and find an officer, tell him we have a situation and need direction." There was a pause during which no one moved. "I gave you an order, Charanjeet. Now get moving! The rest of you, keep these three covered but do not approach them. Deepinder, check on the corporal, is he still alive?"

One of the troopers, I assumed it was Charanjeet, took off at a run back down the corridor while the rest of the troopers kept weapons pointed at us. No one made any move to come closer but another trooper bent down and slowly shuffled to the inert form of the downed corporal. He kept a wary eye on me, examining the body for a moment before looking back to his team and shaking his head.

Something messy dripped off my thumbs to splash on the floor.

Rack up another one to the Valentine kill count.

Chapter 30

WE STOOD AROUND, ALMOST embarrassed for a few minutes until the sound of running footsteps announced the arrival of another batch of troopers. Our space was getting seriously crowded. One of the newcomers must have been an officer because Akal saluted him before quivering to a position of rigid attention.

The officer turned to me, looked down at my empty hands and must have noticed the slight drip coming off each thumb. He raised his pistol and pointed it at my head. "Any reason why I should not shoot you now?" he asked.

Good question. Damn good question. Of course, if had been me I would not have asked the question, I would have shot the idiot in front of me. Look, if you're going to shoot then shoot, don't gab away. More bloody amateurs.

Our little tableau was broken when Layla stepped in front of me, effectively blocking any retaliatory shot at my handsome visage. She put her hands on her hips, thrust out her chin and said, "Back off, bozo."

I wanted to remember this scene for later retelling. That is, if I got to have a 'later'. Layla, the Anipe, came to about my shoulder. I'm a tall lad which means she had a bit of height to her stature. She stood proudly erect, her eye watering yellow garment seeming to flutter in an invisible breeze. Don't ask me how, the Anipe had this way of making their clothes so it looked like they were always standing in a soft wind. Often, they extended the effect to their long hair and stood around giving dreamy looks to anyone passing by, made me want to hit them. They're all dippy.

Layla had recently gained her adult status, thus the wearing of her blazing colour, but she was still that little girl I had rescued from slavers, still a child trying to make sense of the world. But here she was, poking the enemy officer in the chest — she does that a lot — and telling him to back off.

Since he was wearing armour, the finger poking didn't even register but he lowered his pistol and swivelled his head down to look at this chit of a girl who had confronted him with such passion.

"Who are you, girlie?"

Ah, hell. Talking down to the cadets was not good for the speaker's future well-being.

"I am NOT your girlie, you pustulant pile of dog crap. I am a senior member of the NightWatch Cadet section, engaged in making the lives of you and your bloody invaders as miserable as possible. I am a combatant. But most importantly, when it comes to the sergeant here," she indicated me with a casual wave of her hand, "understand he is under my protection."

"Your protection?" stuttered the officer.

"That's right, numbnuts,' she snarled. "I'm his bodyguard!"

This remark was not met with the hilarity I had expected. Rather, confusion reigned for a few heartbeats until the officer growled another order, "Someone had better give me a proper report. Right now!"

Akal stepped forward, saluted, identified himself as 'Corporal Akal' and then gave what I considered to be an outstandingly accurate report of the squad's actions from the time they arrived in the corridor until the officer arrived. He's an idiot, you never tell an officer everything, you spin a tale, you shade the facts and leave unpleasant pieces completely out of the telling. But not Akal, he included the attempted rape from the corporal, he also added the bit where I appointed him as the new corporal. Crazy kid.

The officer stood quietly in thought, looking from me, down to the corpse of the corporal, then over to the girls and so on. "I notice Corporal's Balbir's body is not completely in his armour. That would bear out your allegation he was proposing to rape these two girls."

We all stood around as his mighty brain churned through the facts of the case. "Confederacy military personnel do not engage in acts of rape or unprovoked violence," he said. "Let me make one fact perfectly clear: he had no right to threaten you girls," here he bowed to Patrica and Layla. "For that, I apologise. If I had discovered his actions, I would have shot him on the spot." He turned and looked at the rest of the squad, "And I shall assume you troopers would have informed me of this event, albeit after the atrocity had occurred.

"To be clear, Trooper Akal, this man," he pointed at me, "is an enemy. He does not have the right to confer rank upon you. Still, since you were the one willing to openly express disapproval of his actions, I commend you. And promote you to corporal; the squad is now yours."

Valentine, kingmaker.

The officer had a strong, authoritarian voice and had been using it to great effect over his suit's external speakers. To me and my two companions, he said, "Place your hands on your heads. Stand still or someone might shoot you. Probably me."

He turned to his gang and spat out more orders, "Squads one and two, secure this room and all approaches." The girls and I placed our hands on our heads, I did not want to move anything in case they thought I was about to attack them or do something equally stupid.

"Val," whispered Layla, "please don't do anything stupid."

Hmm. Maybe I do act rashly from time to time, when I have no other choice. Or when I'm tired. Or angry. Or bored. Okay, I'm an idiot. Time to access the brains of the outfit, so I knitted a communication with the Man in Black, he might be able to hear everything we said.

The enemy officer came back after making his men leap about, I took my cue from their reactions and decided to walk softly around this guy. "My name is Sergeant Valentine. Who are you and why are you attacking us?"

"I am Lieutenant Ekveer of the Confederacy and you are my prisoners. Tell me about this dead man." His toe nudged the body of the late corporal, the one without eyes. "Did you kill him?"

Tricky question, not a line I wished to pursue. When in doubt, tap dance, "Have you come to surrender to us?" That should give him something to chew on.

"I do like an optimist, Sergeant Valentine," said the enemy lieutenant. "Who are you? You certainly don't act like Empire troopers."

I did not like this at all.

"Why do you want to know?" I asked. It couldn't hurt to appear vaguely incompetent.

"Because otherwise I shall order you to be shot. And if you hesitate to obey any of my future orders, I shall shoot one of your companions." This guy meant business.

"Surrender your communication bead," he said.

I thought I might be able to stretch this out a bit. As my hand touched my ear, I stopped and asked, "How will we know what you are saying if we all remove our beads? We won't be able to follow instructions." It was a weak ploy, but it might give me a moment to think of a brilliant plan.

The lieutenant pulled out his pistol and aimed it at Layla, the barrel resting against her ear. "Are you refusing to comply?" he asked.

Okay, that'll do me, I whipped out the communication bead and placed it into the outstretched hand of one of the troopers. I was now in the dark, not an unfamiliar location for me.

More troopers arrived, we were shunted up against a wall and decided to stand still, to stand breathtakingly still. Two unpleasantly sized soldiers stood close to us with weapons ready to deal death at the slightest twitch of any body part, especially thumbs.

I could watch and vaguely understand what was going on. Thus, I was able to see them organise themselves in poses all looking up at the closed hatch leading into the assault bay of the battle brig. Good luck with that, I thought. It's designed for this event, nasty men with big guns trying to board the vessel.

Which means I was surprised when the hatch began to slide back. I was even more surprised when an armoured trooper, dressed in the purple colours of Empire and thus indicating the wearer was one of our guys, tumbled through the opening to land at the feet of the enemy lads. The Empire trooper did not look well, the missing arm was my first clue. When it hit the floor, it lay there and moaned.

These suits are amazing. I could see where the arm used to be, where it was once attached to the suit. Now it was a flat surface, the hole sealed by some exotic spacey magic. I hoped the inhabitant of that suit was currently enjoying a pain free rest, hopefully full of the wonder drugs these suits carried for such an occasion. Another moan came from the suit, a voice I recognised. I was looking at Corporal Nadia. Had she opened the hatch? Was she a traitor? If so, how did she lose an arm? Or had Dragos been incredibly unlucky and lost a bit more of his slowly shrinking body? Lots of questions.

There was a pause and then two of the black clad troopers peeled off and knelt beside Nadia. One of them had a bag from which several small cables were extracted with the ends being plugged into various slots and holes on Nadia's suit. One of the medics had already removed Nadia's helmet, her face showed the drawn and gaunt look of someone in great pain, great pain masked by strong drugs. I'd been in that same situation, the body all battered and shrieking for rest while the medications coursed through the veins trying to convince the brain that all was well. But the body knows, the body knows when it is hurt and knows when it is being lied to.

I don't like drugs. And don't talk to me about single malt, that is not a drug, it is the water of life. I know because my nephew, Stephen, is a Scot and he introduced me to the stuff. Always believe a Scotsman when he talks about whisky. I had to stop this line of thought, my sister is older, wiser and far away. I love her dearly but well, haven't seen her in a long time. A long, long time. Bugger. But I digress.

Before I got too carried away, the hatch slid back fully which allowed another body, another Empire trooper, to fall through. This one was dead, the huge hole in the chest being the subtle clue. As it hit the floor, several enemy troopers used some clever attachments on their armour and leapt up into the shuttle bay. I heard more shouting but no more shots before everything went still. After a few beats, Lieutenant Ekveer walked over and checked the new body, he opened the helmet face plate and I could see it was my old mate, Bazli.

What the hell was going on here?

Shortly after this, more troopers went up into the body of the battle brig while others descended. They were bringing two other people with them. One was Dragos, I recognised his stance of terrified stillness and the other was the body of the Confederate trooper shot by Corporal Nadia.

Our corridor was becoming full of bodies and prisoners.

The Lieutenant Ekveer did the same examination on his dead trooper, the fart I had known as Bazli. He must have sent orders to his squad because Dragos and I were soon blocked in by several hard bodies, all capable of taking our lives. I could see the lieutenant's face since he had made his plate transparent, he didn't look happy.

Thus, I was surprised when the lieutenant gave me back my communication bead. I stuck it into my ear.

"You owe me two lives, Sergeant Valentine. One for my trooper and another for our agent."

"Bazli was one of your people?" I asked.

"No, not one of mine. I command soldiers. Bazli was an operative of our Intelligence Bureau." He came and stood before me, "Let us move forward." He assembled his team, inviting more troopers to come join us from their various locations on the frigate. Soon, Dragos and I were pressed back against a wall as many efficient-looking enemy soldiers moved past us and jumped up into the battle brig. while a few trickled down the associated hallways.

The lieutenant guided me to stand under the open hatch leading up into the battle brig. This meant I could communicate with the boss again; I opened up a quick link to the brains of the outfit.

The lieutenant placed a hand on my shoulder. "I gave you back your comm bead for a reason, sergeant," he said.

"Because you like me? We've formed a special bond?" I asked. "Look, I'm flattered and I'm sure you're a wonderful lover but I've already got a life partner." I nodded at Dragos, "Not Dragos here, he's just a mate.

But I do know some of the crew from the frigate who might appreciate your rock steady charm."

Dragos, having heard everything I said and understanding it because I spoke in our common tongue, groaned. "You're going to get us all killed, dickhead," he muttered. "Me, especially."

Something hard hit me in the back causing me to stumble a step or two, one of the lieutenant's larger troopers was standing behind me and administering behaviour modification suggestions. A blow to the back of the head generally modifies my behaviour when I was become my normal abrasive self. "I did not ask you to speak, sergeant," he said. "Do not be flippant with me, I have no sense of humour." He nodded to the person behind me who gave me another thump. Okay, lesson learned.

Kidding. I opened my mouth and asked, "So why did you give me back the comm bead, if it wasn't to ask me out for a few drinks? You do have a certain sullen charm but I generally like my social partners to have better personal hygiene. Yes, matey, you stink."

This time I fell to the floor after the blow. Dragos said to the lieutenant, "You have to make allowances for Sergeant Valentine, he has the misguided belief he is a funny man, when really, he is bloody annoying. If you hit him every time he mouths off, we'll be here all day and he'll end up as a grease smear on the floor and, I have to say, not a lot of people would be too disappointed at that outcome."

This was an impressive little speech from Dragos, especially considering he knew he would not be able to understand any reply. Still, his words hurt. Surely, I would be missed by one and all?

"Sergeant," said the lieutenant, "before you say anything else which may cause you to be killed, allow me to tell you why I gave you the bead." He signalled and another blow hit the back of my head. God, I hate punctuation.

"I want you to contact your leaders and inform them of the current state of affairs. We, the Confederacy, have over a hundred troopers still ready to fight. We are slowly cleaning up the resistance on your frigate and are now engaged in the reclamation of our vessel. Nod if you follow me so far."

I nodded and tensed for another blow. None came.

"Excellent," he said. "You are capable of learning. Count the troopers I have in this corridor, Think how many more soldiers I have on this frigate. I still have several squads quelling any insurrections and taking prisoners."

I did so and agreed there was a bucketload of enemy combatants cluttering up the corridors. I grunted an agreement at him. "Okay," I said. "I can see you've got lots of guys. What happens now?"

"Now," he said. "You surrender."

Chapter 31

SOON AFTER THIS EXCITEMENT, a Confederate trooper leaned back over the edge and signalled they had control of the assault bay and the attached corridors. This was not going to end well for our guys aboard the battle brig. More enemy troopers ran past and jumped through the empty hatchway, lots of enemy troopers.

This was not looking good for the home team. The reason you would release combatants back to the battle brig is because they were not needed on the frigate. And the reason they would not be needed on the frigate is because it had been captured.

I think we were deep in the cesspit, well and truly.

Lieutenant Ekveer continued speaking as the organised chaos unfolded around us. "Use the comm bead to contact your superiors, tell them what you can see here. Inform them I require their unconditional surrender. If I do not hear from them — through you — by the time I walk one circuit of this room, I shall assume my offer has been refused. In that case, I shall instruct my men to kill everyone they find. We will not keep prisoners; be aware, we already have several prisoners on board the frigate. Mainly useless men who tried to fight us with swords and clubs, the Empire soldiers all died at their posts as they should. We also have a handful of women and children. I would be most interested in knowing what they are doing aboard an Empire naval vessel." He looked into my eyes. "They will also be killed. Do you understand, sergeant?"

Yes, I understood, this guy played hardball. I nodded and spoke to the Man in Black. I didn't need to give much of a background briefing since I had opened his comm channel as soon as I got the bead back in my ear. My little song and dance, including the thumps on my head, were for the boss to hear what was going on and give him time to come up with a plan. A clever plan. Maybe even a cunning plan.

Heck, he'd had a couple of minutes, surely that was enough for his mighty intellect to devise a sneaky solution. I watched the enemy lieutenant strolling along our room and asked my aspirational question, "What are we gonna do, boss?" I suspect my voice had a slight squeak.

"It's an easy one, Val, "said the boss.

"Tell him we surrender."

These guys were efficient, I'll give them that. After I told the lieutenant what the decision was, he had me relay several instructions to the Man in Black. Basically, these instructions consisted of all our side placing their weapons on the ground and sitting cross legged on the floor with their hands linked on their helmets.

He took back my comm bead, shouted more orders to his people and then turned away from us. Other troopers indicated we should start walking, we were taken deeper into the frigate, soon entering the training room. Since this had been, according to Layla and Patricia, where the NightWatch had gathered, I could assume they had lost control of the space. I hoped the idiots had surrendered and not fought to the last man. Or woman. Or child.

I needn't have worried, this was, after all the NightWatch. We don't go in for last stands. We're more of the give up quickly or run away sort of people. And before you argue, allow me to point out we are still alive.

Thus, inside I was happy to meet lots of our guys and girls. They were all seated on the floor, sitting on their hands, while enemy troopers stood around them in numbers all uneven. I spotted Right Honourable in the front rank and moved over to join him. Before I sat down, a trooper stopped the three of us and took away any remaining comm beads. So much for hatching a cunning plan, most of us would not be able to understand each other.

Layla sat beside me, gave me a poke in the ribs and said, "What do we do now, Val?"

God, I was sick of that question. "Look, Layla," I began, turning to face her smiling face. Her smiling, secretive, clever face. Neither of us had a comm bead, yet she was talking to me in English. "How come I can understand you? And do you understand me?"

She shrugged, "Remember my father?" she said. "The scientist who invented the communication nanobots? He injected me with them because he wanted to see what would happen." That's right. The mob killed him when they were tidying up loose ends but I remember Layla telling me her father used her as a test case, he wouldn't win any dad of the year awards. Not that he would be worried, given he was dead.

"Your nanobots still work?" I said. "How's that possible?"

"Because I wasn't exposed to any of the blasts from that bloody huge spaceship. Anyway, I don't know what good it will do us but I thought you should know."

Clever girl. Right, we now had an edge. A tiny, tiny edge but an edge. The big question was, how was I going to use this fact to ... do something clever.

I sat in thought for a while, eventually coming up empty. Right Honourable and I could chat, as could any of us from Earth so sporadic conversations popped up and down. I looked around at who was in the room, recognising the old NightWatch veterans, the ones Magic had deemed too stupid to use in the fight for the frigate. As I looked at each face, I reached two conclusions — some of these guys would still have functioning nanobots which was a good thing. The other realisation was these particular guys were as dumb as house paint, not the sort of people with whom you want to discuss devious strategy. They liked to chat about beer, girls and sports but beyond those topics, anything requiring more than two syllables confused them and then they hit you.

Into the hall came the remains of Lonely's team, led by the man himself. They were all a bit battered and bruised and I suspected we had lost a few of them. They staggered, some leaned on others. We used to have a colourful scarf, originally a soft yellow colour — not as eye watering as Layla's robes — but they had been getting well-worn over the recent months. I saw several of these scarves wrapped around heads and arms, blood seeping through, adding a bit more to the degradation of the lovely piece of clothing. Damn things had saved our lives a few times.

Lonely slumped beside us, plopping down on the other side of Right Honourable. "Hello, fungus face," he said to me "Are we winning yet?"

"I think we're losing, mate," I said. "When I was captured the Confederate troopers were storming into the battle brig. God, there's a lot of the mongrels. Any word on Captain Blund and the others?"

"As far as I know, everyone's been captured. We've lost the frigate, we've lost people and," he nodded at the doorway, now filling with the Man in Black, Lydia and other survivors, "it looks like we've lost the battle brig."

Lord Franz sat in front of us but swivelled a little so we could all chat. Lydia sat beside me after Layla pushed everyone along some more. She and Lydia hugged and fell to quiet whispering. Sometimes Layla would giggle. Wallace and H'Nuth sat with us, Sergeant Gorka staggered in, supported by her remaining troopers. They all looked beaten up. I don't think Gorka was fully conscious, her team picked a bit of floor and sank into slumps of exhaustion.

Well, I thought, that's it for us. No more freewheeling through the galaxy, chasing bad guys and rescuing fair maidens. I used sign language and asked Lydia to drag Layla closer to the centre of our little huddle, she looked surprised but shuffled along. Layla could translate for all of us.

A thought came to me, a wonderful, mean-spirited thought which should have been discarded, these words did not need to be said. We did not need a reminder of our helplessness. Naturally, my mouth opened up and I said to the Man in Black, "What are we going to do now, boss?" God, it felt good to get that out, to deflect any sense of hope away from me and lay it at the feet of the big guy.

The smug bastard smiled at me.

And so, we all sat around in the training room waiting to see what would happen. I was next to the boss when Captain Blund was brought in, along with his command crew. They all looked bloodied and bruised, a sure sign their capture had not been without cost. Captain Blund did not intend to go quietly into that long goodnight. Tough guy, I liked him.

The room gradually filled up with the remaining crew and any surviving Empire troopers. The cadets entered, being shepherded by Emilii; they were not the crying sort of children, they'd been down this road before. Last time it was slavers and a child rapist — ex-child rapist, I should say. I shot the bastard in the head in front of the kids so they might have some sense of safety from the world. Jeremy was standing next to me when the rest of the cadets rolled in and he decided to move over and join them. There were some hugs and soft mutterings of welcome and I thought I caught a glimpse of Jeremy slipping something to a couple of the other kids. Probably food.

Then came the NightWatch, or what was left of them. We'd obviously taken casualties and I saw lots of bandages and blood on faces and skulls. Still, the gang looked good, even though they were all shuffling along like the world's biggest losers. Definitely a defeated bunch, old, tired and used up. The girls among them were bedraggled and sported ripped clothing, every one of them wearing that wild eyed crazy look I've seen on those without hope.

Lying bastards, the lot of them — they were putting on an act, giving the Confederacy the old 'defeated and demoralised combatants' routine. I knew they were okay because Meataxe caught my eye and gave me knowing wink, if anyone else had seen it the jig would have been up. Meataxe does not do devious. I quickly looked away and found Magic staggering between two of the less hurt NightWatch. I thought about stepping closer to check on him but caught his look of warning.

The were a lying deceitful bunch, possessing no shame at all, every one of them a gold-plated ratbag. These were my people, I realised with quiet satisfaction, my tribe.

Finally, we were all seated on the floor, legs crossed and hands clasped on our heads. Lieutenant Ekveer was deep in conversation with a group of other people, I guessed this was the brains trust of the battle brig. Occasionally, fingers were pointed at various prisoners until they all finally nodded and another officer came over to the boss to give him a comm bead. This allowed him to have a discussion with the Confederate officer but I was restricted to understanding the boss.

The officer said something and the boss replied, “No, I’m not in charge here. Captain Blund over there,” he nodded to where the captain sat, staring daggers at all and sundry. “Captain Blund is the ranking officer, I am a passenger on the frigate.”

Another phrase came from the Confederate officer.

“No, I do not know where Lord Phillip, the Duke of Kent is,” said the boss. “Last I saw him, he was moving back to our assault shuttle.”

At this point, Phil walked in accompanied by Greenash, Sylvia and our wounded from the shuttle. Sylvia tucked her charges into a corner and sat protectively before them. Phil and Greenash came over to us.

The Confederate officer spoke again. The Man in Black responded with, “Yes, this is the duke. The man beside him is one of my team.”

Phil rolled up with his big smile, Greenash slunk down behind me and whispered something but I had no idea what it was. I did miss my comm bead.

Phil said something to the Confederate officer then pulled his own comm bead out of his ear and placed it in the officer’s outstretched hand. Another trooper went over to Sylvia and the lads to take theirs. Greenash hurriedly pulled his out and held it for anyone to take.

Fine examples of the NightWatch’s ability to give up.

Chapter 32

I COULD NOT SEE how we were going to get out of this mess. Confederate troopers lined the walls, all bottled up in their scary armour with huge weapons pointed our way. Looking around, I couldn't see anyone missing, Lydia had managed to shuffle over next to me and we leaned into each other for emotional support. I couldn't even talk to my girl since neither of us had a bead.

Bloody nanobots, when we needed them, they decided to stop working.

The boss said to the Confederate officer, "Sir, I have a proposition to make to you and your leadership." The officer looked puzzled but must have sent a message to the Confederacy leaders because three other senior looking guys wandered over. One of the guys turned out to be a girl. she appeared to be in charge.

She said a few words to the boss and I felt I could almost make them out. It was like a buzzing in my ears, a slight tingle in my body. What the hell were my nanobots doing?

The boss asked permission to stand up and was allowed to climb to his feet. I saw the whole thing from my position on the floor; I could see the boss change posture and become our leader, the man who could cow the entire NightWatch by a raised eyebrow. He turned to those of us near him and said, "This is the captain of the battle brig, the naval officer in charge of the entire force."

He turned back to the Confederate captain, bowed his head in respect and said, "My name is Lord Franz von Palmerland, I lead the Night-Watch. We are a company of police, we render security services to the Empire." He was interrupted by the female leader of the Confederacy saying something.

"No, captain," said the boss. "I am not offering our services to the Confederacy. I am attempting to explain our position to you. As I said, we supply security to the Empire. Part of our recent responsibility has been to safeguard Duke Phillip of Kent. We feel responsible for the ongoing safety and security of our frigate, the ship you now believe to have captured."

Another burst of language came from the female captain, she sounded a tad cross at first but then waved her hand around all us prisoners and gave a small laugh.

"Indeed," said the Man in Black. "I do understand why you believe you have us at your mercy. But let me assure you such is not the case. I stand before you to offer you, and all of your people, a chance to live. If you surrender yourself, your crew, your troopers and your ship to me, I will endeavour to guarantee your safety."

The Confederate movers and shakers exchanged glances before sharing a few chuckles before the female captain spoke again. I heard a murmuring in my ear, were my wee beasties getting their act together at last?

Hang on. If, as was indicated, my nanobots were coming back to do their job — how was this happening? The bursts we had received from PILOT when we invaded the *New Rome* had been severe and caused our internal comms to fall apart.

All who had been in the boarding party when we assaulted the giant intergalactic spaceship felt the little tingles as PILOT sent burst after burst into us; bursts which would have exploded any comm bead in our ears. But we weren't wearing comm beads during the assault, all we felt was the tingling and then the slow death of nanobots and the degradation of our comms, including the translation function.

So why was I now getting some noise? Were my little guys coming back to work? Where had the extra nanobots come from? Greenash thought the bursts from PILOT had destroyed all the nanobots but maybe some survived. And then they started to multiply again. Oh, God, I thought, my body is home to a sex orgy for wee machines as they hump each other and make more wee machines. I felt ill. This realisation took me a few seconds, I came back to focus in time to hear the boss give his ultimatum.

"Surrender now," he said, "or every one of you will die. There will be no prisoners. All your troopers, all your crew will die. And it will happen at my command." He held up one arm and made a pistol out of his right hand with the index finger pointing at the female captain.

This woman laughed and drew her own sidearm. She raised it to the boss's face and smiled, I could see her finger tightening on the trigger. Was this another time for me to do something else heroically stupid? I started to rise to my feet with some vague thought of taking them all on, stupid, stupid man that I am.

The Man in Black dropped his thumb, firing his pointed finger. Nice bit of drama, boss, I thought, at least you're going to go out with a significant hand gesture. I was on my feet and lunging towards the female captain when I saw her eyes widen.

She died.

They all died.

Around me, alongside the walls and everywhere there was a Confederate trooper or crewperson, they collapsed and died. Bodies slid to the floor, dozens, scores of bodies. There may have been over two hundred of them across both ships, crew and soldiers. Every one of them collapsed.

My bloodstream bubbled, I felt an ache run through my entire body, enough to have me double over in pain. I gasped, gritted my teeth and plunged to the floor as the wave of torment subsided. And it did feel like a wave, the pain peaked with a combination of tingling and itch and then subsided, faded away.

I knew what had happened. Caesar had sent a pulse into our ship, a big pulse capable of destroying delicate machinery and exploding comm beads.

Killing hundreds.

Chapter 33

SILENCE DESCENDED, THE WHOLE world went still. My heroic lunge and dive had stuttered to a halt as I fell down with the aftereffects of what had killed all those enemy troopers. All the rest of the prisoners remained sitting on the floor. Standing before us was the lone figure of the Man in Black, the only person on his feet.

Bodies lay around us, around him. All were slumped in that pose of utter relaxation — no, not relaxation, the pose of death. Some had slid down a wall to land in a semi seated position, I watched as one of the bodies slowly tilted to one side and collapsed. In front of the boss were the command cadre of the Confederate troopers, the captain of the battle brig and some undoubtedly big noises in their world. Now they were all quiet in the grasp of a death they had not expected.

The boss turned to Layla, bent down to her ear and whispered something. She nodded, he patted her shoulder gently, gave it a final squeeze and stood up straight again.

The last man standing.

A closer look at Layla's face showed me someone experiencing hell. I moved across, sat behind her and reached around to gather her in my arms. She leaned back into me and sobbed. "I didn't know," she whispered, "I didn't know." Lydia came and sat beside Layla, softly stroking her head. Slowly, Layla began to cry, the tears running down her cheeks and sobs wracking her frame.

"You weren't supposed to know," I told her. Lydia gave me a puzzled look. Not understanding anything except Layla's tears. "The boss had you talking to Caesar, didn't he?" I asked. The little girl nodded. "He told you to send a specific message to that giant bloody spaceship if he gave you a signal." Again, she nodded.

"He said he was going to mime shooting them with his finger," she said, her voice laden with anguish. "And when he did that, I was to communicate with Caesar and say 'Now'." She buried her head in her arms. "But I didn't know what was going to happen, Val!" She was pleading now, "I didn't know everyone was going to die!"

"He kept that from you, at least, the cold-hearted mongrel," I said. "Lord Franz von bloody Palmerland didn't want you to know in case you acted like someone with any decency." I got to my feet after leaning Lydia into Layla, others came and sat with them giving what comfort they could.

I strode over to the boss, he had remained standing, carrying the burden of what he had done. I watched him slowly scan the room, lingering on every dead body for a moment before moving on to the next. He was looking at what he had wrought, gazing squarely at the consequences of his actions. "Did Caesar know what you had planned?" I demanded.

"Not entirely. I allowed him to assume I may have wanted to take out a guard or two. Give a small demonstration of what the surge would do."

"Then why didn't you? Why didn't you do it differently, have them take out their comm beads and watch while the surge was sent through. Why not give a demonstration? Why go straight to killing? Killing everyone!" I had raised my voice, anger and spittle spewing from my lips.

"Have you forgotten who we are, Val?" He paused and looked at me, Magic, Teddy Boy and Right Honourable had joined us but no one was stepping between me and my tirade at the boss. "Have you forgotten how we keep the peace, enforce our will on those bigger, meaner and stronger than us?" He scanned our faces, he showed no emotion, no rancour, shame, embarrassment or anger. The ultimate stone face.

"Why do people hate to deal with the NightWatch?" he asked. "Why do the bad guys step softly around us?"

I sighed. I understood what he was saying, and it was true. He had given a visible demonstration of what the NightWatch could, and would, do.

"Because we are the biggest bastards around," I said.

"More than that, Val. This Empire is probably full of cruel and awful people, showing we were merely bad wouldn't be enough. We had to show we were worse than they could ever expect. I showed them," and here he nodded at Phil, Captain Blund and the rest of the Empire people, "I showed them who we really are. I showed them we are utterly ruthless."

He sighed, straightened up, adjusted his clothes and looked over to where Captain Blund was getting to his feet. "I better go and see what else we need to do. Right Honourable, come with me." He stepped forward, stopped and turned to face us.

"Just bear in mind, gentlemen," he said, "I am the biggest monster of all."

I don't want to be him anymore.

Chapter 34

I REMEMBER, FROM OSTEND and other godawful experiences, that period after a big explosion or fight. The sense of unreality, the buzzing in the ears, the feeling time has stood still. We didn't have the accompanying dirt and debris drifting down from the ceiling, but the emotional desolation was still the same.

Except for the old NightWatch, of course. These guys stood and stretched, wandered about looking for something to eat. Or drink. Meataxe had already begun to go through the dead troopers' gear and was soon joined by his all-female squad. He was passing on his valuable knowledge about looting the dead. Way to go, ladies.

Magic turned to me. "He had Caesar send through a surge, didn't he?"

"Yep," I said. "He knew Layla had her comm ability because she still has fully functioning nanobots. I guess he picked her rather than any of our guys because she has a brain. The ones from our side with functioning nanobots would not be the guys I would use to save the world. And those of us with half a brain have had our nanobots butchered by our recent frolic as we assaulted the *New Rome*. Goddamned stupid name."

"So, he had Layla ready to send the signal to Caesar. Hmm..." He scratched his chin, "Do you reckon Caesar knew his surge was going to kill so many?"

"Don't think so. I think the boss probably told him, or it — can we get some more pronouns, please? — I think the boss told him it was nothing big, probably told Caesar it would be a small, innocuous demonstration."

Magic looked over at where the Man in Black was deeply engaged in conversation with Captain Blund. "Our boy is something else, isn't he? Don't know if I could have given that order, to kill so many at once." He turned to me, studied my face for a moment and went on. "You, I'm not so sure about."

"Thanks a bunch, Mr Soul of Gentleness. And you can go screw yourself, too."

"Nicely said, Val." Magic looked around, noted the lack of direction from everyone, the aimlessness and shock. "I guess I better get this lot sorted out, give them something to do. I'll get Senior Sergeant Thulani to start running some pointless drills, possibly even the odd lecture."

"No, you won't," I said. "Thul can't communicate with anyone. No comm bead, remember? You'll have to use the old NightWatch and those of Meataxe's girls who have nanobots. Ones that work, anyway. And Layla, mustn't forget Layla."

"God, what a mess. Okay, I'll sort things out, I'll sprinkle the nanobot people throughout the rest of the gang; I'll give one to Thulani so he can shout orders. Layla can stay with the cadets and help keep them settled. Ted can stay with Sylvia, he might be able to run interference for her as she yells at everyone. Hmm, yeah, I've got a few ideas. What are you going to do?"

"Don't you want me to help out?" I was both surprised and relieved Magic hadn't delegated any tiresome task to me. Surprised because I was, you know, his sergeant — but mainly relieved because I am not good at bringing order into chaos.

He gave me a funny look. "You? Help out? Give me a break, Val. I know you'll start off with the best of intentions but after five minutes you'll have started a fight or some mad game involving lots of running and yelling. No, how about you shoot through."

I wanted to feel hurt, but I could see his point. Then I caught sight of Dragos wandering about. "I might leave you to it and speak to Dragos, find out what happened up there in the assault bay. I'm interested in learning why Nadia lost an arm and how Bazli was killed.""Good lad," murmured Magic. "Off you go, sunshine, make sure you're home before dark. Don't talk to any strangers and don't accept any sweeties from hairy men." We abused each other some more before drifting off on our separate ways.

I sidled up to Dragos and gently poked him on the shoulder. Since we had all removed our space armour — a stern directive from the now dead enemy troopers — I was able to poke my finger into his flesh to some depth.

"Oww!" he yelped, a yelp quickly cut off as he turned to see me grinning at him. "You are such a dick, Valentine!"

"You betcha, pal," I replied. "Tell me what happened up in the assault bay. What happened to Nadia and how on Earth did Bazli end up falling though to us with a hole in his chest."

He sighed, leaned back against a nearby wall and slowly slid down to a seated position. Other NightWatch were already sitting or lying around, I pushed one aside to give me some space — more bad words came my way — and settled in beside him.

"It was Bazli," he said. "He shot Nadia."

"Walk me through it, mate. Pretend I wasn't there, use small words."

He rolled his eyes, took a breath and went on. "Okay. Nadia and I were standing near the controls, keeping an eye on things. She suggested

I might be more useful watching the entrance door to the assault bay, away on the other side of the room."

"She got sick of you leering at her, didn't she? What happened, were you doing some heavy breathing in her ear?"

"Nothing like that!" He had taken offence, yawn, like I care. "I may — 'may', mind you — may have been standing a tad too close. She's a damn fine-looking woman, Val!""How the hell would you know, dipstick? She, and you, were both in space armour. Unless you had smoothly talked your way into some disrobing. Don't tell me, you didn't flash the old appendage, did you?"

His face took on a nicely mottled hue. "Bloody hell, Val! I wouldn't do that! For starters, you and Magic have made it abundantly clear what we can expect if we, er, make unwanted suggestions to any of the females. Or males, for that matter. Plus, and I emphasise this, I would never, NEVER, willingly expose myself as you suggest. And you are a complete low life to think I would." He dropped his chin in a sulk.

Bloody hell, I had gone too far, I had actually offended a member of the NightWatch. Who knew this could happen? I tousled his hair and said, "Sorry, Dragos. I can be insensitive sometimes. Go on with your story. I'll try to be better."

"Yeah, well, try real hard. Anyway, I went and huddled in a corner, there was a piece of heavy equipment near the doorway, so I hunched down behind it and kept an eye out. It was a good idea from Nadia, there were still a few random Confederate troopers wandering about."

"Let me get this straight. Nadia was standing near the seal over the assault hatch, probably near the control panel. And you were dozing off behind some machinery and pretending to be alert and watchful?"

"Still a dick, Valentine. But yes, that's about it. Oh, and there was the dead body of the trooper Nadia had shot. It was lying off to one side.""Okay, what happened next?"

"Yeah, right. Well, that's when one of our team entered, a trooper dressed all in armour but it was Empire armour, so I wasn't too worried. He crossed over to Nadia and they must have exchanged a few words. I don't know what was said because I wasn't in their comm loop."

"This new guy, he didn't use the suit's external speakers?"

"Nope, he walked over to Nadia and chatted, I went back to watching the door. That's what I was doing when the scuffle broke out. I looked around and saw Nadia pushing the new guy away, he wanted to get at the control panel. I moved out towards them when Bazli, because that's who the new guy was, pulled his pistol and shot Nadia."

"That dog's breath!"

"Yep, agree with you there. He didn't get a clean shot at her because he was using one hand to manipulate a control and the other to shoot. He'd never make it in Ted's group, we have to be accurate with both hands, no matter what.'"Yeah, great, Dragos, you're all rootin' tootin shootin' heroes. What happened?"

"Bazli hit a control, it must have been the one to slide back the covering panel because it began to slide back. Nadia was dancing around on top of it, trying to draw her weapon when Bazli got a shot off. It missed, well almost missed. The shot took her arm off and she screamed — I heard it through the external speakers — she dropped her weapon and fell to the floor. Then the panel slid open, and she fell through to where you guys were waiting. I understand her suit did some sort of seal and medical aid?"

"Yeah, she'll be alright. I saw her when she landed, the suit must have established the seal during her short fall. Damn, those suits are good. I understand she's receiving, or was receiving, medical treatment from the Confederacy guys before ... before ..."

"Before the boss killed everyone," he finished.

"Yeah, then. But how did Bazli end up falling after her with a hole in his chest?"

"Oh, that's easy, I shot the dork. He'd done his trick with the control panel and shot Nadia, so I knew he wasn't one of the good guys. My pistol was out and pointed at him before I realised it — Ted's training kicking in — all I had to do was pull the trigger."

"You didn't miss, then?"

He gave me a jaundiced look. "Ted's squad, dipshit. We don't miss. Not if you want to stay in his squad."

I patted him on the shoulder and then used it to lever myself up. "Well done, mate. I'll be sure to tell Magic what you did."

He brightened up. "Thanks, Val. Sometimes you can be almost ... okay."

"Let's keep that to ourselves, Dragos. I wouldn't want people to be going all soft and gooey on me. But how come you're still upright and breathing? I saw several Confederate troopers leap up into the assault bay after Bazli did his faceplant onto our deck."

"Yeah, I figured they might be a bit cross so, as soon as I saw them jumping up, I threw down my weapon and raised my hand. Plus. I did my best to look useless and harmless."

"Not a stretch there, mate."

"Dickhead ... uhh, Val," said Dragos. "What are we gonna do about all these bodies?"

I looked at him. I looked around the large room. Most of the people had left, I assumed Thulani had given them stuff to do. Probably colouring in pictures or join the dots puzzles, something critical. The boss and other movers and shakers had also shuffled off. Again, I assumed they wanted to find a more comfortable room to discuss whatever they needed to discuss. Someplace with large, comfortable chairs and snacks. I could do with a snack, myself.

Dragos elbowed me. Okay, where was I? Oh, yeah, surveying the room. The room now obviously containing dead bodies. Lots of dead bodies.

"Someone should do something, Val," said Dragos, he gave me the old look. Yeah, sure. That would be me. Got a mess to clean up? Call Valentine. Want someone killed? Call Valentine.

I should hang out a sign — dirty deeds, done dirt cheap.

Chapter 35

I BENT DOWN AND grabbed the shoulders of one of the bodies, perhaps I could pile them into some sort of neat heap. God, it was heavy. I could heave a normal body about without too much trouble — one of the key social acts in the City for members of the Watch was to move the morning's crop of dead people off the streets and into alleys. Or the river. Anywhere out of sight so the eyes of the burghers would not be offended. But these guys were in full armour which made them heavy. Bloody heavy.

"Grab his feet, Dragos," I commanded. He struggled with his one arm so I waved another bulky lad over to help. You can't have bulky lads standing around doing nothing, they might start to think for themselves.

Together we heaved and grunted and managed to lift the dead weight. Yes, I see what I did there. Then I dropped my end, this allowed Dragos to drop his and we were back to our starting positions. There was no way we could move all the bodies in this room without risking pulled muscles or other work-related injuries. I'm not a fan of work-related injuries, although, to be fair, that term usually has a different meaning while working for the NightWatch.

A hand tapped me on the shoulder, and I turned to see Sergeant Gorka standing behind me. In her other hand she held out a comm bead. I took it gratefully and stuck it into the appropriate orifice.

"Having trouble, fellas," she said, nodding at the recently dropped body. "Can't get it up anymore?"

Standing with Sergeant Gorka were several troopers and two sizable machine thingies. One of these was a large flatbed about the size of a big cart while the other was some sort of crane, an articulated post with a cable and hook at the end. Both were pushed by individual troopers who must have been extremely strong given these machines looked bloody heavy. Or they had lots of tiny wheels, or itty-bitty rockets to hold them up. Yawn.

"You want to step aside and let the professionals work?" said Gorka. Dragos and I stepped back and watched as they proceeded to use the crane to pick up a dead trooper and place the body on the cart. Each trooper's armour had a pair of loops integrated into the armour, one on top of each shoulder. The crane latched on to these, raised the body, swivelled it over to the cart where a pair of Gorka's team guided it into position. Soon they had a pile of neatly stacked dead people on the cart. Like firewood. Yukk.

"What will you do with them, Gorka?" I asked. The first cart thing slid away and another took its place. I bent down to look for little wheels and saw nothing except a shimmering glow under the cart. The damn thing hovered over the glow which allowed it to be manoeuvred by one person. These space people were clever bastards.

"Captain Blund told me to find somewhere on the battle brig to put them," she said. "We'll strip them of anything useful — armour, weapons, stuff like that." She looked at some of the nearby bodies. "I see your people have made our job easier in this regard. Been doing a little looting of the dead, Val?"

"I'm shocked, Gorka," I replied. "Shocked, I tell you; that you could think I would engage in such pursuits as robbing the dead." She shrugged which I took to be her complete indifference to the recent activities of Meataxe and his girls. "Where'd you get the comm beads, Gorka? I thought the surge destroyed them all.""Yeah, that surge is bad news. Fortunately, we keep spare beads, some on assault shuttles and others in special lockers on the ship. All these lockers are secure against any sort of electromagnetic pulse, it's a standard precaution."I didn't know what an electromagnetic pulse was and cared even less. "Do you have any more? Dragos could use one."

"Yes and no. We don't have enough for everyone, so Captain Blund told me to distribute them to officers. Naturally, I gave one to all the girls in Meataxe's squad because, well, because they're girls. I had one left over and thought about giving it to Jeremy because he's so cute."

"But you gave it to me because I'm important?" I prompted.

"Yeah, sure, dickhead, go with that dream. No, I couldn't be bothered to find the little guy, saw you two bozos and thought 'problem solved'. Now sod off and let my team work."

Dragos and I left them to it. We were both relieved to get out of that room of death until we hit the corridors and found more dead bodies against walls and in random rooms. Other carts and cranes were busy clearing away the consequences of the Man in Black's ruthlessness. I told Dragos to rejoin his squad wherever they were while I decided to do a small tour and check on the mental health of the NightWatch. Not that I cared, but it might make someone think I was interested in them. Mainly, I had nothing else to do and didn't want to be given a job, so I decided to look busy in case an authority figure wanted me to do something actually productive. It's all about appearances with officers. Never let them think you are standing around and relaxing, they hate that.

My first visit was to Meataxe and the girls, his terrifying women. I found them in their squad room, all seated on the floor in a circle. They were listening to one of their team, so I leaned against a wall and listened.

"Hello everyone, my name's Mary," said the girl.

Everyone responded in a clear voice, "Hello, Mary."

"When the frigate was boarded, I was in the galley with the cooks." She proceeded to describe her initial encounter with the Confederate troopers when they stormed into the galley, killing the two cooks and hitting her in the head. She was left unconscious and presumed dead, regaining consciousness after the enemy left the galley.

"So, I took some knives and went after them. Managed to kill two before I was restrained. Knives are good for slipping in the cracks in space armour. It's like Peter told us when he described how to kill those armoured knights on Earth. Thanks, Peter. That's my story." They all had a comm bead because Gorka liked girls and, for some unfathomable reason, some of these girls liked Gorka. Unbelievable.

Others mumbled similar thanks and then Peter — sorry, Meataxe; ridiculous the way these girls insist on using his proper name — said thanks and asked if anyone else wanted to share.

He saw me before calling on the next raised hand and said, "Hello, Val. We're having a debrief. Like one of our regular encounter sessions, want to join us?"

"Regular encounter sessions?" I asked. "You have these often?"

"Usually once a week," he replied. "Good for the emotional health of the team."

I scanned the faces of his 'team'. Looking back at me were about twenty of the most bloodthirsty women you could ever hope to meet. Or not, if you desired to keep on living. I was having enough internal warfare dealing with mood swings brought on by my damaged nanobots, I had no more emotional space to think that Meataxe — our most slovenly, disorganized, smelly, uncouth watchman — was running an encounter group for girls. My brain refused to consider it. Meataxe was smiling at me but his was the sole welcoming face, the rest of the girls stared back at me with various gazes covering the entire gamut of dislike and disgust. I could tell my presence was not required nor desired.

I left, tail between my legs.

I felt more bubbles in my body, this made me suspect my nanobots were again procreating. Pulling my comm bead out of my ear, I tried to message anyone on the off chance my wee beasties were back on the job, but there was no response at all. Teddy Boy's gang had a larger room larger than others because they said they had so much equipment, lots of guns and things which might explode. We agreed and hoped any blast would be contained within their walls.

As I entered their room, I caught a few words from some of the lads. Nothing definite but I distinctly heard phrases like, "Here's old what's his face' and 'It's Val! Look busy!' This cheered me up immensely because it meant my inner machines were slowly coming back together and getting on with the job. About time, too, the plonkers. To be safe, I plugged the comm bead back into my ear.

"Hi guys," I said, in my cheeriest voice. "Watcha doin?"

Some had still functioning nanobots, one of these looked back to me and muttered, "Cleaning." All heads were bent over large tables upon which rested a fearsome array of killing implements. Some I recognised, most I did not but I felt sure I could work out how to operate each weapon if needed. I reached for one.

A set of censorious murmurings surrounded me until a clear voice said, "Please don't touch anything, Val," I stopped my hand over the weapon for which I was reaching and looked into the speaker's eyes. She was a small, nugget of a woman, black hair, aquiline nose and a rather fierce cast to her visage, she must have had nanobots. I think I detected small fangs although this could have been my imagination. I pulled my hand back.

"Sorry, what?" I queried.

"We would prefer it if you did not manhandle the weapons, sergeant," said the wee girl. "They are sensitive to severe knocks and cannot withstand harsh treatment.""What makes you think I would pursue a 'harsh treatment' course of action?"

"Is your name Valentine?"

"LUCILLE," I said, for that was this slip of a girl's name, "I outrank you, I am also bigger than your slight stature." I grinned at her. "I can pick up any damn thing I wish."

"Touch anything on this table," said Lucille, "and I'll kick you so hard in the crutch that Lydia will looking for your pecker with magnifying instruments." She smiled back at me, fangs were in evidence.

"Lucille," I asked, "are you a vampire?"

"Sod off, Val," she replied. "Ted's over there checking on our new toys. Go and annoy him." She returned to her work but gave me a parting shot, "No, I'm not a vampire but I do have prominent canine teeth. Good for biting idiotic sergeants."

Lucille is one of my favourite people in Ted's squad, she's feisty, brave, cheeky and unstoppable. And slightly terrifying.

Teddy Boy was indeed hunkered down examining some inner part of his new toy, the assault cannon we had purloined from the battle brig. Looking around, I spotted several other new things which I suspected were once the property of the Confederacy but had now fallen accidentally into the arms of this light-fingered squad. And they were all weapons, I suspected. Nothing as trivial as armour, food or other vaguely useful trinkets. If it didn't go bang, Ted and his lot were not interested.

I chatted with Ted for a few minutes in my never-ending endeavour to raise morale. But their morale was fine, no one was too affected by the copious number of bodies we had witnessed. No one was disturbed by the Man in Black's casual destruction of over a hundred human beings. No, give this bunch some toys and their minds and hands were happy. I left them to their arcane ceremonies and left their room. As I walked past Lucille's worktable, I knocked a pistol onto the floor and managed to escape with the normal level of abuse ringing in my ears.

You take your fun where you can.

Next were the cadets, our seemingly endless bunch of preteens and assorted little guttersnipes. I entered their room to find them playing some sort of game with H'Nuth, our resident Tharl. H'Nuth was a good guy, albeit one who looked like a devil — red skin, little horns, protruding teeth and muscles on top of other muscles. And he was head and shoulders taller than me. Talking to H'Nuth meant speaking to his chest and interpreting the bass growls he gave off. Heck of a guy.

The kids were trying to see how many could climb on him before he collapsed, or until they all fell over. He had about ten on his head and shoulders with Jeremy playing a fierce game of 'king of the hill' from atop H'Nuth's head. Patrica was yanking the little snot's ankle, endeavouring to pull him off so he might fall to his death. He replied by kicking her in the face. Other children climbed the Tharl's legs, thighs and other body parts while Emilii sat nearby on a large, comfortable looking chair and smiled at them all.

Everything normal here.

"All good, Emilii?" I asked. She gave me a thumbs up so I decided to leave them to it. As I left their room, Paticia gave a yell of triumph and supplanted Jeremy on top of the big guy's head. He stopped his death dive by catching hold of another cadet's waist where they both hung on and screamed about fair play. H'Nuth kept smiling and occasionally giving a reassuring growl. The idiot loved the cadets, and they loved him.

Bloody kids.

Chapter 36

MY LAST VISIT WAS for Lonely and his bunch of goody two shoes. Lonely was an aberration for the NightWatch — alert, organised, efficient and always correctly turned out. His squad attracted those men and women who believed in doing things the right way, things like being on time for duty, wearing clean underwear and thinking before acting. All the stuff with which most of us have minimal knowledge.

I paused before entering their room, taking a moment to mentally readjust my thinking from slovenly casual to alert and efficient. I pushed open the door, walked in and stopped in surprise. The room contained three people, Lonely and two of his squad.

"Sergeant Lonely," I said, using my most soldier like voice, "Where is your squad?"

"It's Sergeant L'On-li," he replied. "And most of my squad is dead or wounded."

This was not the happy homecoming I was expecting. "What happened, mate?"

He sat down at the table in the centre of the room, asking his two squad members to join him. His face wore that look I had seen in my own mirror far too often. The loss of those with whom you served, the questioning of why it was all necessary, the furious demands to God about it all. The whole thing. Usually, it was followed by lots of alcohol or other drugs, anything to make the pain go away. But Lonely and his people did not go down that route, they were upright, decent, hardworking men and women. Why they stayed with the NightWatch was beyond me.

We all sat together, I let the silence settle with us. Silence can be healthy, there is no need for every group of people to be always talking. Sometimes it is best to shut up and be together, I believed this was one of those times.

Lonely took a breath and began to speak. "My squad was spread out on various duties when the frigate was attacked. It was our turn on the rotation of guard duties, so we were scattered throughout the ship. When the assault was made, we, well, we did our best. I had teams of two doing random patrols when the assault happened. No particular reason, we weren't concerned about anything, I thought we should be doing something productive."

I didn't say anything, no point.

"As a result, several of my teams were taken out quickly, before we even knew what was happening. I know I lost six people in the initial attack with another four being wounded. They're in sick bay now with Sylvia."

"How many left?" I asked. "How many fit and capable of duty?" I kept my voice on an even level, straightforward, soldierlike and all business. No compassion in any of my tones.His eyes flared at my question. And it was a dick question, I was indicating all I was interested in was who could front up and do the job. I wasn't, but I wanted to see how Lonely was coping. Hence, my verbal prod. If he was over the edge, I needed to know about it. If he raged at me then he would have to be pushed to one side. Protracted fighting in confined spaces takes a toll on the mind, far more than the body. The sense of uselessness, of never-ending toil, the blackness of eternal night closing in. If a leader gave way, then all who followed would collapse in despair.

I needed to know if Lonely was falling apart. I wasn't concerned about his squad, they would follow his lead, he set the standard. I needed leaders who could look that beast in the eye, and spit in it.

His eyes held mine for a moment, the anger fading as he saw something else in mine. "You continue to be a first-class dick, Sergeant Valentine," he said, his voice calm and controlled. Not the control of a person about to run amok with the good scissors, but the voice of someone with a deep strength, the voice of a leader.

"I have four people in sick bay and six dead. Damien and Zoe here are my ready reaction team," he nodded to the two troopers beside him. Both looked beaten down but not defeated. Exhausted but not finished yet. Good people. "My last four I sent to the brig, we're still responsible for at least one of the prisoners."

The prisoners! I had forgotten about them. I'm glad Lonely is such a stickler for doing his job. I was aware of two prisoners, Mr Grey and S'eenyur, the Anipe working with Greenash. And then, I remembered, there was the mysterious woman who had come aboard with Phil, the lying greasy toad. Was she in a cell somewhere? Were they all dead with exploded comm beads?

I stood up. "I need to go to the cells, L'On-li," I said. "You three come with me and show me the way."

Lonely gave me a surprised look, and it could have been for a couple of reasons. One, my correct pronunciation of his name, and two, the fact I had no idea where the cells were on the frigate. A serious sergeant would know all this stuff. Yep, that's not me. He didn't say anything, stood up, waved at his two troopers and took us out of the room. I did see a little smile on his face. "You do good work, L'On-li," I said to his back as I followed him and the other two.

And then, because I am, indeed, a dick, I added, "Try not to stuff it up."

We walked the corridors and saw again the detritus of battle. Scorch marks on the walls, sometimes an appendage or blood smear plastered across the floor. Bodies were becoming less and less frequent, a sure sign Gorka and her efficient team had been on the job. I found the lack of other people remarkable. Sure, we occasionally encountered a crewperson or a pair of troopers patrolling but nowhere near the level of activity I had seen when we first embarked on the frigate. Way back then, dirt, dust and grime had been attacked with passion. Walls gleamed, floors were litter free, people moved with a relaxed sense, that stance which comes from knowing one is safe.

Now, the place looked beaten up. Even the air held particles of mist or rubbish as the circulation system grappled with the many noxious weapon discharges. And the smell of open wounds and flowing blood. Not as much as would have been observable back on Earth in any city undergoing a siege; back then, filth, grime, pus and blood were what we called the floor.

Eventually, we came to a secure door. Lonely produced one of those magic cards and slid it through a slot, the door opened and in we went. This room was obviously a holding space or reception area for people being processed before heading into a lock up. Two of Lonely's people were in the room, both with weapons aimed at us as we entered. On seeing their boss, they lowered their guns, an action for which I was deeply grateful. In any other squad, I would have been apprehensive about receiving some friendly fire but not with Lonely and his team. They were quiet, stable people who didn't leap about and yip at the first hint of outrage. I thought they were all incredibly boring. Safe, but boring.

"Anything to report?" asked Lonely.

I understood what he was saying because of the comm bead in my ear, and I knew Lonely had one. But these guys were rank and file. Unless they had functioning nanobots then they would not be able to understand Lonely or communicate with anyone else.

Unless they shared a common language. And now I could see the cleverness of Lonely and why I was pleased with him as a squad leader. One of the people, a man, spoke back to Lonely in his own tongue. This guy must be from Lonely's language group. My clever lad must have paired up his team so at least one of them could communicate with others. Smart lad,

"Mr Grey is alive and well, moving around and talking although we have no idea what he is saying," said one of the guards, obviously one of those who could understand Lonely's lingo. God, this language stuff is confusing. Come on, nanobots, I mentally urged. Go forth and multiply, you little reprobates.

"The female in unresponsive," continued the guard. "She is lying on her bed, still covered from head to toe. We haven't gone into her cell as you ordered so we don't know if she is alive or dead." Lonely grunted, looked at me for direction. I returned his stare with one of my many blank looks, perfected over conversations with anyone asking me a question.

"Right," Lonely grunted at me. "No help from you, as usual, you waste of space." My mouth twitched as I endeavoured to hide my smile.

He turned back to his team. "Bring Mr Grey out here, let's have a look at him." We stood around as his orders were carried out until a fragile and slovenly Mr Grey stood before us.

"Val!" he exclaimed. "So good to see you! What's been happening? Have we been attacked?" he attempted to come within hug range but one of the guards held him back.

"Mr Grey," I said, "Stand still for a moment, would you?" He couldn't understand me without a comm bead, but I'm a master of nonverbal communication. I pushed him in the chest, making him stagger back a few steps. I turned back to Lonely because my mind finally dragged some of the previous conversations up for the brain to consider. "Lonely, what's this about a female prisoner? Who is it? Have you identified her yet?""No, Val, it's that woman brought aboard by Phil. Remember your little interview with the heir to the throne in the corridors before you kicked the shit out of Bazli? I hear he's dead now, the little creep.""Not a lot of give in you, is there. Lonely? Not brimming over with the milk of love and kindness."He looked at me, leaning into the look. Eyes slightly narrowed, shoulders hunched. He was a well set up young man, originally all shiny and new until he joined the NightWatch and became the formidable lad now standing before me. Good shoulders, slim waist, uniform all present and correct, face clean shaven and a look that could either melt a girl's heart or quell a member of the Watch.

I was proud of him.

"Look who's talking," he said. "Sergeant Valentine of the Night-Watch, a man who walks with violence as others breath air. Valentine, I honour you, but I never want to be you."

Yet another fan. "Yeah, righto, Lonely, fair comment," I said. "But if we could move on, we may still have some issues to deal with."

"What issues?""Well, who is this woman?" I asked. "And how did this frigate get ambushed by that bloody battle brig? Was it Bazli, letting them know where we were?"

"Bazli? He was a lowly trooper, nothing more than a corporal on his best day. Are you saying he was some sort of superspy?"

"I'm saying, mate, there are still a few mysteries about this ship, these prisoners and our bloody situation. The reason we have survived is because we have the Man in Black, a complete and utterly ruthless man. A leader who is not afraid," I may have emphasised this last word, "to take the big decisions and carry out the most godawful acts. I'm okay on a one-to-one killing basis, but the boss kills by the hundred. And we should be bloody grateful."

I realised I was raising my voice and stepping about the room in a possibly aggressive manner. I took a breath and tried to calm down.

"Val, for goodness' sake," said Lonely, "Get a grip. You're prowling around like a mad dog. No one feels safe around you anymore."

"GOOD!" I spat. Another pause as I realised I was holding my hammer in one hand and my knife in another. Whoops. I put them away, swallowed, calmed my voice down to a rasping croak and ordered, "Okay, now show me this bloody woman. I want to see what one of Phil's, or the Emperor's, girlfriends look like."We walked to a solid door after ordering Mr Grey to shut his face and wait in the corner. A large guard stood near him, to prevent him making a stupid mistake. Grey was a tech geek, not a fighter but you never can tell with these guys. He might have a sharp pencil concealed on his person — I'd seen what Wallace could do with a pencil. Still, there's a world of difference between Grey and Wallace. I think. I hoped.

My head hurt.

I opened the little viewing slot in the armoured door and peered in. Sure enough, the woman was stretched out on the bunk against the far wall. Her back was to us and the door, it was impossible to see any signs of life. Perhaps she was dead or unconscious?

"Anyone been inside, Lonely?" I asked. "Any of your guys done something nasty to her?"

"No, sergeant," he replied. I noted the form of address and understood I was back to being his heavily worried about superior. "Captain Blund set up security for this prisoner. Or rather, one of the lieutenants did. He organised the guards, the food and everything. We were given clear instructions to stay out of the cell; we couldn't even look in through this slot."

"Right," I said. "Open the door." He paused, I understood he was considering my order as a request, especially as my order went against those of Captain Blund. A small refresher on my authority level was called for, "Open the bloody door, Lonely!" I snarled.

My voice must have contained the required amount of menace because he nodded to one of his team. This guy stepped forward and did something with the door controls.

The door opened and I walked in. "Stay outside," I said, over my shoulder. "Keep the door open and kill her if she ..." I paused, unsure what to say.

"If she ... what?" asked Lonely. "Says harsh things to you? Gives you a well-deserved slap? Val, do you honestly think this girl is capable of taking on a thug of your calibre."I stiffened, because the girl had rolled over and removed her masking headdress. Poo, bum, tit, fart ... enema.

"Yeah," I replied to Lonely. "I reckon she could. And then she would go through you lot like a dose of salts." The girl stood up, unclipped her covering garment and stood before us in a figure-hugging dress. A red dress. She smiled.

"Why, Sergeant Valentine, what a pleasure to see you again," she said. "And in such good health, too."

I felt my bum go into full pucker mode.

"Hello, Louise," I snarled. "You bitch."

Chapter 37

It was indeed Louise, the sadistic, seductive and possibly psychopathic member of the criminal fraternity known as 'The Syndicate'. A fraternity which no longer existed. A fraternity which had tortured me over many days before I escaped and then freed their child slaves. They had been using children to transfer black market nanobots around the planets with no regard to whatever damage the bloody machines would do to their young bodies.

God, I hated nanobots.

Now she stood before me, one hip gracefully posed in a possibly unconscious stance, the one which had caused many men to miss the evil in her eyes. They usually found out when she slipped a knife into their ribs, or worse.

"Why, Val, darling," she husked, "is that any way to greet an old friend. After all we've been to each other? I thought we could move past our unpleasantness. How about we start again?" she bent forward and jiggled, her cleavage bubbling over and her lips wet with desire. Louise was the whole package.

I stepped back out of the room and slammed the door shut. For good measure, I slammed the small viewing hatch shut and ensured everything was bolted down. For some moments, I stood with my head against the door, breathing heavily and trying to get my emotions back under control. Louise could make you want to bed her and kill her in the same moment. I generally leaned towards the 'kill' option.

A soft voice behind me coughed. "You okay, Val?" asked Lonely. "Isn't that ... Louise?"

My eyes were having trouble, some sort of red mist covered my vision. I pushed past Lonely and snarled, "Keep that door locked, including the viewing port. No one, I mean NO ONE, is to enter that cell. Or I will kill them — and then you, Sergent L'On-li." I left them standing with mouths open in surprise.

As I left the area I heard Lonely say, "We're in trouble, people, he is off the deep end. Everyone, stay away from this cell."

I travelled in a sea of rage, the red mist over my eyes but not impeding my vision. I entered the bridge area, brushing past the trooper on duty who must have recognised me, or the state I was in. A quick glimpse of the bridge showed no sign of Captain Blund or the boss but two other troopers stood guarding the door to their little conference room. I moved towards the door, noticing the two guards making a soft movement with their hands, a gentle suggestion I might like to stop and ask for entry.

To hell with that. As I came closer, I stepped between the two of them and gave the guy on my right a closed fist punch to his ear, full force, no holding back. As he was falling, I used my other fist to do the same to the other, now surprised, guard. He, too, collapsed. I pulled out my hammer and kicked the door open.

My entrance must have caused a slight stir to the room's occupants. Captain Blund was seated at the far end of the small conference table with the Man in Black and Right Honourable seated down one side. Along the other side sat two of the frigate's lieutenants, I don't know their names — there used to be three of them but one died from an exploding comm bead when we first met Caesar and his mad mate,

PILOT. Standing against the wall behind Captain Blund was Sergeant Gorka taking a guard stance. Those seated at the table turned to look at who this clod was kicking their door in. Right Honourable and the Man in Black were already on their feet because that's how you get to stay alive in our profession — quick reaction times. The other officers were beginning to move their chairs back, but my eyes went to Gorka and the person seated with his back to me. Phil. Bloody Phil, liar extraordinaire.

But Gorka needed some attention, she was beginning to draw her sidearm, too slow, far too slow. I threw my hammer at her, the damn thing had a spike on one side plus another spike at the end of the handle; either of these would kill her if they hit her unprotected body. None of the troopers I had encountered so far had been in any armour, this meant Gorka could easily die in the next few moments. I wasn't intending to kill her, but I didn't care. The red mist was singing through my head and my ears. I was raging.

The hammer hit Gorka in the nose, the head of the weapon landing with a solid thunk but mercifully avoiding hitting her with any sharp bits. Still, her nose squashed and a colourful stream of blood burst forth as she dropped her pistol. I know about broken noses, having picked up a few myself over the years. It's not the pain and blood which incapacities you, it's the fact your eyes tear up in sympathy. The whole face howls in protest, plus it's awfully embarrassing. This meant Gorka was out of action for a few moments, giving me time to fully enter the room.

I grabbed Phil by the shoulders, flung him out of the chair and against a wall. As he stuttered to a halt I was on him, spinning him around so he was standing with his back to the wall and my war knife at his throat. My huge war knife, a thing of beauty. I jammed the point slightly into his throat causing him to stand on tip toes and attempt a brief growth spasm. I believe he said something like "Ungh.

"YOU BASTARD!" I roared. "YOU UTTER, UTTER BASTARD!" I could hear movement behind me, undoubtedly the rest of the gang were drawing weapons ready to shoot me down like the mad dog I was. The red mist never wavered. "That woman you brought on to this ship!" I screamed, "You knew who she was! You never once told ..." I stopped and stuttered, my rage too much for my tongue. "I should kill you right now, you complete and utter arsehole!'"

"Sergeant Valentine!" snapped the voice of Captain Blund. "Stand down! Release His Lordship at once or we will have to shoot you down."

"Go ahead," I snarled back, my voice struggling through the mess of my emotions. "But I'll still be able to stick my knife into the throat of this sack of pus." I demonstrated my intent by pressing the blade's tip in another finger width allowing a trickle of blood to seep out. Phil's eyes swivelled around seeking help, he gurgled and we smelled his out-of-control bladder.

Two people pushed themselves against the wall alongside Phil, I didn't take any action because my brain must have registered not only who it was but what they were doing. It was the Man in Black on one side of me and Right Honourable on the other. And they were not facing me, not pulling at my arms, not holding any weapon on me. No, their eyes were directed back into the rest of the room, and both had weapons drawn but facing away from me. They were not trying to intercede with me, not interested in rescuing Phil, not at all concerned with stopping whatever brand of crazy I was displaying. Their weapons were aimed at everyone else in the room, not at me.

They were backing me up. Because that's what mates do.

"I suggest," came the calm voice of the Man in Black, "that everyone settles down. Captain Blund, you will notice I have a pistol aimed at you. And I am sure Sergeant Gorka is aware Right Honourable has his aimed at her chest. We are both happy to shoot you down where you stand. Perhaps everyone could raise their hands for me? And place them on your head, interlacing the fingers."

I didn't move, my gaze fixed upon Phil and his now shiny face, his face spotted with runnels of sweat. Behind me, I heard movement.

"Excellent," said the boss. "Sergeant Gorka, would you be so kind as to shut that door. You may appraise others of our situation but do please ensure no one attempts to interfere with Sergeant Valentine. The results would be catastrophic to all in this room." I heard the door shut.

"Lord Franz," said Captain Blund, his voice carrying a mixture of astonishment and resolve. "Sergeant Valentine has one of the heirs to the Empire with a knife against his throat. Such a threat carries a mandatory death sentence. Surely, you are not going to stand by and let His Grace be killed by ... by ... this man?"

"Let me make myself perfectly clear, "said the boss. "I stand with Sergeant Valentine." A small rumble of agreement came from Right Honourable's throat. "If he does end up killing Lord Phillip Kent, then I shall be fully supportive of such an action, consequences come what may. To be clear, the fact he is the son of Prince Clarence of Arenburg and tenth in line of succession to the throne of the Empire carries no weight with me."

"But why has he done this? What possessed him to take such an action?"

"I have no idea," said the boss. "But I trust Val. To the death."

Right Honourable growled agreement, "What he said," nodding towards the boss.

Wow. The red started to recede from my eyes. Somehow, knowing I had two people ready to die beside me, without any question, hesitation or reservation was calming me down. Plus, I had Phil at my mercy so that's a win.

I started to speak but managed a guttural growl. I swallowed and tried again. "Sir," I said, making it clear I was talking to the Man in Black and not to any other authority figure, "I discovered the identity of the female prisoner. The one brought aboard by Phil."

"Ah, yes," said the boss, "we all thought it was one of his girlfriends."

"Might still be," I said. Part of me was intrigued by my own calmness. Although my arms, the knife and my grip on Phil never wavered, I was regaining control over my mind and body. Not so bent on a mass killing spree. But I understood the urge was below the surface, the beast ready to emerge at a moment's notice.

"It's Louise," I finished.

Phil slumped. Not much, given my grip and the location of the knife, but it was a slump, A slump of defeat, of resignation. He opened his mouth to speak so I released one hand, kept the knife plunged gently into his neck and hit him across the ear.

"Shut your lying sack hole of a mouth, you conniving worm," I said. "Do not say a word. Not one bloody word."

Silence descended. I felt the tension from the boss and Right Honourable. Not tension caused by any of the room's inhabitants. Not tension brought on by the need to keep everyone under control. No, this tension was caused by the knowledge that this frigate held Louise, the woman capable of peeling the skin off a prisoner and transmitting the vison and screams to a waiting world. And more. And worse.

I know. I had been that prisoner.

Chapter 38

I STOPPED TALKING, WONDERING what was going to happen next, knowing my rage had placed us at a delicate point. I did not doubt the Man in Black and Right Honourable would kill anyone in this room if push came to shove. I also did not doubt that, if we went down that route, I would ram my blade into Phil's brain.

That's a lot of death. A lot of death with big consequences. I couldn't see the Empire welcoming us with open arms after I had filleted one of the family. And I was damn sure Gorka would charge into our guns, she would not go down easy but go down she would. And what then? Wholesale slaughter as the NightWatch were either attacked or took out everyone else. Where would that leave us?

We would be left alone on this frigate, still attached to the battle brig. Sure, Lydia might be able to keep us alive for a while but essentially, we would have neutralised anyone with the skills needed to fly this conglomeration of potential space junk. Stories would be told about us after our desiccated corpses were discovered by some wandering explorer. We might even go into legend.

God, my mind infuriates me sometimes.

"Boss," I said, speaking softly out the side of my mouth, "I might need your help in getting us out of this one."

"You think?" muttered Right Honourable.

"Yeah, no worries," said the boss. "Want me to take over now? You good? Back with us again?"

I nodded, swallowed and nodded again. "Yeah, I might keep my knife against Phil's throat but, aside from that, I'm stable. Reasonably stable. Don't ask me to do anything complex."

"Like thinking before acting?" asked Right Honourable.

"Like asking me bloody stupid questions, you po faced son of a ..." I reined it in. "Sorry, mate. I seem to fly into a rage whenever I'm threatened."

"Noted, "said Right Honourable. Then he raised his voice, to the rest of the room. "Sergeant Gorka, if you keep slipping your hand towards that weapon, I shall shoot you dead." He took a breath, "Now listen to me, everyone," he was speaking calmly, authority and integrity rolling off him in waves, "Sergeant Valentine has discovered a serious danger to this ship. A passenger, or prisoner — not sure which — is aboard, and this person is exceedingly dangerous."

When did my mate acquire this level of calm authority. He was speaking in decisive tones, being reasonable and direct. He was being a leader. Hanging around the boss all this time must have rubbed off on the lad. I've been around the Man in Black for a long time, but I hadn't improved my leadership ability at all, I certainly couldn't do the stuff he does. He thinks, I hit. Must be hard being him.

As I was engaged in this silent debate, the boss spoke up. "Thank you, lieutenant, I'll take it from here." Heck, was Right Honourable doing his little dialogue to give the boss some thinking time? Probably, because both are devious low life mongrels. But how did they communicate this plan? I was out of my depth in this company.

"Please listen to me carefully," said the boss. "If we remain calm and take things slowly, we may all live to see another day. And if we don't, well, I'm ready to die. Not a problem."

He stopped talking and waited. I don't know why he waited, but he did. I felt the atmosphere in the room change, people exhaled, I could hear behind me the sounds of bodies shifting. Finally, I heard Captain Blund's voice.

"We cannot negotiate," said Captain Blund, "while Sergeant Valentine holds His Grace at the point of a knife. Release the prince, and we may be able to talk."

"Yeah ... no, we won't be doing that," said the boss. "What we will do is all sit down at this table. When we are all seated and you are suitably disarmed, I will ask Sergeant Valentine to move the prince into a chair. But he will stay standing behind him with that marvellously sharp blade held against His Grace's neck. At that point, I shall ask Val to tell us what he has found."

Neither the boss nor Right Honourable had moved, their weapons remained steady, their voices calm, their breathing even. No hint of wild-eyed panic, simply the irrevocable message that here were two bloody scary people capable of any level of immediate, outrageous violence.

God, I love being in the Watch.

There was a bit of back and forth banter, feeble attempts at negotiation, but they were up against a master. The Man in Black was used to dealing with the royal courts of Earth, rooms full of conniving, backstabbing, traitorous swine. A few naval officers and one musclebound sergeant didn't even make him break a sweat.

And so, we gathered around the table as directed. I made sure Phil knew I hated him, a small incentive for good behaviour. He sank into his chair with a slightly wet splosh from the damp patch between his legs, I didn't mention it then but would at some point. His legs trembled with stress and nerves. And fear.

"In your own time, please, Sergeant Valentine," said the Man in Black. He was leaning back in his chair, shoulders down, arms comfortably resting on the table. On the floor behind him was a pile of weapons from the assembled officers and Sergeant Gorka. She was a peach, she had given up another pistol and several knives. Terrific gal.

One of the boss's hands was resting on his own pistol as it sat on the table. The barrel still pointed at Captain Blund — accidently, I'm sure. Yeah, right.

Further along the table was Right Honourable, across from him sat Gorka who had, at our lad's terse instruction, placed both her hands on the table top, palm down, fingers splayed out. Right Honourable kept his pistol in his hand and pointed directly at Gorka.

That left the two naval lieutenants sitting between their captain and Gorka. Of these two guys, I knew one due to him being the officious prick who had met us when we first boarded the frigate. The other guy was slightly smaller, his uniform rumpled and his reddish hair plastered by sweat across his skull. I gathered my two mates did not feel these two presented the same level of threat as Gorka. Probably right, but I could throw my knife at either of them with both accuracy and force. I saw them flicking their eyes to me and the knife so I waved it to them briefly before pricking Phil's ear again. I also threw in a small smile, keeping things civilised. The first lieutenant sneered but his companion, the second lieutenant, shuddered.

I took a breath and started speaking. "We discovered in the cells, both Mr Grey and Louise. Mr Grey we knew about, we have a good relationship with him and he has never given us any trouble. Sergeant

L'On-li's squad had been responsible for his security and there had been no problems. I understand he is travelling to the capital to give evidence against the remaining members of The Syndicate, a group led by Phil's batshit crazy relative who likes to run criminal enterprises."

The room had settled into a state of tolerance now. No one had died in the last few minutes so they probably thought they were safe. Ahh, the folly of youthful dreams, we'd kill them in a heartbeat.

"Tell us about Louise," said the boss. "How do you know her?" Okay, it was going to be like that, was it? The boss wanted me to recount my awful experiences, I got that. But how far did he want me to go?

"And don't leave out anything to do with necks or biting," he said. Damn, I was going to have to tell them of a few of my darker deeds.

Okay, so be it. I talked for some time, describing my capture by the Syndicate and their subsequent plan to torture me to death over days or weeks. One of the highlights of this little project was the presence and guiding hand of Louise. It didn't take much for me to highlight her joy in the whole 'torture Valentine' thing, given she stage managed these unpleasant sessions — and sometimes joined in with enthusiasm. I included the salient fact that the whole thing was transmitted to screens through some sort of computer network. I dunno, people don't want to sit and talk anymore; everyone is on a screen somewhere.

Then I described my escape, including the ripping out of the chief torturer's throat with my teeth. I told them of rescuing the kids, our eventual escape — with the assistance of Mr Grey —and the capture of Louise.

In some future, I shall recall, with some satisfaction, the slow understanding as it dawned on each of my listeners' faces, the understanding they had, as guest or prisoner, a nightmare. Even Sergeant Gorka looked a little green when I hit some of the high points of the sessions.

Phil, I wasn't so sure about. Had he known who she was? He always claimed the mastermind of the criminals was his wayward look alike relative and he had supplied evidence to this fact. Evidence which satisfied people I trusted but all and sundry knew my judgement was poor. Bloody stupid, in fact.

Phil may have been in on the whole thing.

As I mused on this concept, I felt his shoulders shaking. So much so I withdrew the knife because his agitation could easily have sent the blade into his neck, thus ensuring a messy end for all concerned. I stepped back to check on the lying bastard, wondering what was going on with the conniving snot.

He was crying. Huge wracking sobs, his nose running, eyes streaming and he shook his head over and over again. "I'm sorry, Val," he was husking, "I'm so sorry. I had no idea ..." then he'd gurgle some more.

"And that, gentlemen and sergeant," said the Man in Black, "is why Sergeant Valentine was so understandably upset when he discovered that this ... individual ... was present on this ship. With the full knowledge of both you, Captain Blund, and you, Phil, you deceitful nosewipe."

He let silence reassert itself, everyone composed themselves, Phil blew his nose a few times and we all relaxed some more. Except for the boss and Right Honourable, they never relaxed their willingness to shoot the bastards. The benefit of experience and living with treachery on a daily basis.

Finally, Phil spoke in a halting voice. As he went on, he sounded more composed and his tones became closer to that of someone with authority both on this ship and in the Empire. "I did know of Louise's identity," he said. "But only as a member of the criminal fraternity. She had contacted me through her legal team and offered to surrender more information on the Syndicate and its tentacles on other worlds. Since she was a high-ranking member of this group, second to my cousin Egbert, I agreed to her offer. I deemed her information was of such significance it merited taking her to the capital for a possible interview with the Emperor — given her testimony would implicate a member of the royal family."

"What about Mr Grey?" I asked. "Wasn't he going to give the same sort of evidence?"

"Yes, "said Phil. "That's why he was on this frigate and Louise was with me on my yacht, I wanted them to testify separately with no chance of collusion. While I recognise Mr Grey has been of some service to us since aiding in Valentine's escape, he was still a criminal. Albeit a low-level operator. Louise was in another category. Of course, when I learned of the presence of the battle brig in the area, I was forced to move her onto this frigate for safety, while I endeavoured to locate our missing scout ship and contact Caesar.""Hell, Phil," I said, "How do you keep so many balls in the air? You're running around in your swanky yacht playing at being a rich, playboy doctor and being an idle royal with the necessary parties and lifestyle. At the same time, you're hatching plots to transport high ranking criminals like Louise — and then you go and attempt to make first contact with an intergalactic diplomat."

"Yeah," he agreed. "Not a lot of downtime in my line of work."

"Plus, you have to run little errands for the Emperor. Errands which allow you to invoke his authority and give orders to Captain Blund. Who the hell are you, Phil?"

"I'm just a messenger," he replied. "As I've told you many times."

"Bullshit," I said. I glanced over to my boss and asked, "What do we do now, mate?"

"Hmm," said the Man in Black. "I think that is up to both Captain Blund and Phil. What are your intentions now that you know the reasons behind Sergeant Valentine's actions? Actions, I might add," he stood up, picked up his weapon and holstered it, "which I think showed considerable restraint."

"He held a knife against the throat of a member of the royal family," stated the first lieutenant, the arrogant pushole.

"Yes," agreed, the boss, "and that proves my point. I would have stabbed the bastard on the spot but Val quite wisely held himself in check. A strong demonstration of his personal self-control, as I'm sure you'll all agree."

Well, this was some world class bullshit, right there. He was spinning my rage-filled entry and subsequent murderous intent as an example of quiet self-restraint. I, again, admired the man's ability while also commending myself on my own personal self-control. It's all about how we deceive ourselves after we have done something particularly bone headed — and I am good at self-deception.

I'm a hell of a guy.

Chapter 39

"I wish no repercussions to be taken against Sergeant Valentine for his actions or his words," said Phil. "That is my desire and, if necessary, my command."

Okay, I was out of the cesspit. Well done, me.

"As for Louise," he said, "it is essential she is brought before the Emperor. He must hear her testimony about cousin Egbert and his actions. While the Empire can overlook some crimes, child abduction, slavery and torture are not forgivable. But the Emperor will not believe any member of the family is capable of these things without direct evidence. Hence, I need Louise. I need to have the Emperor hear her words."

"What about Valentine's attacks on the troopers? "demanded the first lieutenant. "He assaulted the guards outside this door and then there was his brutal attack on Sergeant Gorka which has left her injured!'

"Want me to kiss it better, sergeant?" I asked.

"Drop dead, Valentine," she replied. "Bring those lips near me and you won't be playing any more hide the sausage with Lydia."

Ouch.

Captain Blund stood up. "No action will be taken against anyone in this room," he said. "I want this Louise person watched carefully, I do not want any of the NightWatch involved in her guard, she may have an 'accident'." He looked at his second lieutenant, "Lieutenant Jerkyn, spread that word through the ship, please."

Yep, he was beginning to understand us now. Everyone stood up, looked about with some shuffling embarrassment until the boss said, "Val, Right Honourable, let's shoot through and leave these guys to work out what happens next."

"Please wait," said Captain Blund. "We still have issues to decide, some of which will concern you and the NightWatch." We all sat down again, I planted myself next to Phil and shuffled my chair closer to him. He didn't look at the top of his game, looking decidedly weak and peaky with a slight hint of urine.

Excellent.

"Such as?" asked the boss.

"Look," said the captain, "I lost a lot of my crew and most of my troopers during the assault. I can organise the crew, we can spread ourselves out between both these ships so we have operational capability. But it will be severely limited. The two ships must stay joined if the frigate is to survive. Certainly, the battle brig can cover its assault hatch and uncouple from us, the whole damned vessel is designed to do that very thing." He stood up and walked around, I noticed his top button was undone and his hair was beginning to look somewhat unkempt. I assumed this was an indication of his stress levels. I liked the guy, he was a good man, he had an inner decency. It's something I recognise in others, mind you, not a drop of it in me.

"But we cannot cover the breach in the frigate's hull, the one caused by the battle brig's assault. If the vessels uncouple, we will have the entire ship open to vacuum. We could stay in suits for a short time, we could drive the ship to some extent but we could not enter the channel. That means we would be limited to standard engines, we would never reach any planet, certainly not the capital."

I didn't follow all of this but it sounded bad. I did the sensible thing and kept my mouth shut. Amazing.

"And I have to get back to the capital as quickly as possible," said Phil. "I still intend taking the scout ship but there is not room for Louise. Not if I value surviving the journey. Sergeant Gorka, do you still have two of your troopers to spare as my crew?"

Gorka looked at Captain Blund who gave a small nod. Another big tick for the captain, if he could command that level of respect and obedience from someone like Gorka then he was a man worth knowing. Not that I ever would, of course, I usually don't hang around captains of spaceships.

"Certainly, your Grace," Gorka said. "The two I had previously selected survived the assault, I can send them with you." She turned back to Captain Blund, "But sir, we will need to reorganise all the remaining troopers. Reports indicate we will have about twenty of them fit and ready for duty. Others are injured and may return to duty, I haven't had time to check all those numbers."

"Go ahead, sergeant," said the captain. "Do as you see fit."

"Thank you, sir, but that brings us to the heart of the problem. All the officers were killed. While I am the senior rank of the remaining troopers, we need an officer to issue legal orders, orders at this level."

"Consider yourself promoted, sergeant," said the captain. "You are now Lieutenant Gorka. Or would you prefer 'Captain'?" Yep, this was the standard way to get promotion in the armed forces, wait for anyone senior to you to die and then step into their shoes. Great system.

"No, sir," replied Gorka, her voice level, strong and implacable.

"I beg your pardon?"

"No, sir, I will not become an officer. I am a banner sergeant, making me a lieutenant would actually diminish my authority within the armed forces. Even a captain would be stretching it. No, sir, I need an officer, a military officer, to give me legal commands. I can then carry out those commands in the way they should be done."

I knew what she meant. When this was all over, everyone's actions were going to be scrutinised in fine detail by idiots in fancy uniforms and pompous attitudes. If Gorka put a foot wrong, exceeded her authority at all, or appeared to have manipulated the situation for her own benefit, then she would be in big trouble. Her enemies would be rubbing their hands in glee and, judging by my brief knowledge of this fearsome woman, her past history would have offended many idiots keen on seeking a little revenge. Yes, I understood she had to walk carefully, she needed a figurehead, some dumb pillock who she could point at and say, "I was given orders by that officer!"

"What about me?" asked Captain Blund. "Surely my decisions carry some weight with your superiors. I can give you orders."

"Yes, sir, certainly sir," Gorka replied. I recognised the old trowel coming out, she was about to lay it on a bit thick. "You can give me orders as captain of this vessel but you cannot, with all due respect, take the role as an army officer. I am bound by a strict hierarchy, a chain of command which has a different pathway to you, While on your ship, I work for you but in the greater scheme of things, I must take promotions and larger orders from someone in the army. Otherwise I can be accused of mutiny or corruption."

She was probably putting some spin on this, but essentially, she was right. The military, the generals and bigwigs in armies, took a dim view of any jumped up naval officer interfering in their realm. Gorka would be the one to suffer.

A gentle cough came from beside me. “I may be able to help, there,” said Phil.

We all turned to him, I leaned back in my chair, fascinated at how decisions were made at this level. They made it up, there was no moment of serious discourse, not layers of wisdom and sensible pronouncements. No, these guys made it up as they went along. Oh, the humanity.

“As a member of the royal family and a functionary in the royal household, I have some small authority over many areas.” He began to smirk and shifted his bum but stopped when we caught a whiff of wet pants. “One of my powers is the raising of regiments. I have the power to ask any prominent personage to raise a military force as needs arise.”

“What,” I said, “like “Lord Phil’s Regiment of Pissheads?”

“Not the phrase I would use, sergeant,” he replied, “but you are essentially correct.”

“How does that help us?” asked Captain Blund.

“I suggest,” said Phil, “I appoint Lord Franz as the colonel of a new regiment, this regiment to be initially made up of the NightWatch. I may also transfer Sergeant Gorka and all her troopers into his new organisation and the new colonel may give orders as he sees fit.”

A stunned silence greeted this announcement. I did not like this one bit, none of the NightWatch would be keen on rejoining the military. My body language must have sent off a few messages because Right Honourable said, “Sit down, Val, put the knife away.”

I blinked and realised I was standing with my knife in an angry hand. Where did all this rage come from? I sat down again but sent the boss several pleading looks.

“I agree with Sergeant Valentine,” he said. “We in the NightWatch have no desire to be part of any military organisation. Such an act would send horrors through many of them and rebellion from the rest.”

"Well," continued Phil, unabashed by this determination, "in that case, I have an alternative suggestion. Lord Franz does indeed become a colonel of a new regiment, but this regiment has no members. It is a legal fiction and allows Lord Franz to have authority over lesser ranks. Sergeant Gorka and her people would be attached to his somewhat fictional regiment as auxiliaries."

Silence greeted Phil's comments, my mind was trying to grapple with the existence of a new regiment which did not actually exist but which could have regular troopers attached as auxiliaries. His whole plan reeked of mental contortions, borderline illegalities and straight out cheating. Which, I reflected, described Phil most accurately.

The boss stood up, extended a hand across the table and said, "I welcome Sergeant Gorka to the NightWatch. I emphasise they join us, we do not join them."

Yep, I could see the boulder rolling down the hill towards me.

"That would work, Captain Blund," jumped in Gorka. "We could be attached to the NightWatch by order of His Grace. Then I would be able to carry out my, er, actions, under the ostensible covering of 'Colonel Franz'." She beamed at them and shook the boss's hand while I groaned.

"A word of caution may be in order," said the boss. "If I accept your service, Banner Sergeant Gorka, and that of all your troopers, we will need to discuss your rank. You join the NightWatch. You do as we say, you follow our organisational structure and you fit into our culture. Not the other way around. Do you agree?"

Now Gorka was beginning to smell a rat. I decided this could be worth watching and settled back in my chair, nudged Phil and whispered, "Time to watch a master at work, dog breath."

Gorka straightened to a more erect position, her smile becoming that ever popular neutral visage so beloved of the other ranks while addressing senior officers. "Perhaps you would care to expand upon that comment, sir?"

"Certainly," said the boss. "Lieutenant Manfredi, would you please explain our organisational and command hierarchy to the banner sergeant." He sat down again and relaxed as aristocrats learn to do after shafting the peasants.

Right Honourable sat up, coughed and said, "Uh, yeah, sure. No worries." He paused for thought, took a breath and launched into one of those explanations I would have paid good money to hear. "The NightWatch consists of Lord Franz as its leader and ultimate authority. Under him is Captain Charles Althorpe who is the operational commander of the unit. I am the lieutenant while Ensign Franco rounds out the officer corps. Then come the non-commissioned officers; Senior Sergeant Thulani has under him a range of squad leaders, all with the rank of sergeant. Then we have the various corporals and other specialists such as medical support, technical support and our cadet corps. The cadets are under the authority of Cadet Officer Emilii assisted by Cadet Sergeant Layla."

He paused and gazed upwards in thought before finishing with, "That's about it, I think."

Slowly, other eyes at the table moved to me. Right Honourable had described a straightforward structure which included an almost throwaway reference to the ordinary rank of sergeant. My rank.

"Thank you, lieutenant," said Captain Blund. "Er, does that mean Sergeant Valentine here is under the authority of several officers as well as your senior sergeant? He follows their orders?"

"Not a chance, sir," said Right Honourable, with some vigour. "Val does as he bloody well pleases. I think Lord Franz and Captain Althorpe may be able to herd him a little but we generally find it best to do whatever he tells us."

"But his rank is sergeant," said Blund, plainly struggling.

"Ahh," said the Man in Black, "I see your confusion. Perhaps it would be best if I gave you Valentine's full rank."

Oh, boy, I thought, here it comes. I'm going to be a 'Super Sergeant' or 'Super Senior Sergeant' or maybe even "Big Man." I was hanging on the boss's every word, as was Right Honourable.

"Valentine's rank is 'NightWatch Sergeant'," said the boss. "a rank which gives him considerable authority over everyone in the Watch including a copious amount of freedom of action." He smiled down the table at me. "Lieutenant Manfredi, whom some of you know as 'Right Honourable', has summed it up succinctly. Basically, Val does as he damn well pleases." He looked over at Gorka and finished by saying, "He will outrank you, Banner Sergeant Gorka."

Well, talk about happy. Me, I mean. Gorka did her best to swallow this outrageous command structure so I attempted to smooth the communication by giving her a wink and blowing a kiss. She sank down, lowered her head into her hands and groaned.

"Still willing to come over to the dark side, Sergeant Gorka?" asked the boss.

She looked up, gazed at me with distaste before nodding. "Yes, sir," she said. "But I may have to hit Val from time to time.""Feel free, Sergeant. Many people do," said the boss.

Chapter 40

I WANTED TO GET up and roam about, I wanted to lie down and sleep, I wanted to go somewhere else, be someone else. I wanted all this bad stuff to go away.

Instead, I slumped in my chair, letting the knife droop. I didn't drop it though, I'm not a complete noob.

"That seems to bring us to some form of conclusion," said Captain Blund. "Although, to be honest, I'm not exactly sure what we have decided."

"Phil is going back to the scout ship with two of Gorka's people," said the Man in Black. Again, he was speaking with confidence, his brain capable of lining stuff up efficiently and neatly, his response time to chaos was amazing. I may have been deflated but we were safe, the boss would sort us out. "He will fly back to the capital and, with any luck, we will never see his dishonourable carcass again.

"Banner Sergeant Gorka and her people will come under my authority as a colonel of the Empire. Until further notice, they will function as auxiliaries to the NightWatch. The criminal Louise will remain in custody, under a strict watch. Banner Sergeant Gorka will supply the necessary guards, I do not think Louise would survive if I placed any NightWatch in a position to cause her harm. Captain Blund, I ask you to delegate one of your lieutenants to liaise with these guards for her meals and other necessities. I think that's about everything." He stood up, flicked a gaze around the room before adding, almost as an unneeded afterthought, "And, of course, there shall be no recriminations or actions taken against NightWatch Sergeant Valentine for any of his actions. Are there any questions?"

"I'll assist with the prisoners, captain," volunteered Lieutenant Jerkyn. Okay, another small detail taken care off, this guy must have been looking for ways to impress. I found staying alive and undamaged was enough for me.

Everyone, me included, was exhausted. Right Honourable whispered to me as we stood up to accompany the boss out of the room, "He's done it again, hasn't he? Found a way through."

I nodded. "And saved my worthless carcass," I said.

"We all do it at some time. Probably his turn," muttered my mate.

Bastards. I'm surrounded by bastards.

Outside the room, the boss stopped us. "Val," he said," you're not right. I want you to go to Greenash, possibly Sylvia, and see what is going on. Stay out of things until you are safe to be round.""Hang on, sir," I said, "I'm okay. You'll need me to ... do stuff. What about incorporating Gorka and her lot with our people. Oil and water, sir. Bound to be some fights, possibly a little bit of the old Valentine magic will be needed in sensitive negotiations.""Val, you intimated you could be 'sensitive' and carry out 'negotiations'!" said Right Honourable. "Do you ever actually listen to anything you are saying?"

"Hell, no" I replied, "where's the fun in that?" We continued walking while I let the boss's words wander through my mind, I was surprised at the welling of anger they had produced. Real anger, not some of the pretend stuff I trot out from time to time. And then, when Right Honourable spoke, I again felt my cheeks burn as he questioned my thinking. How dare he! How dare either of them talk to me like that!

We had stopped, or rather, they had stopped. I was a couple of paces along the corridor when I realised they were both still behind me. I spun quickly, pulling out my knife and dropping into a combat stance. What were they up to?

Both of my friends were standing quietly, empty hands and looks of worry on their faces. There was no threat there, yet I had pulled a knife on them. I don't do that. I don't pull out a weapon unless I plan to use it, usually to kill someone. But here I was, crouched and ready to spring into mayhem against two of my dearest friends because ... because they had said something to upset me? I had taken murderous offence at an order from the boss and some typical banter from Right Honourable. They both looked worried now. Worried and possibly a little concerned over their future wellbeing. Oh, God, what have I become?

I reversed the knife and handed it to Right Honourable, then I disarmed myself completely, giving them equal shares in the various implements of destruction I keep stored on my body. Knives, pistols, more knives, little club like things that hurt like hell and broke bones when used correctly. And a few more knives.

"Oh, God, I'm so sorry, fellas," I said. "You're right, Franz, I need help. Right Honourable, do you reckon you could help me get to Greenash before I kill someone?"

"Yeah, righto," he replied. His voice had a slight tremor, can't say I blamed him.

We eventually found our way to the rooms used by Greenash and S'eenyur, H'Nuth was with them in his capacity of sheep herder of cadets and random prisoners. It was his job to ensure S'eenyur was guarded — because he was supposed to be yet another prisoner — and also stop Greenash from doing something stupid, like breaking the kaffe machine.

When we arrived, I was feeling narky so I went and made myself some of the life-giving drink while Right Honourable filled them in on my recent activities. A variety of astonished expressions were uttered, especially when we got to the knife and Phil's throat. I drank my kaffe and wandered over to their workbenches where I climbed up onto something which resembled a hospital bed. Narrow, on wheels and not even vaguely comfortable.

"Fellas," I said, still slurping my drink, "I think you better check up on my wee beasties. Could they be affecting my behaviour? Making me feel slightly more murderous than normal?"

Greenash and S'eenyur looked at each other, bent their heads together and began muttering, I finished my kaffe and passed the empty cup over to Right Honourable. As I considered dozing off, Sylvia entered the room in her battleship mode. This consisted of demanding immediate attention to her needs by all and sundry and God help you if you weren't snappy about it.

"Greenash!" she yelled. "Get yourself down to my sick bay. Franco has collapsed and I think it's your fault! Yours and those damned machines you injected into my lovely man." She must have been extremely upset, she was referring to Teddy Boy as 'Franco' with the added secret sauce of 'my lovely man'. Perhaps I should sit up and watch the fun. "And what is Valentine doing in here?" she further demanded. "Is he having trouble, too?"

Okay, I was staying put and pretending I was asleep. No such luck, she came over and poked me, lifting up an eyelid to check out whatever and finally squeezed various parts of my anatomy. No idea why, she's weird.

"Right," she commanded, "Christopher, take Val to sick bay!" Right Honourable leapt to obey. "Greenash," she went on, a full head of steam powering her engine by this time, "you and S'eenyur get yourselves there as well. Take some of your analysis machines. I want to know what those nanobots are doing to these lads. And I want to know NOW!"

I won't bore you with the rest of the circus. Soon I was ensconced in a bed beside an unconscious Teddy Boy. He was in a coma and hooked up to various machines which did stuff to him. I couldn't move too much because I had my own gaggle of machines beeping over me. Greenash and S'eenyur had waved various instruments over both of us, conferred, disappeared and returned with bigger and bulkier machines which they also plumped around us. I drifted off into sleep, at least, I hoped it was sleep and not a coma like Ted.

Some time later, I was awoken by someone sticking a needle into me. It didn't hurt but it was the principle of the thing so I attempted to hit the poor innocent slob. I discovered my movements were restricted because my arms and legs were fastened to the sides of the bed making me effectively immobile. I lunged at my assailant, finding it was Sylvia herself. She straightened from my flailing body and showed me a vial of blood. My blood, My blood which she had recently extracted. I thrashed about with some growling.

"You're sick, my poor boy," she said. "No one else wants to come near you, especially after you laid out two of my helpers. We've had to restrain you for our own protection." I ignored her entreaties until my brain registered she had called me her 'poor boy', if Sylvia was this worried then I was in a bad way.

It didn't stop me from trying to grab her by the throat and squeezing but a combination of her fast footwork and some truly excellent restraining straps rendered my actions impotent. I think I was gnashing my teeth, possibly dribbling a little. In any event, I was not the picture of calm. Sylvia adjusted something on one of the tubes going into me. Someone was going to pay for all these indignities. Throats would be torn out, I would kill any and all in this room and then see who else had offended me. People were going to die, and die messily.

With these as my last conscious thoughts, I fell back, relaxed and drifted off into dreamland yet again.

Time passed, hours, possibly days. I would regain consciousness from time to time, still restrained. Each time, someone was sitting in a chair beside my bed. Often two or three someones. Lydia was there a lot, so was Jeremy. I think there was always one of the cadets in the room, either sitting in a chair or squatting on the floor. Layla came in a lot. Wallace stopped by.

The red haze was not as prevalent. At first, it descended across my eyes every time I woke but eventually it receded until one day I woke up, blinked and realised I was seeing things normally. I was still tied to the bed but it didn't bother me as much. In fact, as I thought back over the last days, I realised it would have been a sensible action. Keep the mad dog killer tied up.

I lay there, seeing Jeremy on one side and Meataxe on the other with a worried look on his face.

"Meataxe," I said, more of a rasp than a clear voice. I coughed and tried again, "Meataxe? What's going on?"

"I dunno," he said. "I think it's my turn."

Colour me confused. "Your turn?" I asked. "Your turn for what?" My voice was growing stronger, Jeremy came and held a bottle of water to my lips. I smiled my thanks at him and he tousled my hair before stepping back quickly with a worried look on his face. "It's alright, Jeremy," I said. "I'm not going to bite you."

"You've been trying to, Val," said the little weed. "We've had to reinforce those restraints and stay away from your teeth." He put the bottle down and headed for the door, "I'll get Sylvia and Greenash." I dropped back onto the bed. Was I a menace to one and all? Had my nanobots turned me into some version of those undead killing things we had fought on the ship so long ago?

Shortly after this, my room filled up with people. All stood some distance from me, usually pressed against a wall. Lydia came over and bravely held my hand while Sylvia shone a light into my eyes, looked at the machines and said "Hmmm," a lot.

"Feel like killing anyone, sergeant?" she said.

I opened my mouth to make some glib remark but then saw her eyes. She was serious. I looked over at Lydia who had a death grip on my hand and a pleading look on her face. Everyone else in the room tensed up, waiting for my reply.

Oh, dear.

"Uhh, no," I replied, keeping my voice gentle. "I suspect, um, I may not have been myself lately."

"Well," offered Greenash, "that's exactly it, isn't it? You have been yourself. The damaged nanobots have been strengthening your inner urges, reinforcing your desires and shortcutting a lot of higher brain function."

Lydia stroked my cheek. "You've been a nasty man sweetie."

Chapter 41

THIS WAS NOT GOOD. I never had a life plan, never considered settling down and living the quiet life with my one true love — that would be Lydia — I had never had daydreams about sitting in a chair in my declining years, soaking up the sun while adoring grandchildren played at my feet. I wasn't one of those people who looked down the long years of their life and planned ahead. Often, I considered making it to the next day a win.

But even without this rosy future, I had never imagined I would develop into the real bad guy. The one who destroys rather than builds, the scary man, the one capable of invoking fear in the innocent. I did not want to be a permanent nightmare.

I looked from Lydia to Sylvia and back to Greenash. "Help," I whispered. "Save me, please."

An embarrassed silence met my words; was it because of the message of my plea or because there was no going back, was I doomed to be a nutter who attacked anyone and everyone?

Lydia glanced at Greenash and then did something truly heroic. She kissed me, full on the lips. It wasn't lust I felt, inflaming my loins, it was something else. Sure, I responded to the pure physical nature of the kiss, but more than that, somewhere inside my battered mind and body a warm glow spread thought my entire being. Lydia loved me, she demonstrated she would stand by me, no matter what I became. I felt a lurch somewhere inside my system, up and down my arms and legs; a definite tingle, a river of warmth.

When she released my lips and the world went back to normal, Greenash was speaking. "I took some of your blood while you were unconscious," he said. I did commend him for his timing, taking my blood while I was conscious would have led to a lot of screaming. "We've been running tests and analysing results to see what has been happening with your nanobots." He looked at several other people in the room before continuing, "We think that your, er, condition, is solely due to malfunctioning nanobots. If we can track down the ones causing your mood swings, we might be able to turn them off. But we have to do it quickly, before they multiply and become the dominant force in your body and mind."

"What about Teddy Boy?" I asked. "Why isn't he in a bed beside me? Is he strapped down somewhere else? And what about everyone else with nanobots? Is everyone else going to go crazy?"

"No," said Greenash. "Again, it was the surge. Each time one hit your bodies, more damage was done to the nanobots. Everyone else is fine, a bit groggy but they're recovering nicely with a bit of rest and food. You and Ted got the most damage. Him because of his extra time on the scout ship and the surges he experienced there. You, because, er ... um, because we had tweaked your nanobots to have extra functions. These put too much of a load on your system and the final surge by Lord Franz — the one which killed all the Confederate personnel — finished off the damage.""So, it's your fault," I asked. "Is that what you're saying?"

The room went quiet again, Lydia and Sylvia stepped away from me but then Lydia moved back and held my hand. For some bizarre reason, I noticed the wounds to my hands — the missing finger bits — had been bandaged and were now covered in some form of flexible dressing. Lydia gave me a squeeze, drawing my attention back to her. I could see her face glistening, she licked her lips but stayed by my side. Wallace had stepped forward and looked ready to jump in if I decided to rage about.

Finally, Greenash coughed and stammered a reply. "Well, yes," he said. He stood at the foot of my bed, his shoulders slumped and he presented the picture of regret. He looked me in the eye. "I did this to you, Val. You are correct, it's my fault."

"Greenash," I began, endeavouring to sit up. My movement was stopped by the restraining straps and Lydia's firm grip on my hand. "You are a better man than I will ever be." I lay back down. "No, it's not your fault. It's not anyone's fault, unless you want to blame an uncaring universe. We didn't have to be here, on this ship. We didn't have to walk through the bowels of Caesar's ship and fight his maniacal hordes. We didn't have to leave Earth. If we always seek to find someone to blame, rather than accepting the consequences of our actions, we will always be miserable. Because life isn't fair. It sucks, and then you die."

I gave Lydia's hand a small squeeze. "But if we are lucky, if we are very, very lucky, we get to fall in love," I looked up at my girl and then back to the people in the room. "And we get to journey with heroes, heroes like these nutcases. Heroes like you, Greenash, willing to face up to a murderous thug like me and tell it straight. No blame, my friend, not from me, not ever."

"I think I'm going to be sick," said Wallace. "I hope someone wrote that down, I want to read it back to him when the drugs have worn off."

The room relaxed, Lydia's thumb was caressing the back of my hand. Okay, nanobots, I thought, do your worst.

We all chatted for a while longer before I fell asleep while listening to how Phil had been taken to the scout ship and departed for his journey to the capital. Nothing bad happened to prevent his journey which I thought was enormously unfair. Louise was behaving herself and that's all I remember before the snores cut in.

The next time I awoke, it was to find Greenash in the visitor's chair. He was smiling. Jeremy and Patrica were my other two escorts, or guards. "We've got something, Val," said Greenash.

I perked up, the restraints were still in place so I guessed I wasn't seen as harmless yet. No matter how honeyed my words. Since I couldn't sit up and beg him to go on, I resigned myself to raising one eyebrow.

"We can inhibit the procreation of your nanobots, even select which ones we want to regulate." Okay, this made no sense to me, so I nodded in my most sage like fashion, hoping he would keep talking until I got words I could recognise.

"It's a matter of finding what affects the particular nanobots causing you to, er..."

"Act like a psychopath?" I suggested.

"No. you'll always be that. But you can generally control those urges. S'eenyur and I have some good ideas, we're testing out various chemicals to see which ones isolate the rage nanobot without diminishing the others. Or changing their programming so that you end up as mindless vegetable in a chair, dribbling on Lydia."

"You do know who you are talking to, Greenash?" I said with the merest hint of a snarl.

"Yes, Val. You. Look, this episode has shown that you have been able to bury your violent tendencies down deep, but they will always be with you, they are a part of you. Somehow, over the years, you have learned how to cope, how to rein in those tendencies." He scratched the back of his head. "I must say, it's impressive, the self-control you exert when you are at the top of your game. You must have had an awful time growing up and grappling with whatever happened in your life. You've had it tough, mate."

I shrugged. Eh, so what, you play the hand your dealt. You suck it up and never whinge. Push through, get the job done. I yelped as something poked my shoulder. Looking down, I saw Jeremy standing there with a pencil ready to jab me again.

"Oww!" I said. "What the hell, Jeremy?"

"Are you going to get all sooky again, Uncle Val?" he asked. "You had a vaguely noble face and I was worried you might say something wise and endearing. I'm supposed to write down everything you say, but that would be embarrassing."

I managed to reach his pencil and snatched it away, my restraints had been sufficiently loosened for comfort, they kept my upper arms tied to the bed but my forearms were available for duty. I'm living the good life. "You little piece of crapulence, I know what you were doing, you were trying to make me feel better." I twiddled the pencil, "And why are you using this thing for writing? Why haven't you got one of those electronic tablet thingies?"

"I love hearing you trying to talk about technology, Uncle Val," said the youthful boil. "Emilii says I need to learn self-control and she thinks having me write with pencil and paper will slow me down and make me think."

"Is it working?" I asked.

"Nah," he said, a big grin spreading across his beaming face. "I'm capable of multitasking at an astonishing level. I can shift to a multi modal pedagogy whilst retaining an inherent understanding of the needs and cares of the everyday personnel with whom I interact."

"Anyone hit you yet?"

"I'm also quick on my feet."

"If I might continue," interrupted Greenash, "we should be able to distil something for you in the next couple of days. We've had great success with certain cheeses, sugary bread products and, to a lesser extent, fermented malt grains. Barley seems to be the best."

I thought about this for about two seconds. "Do you mean to tell me that you have had those idiots in the original NightWatch drinking beer while eating cheese and pastries?"

"Certainly," he said. "They all benefit from the treatments, I'll bring some down to you."

I lay back and fell asleep in disgust.

Chapter 42

THE NEXT DAY BROUGHT me my expected visit with Greenash. He came bearing a container holding various food products and two bottles of liquid. He fed me some of the bread and cheese and then gave me the choice of a sweet, sugary drink or a beer. Obviously, it was no contest, I chose the sugary drink. I did consider the beer, I wanted that beer in the worst way but I was not at my best with any sort of alcohol. One drink would be too many and I decided that, given the state of my current mental and emotional state, getting hammered may be a bad idea.

Sometimes, I'm so sensible I hurt myself. I drank the sugar water and ate some more of Greenash's goodies.

The morning also brought Sylvia on her rounds, she looked at Greenash's offerings and dragged him and them off into a corner, for a consultation. "What the hell do you mean by bringing these things down for one of my patients, Greenash?" she demanded. She had him backed into a corner while pointing at the offending items on a table near my bed.

I enjoyed this little tete a tete. It was always worth a watch, anytime Syliva went into full matron mode. She could make Meataxe quail and I even caught Wallace looking vaguely embarrassed when she had a go at him. I also believed she was lucky to leave that particular conversation with all her fingers and toes still attached.

With this level of distraction, I did not pick up on who was now fiddling with the machines near my bed. These things were attached to tubes which were eventually attached to me. Thus, I had a keen interest in knowing who was playing with the damn things. I turned my head, got a good look at the person in question and lunged for him.

It was Don'elk, Sylvia's no hoper of a brother, a man to whom I had taken a hammer with some delight. That occasion cost him two fingers. He had returned the favour by delivering me to the murderous Louise and her sadistic henchmen. But, as these things go, our journey was destined to be shared together, especially when the boss previously spoke to me in his most reasonable tones about allowing Don'elk to join the NightWatch. His bloody, infuriating reasonable tones. I won't go into it here, but my boss can be a right dickhead sometimes.

And so Don'elk joined the NightWatch with promises from me he would not suffer any accidental injuries. No problem there, I intended to cause him a few injuries here and now, none of which would be accidental.

"VALENTINE!" yelled Sylvia, realising what I was doing because the bloody restraints had prevented me from wrapping my hands around Don'elk's neck. My rage blossomed and I wrenched the bed enough for it to shift sideways and jostle something standing beside it. Some form of tall pole holding a liquid in a bag, all of which now fell onto the other machine which then cascaded onto Don'elk. He ended up on the floor with bits of broken machinery around him while I lay panting, my torso stretched over the side of the bed and a bruised arm still held by the restraints.

Sylvia bustled over, yelled for assistance which came in the form of two burly attendants. They managed to get me back on the bed. I wasn't helping. Rather, I was rolling about, thrashing and threatening death and destruction to all. More restraints were added, my arms were again tied down some more as I was given another injection.

Out I went, back to dreamland.

And so we passed into the next day. This time, I awoke to a few more visitors. Lydia was in a chair beside me, holding my hand. Don'elk sat in another chair against the far wall, in my line of vision but far outside my reach. I detected Lydia's hand in all of this.

"Hiya, sweetie," she said. "Feel like killing anyone?" That's my girl, alright; a little light banter in the morning, some slow and gentle pillow talk.

"No," I said. And then realised I meant it. She had obviously placed the trembling Don'elk within my line of sight in order to assess my rage state. This could be a smart move but I considered it borderline stupid. On the plus side, I was not feeling like running amok with any nearby pointy objects. Speaking of which, I moaned, rolled over and pulled out the pencil I had taken from Jeremy. In all of yesterday's ruckus, it had ended up under my body attempting to insert itself up my bum.

I placed it carefully to one side, intending to give it back to Jeremy at my earliest opportunity. I would watch him use it before telling him where it had been. Jeremy often chewed the end of these pencils.

Another figure entered the room, another one of Sylvia's attendants. Hard to tell if this one was male or female because they all wore floppy white gowns, this one wore a medical mask, the sort I've seen Sylvia use when she didn't want to breath in the noxious fumes coming from the unwashed NightWatch. Sensible girl, Sylvia.

This attendant came over to stand behind Lydia and leaned over to look at some of the machinery near the head of my bed. She disappeared from my view for a moment before reappearing suddenly in a burst of activity.

She grabbed Lydia, pulled her up and jabbed her neck with one of those little knives they use in surgery. These things were immensely sharp, far sharper than anything I had ever seen before, they always caused me unease, being so small — a tiny blade at the end of a metal handle. It could slice a person open from neck to groin, allowing the skin to peel away while the recipient stood and watched it happen. These things were so sharp they scared me.

And now, one of them was held against my love's throat by this maniac. This maniac who now came into view, pulling her mask off with a brief flick. I groaned, seeing a face I had hoped never to encounter again.

"Hello, Louise," I said.

"Val, darling," she cooed. "How simply marvellous to see you again." She stood triumphantly before me, Lydia held by one hand while the other pressed the tiny, evil knife against my girl's throat. She spotted Don'elk who had half risen in shock. "Don'elk!" Louise exclaimed. "How fortunate! Go and shut that door, dear boy, lock us all in."

"Louise," stammered Don'elk, "what ... what are you doing?" He hadn't moved, his stance resembling that of a mouse discovering a cat nearby.

"Why, I'm going to kill Valentine, of course," replied Louise. "Surely, that's obvious. But first," she turned back to look at me, her long hair framing a face made for seduction, for pleasure and at the moment, for murder. "But first," she repeated, I'm going to slit the lovely Lydia's throat in front of him. I'll do it so her blood jets over his bed, he can be awash in his lover's bodily fluids. Won't that be fun?" She flicked a glance back to Don'elk and changed her tone to that of the imperious majesty, the voice of a woman you never disobeyed. "Don'elk! Shut the door!"

Don'elk slid across and did as he was ordered. Then he turned back to face Louise and did, to my mind, a brave thing. "Louise, don't kill her," he said, the lovely man. "Put the knife down, surely we can talk about this?" He took a step forward towards the murderous bitch. Lydia remained motionless. Smart girl.

"Don'elk!" snarled Louise, "What's gotten into you? Of course I'm going to kill him. And no, I don't 'have to', I'm doing it because it pleases me." Her smile broadened, I could see her muscles begin to tense, the blow was about to fall, the slice which would end Lydia's life and my world.

I wrenched at my bonds, rolling from side to side, thrashing and howling. Blood seeped from under my restraints where they tore at my skin, the muscles on my neck were steel cables. The red rage started to descend but then diminished, my eyes were clear, my brain was functioning and I knew what was going to happen. I threw myself against the restraints.

All to no avail, except to make Louise laugh. "Oh, that is so, so precious, isn't it, Don'elk? Look at the poor, dumb fool." She was right, there was nothing I could do. Louise would kill Lydia in her particularly gruesome way and then kill me. And at the point, I would not care. If Lydia was not in my life, I didn't want it anymore.

Don'elk lunged. He had been slowly, slowly sidling towards Louise and now he leapt at her. Or rather, at the arm holding the blade. Louise had raised it on high, ready for the slash across Lydia's throat; her attention was fixed on me and my face, her anticipation of my grief and the death of Lydia shining from her eyes.

And then Don'elk grabbed her arm.

Louise spun, she was fast, fast and ruthless. She voiced no surprise, no confusion at this attack from one she considered an ally. No, she used her strength to brush aside Don'elk's ineffectual arms before thrusting the blade at his face.

The point of the blade entered his eye, causing it to pop. Her thrust then became a slash, she dragged the blade out of the eye socket, down his cheek and along the jaw, I saw Don'elk's face open like a carved piece of fruit. His cheek peeled away, bits of eye dribbled over his shattered face and he fell back a step. As yet, he was feeling no pain. These knives did that, they opened the flesh so quickly, so neatly the brain was astonished. Nerves were taken by surprise and were laggard on letting the mind know great pain was on its way.

I saw Louise's face in profile, the fierce grin, the head tilted back in victory, the eyes soaring in exhalation. Her face glowed.

And then changed. It went from victory to confusion in a heartbeat. Her brow furrowed, a question tugged at her lips and she began to turn her head back to me, possibly wondering what I had done, how I had escaped my bonds.

I had not moved.

But Lydia had. As soon as Louise took the blade from her throat, Lydia leaned over and scooped up the pencil from where it lay on the covers at the side of my bed. The side closest to Lydia. She swivelled to Louise who was preparing to deliver a final slash at the cowering Don'elk — and then my girl plunged the pencil into Louise's ear.

Into her ear.

The pencil sank in a short distance, enough for Louise to halt her attack on Don'elk and wonder who had assailed her. She began to turn her head back to Lydia, her arm holding he blade rising, ready to come back and slash at this unexpected resistance.

I saw it all. I saw Louise begin to turn, I saw the sharp, sharp blade prepare to eviscerate the threat. And I saw Louise's eyes glaze over. They no longer held a question, they no longer held an anger at this usurper of her will; for now, her eyes held the knowledge of death.

Lydia, my wonderful, magnificent, heroic Lydia, had used a palm strike on the base of the pencil, driving it forward, plunging it into the depths of the mad woman's brain. Louise died in an instant, collapsing to the floor.

Around this time, the door burst open and every man and his dog surged in.

There's always a party at Valentine's place.

Chapter 43

MAGIC WAS FIRST IN, quickly shouldered aside by a ferocious Sylvia before he was further shunted back by several Night-Watch veterans. Sylvia went straight to the downed Don'elk, the Night-Watch guys looked for other dangers, saw none and then backed against a wall to stand guard. This allowed Magic to get into the room.

"Why aren't you dead yet, Valentine?" he asked.

"That's getting old, sport." He looked over at the downed Don'elk, then casually turned back to me with one raised eyebrow. It's a neat trick, took me months to master but it looks cool. "The little toerag saved us, Magic," I said. "Louise was all set to kill Lydia and then me, not a damned thing I could do." I rattled my bonds to indicate my inability to contribute to the mayhem.

Lydia gathered herself, adjusted her clothes, brushed some hair behind an ear and finally sat on my bed with one hand casually resting on my leg. I was close to heaven in her presence.

"Don'elk grabbed her arm, she was about to cut Lydia's throat," I went on. "In return, she opened his face up like a melon. You're probably standing in what's left of one of his eyes." I derived some small satisfaction from seeing my captain shuffle his feet and check his boots.

"Don'elk saved you?" he asked, a small note of wonder in his voice. "Don'elk?"

"Well, more Lydia than me."

"Don'elk. Saving Valentine. What a time to be alive," he muttered.

We watched as Sylvia did things to Don'elk's face, folding up his cheek and holding it in place as other minions entered and lifted the semi-conscious little snot onto one of their mobile beds. He was wheeled out of my room, leaving Magic and a few old NightWatch hanging about.

Greenash burst in, he was wild eyed and frantic, arms and legs waving about. "Has Val gone crazy again?" he blurted, before seeing us all standing about and casually chatting. I, of course, was still on my bed but you get the idea. He spotted me and stumbled to a halt, "Ahh," he concluded, "You're not, um, not, um ..."

"Running amok?" I suggested.

He coughed, "I heard shouting and suchlike from your room and wanted to make sure your nanobots hadn't, er," Again, he dribbled to a stop. I remained silent, enjoying his consternation and wondering how long I could play this scene out.

"Val's fine," said Lydia, "he lay there and did nothing while those around him defended his honour."

"Sorry, what?" asked Greenash. He had stepped forward and was noticing my dishevelled bedclothes and became particularly concerned with the amount of blood around my restraints. "What happened?" he asked.

I went through it again, this time in detail, giving a blow-by-blow description. While this was going on, Greenash was running some sort of scanner over my arms and legs, he even scooped up some of my blood and put it into a small sliding drawer in a machine set against the far wall. I'd never noticed it, I assumed it was part of Sylvia's medical arsenal. I finished my tale as this machine gave a beep and Greenash bent to study a small screen on the front of the thing.

"Hmm," he said.

Magic told the two NightWatch to fetch another mobile bed and take Louise's body away. Greenash turned and gave me a self-satisfied look, "The amount of damaged nanobots in your system is falling, I think you're safe to be around civilised people now. Light duties for a while, and maintain a good fibre rich diet with lots of liquids. We have to get those dead nanobots out of your system. How have your bowels been?"

I ignored this stupid question and emphasised Greenash's diagnoses to Magic. The one where he had said I was safe to be around and could he get me out of these restraints, please. He gave me a slow look but bent down and got me loose. Lydia found some medical cloths and wiped the blood away from my arms while also examining the rest of my body for damage. Since I was wearing a silly hospital gown, the others got to see much more of me than we would normally allow in public.

"I may never eat again," muttered Magic as I bent down to get properly dressed in my clothes after Lydia hauled them out of a nearby cupboard.

I stood up, straightened myself out and asked, "What now, mate? And how did Louise get out of her cell?"

"Damn good question," he replied. "Come on." We both stepped over Louise's body as a mobile bed was wheeled in. "Put her somewhere safe and keep an eye on the body," instructed Magic. "Val and I are going to the cells to see what happened. We may want to come back and search her."

Greenash kept eyeing me speculatively until I growled at him, he left to spread the good news of my partial recovery. Lydia came with us, because I had grabbed her by the arm and pulled her along. She was not ready to be left alone, especially after stabbing someone in the head with a pencil.

A pencil! What is it with people and pencils? First Wallace and now Lydia! Perhaps we should forgo any other weapons and equip the entire NightWatch with stationery!

Magic called a halt as we entered the corridor before the cell block. I still held Lydia's hand, both as a message of my love and care as well as a mechanism for keeping her moving. She walked with us but was not with us, if that makes any sense. I needed to remind her of her value, of her goodness and of who she was, deep in her heart. Not the killer, capable of punching a pencil into someone's head, but as the young, intelligent woman both loved and admired by the entire NightWatch. Especially me.

I did not question the reason for the halt because my attention was fixed on Lydia. This meant I was not as aware of Magic, his position or his speech, as I possibly should have been. He turned back to face us and began spewing insults.

"You are the biggest dropkick I have ever encountered, Valentine," he said. "I am sorry I ever laid eyes on you, let alone promoted you in the NightWatch. Lydia barely tolerates you, the rest of us hate you. Personally," and here he poked me in the shoulder with a stiff finger, "I'll be happy when your stupidity finally gets you killed."I couldn't believe what I was hearing, it certainly drew my attention back from my focus on Lydia. I turned to face Magic, while also rubbing my shoulder where he had poked me. When I turned, he stepped forward to be right in my face and shoved me in the chest. "Did you hear what I said, you fatuous lump of lard?" he said. "What are you going to do about it?"His push forced me back a couple of steps, causing me to drop Lydia's hand or pull her off balance. What was going on here? Magic was saying things about me which weren't true. Or were they? Had I been fooling myself all this time?

He pushed me again before folding his arms across his chest and laughing at me. One of those derisory laughs so beloved by bullies and thugs. I could feel myself responding, could feel my body start to crouch in anticipation of a fight. A fight with Magic! What was happening?

He stepped back dropped his arms and changed stance, now he was the caring leader, the vulnerable friend. "How are you feeling, mate?" he asked. "Want to have a go at me? Feel a bit of rage coming on?"

I opened my mouth to respond, considered snarling a few words before punching him in the face. He smiled at me. Not a sneer, but a warm smile. I stopped and examined myself — where was my rage? He was right, I should be about to go berserk by now, if my recent behaviour was any guide. But there was no red mist over my eyes, no screaming need to respond violently to this unexpected attack.

"You dropkick," I said, lowering my hands and sucking in deep breaths. "You absolute, gold-plated mongrel. You had me going there."

"Did it work?" he asked. "Do you want to kill me?"

"Hell, yes," I muttered. "Preferably by making you do paperwork for the rest of your miserable life. Or asking H'Nuth to teach you how to sketch and paint."

He shuddered. "Fair go, mate. Sure, I insulted you, but there's no need to make those sort of threats."

"Magic, you mad damn fool," I said, "If my rage was still lurking inside me, I could have gone for you. I could have killed you."

He laughed, "Sure, you could, dimwit. Hah! You — kill me? In your dreams, junior." He clapped me on the shoulder and went on. "I had to know, Val. I had to know you were safe to have around, because I need you; I need you to be a copper, a damn good copper. Through that door," he nodded at the closed door leading to the cells, "we'll find out what happened, how Louise got out, what happened to her guards.

Everything. And it won't be pretty. So, if you were going to do your nut, I'd prefer to find out now, and not when you have some weapon to hand.""My whole body is weapon, dickhead."

"That's my boy, full of self-delusion." He looked at Lydia and said to her, "How about you, Lydia? Back with us?"

She swallowed, reached out and tugged my shirt until I stood next to her. "Yes, Magic, I'll be fine. Val will help me." She gave me hug, "and I'll help him."Magic quietly studied us and said to me, "You lucky, lucky bastard, Valentine."

No argument from me.

We sorted ourselves out, Magic produced a pistol, noticed I had no weapon, smiled and shrugged. "Let's go, team," he said, pushing open the door into the cell area.

In we walked, into a mess of murder, blood and chaos.

Chapter 44

ONE BODY LAY SLUMPED over the reception desk. Mr Grey's cell door was still locked, we left it alone and gathered outside the remaining door, the open door — the one to Louise's cell. We took our mental breaths and entered, looking for the missing guard.

He was inside the cell, dead, his throat cut and a stab wound to the chest.

"Whoever killed this guy was into overperformance," said Magic as he squatted down to examine the corpse. "Lydia, would you please check these rooms, especially the control console at reception, and let me know if anything has been tampered with? Look in any drawers or cupboards, look for anything unusual, out of place or missing."

Lydia nodded and started moving around Louise's cell, examining the walls and furniture. She eventually left us to go back to the reception area. Her up bringing in this modern, space era should allow her to spot something out of place whereas Magic and I could be looking at something significant but have no idea. We weren't stupid — well, Magic wasn't — but we also did not have the cultural baggage people familiar with space travel would have. Since Lydia was a technician and an engineer, she would have the best chance of spotting such a clue.

Personally, I didn't think she would find anything. I would bet this was a simple jail break. For whatever reason, the guard had ignored the standing order to stay out of Louise's cell. Somehow, she had convinced the guard to come in, then killed him. How I did not know, but she did it, the bitch.

The dead guard was one of Gorka's troopers, as was the one outside, the one slumped in a chair and supposedly guarding the place. I joined Magic down beside the body of the guard, careful not to touch anything and asked him, "What do you think happened here, Magic? Do you think she used the old sex gambit to tempt this young fellow in here for a quickie?"

"You have a remarkable touch of the poet in you," replied Magic. "And that could be true, but let's pretend we are good coppers and see if we can work out what actually took place." He pointed at the two wounds and said, "On first glance, it would appear this poor fellow walked in and was stabbed in the chest by Louise, and then she cut his throat."

"Could she have done it the other way round?" I asked. "Cut his throat first, then stabbed him in the chest?"

He put his hands on his knees, both of us being careful to point at various bits of the dead guy's anatomy. No touching, that was Magic's rule. You look, you think, you smell, you think some more, you listen and then think again. "Tell me the story," directed Magic, meaning he wanted me to construct the actions leading to this poor sod lying here like a lump of meat. Someone's son, possibly someone's lover, now a corpse, all future gone.

I looked around, shifted my squat and shuffled about before talking. "Right," I said, "He came in the door — don't know why — he stepped in and she attacked him."

"Let's leave why he came in until later. Consider the attack. Would she have been lying on the bed?" he suggested, "looking all casual and sensual, panting for it?"

I gave him a judgemental look over his word choice before going on, "No, if she was on the bed, she would have to get off the bed, take at least two steps to reach him before carrying out her attack. This guy, this guard, would have seen her attack and had time to respond. Anything, a defensive pose, a step back, a shuffle of feet, any movement at all would have left some marks on this floor. See how his boots have that shiny black coating, it's what they use to polish their boots because Gorka likes them to be all shiny. Don't ask me why. It's fine when the boot is placed down straight, but any twist of the foot and a black streak marks the floor. This cell floor has no markings. Louise was wearing slippers when she came into my sick room, so we wouldn't expect any markings from her footwear. This guy," I pointed to the dead guard, "walked in and collapsed, he never moved his feet at all. No way she leapt from the bed and killed him with a chest stab."

"You don't think it was the neck wound, the cut throat that did him in?"

"No. Look at the wound. Minimal blood around the neck or across the room. When you cut a throat, blood sprays out everywhere, and if you are standing in front of the victim, as Louise would have to have done, then she would have copped a blast. There was no sign of blood on her when she attacked us. Sure, she might have cleaned herself up but it would have been a quick rub down. She had no evidence of blood in her hair or any of the wrinkles on her skin.""When did you get to be so observant, Val?"

"I tend to focus my attention when homicidal sociopaths threaten to kill me."

"Um," he said, "okay, I agree with you. He was stabbed in the chest first, then had his throat cut. Why? And to do it, she would have to have been standing close to the door when the guard came in. As you said, he didn't fight back or attempt to defend himself or shuffle his feet or anything like that. It would appear he walked in and stood still while Louise stepped forward and killed him. And where did she get the weapon? This doesn't make sense."We stood up, I heard knees pop so I gave Magic a censorious look. He shrugged and muttered something about getting old. I grunted — we have our own verbal shorthand. I looked at the room, gazed steadily at the body and tried to picture the guard calmly walking in, standing still and waiting to be skewered. The more I looked at the body, the more I didn't believe it.

"He's too far to one side," I said. "If he was stabbed as he entered, he should be here." I moved and gestured at the space in front of the door. "But he's off to one side. I think he was stabbed while he stood against the side wall."

"She threatened him when he entered?" suggested Magic. "Forced him against the wall?"

"You're kidding. A guard walks in, sees a prisoner with a knife and doesn't yell out or step back. Simply waits to receive instructions?"

"Could be," said Magic. He bent down and closely examined the victim's chest. "Something's not right about this wound."

I joined him, the wound was huge, certainly wider than any blade I had ever seen. "Heck, what did she stab him with, a table leg?" I asked.

"No, it was a knife, but she made several blows. Over and over. You can see the hole has gashes all around it from when the knife was plunged in again and again.""Well, she is, or was, a nutcase," I said.

"What, she stabs him a few dozen times, then cuts his throat? And the guy outside never hears anything? No sound of a scuffle, no scream from the dying guard. No, something's off here."

I stood up, having finished my close study of the chest wound. "He was shot first, then stabbed," I said. "I think the stab wounds in his chest were made to cover up the blaster hole. If we cut him open, I bet we would find a bullet inside him, or darts, or blast burns."

"Damn and blast," said Magic.

"Yep. He was shot, then the knife wounds — the chest stab and the cut throat — were done to mask the fact he was killed by a pistol."

"Where the heck would Louise get a pistol from?" asked Magic.

"I don't think she did," I replied. "I think someone else was here. Someone else shot both guards and set her free.""Well, aren't you Mr Cheerful," he said. "That means we have another traitor on board. Bazli was not alone.""It makes sense. Someone was contacting the Confederate battle brig and telling them where to find Phil when he was in his yacht. That's how he was ambushed. And then, the same someone helped that enemy locate this frigate and latch on for their assault. I don't see Bazli as being the one who knew that level of information." A thought came to me, a remembered conversation with Phil way back when he first boarded the frigate after his rescue. "Phil did say there was a traitor in the officer corps somewhere. It must be one of those lieutenants.""Or Captain Blund," said Magic.

"Or Captain Blund," I agreed.

Poo. Bum. Tit.

Lydia re-entered the cell. "I've found something," she said. "I was checking the logs to see who had entered the brig area. One of the lieutenants was here recently."

"How recently?" I asked.

"Recent enough for him to have helped Louise escape," said Lydia.

"Show me," said Magic. We went back to the reception desk in time to be greeted by Banner Sergeant Gorka and several troopers, none of them looked happy. Gorka became particularly incensed when she saw the body of the trooper draped over the reception desk.

"Valentine!" she exploded, "What have you done now?"

Weapons were pulled out, many aimed at me, a few at Magic and even one at Lydia. Wow, this could be serious.

"What are you doing, banner sergeant?" asked Magic, in his best 'let's everyone calm down' voice.

"We know about the attack in sick bay, we were interviewing Sylvia and others when I was informed these guards had missed their last check in. And who do we find here when we arrive? You three, and the body of a dead trooper."

"There's another one in Louise's old cell," I said.

"Not helping, dog breath," muttered Magic.

Gorka waved at two of her people who checked out the cells. Guns remained pointed at us so we all stood and looked at each other until they came back and reported there was, in fact, another dead trooper in the cell.""See," I said, "you only have to ask." No, I don't know why I do this, keep on prodding a situation. Part of me wants to see how close I can go to the edge without everything exploding. Usually, it's bit of fun but I try not to do it to people holding lots of guns pointing at me.

Gorka sighed, put her weapon away and told her team to do the same. "What happened, dickhead?" she asked. I assumed she was addressing me, since no one would use that name on Magic. Oh, except me. Sorry, forgot.

"That would be Sergeant Dickhead, banner sergeant," I replied. "And, by the by, I outrank you. If there is to be any name calling around here, I will be the caller and you will be the callee."

"Why are you still alive, Valentine?" she asked.

Magic stepped forward, taking control of the situation. "We have a traitor on board, banner sergeant. We have reason to believe that person is still with us and is one of the three remaining officers. That would be either of the two lieutenants or," he took a breath, "Captain Blund. Whichever one it was, he was the one who came down here, killed your people and released Louise."

"Any clues as to who the traitor would be? Surely not Captain Blund?" asked Gorka.

All eyes, moved to Lydia. Magic smiled and said, "Lydia was about to tell us a name. The name of the officer who so recently entered the cells and, we suspect, freed Louise."

She said, "Lieutenant Jerkyn."

Gorka swore and said, "That's the second lieutenant."

Chapter 45

"Gorka," Magic yelled, "Where's Lieutenant Jerkyn now?"

For the first time in our acquaintance, I saw Gorka stammer. "Uh," she said," He's, er..."I stepped into her personal space and gave some added oomph to my words, "Get yourself organised, Gorka! Where is that weasel?"

"I," she stammered, "I don't know, sir." Good to see she was keeping the courtesy of rank when addressing a senior officer, that person being me.

"I think he ..." she said, her mind coming back up to speed, "I think he's supposed to be on duty in the comms room." I took off at a run, closely followed by Lydia and Magic. We left the Empire's best behind us, still scratching their collective mental bums, which is a dreadful visual image.

To be fair, both Magic and I were reacting using our learned behaviours from walking filth-encrusted streets. If you wanted to get some news out, you ran somewhere and yelled a lot. We had forgotten, of course, about comm beads and associated technology, fortunately, Gorka had not. By the time we hit the comms room, we were met by two more of Gorka's people, both saluting Magic and reporting Jerkyn had, indeed, been with them, but he left the room some time ago.

Our comm beads were insisting on answers, I shut mine off and hoped Magic could handle all the questions but I kept a line open to the Man in Black and Magic. Time for some thinking. Oh, God, this was going to be hard.

"Where are we, Lydia?" I asked.

"We're in the comms room, Val," she said, giving my arm a reassuring pat. "How are you feeling?"

"Not us, I said. "I mean the frigate. I know we are still attached to the bloody battle brig, but are we still travelling? Are we in that channel thingy, whatever it is?"

"No, Captain Blund and his people worked out how the two ships could traverse the channel, even while attached, we've completed the whole journey. It's not an unusual manoeuvre, they use it a lot after a battle with the more damaged ships and ..."

"Yeah, yeah," I interrupted. "So, where are we?"

"We're docked at a small repair station in orbit around the capital, we arrived a couple of hours ago."

"Okay, can the second lieutenant get off this ship? Can he get onto this station? And what the hell is a station?"

"It's space station sweetie.""Why would you have station in space? Is it like a caravanserai? A place to rest and recuperate after a journey. An inn or something?" My head hurt. "Are we attached to some sort of space pub?" A hint of pleading had entered my voice.

"No, Val, a space station is like a giant spaceship, except it stays in the one spot, usually around a planet. Since we are at the capital planet, there are several stations in orbit. The main one is called *The Darkling Plain* but there are several others like this one. It's called *Gallifrey,* old but still capable of restoring the damage to the frigate before sending us off to a proper repair facility."

Oh, God, this was so hard, I didn't know what to do or say. I knew I should be asking insightful questions and formulating a brilliant plan, but my mind was full of the mental image of a tavern floating in space. Quietly rotating with a warmth coming from the lights and the open fire. But where would you go if you wanted to have a quiet brew outside. Sometimes, my mind worries me.

Some direction was called for, especially since I had a new title, I was the 'NightWatch Sergeant'. "Urgh..." I gurgled.

"Val," put in Magic. "I'm going to see the Man in Black. I've arranged for Gorka to meet me there with her team, You wait here and look after Lydia!" he disappeared, followed by the remaining troopers until it was just me and Lydia.

"Ahhh..." I continued. Totally in charge.

Lydia had not heard me, she had been doing things on the big board in the comm room but now turned back to me as I made my inane noise. "What was that, sweetie?" she asked. "Doesn't matter. I think I can track down where the second lieutenant is now. Remember our ability to locate everyone with a comm bead?" She did something and the big screen changed to show our deck with lots of green lights.

"Can you identify which one is the second lieutenant?" I asked. Heck, why not. These people all believe in their own version of magic, they call it technology. I call it weird. And scary.

"Yep," she said. All the lights disappeared except one. We watched it enter a small room and then disappear.

"What happened, Lydia?" I asked.

"He's entered a lifter, going to another level. Give me a moment." Again, her hands danced across the controls while on the big screen I saw other decks appear until finally it stopped and we saw the single green light moving along what I assumed was a corridor. “Got him,” announced my heroine.

What to do, what to do? Ah, hell, I was overthinking this. I took off at a run, exiting the comm room and heading down the main corridor. As I ran, I commed Lydia and asked her — ask, never order — asked her to guide me to wherever Jerkyn went.

What ensued was one of the strangest pursuits of my career. Normally, I would be able to see my quarry or at least catch a glimpse of the malefactor. But not now, now I had to hurtle through the ship, turning left or right at Lydia’s instruction in my ear. My brief rests came when I used a lifter, and I needed the rest after my long sojourn in bed. I hoped my bloody nanobots were struggling, the bloody things. A bit of tiny machine panting would be good.

The recent fighting had decreased crew numbers, plus there was a need for some to be aboard the attached battle brig. This meant my progress was not impeded by corridors full of wandering people. Even so, I scared the stuffing out of a few crew as I burst around a corner, yelling for them to get out of the way. Given I am a large lad, any slowpokes got shoved vigorously into a wall. My run was accompanied by lots of surprised yelling and some disappointingly ordinary swearing. These naval types were not up to scratch when it came to cussin’.

“He’s cycling through an airlock in the next room,” shouted Lydia, her excitement evident in the damage she was doing to my ears. I got into the room in time to see the inner airlock door shut while the face of the second lieutenant glared at me from within the outer room. I could see his face because these inner airlock doors had a circular window in the middle, something to do with safety and the need to observe the state of anyone in the airlock. Don’t know, don’t care. If I ever get a family crest, that’s going to be my motto.

I pounded on the door and watched him clamber into one of the emergency survival suits. These are flimsy things, intended to keep the occupant alive for a short time. A small air bottle could be attached to lengthen your survival time but they were not designed for hard use. Certainly not hand to hand fighting, a lesson I had painfully learned earlier in my stupid career, a career full of stupid decisions.

I could see his mouth moving so I activated the speakers on the inner door, I knew these were another safety feature. The designers of this warship were unfathomably concerned with safety considering the vessel was intended to wipe out people by the hundred.

"You killed her," he was saying. "My truest love, you killed the most wonderful woman in the world. Now you can all die."

Okay, I had to assume he was talking about Louise. I also assumed she had done a number on the sap and seduced the poor, dumb fool. "We were going to escape together but she wanted to make one last visit to see you, Valentine. To make peace and ask for forgiveness. You barbarian! You killed her!"

This was going too far. "Actually, I didn't kill her," I said.

He stopped his dressing and looked back at me through the window, "What?"

"I said, 'I didn't kill her'. It wasn't me who stuck a pencil in her brain."

His face changed, taking on a more mottled look. "A pencil!" he choked. "You stuck a pencil into her head! What sort of animal are you?"

"Look, mate, as I said, it wasn't me,"

Now his face was pressed against the window, "What do you mean? She said she was going to say farewell to you. You're the murderous animal with the reputation for cruelty. If you didn't kill her, then who did?"

"Well, to be fair, it was a team effort," I said. "Don'elk distracted her while Lydia stuck her with the pencil. Totally worth watching, I've got to say."

He became inarticulate at this point, possibly having some sort of medical episode. About this time, Captain Blund arrived, followed by Gorka, the Man in Black, Magic and a host of others who could not possibly fit into the small room. I found myself wedged up against the inner airlock door with my face plastered against the window. I was separated from the mooshed cheek of the second lieutenant by the thickness of safety glass.

"Lieutenant Jerkyn! Florian!" cried Captain Blund, "What are you doing, man? Whatever it is, we can sort it out. Talk to me!"

Lieutenant Jerkyn, or Florian, finished climbing into his suit, attached the air bottle and picked up the last piece of gear, the helmet. "I'm sorry, Adem, I truly am. But Louise and I were going to go away together, find somewhere far away, a place we could build a life. I loved her, and she loved me. She was a delicate creature, misunderstood and ill used by the Empire. She needed gentleness, she needed kindness."

"She needed a kick in the teeth," I snarled. "Followed by a knife into her heart."

"Not helping, Valentine," suggested the Man in Black.

"This is on you, Valentine," said Jerkyn. "Louise told me how you had attacked her, how you had forced yourself on her. What sort of man are you, to ravish such a timid flower as my Louise?"

Okay, he won. This little speech left me without any sort of verbal comeback, not a word passed my lips as he attached the helmet and activated the mechanism to exit the air lock. As far as I understood it, all the air had to be pumped out of his little room and then he could open the outer door and leave the frigate. But why? He took another air bottle from the remaining emergency suit inside the airlock. Again, safety standards must have indicated each airlock should have two of these suits. Sucks to be number three, eh?

I couldn't talk, but Captain Blund could. I registered both the Man in Black and Magic were, sensibly, keeping quiet. None of us had a lot of experience at negotiations involving airlocks, spaceships and space stations. Or, as I liked to call it, a flying pub.

Not so Captain Blund, "What are you going to do, Lieutenant Jerkyn?" he asked. "You can't escape, there's nowhere for you to go. You have a limited amount of air inside that flimsy suit. Come back inside, we can talk this through."

A hand clamped over my mouth, a hand about the right size for Magic, a man who knew my tendency to inflame situations. A wise, wise man.

The outer door opened and Jerkyn exited the ship. Through the open door we could see the space station, hanging in space close to us. Not so close you could jump from one to the other, but still close. One of Lydia's clever backpacks would be capable of jetting a person over in a few heartbeats. But Jerkyn did not have such a backpack. How was he going to move? You can't swim in space, God knows, I've tried.

The traitorous lieutenant faced the space station, adjusted his grip on the spare air bottle, the one he had taken from the other survival suit, and opened the nozzle. The air jetted out and he began to move towards the space station. He was moving slowly.

But still moving.

Chapter 46

WELL, I THOUGHT, THAT'S it. Some of Gorka's people suit up in combat spacesuits, attach proper backpacks and easily fly over and catch this nutcase. There was nothing he could do.

"He's going to blow us all up," announced Captain Blund.

My mind did what it always does in these situations and went blank. The Man in Black stepped into the breach and said, "What do you mean, captain?"

Good question. Another damned good question in a long line of damn good questions.

"He's heading towards that hatch over there, the one we can see on the space station," replied Captain Blund.

"Is that a problem?" asked my boss. "Surely we can alert those on the station, or even send our own troopers after him?"

"Yes, we could and we will. Unfortunately, *Gallifrey* is an old station, incredibly old. It was built in the early days of space travel when things were still dangerous out here. Especially power sources. This particular station was originally designed to have a delicate power source, one which had an unfortunate history of exploding."I didn't like where this as going. As I understood it, we were attached to a pub which could explode at any time. What about all the bloody safety standards.

"Of course," went on Blund, "we have since replaced those earlier power cores. Now the station is not in danger of being randomly destroyed."

I breathed a sigh of relief.

"However," he said and my bum resumed its clench, "part of the original safety design included a mechanism for expelling the core if it began to go critical. That hatch over there," and here he pointed to the hatch towards which Jerkyn was slowly moving, "it leads directly to the current core."

"And when he gets there?" asked the boss.

"When he accesses the hatch and enters the tunnel leading to the current core, it is a simple matter to initiate a critical shutdown especially if he has any sort of explosive strapped to his chest. One that will destroy him, the station and, of course us."

"Lieutenant Jerkyn would have had access to explosives," said Captain Blund. "He may well have rigged up some sort of harness and an initiator."

"An initiator?" I asked. Poo. Bum.

"Yes," replied Gorka, "we make up simple explosive packs for use in an assault. They all have a button or trigger. Push it, count five and it goes boom."

It's always a count of five. I preferred a count of five hundred or more but these gung-ho types liked to activate the bomb and then chuck it. I wish Ted was here.

"Can we get out after him?" asked the Man in Black. I noticed Magic was letting the big guy run the conversation and filed this piece of good judgment away for next time. Yeah, right, the next time I'm stuck in space next to a homicidal maniac about to destroy everything within reach. That time.

Gorka jumped in, "I've sent for suits and backpacks, sir, but it will take time for them to get here. He will probably make it to that hatch before we even exit this frigate."

The ensuing silence was broken by Magic asking a question. "Valentine," he asked, "What are you doing?"

He said this because I had, or rather my body had, decided it would do yet another incredibly random action. I had entered the airlock, shut the inner door and began dressing in the remaining survival suit while Captain Blund was explaining how we were all going to die. I'd like to take credit for being the man of action but, honestly, I was simply a passenger and running on some sort of survival instinct. Many times, over the years, my body had done things even before my mind registered a dangerous event. I don't know why I reacted this way and, frankly, it scared the crap out of me. Like now.

"Sergeant Valentine," said Captain Blund, "that suit has no air cylinder. You cannot survive if you leave this ship."

"And, you absolute dickhead,' put in Gorka, "you have no means of propulsion. No backpack. What do you plan to do, wave meaningfully at that bloody traitor?"

I ignored them, mainly because my brain had caught up and I realised what I had to do. I had to stop Jerkyn; at least long enough for Gorka and her team to come cross and grab him. None of that plan included the necessity of me surviving.

Poo. Bum. Tit. Fart.

The survival suit inflated with air from the airlock, I took several deep breaths, sealed my helmet and evacuated all atmosphere. When the appropriate light came on, I opened the door and stood in the doorway, open to space. I had a hand on each side of the hatch, the toe of my boots jutted out into the eternal nothingness. But all I saw was the far figure approaching the space station. By using the emergency air bottle, he had managed to travel most of the distance. Not all of it, but most.

I crouched down on the lip of the hatch, took a mental breath because I couldn't afford to take a real one, and dived into space. My legs pushed hard, I thrust with every bit of muscle I had, praying I would not tear the bloody suit with the strain of the action.

An interesting titbit — leg muscles don't produce a lot of thrust, but they produce more than a piddly little air bottle. Some part of my brain had remembered my idiotic action when I rescued Lydia by cutting the fingers off my spacesuit. The little bits of air ejecting from each hole moved us at a snail's pace. With this in mind, I thought I would have good chance of catching this ratbag before he got to the opposite hatch.

Good plan. Not a great plan, but a good plan. Didn't work.

He reached the hatch leading to the space station's core before I got to him. If I survived this little episode, I intended to put in a report about the utter stupidity of putting an exterior hatch leading into such a sensitive location. For goodness sake, people, safety first!

He punched various buttons on a panel beside the hatch and lights changed colour. The hatch unlocked and he began to pull it open.

That's when I got to him.

Because I am a world class idiot and not one of your everyday idiots, I had not brought a weapon with me. At least, not one I could access while wearing this bloody suit. I had not thought how I was going to kill or injure this soon to be deceased human snot rag.

But maybe I could hold him up, give the others time to get here.

Yeah, good plan. I liked the plan. My lungs, on the other hand, had an alternative point of view. They put in a bid for more air, air I did not have. Well, not completely true, I had all the air held within the suit, the stuff currently lurking around my armpits and the rest of my sweaty body. I let out my first held breath and took another. How many fights have you gone into where you had to hold your breath? This was my first and, I hope, my last; I do not recommend it. I knew my body would suck the suit dry of air if I did my usual frantic hitting and panting. No, I could not do that, I had to fight and hold my breath as long as possible before taking another lungful.

Are we having fun yet?

I caught up with Jerkyn, grabbed his shoulders and spun him around, away from the now open hatch. I have some experience fighting in zero gravity and I do not recommend it, there is no way to launch a huge punch at the other party. The punch pushes them away but also knocks you backwards. Most of the force of the punch is lost.

I wrapped my legs around his torso to give me some stability while I considered how best to hammer this loathsome piece of human faeces. I exhaled, took another breath and held it, feeling incredibly ridiculous, what the hell was I going to do now? If he could shake me loose, I would not be much of an obstacle. With no air, no weapon and no plan, I would not be able to fight him for long — I should think these things through before taking any action. All he had to do was push me away and I would float off into the eternal night and die screaming. Now there's a mental image I could have done without.

Therefore, letting go of this bedwetter was not an option. I squeezed him with my legs and wrapped my hands around his helmet. No way he was going to get rid of me. At least, that's what I thought until he hit me with the spare air bottle.

It wasn't much of a blow, little more than a light tap on my helmet but I knew how fragile these suits were. A couple of good whacks would shatter the faceplate and the it would be good bye Valentine. The air whizzing out the back of the spare bottle, the one he had used as a miniature engine, also contributed to the chaos. He couldn't get a clean swing because the damn thing kept twisting in his hands. Honestly, we must have looked hilarious, spinning around as a conjoined lump while he grappled with a weapon that wouldn't behave and I tried to choke him through his suit. Yes, I realise now this choking idea was possibly silly, but you had to be there.

Hmm, fragile suits. Okay, snotbreath, two could play at that game. I ignored his beating and took a good grip on the base of his helmet, the ring which joined it to the rest of the suit.

My air was both getting foul and harder to take in. My sucking had taken on a certain urgency, a definite frantic intensity, plus I smell bad when I get into these situations. I continued to pull at his helmet, jerking upright against the balance given by my legs around his waist. And we spun about.

Then his helmet popped off.

I saw his head turn to me, saw the surprised look on his face, saw his eyes become saturated with blood as all the inner bits collapsed. He exhaled, the air in his lungs exploding outward as attempts were made to equalise the pressure. He spasmed, his legs kicked erratically and then his face began to freeze into the rictus of death.

He managed one more glare at me, one more smile of contempt and then he hit his chest, hard. His last action before dying and one which, I strongly suspected, activated the explosives. Five seconds.

I unwrapped my legs and kicked his body away as far as I could, the bloody spare air bottle had jetted off to parts unknown so no rescue there. I took a breath, it was like sucking molasses through a straw. In my head, I had started a count, Jerkyn's body drifted slowly away from me and, fortunately, away from the space station and the other vessels. I gently drifted back from him until I reached number five.

That's when Lieutenant Jerkyn's body exploded.

Thank goodness there is no atmosphere in space. It is the air pressure of an explosion which knocks things down, no air pressure, no nasty force coming out of a bang. If Jerkyn had detonated his bomb inside the space station it would have been in a confined space, causing damage to everything nearby and setting off a bigger explosion from the core. But out here, his body did the exploding with pieces of Jerkyn conducting a redecorating routine. I caught particles of frozen blood, something wet slapped my faceplate and I was aware of other body parts floating past my vison and probably entering the open hatch into the space station. Clean up on aisle three, I thought.

That is how I finished up, looking at this sight while also holding the helmet I had torn off his head. About this time, my air did run out, my last suck got me nothing and I realised I was about to die.

Yeah, no bigee.

A gloved and armoured hand grabbed my shoulder as another hand jammed something into my suit. Then I felt air hissing in, wonderful, glorious air. I sucked away, heaven on a stick as the gloved hand attached a cable to my suit and we sped back to the frigate, I suspect I was shedding particles of Jerkyn during the journey.

Once back through the airlock chambers, I stood before Captain Blund, Magic, the Man in Black and Gorka, all staring at me in open mouthed surprise. I unlatched my helmet and allowed them to experience the full aroma of Valentine, complete with optional fear scent, sweat and, I suspect, some minor bladder issues.

A certain amount of gagging took place. Lydia arrived and slowed her headlong rush into my waiting arms before stopping completely and saying, "EWWW! What is all over you? And why do you smell so bad?" Right about then, a piece of Lieutenant Jerkyn's small intestine slid from my shoulder to land on the floor with a soft moosh.

"Hi honey," I said, "how about a kiss?"

Chapter 47

We spent the rest of the day in the frigate, Greenash wanted to check my nanobots again and Lydia insisted I get clean. This meant several showers, the last one being with Lydia and this was, by far the best one. After we had, er, finished, we had to take another shower.

Then I did my rounds again. Talking to as many NightWatch as I could find, asking after their welfare and ignoring their answers.

While I wandered throughout the NightWatch, I noticed one common element, one symbol which every last one of them had on their clothes somewhere. It was the NightWatch patch, the old one we had brought with us from Earth. This had me thinking, we needed a new symbol, something which showed all of us were in the same bunch. Not just a hangover from Earth, we needed a new emblem. Preferably something scary, I was heavily in favour of skulls. Skulls with flames coming out of them.

I approached Magic with my ideas and showed him preliminary sketches I had made of a human head with red glowing eyes, wreathed in flame. I suggested several skulls, plus other inane additions.

“Not sure if I like the idea of blazing human skulls, Val,” he said, drenching my positively brilliant idea in the cold water of common sense. “Human skulls are a bit, I don’t know, overdone.” He thought for a moment and sent for Wallace and H'Nuth, our two resident artists. When they arrived, he showed them my drawings and they both laughed.

Bastards, I'm surrounded by bastards.

"Val's right, sir, "said H'Nuth, "we need a new badge. Symbols are important, they help identify who's in our tribe.""And our tribe," put in Wallace, "is very diverse. Men, women, children. Aliens, nutcases." He looked at me as he said the last word but I took it on the chin, all manly and brave. And because I'm scared of Wallace. "Leave it with us, sir," said the burly hit man. "I'm sure H'Nuth and I can come up with something."

I left them to it, discussing colours, symbols and other exotic issues. And because H'Nuth walked me to the door of Magic's office, pushed me through and shut it in my face. Right, I know when I'm not wanted. Obviously, the final design will look hideous since it will be designed by committee and not by a single, far-sighted artist. Like me.

Several times I was approached by various troopers who gave me one of this age's marvellous electronic tablets. When I asked them what it was for, they told me I had to write a report of the action from my point of view. Yes, I was being asked to write a report. I could read their text now, Greenash's nanobots were all functioning at full bore so I was capable of listening and speaking in any language I heard, I had a built-in short-range communicator but I kept the earpiece in on Magic's orders, as all of us with nanobots were instructed. And we were told to keep their existence confidential. My wee beasties also had some extra wrinkles, a slightly improved healing rate and the ability to learn any written language, given time. But could they write a report for me? Hell no. I accepted the electronic tablet from the troopers each time and then threw it away.

I was a happy lad that night as we retired to our cabin, right up until the communication from Magic. "You and the boss have been summoned, fartface," he said. "And you still have to give your report. It can be verbal, you can record it and pass it on, you lazy sod. Ask Lydia for a storage chip, record your report and then report to the shuttle bay tomorrow. You and the boss are off to see the Emperor."

I did my rounds of the troops next morning, chatting to as many individuals as possible. I was testing the air, seeing how the NightWatch was getting on. Were they nervous about their future? Were they overawed by it all? What were they thinking?

Mainly, they were thinking about lunch. No one was disturbed or concerned. Whenever I gently suggested that some nervousness could be normal in our situation I was met with a disbelieving look and often a meaty laugh.

"We're the NightWatch, Val," was the most common refrain. "We don't do nervous. We make other people nervous. Besides, who'd want to mess with you, our fearless sergeant. The mad bastard who can pull a man's head clean off his shoulders!" And then they'd laugh. They were referring, of course, to the way I had removed Jerkyn's helmet. The story had morphed from our chaotic melee and the removal of a lightweight helmet into a grand battle where I disregarded using any suit but went after Jerkyn in my shipboard clothes, grabbed him, pulled his head from his shoulders and then kicked a bomb out into space before casually swimming back to an airlock. Telling the real story had no effect, fake news.

I gave up and went to the cadets, they always made me laugh. When I joined the rugrats, I had to go over my escapades again, I stressed it was the helmet I removed, nothing else. They gave me a lot of side eye, several spoke strongly about the errors in my story but quieted down when Jeremy stood up and told them I had, indeed, pulled a man's head off. Then they cheered.

My eyes were drawn to Sparky, or rather, several Sparkys. Jeremy, Emilii and Patricia each had one of the little machines, each perched on a shoulder, each clapping mechanical hands. I guessed this was what Jeremy had been slipping to his co-defendants when I saw him in training hall. I wonder if Teddy Boy and the Man in Black knew they had 'donated' their gifts from Caesar to the cadets.

Their infectiously casual attitude to truth gave me an idea. I had been receiving a constant stream of messages from all manner of people, all asking for my verbal report. And could I get it done now, please. Sure, I thought, I can give them a report, I'll get the ankle biters to help me. We'd even do it in song. I activated the record function on the stupid thing Lydia had given me and we launched into "The Good Ship Venus." The kids all loved it, but I had to answer several questions after the song was recorded. Most of these, I referred to Lydia. I sent the recording off to the appropriate people and ran away.

Magic called me into his office to meet with Wallace and H'nuth, they had a design for the NightWatch and probably wanted my blessing on the stupid thing. They showed me their design, not a human skull in sight, no flames, no red eyes. But scary as hell. "Is this," I swallowed," is this a Tharl skull?" I asked.

The emblem showed a grinning Tharl skull, empty eye sockets, horns coming out of the head and lots of teeth. Behind it was a circle and a star, all done in dark colours. No red eyes, just two huge eye sockets looking into the viewer's soul.

"I think I just wet myself," I stated. "This is perfect. Can I get one on a kaffe mug?"

Then it was time to get on the shuttle and report to the Emperor. Mum would have been so proud of her wayward boy. Dad would have been amazed. I was a little surprised myself. "What's the go here, boss?" I asked the Man in Black as we journeyed down to the planet's surface. He was trying to read something from one of those tablets and I believed I had a mission to annoy him as much as possible. "Why are we seeing the Emperor? You, I can understand because you are such a high mucky muck, but why me? And should I be wearing clean underwear?" He was a tough nut to crack, I'll give him that. The trip lasted about an hour and I think he read for a total of fifteen minutes between my ramblings and his inherent courtesy in answering my ridiculous questions. I'm amazed he didn't hit me, most travelling companions do after a while.

We were met at the landing area by a bunch of mean looking individuals who bundled us into a large, black ground vehicle before speeding away into the interior of the palace. I want to say city because it was so huge but it was merely the Emperor's place. The place from where the Empire was run.

We were taken into a large hall and escorted through various corridors before being left in a well-appointed and garishly decorated formal reception room. It even had a throne on a raised dais with every possible surface area covered in gold, jewels or other undoubtedly precious stuff. I was dead impressed. And a teensy bit nervous, this was way out of my comfort zone. Guards stood around walls, all dressed in glittery armour with swords, shields and other ridiculously useless weapons for this day and age. Still, it looked good. Several other well-dressed people were also in the room, many of them clustered in small groups and talking quietly.

A man sat upon the throne, he was dressed in comfortable but beautiful clothes. The entire room reeked of wealth, class and power yet the people in it acted as if they were visiting friends. There was a definite air of casualness about it all, the Emperor sat chatting quietly to a man standing near him, one of them made a comment and they both laughed. A good, honest laugh, not a maniacal giggle or a hearty, drunken roar; the laugh of two mates telling each other outrageous lies.

We were waved forward, I let the boss precede me while I took up what I hoped was the position of flunky behind him. I kept my head lowered, partly out of respect but more out of terror. The terror of embarrassment for when the moment came when someone noticed me and yelled for the guards to toss the riff raff out onto the street. I'm comfortable being riff raff, you know where you stand. It's not at the foot of an Emperor's throne while he talks softly with my boss. Softly talking and with some affection, I realised.

"We thank you, Lord von Palmerland, for your services to the Empire," said the Emperor, his voice gentle but full of warmth and something else — power, I guessed. "It is our pleasure to take you into our service. You will retain your title and rank, I have been advised some of our loyal space marines have been temporarily attached to your company as auxiliaries. I shall make this a permanent arrangement. Please take them on the strength of your," here he paused and looked at the man standing beside him. This bloke leaned down, whispered something and the Emperor continued, "your NightWatch," finished the Emperor. He paused, pressed his lips together and appeared to have glimpsed something or someone over my shoulder.

"Ah," he went on, "I almost forgot. I understand that Captain Blund and the crew of the *Immortal*, our loyal frigate, have become used to your ways, your, er, methods. Please consider them as NightWatch Auxiliaries, along with Sergenat Gorka and her people. I shall give instructions that you, Lord Franz, have the authority to use this vessel and crew whenever you desire. You will not need to go through any tiresome layers of bureaucracy."

Were my ears deceiving me? Had our bunch of ratbags now picked up its own army and naval force, to go along with the whacko sentient machine known as Caeser? We're going to need a bigger boat. I managed to squeeze a peek at all of this but mainly concentrated on keeping my head down.

"And this is Sergeant Valentine?" he asked.

"It is, sire," said my boss. He stepped to one side so the Emperor had an unobstructed view of me, quaking before him. "Step forward, Val," said the Man in Black.

I shuffled forward, head down and muttered, "Greeting, your imperiousness." Yes, I was ridiculous. How do you talk to an Emperor?

"Sergeant Valentine," said the Emperor, "we particularly thank you for your efforts in saving our precious station, not to mention the ships and people attached to it. Your bravery has been mentioned to me in many reports but I was particularly taken with your own verbal recording of the incident, it was an extraordinary insight into the workings of the NightWatch."

Oh, God, I thought, I'm going to die.

"However," he went on, "I question the verse concerning the cabin boy who filled his rectum with broken glass, I understand there was a desire to perform minor surgery on the captain. Perhaps such a procedure may have had unwanted side effects?"

Why doesn't the earth open up and swallow you when you want? My face heated up, I dribbled some inanity until the boss took my arm and gently guided me off to one side. "That was so worth it, dickhead," he muttered, the smirk reeling through his words. Eventually we were taken out of this large formal room into a smaller, more comfortable space filled with plush chairs, books and a well-used couch. Books lined the walls and a large desk stood on beautiful carpet, the Man in Black almost swooned at the place. We were told to sit and wait.

Since I cannot stand silence or inactivity for more than two heartbeats, I took this opportunity to quiz the big guy on our situation. “Where do we stand now, Franz?” I asked, desperate to find some normality in our lives. Illusions of a warm and snug Watch house drifted through my mind.

“Val we’ve been moving, running or fighting for almost a year now. And not in our known environs, the City, the world we know. You and I, plus the other original NightWatch, have encountered strange things. We’ve seen spaceships and aliens, we’ve talked to sentient boxes which have travelled across galaxies and fought off everything from bandits to machines. We need time to rest, to regather. We need time to reorganise ourselves and concentrate on our place in this universe.”

“Have you seen the new emblem, the one designed by Wallace and H’Nuth?” I asked.

“I have, thank goodness they didn’t use any human skulls.”I coughed. “Yeah, because that would be silly. Are we going to use it?”

“Absolutely,” he replied. “It sums up nicely who we are.”

“And who are we, sir?”

“We’re the NightWatch, Val, and we keep people safe. Look at you, for example. Why did Don’elk take on Louise all by himself? Why did he change sides permanently. Yes, I know he joined us, but they were just words. I don’t think you can suspect the motives of a man who, unarmed, takes on a knife wielding maniac.”

“I dunno,” I wanted to despise Don’elk, I wanted him hurt, but not necessarily dead. I just wanted him gone, to be somewhere else. “But he saved Lydia. For that I’m grateful.”

"And he saved you. Probably the man who scares him most. You owe him, Valentine, you owe him for what he did, for the lives he gave to both you and Lydia."

Damn and blast, he was right. It wasn't going to be enough for me just to tolerate Don'elk, I had to accept him. He deserved my respect for what he had done. By saving Lydia — never mind me — he had allowed my life to have some sort of hope. As long as my wonderful girl was in my life, I believed I could keep myself under control. "I understand, mate. Next time I see him, I'll have a quiet chat and let him know he really is one of us now. With nothing to fear from me."

"Well," said the boss, "No more than the rest of us."

"Prick," I muttered.

"Dropkick." He smiled.

After enough time had passed for me to get bored enough to doze off, and for the boss to closely examine the shelves, gently caressing books and spines, the door opened again and the Emperor came in. The Man in Black and I leapt to our feet, I bowed and scraped while the boss nodded his head in respect.

"Sit down, gentlemen," said the Emperor, "In this room, I work. I am an administrator here, a man who must actually work at keeping the Empire together. Sit down while I outline your duties." We did so, the boss looking comfortable and relaxed while I perched on the edge of a chair and sat to attention.

"You, Lord Franz, will continue to lead the NightWatch and the Auxiliaries. They shall function as the armed force for my intelligence network. As you may understand I cannot use the military for these purposes, nor are the normal police the answer. I need a group which act on their own initiative." Here he looked over at me, "And I believe initiative is something the NightWatch has in abundance."

The door opened and a man walked in, a man I recognised. I started to rise from my seat but stopped when the Man in Black placed a gently restraining hand on my arm.

"Let it go, Val," he said.

The Emperor waved a hand as introduction to the newcomer, "Gentlemen," he said, "allow me to introduce the head of all intelligence services for the Empire. Your new master."

The man stepped forward to sit on a corner of the Emperor's desk.

"Please," he said, "call me Phil."

"My life is over," I groaned, dropping my head into my hands and sliding down in a dead sulk. I noticed the boss, I mean the Man in Black, not Phil — Phil will always be a dick — had maintained his air of casual elegance. This caused me to wonder, so I said to him in a soft voice which may have come out as a low growl, "Did you know, sir?" I asked. "Did you know Phil was this high mucky muck?""No," he replied, "but I had my suspicions. Phil is wonderfully well informed about the doings of the Empire. And he also possessed a wide range of contacts, plus the ability to invoke the Emperor's authority." He did his own small slump but then I guess his higher breeding came through because he sat up erect again, leaned forward and looked at the Emperor.

"If I may ask a question, sire?" he asked.

"Certainly, Lord Franz," said the ruler of worlds, "be my guest."

"What is it you want us to do? The NightWatch, I mean. We're basically coppers and not good ones at that. Some of us have been soldiers but we are not a military force. So, if we're not coppers and we're not soldiers, what are we?"

"You are," said the Emperor, clasping his hands on the desk and doing his own lean forward, "**my** people. **My** arm, **my** will. Your previous role was walking through the darkened streets of a city, keeping the peace.

You went into dark alleys, you gave ordinary people a chance at a normal life.'

Well, sure, I thought. Our actions could be seen to be noble and honourable. On a good day, going downhill. But most of us just wanted a free drink and the chance to stay alive another day. Sometimes that resulted in kicking the stuffing out of bad guys. Occasionally each other. A bit of self-delusion never hurt, I liked the noble outlook of our previous roles. Bloody saints, we were. Goddamn saints.

"Now," continued the Emperor, "I ask you to walk through the Empire, I want you to go into **our** dark places, find things which might endanger our Empire and destroy them. I want you to keep the Empire safe."

"But you must have better police," I interjected. "Clever lads capable of solving crimes or rousting troublesome crowds. I know you've got some bloody good soldiers. I've met some of them and they are frightening. "

"Yes," replied the Emperor. "I have a police force, I have a military. But the police are governed by rules. They function within a framework designed to keep the peace, while at the same time demonstrating they are accountable to those laws and rules."

Yeah, okay, that's definitely not us. We can certainly keep the peace, no problem there. We're all for enforcing laws and rules as long as the NightWatch is doing the enforcing. That word 'accountable' could be a problem. When asked why we did some particularly violent act, most of the gang gave the questioner a surprised look. It all boiled down to having sensible, reasonable discussions with people until they agreed with you. Or you killed them.

The Emperor was going to great pains to explain his reasoning to the Man in Black. Frankly, I didn't need any explanation. I trust the boss when he tells me to jump. Ahhh ... I was beginning to get it. The Emperor wanted us to trust him.

Trust an aristocrat? Trust one of the ruling party? Don't make me laugh. Still, if his yakking made him feel better, let him rabbit on. The boss was doing a great job pretending to be interested. Or maybe he was interested. Don't know, don't care. Words to live by.

"And I have soldiers," the Emperor said. I was struggling to stay focussed as he drew breath for more of his rationalisation. Or was it justification? I always get those two mixed up. Along with excuses and apologies; life can be complex for your basic thug. I tuned in for his next words, "I have heroes by the hundred, by the thousand."

He stopped speaking, probably thinking he had made a vital point. I fought off a yawn.

"I don't want people willing to die for the Empire. I want people who make the other people die." He took his weight on his forearms, his gaze holding us in its spell. "I don't want upright and honourable. I don't want honest men and women bound by law. I want a man who can rip someone's throat out with his teeth."

He was looking at me now. Christ on a crutch, I thought, this guy knows everything about us, he's worse than the Man in Black. He went on, "I want a man," he was still looking at me, "capable of pulling a man's head off."

I coughed and muttered softly, "It was his helmet." Maybe the Emperor wasn't as well informed as I thought. Fortunately, he turned his gaze to my companion.

"And, Lord Franz," he said, "I want a person willing to kill hundreds of people with the wave of a hand." The boss's gaze never faltered, he looked back at the Emperor, two strong men defining their world.

Everyone sat back, a moment of stillness settled upon our happy group. He looked at us, his gaze heavy with responsibility, "I don't want heroes, I want you."

"I want monsters."

THE END

www.ingramcontent.com/pod-product-compliance
Lightning Source LLC
LaVergne TN
LVHW041109080826
845145LV00007B/1739
* 9 7 8 1 7 6 3 7 8 2 6 1 7 *